LONE RIDER

LINDSAY McKENNA

ZEBRA BOOKS
KENSINGTON PUBLISHING CORP.
http://www.kensingtonbooks.com

ZEBRA BOOKS are published by

Kensington Publishing Corp.
119 West 40th Street
New York, NY 10018

All Kensington titles, imprints, and distributed lines are available at special quantity discounts for bulk purchases for sales promotion, premiums, fund-raising, educational, or institutional use.

Special book excerpts or customized printings can also be created to fit specific needs. For details, write or phone the office of the Kensington Sales Manager: Attn.: Salcs Department. Kensington Publishing Corp., 119 West 40th Street, New York, NY 10018. Phone: 1-800-221-2647.

Zebra and the Z logo Reg. U.S. Pat. & TM Off.

First Printing: April 2018
ISBN-13: 978-1-4201-4535-9
ISBN-10: 1-4201-4535-5

eISBN-13: 978-1-4201-4538-0
eISBN-10: 1-4201-4538-X

10 9 8 7 6 5 4 3 2 1

Printed in the United States of America

To all my wonderful global readers,
who enjoy a great cowboy love story as much as I do!

Chapter One

Tara Dalton wiped her hands down the sides of her jeans before pushing the doors open to Charlie Becker's Hay and Feed. She stomped her feet on a well-used bristly mat in front of the doors to knock off the slush from the last snowstorm. The wind was sharp, the temperature below freezing, the sky turgid with spots of blue here and there. Her blond hair lifted from her shoulders, flying around her face. Making a frustrated sound, she pulled the hair away with her gloved hands.

Would Charlie have a job for her? A position where she could get paid for something she loved to do and kept her in Wind River, her hometown in Wyoming? Her heart felt like it was contracting in her chest, anxiety threading through her as she entered the establishment. She saw Charlie sitting behind the long L-shaped register counter, slowly counting his receipts for the end of the day. He closed at five p.m. Tara didn't want to be seen by many people from Wind River going into the store. Everyone knew her. And she didn't want what she had to ask Charlie to be heard by anyone else.

The cold wind pushed her into the warm, empty feed store.

"Oh, hi, Tara," Charlie greeted, smiling. "I heard through the grapevine that you'd come home. How are you doing?"

Forcing a weak smile, Tara said, "Hi, Charlie. Yes, I got home a week ago." She loved the smell of fresh, new leather, row upon row of saddles sitting in one part of the large cowboy farming and ranching store. The wooden floor squeaked and creaked beneath her hiking boots as she moved toward Charlie. The red-brick building was a hundred years old and had been owned by generations of Beckers.

Charlie was tall, almost six foot, and skinny as the proverbial rail with thick, silver hair. His face was lined with sixty-five years of living, and he had always been a kind person to everyone he met. He was one of the fixtures of this small town. Tara had always loved coming here with her father to get hay and grain for her horse when she was in her teens. That was a while ago and happy times for the most part. Charlie always had colorful candy suckers in a bowl beneath the counter near the cash register. Every kid from four to ninety, when they left, was offered one. Plus, Pixie, his wife, a baker of great repute, was always dropping something off at the rear of the store on the coffee table there. Lots of people wandered in to have a cupcake or a cookie.

"Finished with the Marine Corps and done being a combat camerawoman?" he teased, setting aside his stack of receipts and giving her an intense, scrutinizing look.

"Yes, I'm done. I didn't re-up," she admitted.

"Have a seat. Coffee? I'd like to catch up with you, Tara. Usually, when your dad comes in here, he'll tell me you're in Afghanistan, and because you worked in black ops, he didn't have much he could share."

Tara took one of the two wooden stools that sat in front of the counter toward her and sat down. "I'd love some coffee, Charlie. Thanks." She pulled her gloves off and removed her bright blue knit cap from her head. Quickly, she smoothed the flyaway strands of hair with her fingers and opened her blue nylon down jacket. "I need some help," she admitted, watching him pour coffee from a nearby coffee station.

"Figured as much," and he handed her a cup. "Cream? Sugar?"

"No, black. Thanks." Taking a sip, Tara watched him sit down.

"So? How can I help you?"

"Well," Tara said in a low tone, "I need a job, Charlie."

His gray brows rose. "But I thought you'd work at your parents' hardware store in town?"

Mouth flexing, Tara avoided his concerned gaze. "No . . . That's not going to happen." She saw the sudden sadness come to his eyes. "I mean . . . I've got PTSD from my years in combat, Charlie. When I came home, all I did was keep my mom and dad up at night, waking them with my flashbacks and nightmares. They want to help me, but right now? I need to try to get my act together alone."

"But you're still seeing them? Keeping in touch?"

"Oh, for sure, Charlie. We love one another. There are no issues between us. They know I'm looking for another job. Something, I hope, that will get me outside, give me a lot of physical work. I—I have a lot of anxiety. I'm super restless and the only thing that helps tone it down is exercise and staying active. Then, I feel better." She gave him a pleading look. "I don't want this getting around to anyone here in Wind River."

He reached forward, patting her hand near her cup. "I'm not the town gossip, Tara. Our conversations are strictly between us. So? You're looking for an outdoor kind of job?"

"Well," she said, "I was hoping you would have an opening?" and she held her breath, praying Charlie did need help.

"No, I'm sorry. I have two men I employ and they've been here for years, Tara. And I don't need another one." He brightened. "But I may have a lead on a ranch that's looking for a wrangler. And I know you grew up with horses at your ranch. Even though your dad started out as an attorney here in the county and then became a judge, your family always had a small ranch to run. You're used to mending fences, changing out bad posts, riding and doing all the things a wrangler does."

Nodding, Tara tried not to look devastated by the news. Her heart had been set on working with Charlie. "That's all true. My dad has two wranglers who run the ranch while he works as a judge."

"Couldn't you stay at their ranch and work?"

Shaking her head, she said, "Dad's wranglers have been there since I left for the Marine Corps at eighteen. He can't fire one of them and replace him with me. That wouldn't be right. Everyone needs a job. And both those wranglers have families and mouths to feed. No, I wouldn't do that to them."

Giving her a twinkling look, Charlie said, "Your parents raised you to be a good person, Tara. There's hope here. You know Shaylene Crawford? You two grew up in Wind River and went through school together, right?"

"Sure, I know Shay. Why?"

"Well, you've been gone a long time and maybe your parents haven't filled you in yet on all the goings on in

Wind River. Shay's dad, Ray, suffered a stroke at forty-five. Shay had to get a hardship discharge from the Marine Corps and come home and take over the reins of the Bar C. Ray, as I'm sure you remember, is an alcoholic. That, in part, caused his stroke at such a young age. It left him incapacitated and in a nursing home afterward. Shay had to step up and become the ranch owner. She had the right to do so because her mother's side of the family has always owned the Bar C and her mom left it to her, not her dad. So now? Shay is the rightful owner of her family's ranch."

"Oh, wow," Tara said, stunned. "I didn't know any of this!"

"Yes," Charlie said, gravely. "Shay's been home for nearly two years and she's taken a broken-down ranch and is slowly pushing it from the red to the black column, financially speaking. It was hemorrhaging money while you were gone. Due to his alcoholism, Ray lost all his grass pasture leases, which gave him a lot of working capital. Shay walked into a disaster and was two months away from foreclosure with Marston, the local banker, when she took over for her father." Disgust filled Charlie's voice. "Marston was waiting for the Bar C to fail. He had a multimillion-dollar condo deal with a New York Realtor who was gonna turn the ranch into nothing but condo rentals for tourists."

"Oh, no," Tara whispered, her eyes widening. "That's horrible!"

"Really. We like our little, tight community. No one wants to see condos built and Realtors running around. But we're a valley that is sliding into economic oblivion, too. So, from Marston's perspective, condos would bring fresh money into our valley, which we desperately need."

"I know everyone drives through here to get to the Grand Teton National Park near Jackson Hole," Tara grumbled. "Or drives fifty miles farther north to reach Yellowstone National Park."

"Well, Maud and Steve Whitcomb, who own the largest ranch in the valley, are working to turn our economy around here in Lincoln County. They've got a lot of new projects under way to invite the tourists driving through to stay and play with us on their way to the Tetons or Yellowstone."

"That's good to hear, because we need jobs."

"Yep, and I'd like to make a call to Shay on your behalf. She's married now, to an hombre who's a retired Marine Corps captain by the name of Reese Lockhart. Stand-up man. Together, they're working hard to bring the Bar C back to life and out of mortgage jeopardy, but it's in a fragile state. Shay, when she took over the Bar C, wanted to hire military vets like herself. She saw firsthand how vets with PTSD and wounds, either seen or unseen, need a hand up. All her wranglers, some men, some women, are vets. And they're all doing well."

"That's wonderful," Tara said softly. "I lost touch with Shay when we went into the Corps. It's nice to hear she's married and happy."

"Well, her father is a huge burr under everyone's saddle over at the Bar C. He's trying right now to get well enough to take her to court to get the ranch back." Charlie frowned. "It's a real bad scene and something that's ongoing. They just put out a restraining order on Ray to stop him from ever setting foot back on the Bar C again."

Tara knew a lot about the law because of her father. "That's pretty serious, a restraining order."

"Yes," Charlie sighed, "it is. Terrible ongoing stress for Shay, especially. That's her father. But that aside? I know they're looking for another military vet to fill an opening they have at the Bar C. Might you be interested in working over there?"

"Sure," she said quickly, hope suddenly filling her. "What do I need to do?"

"Well, Shay and Reese are coming into town tomorrow at noon to pick up a big order of grain for their horses." He picked up his cell phone. "How about I call and tell them you're back and looking for work? Maybe have lunch with them at Kassie's Café in town? It would be a good way for you to catch up with Shay, talk with her and see if you're a fit for her ranch. Does that sound good?"

Did it ever! Tara tried to tamp down her wild hope that this was the perfect job for her. "It sure does, Charlie."

"Just give me your phone number, okay? I'll call Shay right after I get done putting my receipts in my accounting book here. I'll let you know if it's a go or not. You're staying with your parents at their ranch? Yes?"

"Yes," she said, barely able to breathe. "That would be wonderful, Charlie. Thanks so much," and she reached out, gripping his long, work-worn hand, squeezing it warmly. "I appreciate your help."

Giving her a wink, he said, "the people of our valley are tighter than thieves and we always try to support one another where we can. I'll give you a call in about an hour. I'm pretty sure Shay will be more than open to having you apply for that wrangler job at the Bar C, so keep up your hopes."

Tara hugged Shay hello when they met just inside the door of Kassie's Café. The place was filling up fast with lunch patrons.

"It's so good to see you again!" Shay said, parting and grinning happily. "I'd just heard from Garret, who works for us, that you were back in town. I've been meaning to call you, but I didn't have your cell number." She gave her a happy look, releasing her hands. "And stupid me? I should have thought and called your mom and dad at their ranch. I knew you'd be there."

Tara smiled and gestured to a table in the back, near the kitchen. "Don't worry, you are just a little busy out at the Bar C from what Charlie said. Come on, let's sit down in a quieter corner."

Shay pulled off her bright red wool jacket, tucking it over her arm. Everyone knew everyone else. Kassie's was the town's center where everyone congregated. Shay said hello to many of the patrons as she passed near their tables, smiling.

Tara tried to appear relaxed, but she was anything but. Sitting with her back to the wall, she pulled out the other chair that was nearest the wall. She assumed Shay had probably seen combat, too; neither of them would be comfortable with their backs toward doors or windows. Shay gave her a grateful look.

"We're the same when it comes to wanting to see everything around us," Shay said, gesturing toward the plate-glass window. She sat down after hanging her jacket over the back of her chair.

Placing her jacket on her chair back, Tara said, "Are we that obvious?" and she laughed a little as she sat down.

A waitress came over, offering glasses of water and the menu. Tara thanked her.

Shay gripped her hand. "It's so *good* to see you again, Tara! We lost touch with each other. I gave a yelp of happiness when Garret told me you'd come home. He's ex-black ops, so he's always got his ear to the ground when he's in town. I couldn't believe it! You were in for twenty in the Corps. What happened?"

"Let's just say, because I was black ops, too, that I couldn't take it anymore." Tara wasn't going to lie to Shay because if she got the job, she wanted to earn it fair and square. Setting the menu down, she said, "Where's your husband? Charlie said you were happily married."

"Oh, I am! Reese is just wonderful! He's over at Charlie's, helping to load our truck with about fifteen hundred pounds of grain sacks. He and Harper, one of our wranglers, will then drive it back to our ranch."

"But I thought he'd be here for lunch," Tara said. Or did Shay make decisions such as hiring? She saw the gleam in Shay's eyes.

"I packed him and Harper a lunch this morning. They'll have beef sandwiches and chips on the way home. No worries."

"I was hoping to meet him."

Shay pulled out her cell phone and showed off a photo of Reese to her. "He's a real hero and I know you'll like him, too."

"What a good-looking guy," Tara said sincerely, handing her back the cell phone. "Remember when we were in the fifth grade? We'd go ride horses together at one of our ranches? And we'd wonder what kind of boy we'd fall in love with?"

"Oh, that! Gosh, yes, I remember those fun times. But we were so young, so starry-eyed, and we didn't really know anything of the world. I remember I wanted a Sir Galahad kind of boy and you wanted a King Arthur."

Giggling, Tara nodded. "We were way too young and knew nothing!"

The waitress came over, they ordered and she poured coffee into thick white ceramic mugs. Picking up the menus, she hurriedly left. The place was packed with lunchtime patrons.

"You said you had PTSD?" Shay asked quietly.

"Yes. When I became a combat camerawoman in that

MOS for the Corps, the captain of my unit asked if I wanted to work with special ops. I jumped at it because the Corps is still trying to figure out if women can handle combat or not."

Snorting, Shay said, "Yeah, I know. They are so Neanderthal. Women handle it as well as any male Marine does. No more, no less."

"Yes, that's true. But I couldn't re-up after going black ops. I'd had enough, emotionally speaking."

"I can't even begin to imagine what you saw through your lens," Shay said, giving her an understanding look. "But let's talk about something good."

"I'm more than ready for that."

"Great, because when Charlie called me, I was at my wit's end. I'd lain awake half the night, anxious and needing another wrangler. Reese told me not to worry, that the right person would show up." Her eyes sparkled with humor. "And then Charlie calls to tell us about you."

Relief trickled through Tara. She gripped the coffee mug a little less frantically between her hands. "He said he thought you needed another wrangler."

"Yes. And we have two women vet wranglers we've already hired, Kira and Dair. They're doing a great job. They're just as good as any of the male vets. Let me tell you what we need, Tara, and then you can decide if it's a fit or not."

"Sure," she murmured.

"We need a full-time wrangler. But our vets have to have an outside source of income. For example, Kira is an Arabic translator and earns money doing translations between English and Arabic. Garret is a heavy equipment operator. Harper is presently going to college to become a paramedic and he takes care of our horse barn. We rent horses and stable other people's horses as well as selling to the public. He's especially good with our broodmares. Reese, when he first came here, had a CPA and he became the ranch's accountant. He also took on jobs as an accountant for several businesses here in Wind River. Noah was training horses before he went into the Army. Now, he has a huge training program here, and Dair Wilson helps him by being his assistant trainer. Everyone contributes through their other skill sets. And you put twenty percent of those earnings into the ranch kitty because we don't charge you rent to stay at one of our homes on the property. We pay the utilities, you don't. All you supply is food to eat."

"Gosh, that's an easy one for me, Shay. I'm a professional photographer. I already have a website up and I sell my pictures to stock photo sites. I make a reasonable amount monthly and I could contribute in that way."

"Sounds good to me. We'll pay you an hourly wage as a wrangler. We put ten percent of that into a savings account for you, so you can build equity and someday be able to afford your own home, if you want."

"I like that idea. But I saved a lot of my monthly paycheck when I was in the Corps. I have my money in the stock market because of my dad and his broker." She crossed her fingers. "So long as we don't have another crash like we did in 2008, I'm pretty well off, economically speaking."

"Which is unlike everyone else who works here, including me and the ranch."

"I'm using some of it to build the website, plus it costs money to drive to places to take photos. I have to buy new equipment now that the Marine Corps no longer lets me use theirs," and she smiled.

"We have four homes on the ranch, two bedrooms each. Two are filled with wranglers. The fourth one was where my father lived until we permanently kicked him off the property. We're in a legal battle with him because he wants to return to that house, saying it's his. I can't assign it to you under the circumstances." She opened her hands. "The only other house available is where Harper Sutton lives. He was a Navy combat medic."

"It wouldn't bother me to bunk in with him. We'll each have our own bedroom, I'm assuming. And we'll probably share cooking and cleaning duties?"

"Yes, everyone else shares the chores in the home they're assigned to. You two can work that out between you."

"What's Harper like?"

Tara saw Shay's expression start to glow. "He's such a sweetie. Being a medic? You know he's quiet, gentle and gains your trust immediately."

"Especially if you're bleeding out," Tara said, smiling faintly. "Yes, I was with mostly 18 Delta combat medics on the team I was with. They're the best of the best."

"They sure are. But you know the medic type?"

"All quiet, like shadows, they speak softly, gain your trust even if you're hysterical because you know you're dying."

"Yep. That's why Harper is so good with our brood-mares and foals. He's got that special touch of a healer."

"He sounds nice."

"He is. But don't let his Type B appearance fool you," Shay warned. "He was in black ops, too. He was always in the thick of danger, and you know you have to be a Type A to do that kind of job."

"No disagreement. The medics I ran with appeared to be Type Bs, but in reality? They were ballbusting Type As beneath that veneer. I suspect Harper is, too?"

"Well," Shay said, watching their food coming toward

them on a tray carried by the waitress, "I've yet to see his Type A side, but I know it's there."

"If he's working with broodmares and foals, he can't show that aggressive side of himself. Horses wouldn't work with him."

"Right you are," Shay agreed. "Here's our lunch."

Midway through the meal, Shay turned serious once more. "Why aren't you working on your parents' ranch?"

In as few words as she could, Tara told her what she'd told Charlie the day before. She saw Shay's features turn to understanding once more when she finished her explanation.

"But are Scott and Joanna okay with it?"

Shrugging, Tara offered, "Well, not at first, but the more I explained, the more they accepted my situation. It's not like I'm leaving town or anything. My mom was happy when I told her that every once in a while I'd drop in for dinner and see how they were; plus, we'll always have cell phones and emails. And I'll continue to help fill in for her at the hardware store when she needs me. They're okay with it now, but you know civilians who haven't been in combat just can't understand where we're at. It's not their fault. They don't know."

"There are days, even now, when I feel like I'm going to tear out of my skin," Shay admitted between bites of her ham and Swiss cheese sandwich. "Fortunately, Reese does understand."

"Because he's a vet who has seen combat, too. So he knows. My parents are trying to understand, but they can only go so far to grasp it."

"You have to have lived it," Shay agreed grimly, "to know."

"Yeah." Tara sighed.

"I realize you probably don't want to discuss this, but I

have to bring it up. I remember when Cree Elson kidnapped you when you were sixteen."

Rolling her eyes, Tara said, "Believe me, I've never forgotten it. I still get nightmares about that time. About him," and she shivered.

"I heard he's out of prison and working in Jackson Hole doing odd jobs."

Stomach knotting, Tara said, "My dad told me when I got home."

"That's fifty miles away from us. And you know? His mother, Roberta, still lives here, same place, same dumpy trailer on that fifty-acre ranch on the slope of the Salt River Mountains. Remember his three older brothers? Hiram is thirty-one now, Kaen is twenty-nine, Cree is twenty-seven and Elisha is twenty-four. They all live at the southern end of the valley and they're up to their hocks in drug trade and drug movement. While you were in the service, did your parents keep you updated on the Elson clan?"

Shaking her head, Tara muttered, "I told them I didn't want to hear anything about that dysfunctional family. I wanted to leave them behind me once I left town."

"Not much has changed except that your dad sent Hiram and Kaen to prison for three years a piece for drug smuggling. They just got out a couple of years ago, came home and now they're back doing the same thing. Sheriff Sarah Carter has someone undercover trying to get into their ring to prove they're at it again. That toxic family has never changed. They're just as violent and unpredictable as Cree is. Only he never got into selling drugs so much as using them."

Her hope withered. "One of the reasons I joined the Marine Corps was to get strong and to be able to fight off a man like Elson. I never want to be a wimpy, helpless, freaked-out girl like I was back at that age."

"I know. I joined the Corps to escape my alcoholic father. You ran away to leave that kidnapping and threat behind you."

"We both ran," Tara admitted, frowning.

"Did you know Cree was out?"

"Only after I got home. I was still in my PTSD soup and he wasn't on my radar at all. I'm having enough trouble trying to appear normal to everyone."

"Well, if it makes you feel any better, Sarah Carter is the Lincoln County sheriff, and she's already got the ear of the Teton sheriff's department commander, Tom Franks, up in Jackson Hole. She knows Cree's dangerous. Now that he's been released and served his time for kidnapping you, she keeps an eye on him. Sarah ran for sheriff after her dad retired from that position and the folks of the county happily voted her in."

"My dad has nothing but praise for Sarah. He says she's a fine law enforcement officer. Her dad, David, taught her how to be a deputy from the time she was young. She grew up wanting to be one. I was glad to hear she's the sheriff. Everyone likes her. Well, I'll amend that: people who obey the law love her. The people who don't most likely hate her as much as they hated her father. And yes, it makes me feel better. When I got home, one of my worries was knowing Cree was around. That he could try to get even with me."

"Yes, I remember he told you in court he was going to get even with you for putting him in prison. It's the Elson twisted gene: They always seek revenge on the person or group who threw them in prison. Nothing's changed. They're still that way."

"That was another reason why I didn't want to stay at home, put my parents at risk in case Cree was crazy enough to try it again."

Shay nodded. "Well, don't worry about that at the Bar C. We're all vets. We're all licensed to carry concealed weapons. And we all know how to use a pistol if it comes down to that."

"What about Harper?"

"Oh, he knows how to use a weapon, no worries. We all carry weapons, but they're in locked safes in each home when we're not out on ranch property. There's a target range on the ranch, and we go out every two weeks to practice."

"I would die if Cree came onto your property and hurt anyone," Tara admitted. "Really. I've been wondering, because I knew Cree was nearby, if I should just leave Wyoming, disappear and go to another state a long way from here. There's also his three brothers. I worry about what they might do to us, to my family, if Cree is still obsessed with me or wants revenge."

Shay gripped her hand. "Don't you dare run again, Tara. Your family has been here for generations. No one has the right to chase you off with threats. And I feel confident that if he did try? He'd get a very unpleasant greeting when he set foot on the Bar C. The other three brothers are always around, but so far, we haven't had any run-ins with them. No, I want you to stay and I would love to have you as one of our wranglers. Please say you'll take the job?"

Chapter Two

April 3

Harper was just closing the door on Candy's broodmare stall when he saw Shay enter the enclosed area with a woman at her side. He locked the door, turning, his gaze on the stranger. Strong sunlight broke through the clouds across the valley, sending a shaft across the women as they walked down the recently swept concrete aisle toward him.

He liked what he saw, his curiosity piqued.

He took off his leather gloves, stuffing them in the back pocket of his Levi's. Wearing his thick sheepskin jacket, it kept him warm in the chill of the barn. The woman was a little taller than Shay, wearing a dark blue down jacket, a knit cap of the same color over her long blond hair. It was her oval face, and those big blue eyes, that attracted him. She had to be their age or close to it. What tipped him off that she was possibly a military vet was her walk and the way she had squared her shoulders. There was a lot of confidence in her expression as their gazes briefly met.

"Hey, Harper," Shay called, smiling as she came up to him, "meet Tara Dalton. Tara? This is Harper Sutton."

"Hi, Tara," he said, extending his hand toward her. He

noticed her nails were blunt cut. As he slid his hand around her fingers, he felt a callus on her right index finger. That was a potential sign that she used a weapon a lot. He saw her lips, which were lifted into a welcoming smile, curved more as she shook his hand firmly.

"Hi, Mr. Sutton."

Grimacing, Harper forced himself to release her hand. "Call me Harper." He watched her pull on her gloves once more. It was about forty degrees in this section of the barn, which was in the center of the building and well protected from the nasty Wyoming weather and temperature.

"Have you got a few minutes, Harper?" Shay asked. "I thought we might all go to your house to talk. I'm hiring Tara to be our badly needed wrangler. I'd like to sit down with both of you for a bit."

"Sure," Harper said. His mind clicked along rapidly as he walked with them to the door. Tara looked reliable to him, someone who could be counted on to carry her share of the load. That was a good first impression to have about her. Never mind she was attractive, an outdoorsy type of woman who appealed strongly to him. Silently, Harper warned himself off that track of thinking even though his lower body was stirring with more than a little interest.

Opening the door, he gestured for the two women to walk ahead of him. "Welcome to our family," he told Tara. He liked the way her thick blond hair curled around her shoulders. The light briefly touched her hair, turning it to colors of wheat, gold and caramel. His fingers itched to touch those glinting strands as the sun's rays lanced through the windows of the huge arena in front of them. "I've got a couple of horses loose in there," he said to Shay. "I can spend about thirty minutes with you, but I have to get back here to put them away and bring out a couple more to stretch their legs." He saw Tara frown. "We had rain last night," he explained to her as they walked around the outside of the arena to the main door. "It turned to ice. If I put the horses out in the paddocks, they could slip on that ice and maybe pull a tendon or break a leg."

"Not something anyone wants to have happen," Tara murmured, giving him a pleased look.

"These are renters' horses," he added, "so we're a little more conservative about keeping them safe and out of trouble."

"Right," Tara agreed. They halted, waiting for Harper to close the door.

The early afternoon was turning out to be nice, Harper decided. He walked with them up the boardwalk that had already been cleared of snow, salt sprinkled across it so none of the wranglers got hurt on the ice. He walked behind the women, absorbing the warmth of the sun. Too soon, low-hanging, ragged-looking gray clouds blocked it and the cold wind tugged at Harper's black felt cowboy hat. He pulled it down a little tighter, his ears freezing as usual. Tara and Shay wore knit caps to keep them warm and he supposed he should, too, but he was married to his Stetson.

"My house," he told Tara, "is the first one here."

Tara looked at the house and then the others. "They're all the same color and size?" she asked Shay.

"Yes, we built them last summer when we raised the arena. Maud and Steve Whitcomb volunteered their wranglers. A lot of other folks from around the valley came, too, and they all helped us not only finish the arena roof but build these four homes."

"That's great. Is everyone in Wind River Valley helpful like that?"

"Mostly. We have the Elson clan down at the south end of the valley who are no good, but most folks here in Lincoln

County are still the same as when we were young—
generous and willing to help others. Thank goodness," Shay
said. She took the wide concrete walk that glinted with
melting ice and white pebbles of salt scattered across it.

Harper moved ahead of them and opened the door to
the mudroom of his home. As Tara passed him, he caught
her scent, part feminine woman and a hint of mint. He
wondered if she used a mint shampoo on her hair, smiling
to himself at that discovery. Closing the door, he waited
until the two women shed their winter gear and hung them
on huge wooden pegs along the wall before he put his
jacket and hat nearby.

He tried not to be too obvious as he watched Tara. She
wore a pair of jeans, hiking boots and a bright red sweater.
There was nothing to dislike about her. She was tall, but
curvy in all the right places. Her legs were long and sculpted
even though her jeans were loose-fitting. Knowing he
shouldn't be salivating like the lone wolf he thought of
himself as, he put away the rest of his gear, following the
women into the warm kitchen.

"Something smells good," Tara said, halting, turning
and looking at him.

"I made chili earlier this morning," he said, pointing to
the Crock-Pot on the counter.

"You cook?"

He saw merriment in her blue eyes, a reckless curve of
one corner of those lips of hers that called to him. "I do
my best," he joked, pointing to the table. "Why don't you
two sit down? I'll make us a pot of fresh coffee and then
we'll chat."

Shay nodded. "I'll get the cream out of the fridge, and
the sugar."

"Thanks," Harper said. He fell into a familiar pattern with
Shay as they worked around each other in the L-shaped

kitchen. "So? Am I no longer the lone rider here in the house?" he teased her.

Shay laughed. "We just had to wait for the right wrangler to show up. Now you'll have company, Harper."

He grinned, flipping the On switch to the coffeemaker. "That's not a bad thing, Shay."

"I didn't think it would be," she teased, her eyes twinkling.

Pulling out three mugs, Harper walked over to the table, set down two, and handed one to Tara. "You a coffee drinker?"

"Does the sun shine?"

Chuckling, he nodded. "You were in the military?"

"Yes. Marine Corps combat cameraperson. Most of what I did was black ops and top secret."

"I'm a Marine, too. Used to be a combat medic."

"Shay was telling me a little about you."

"Uh-oh, Shay," Harper called, his grin widening as he sat down, "you telling my secrets, are you?"

Shay came over, giving him a wicked look. "Hey, we were all black ops of one sort or another, Harper. I'll let Tara discover you one wart at a time," and she sat down.

He got up and went over and picked up the pot, coming back to pour each of them a cup. Setting the pot down on a trivet positioned in the middle of the table, he pulled up a chair.

Harper liked the way Tara's lips pulled upward. She was at ease, her hands wrapped around the hot mug of coffee, warming up her fingers. "Well, that's a forever task regarding all my warts," he said with a chuckle. He sat down with Shay at his side, Tara opposite them. He could tell Shay was happy, and it was nice to have a positive outlook at the Bar C. Knowing she and Reese were on the hunt for a vet wrangler, he felt her happiness and, most likely, her relief. They desperately needed another hand.

"Oh," Shay said, giving him a light jab in the ribs, "don't make Tara think you're one of those Neanderthal males, okay?"

"Me? Not a chance."

Shay said to Tara, "He's a big tease. But he doesn't play mean jokes on people, so you can relax."

"Good to know," she said. "I don't either."

Mouth twitching, Harper liked her ability to come back and take teasing. That was a good sign because vets usually razzed the hell out of one another.

"Harper, you need to know that Tara is a local. She and I were born here in the valley, we went through twelve grades together and then we both enlisted in the Marine Corps at eighteen."

"So you're tight?" he asked, giving them a glance.

"We were best friends growing up," Tara assured him. "We lost touch when we went into the military, though."

"I would imagine you did."

"But now Tara's home," Shay said. "And I'm really happy she's back with us. She's got a ranching background. Her father is a county judge and her mother runs the local hardware store."

"Oh," Harper said. "I've met your mother, Joanna Dalton. I'm always over there, buying stuff we need around here."

"Yes, she runs the store. My dad has his hands full being a judge, but he helps on weekends."

"Which is why I've never met him. I'm usually at Jo's door at nine a.m. when she opens up," Harper said.

"It's nice you've gotten to meet my mom."

"I can see the resemblance between the two of you," Harper said. "You both have blond hair and blue eyes. Looks like you took strongly after your mother's side?"

She nodded. "But I have my dad's backbone and sense of fairness."

"Was he in the military?"

"No. He went to college and, later, became a lawyer. He was born here, too, so he came home and set up his law office. Then things just sort of took off and he was voted in as a judge for Lincoln County, which is where he works to this day."

"Jo is very mechanically inclined," Harper said to her. "I'm amazed how much she knows about different types of screws and nails."

Laughing, Tara said, "I grew up helping her in the hardware store."

"But your expertise and use of that mechanical knowledge graduated to cameras and videos?" Harper wondered.

"Yes, it did." Opening her hands, Tara said, "I was a little too good in the boot-camp testing and got put into that MOS after I graduated. I thought I'd end up in aviation or jet engines."

Shay said, "But you've always loved photography. You know Kira, one of the other women wranglers, is a photographer, too? She's not a professional like you, Tara, but she dearly loves to go out and take pictures when she can get some time off. You'll have to meet her soon. I'm sure you two will have a lot in common."

"Yeah, Kira's always got a camera somewhere on her," Harper said, "especially on weekends, when we're riding fence line and fixing barbed wire and pulling rotted posts out of the ground and replacing them. She's got lots of photos of all of us doing that."

Tara sipped her coffee. She told Harper about her website and what she was doing to earn money for the Bar C with her skill set.

"That's great," he said. "If you ever want to photograph wildlife, I know a lot of places in the Salt River Mountains to the east of us that has plenty."

"Oh, I'd love to do that. I know some spots where my dad and mom would go for fishing in the mountains, but I could use a guide. I need photos of elk, grizzly and antelope."

"I know where they are," he promised. "When we have some free time, we can plan a few side trips and you'll get some great pictures."

Tara rubbed her hands together, excitement in her voice. "That sounds wonderful, Harper. I'd really appreciate it."

His heart thumped to underscore the winsome pleasure gleaming in her eyes. He wanted to please this woman and didn't examine all the reasons why. Harper warned himself that someone as pretty and wholesome-looking as Tara must be hooked up with some guy. Yet, as he discreetly checked out her left hand, he saw there was no ring on it. Knowing she was a military vet, he also knew wearing jewelry wasn't allowed, especially in the black-ops group. There was no necklace around her slender neck either. Sometimes, women wore one with a ring hanging from it. Trying to tamp down his response, hoping she wasn't attached, Harper said, "Well, we'll work something out after you get used to the rhythm of this place."

"I know you're really busy between school, your handyman jobs around the valley, plus working here, Harper."

"Just a little," he agreed amiably.

"I warned Tara that you might not see a lot of each other under the circumstances," Shay said. "She'll be setting up her computer and other digital camera equipment in her bedroom and working out of there. The rest of the time, I want her to work with you or Noah to get a feel for the ranch in general. With the snow starting to melt off and on, we can ride into some of those lease pastures to start looking for posts that have to be pulled or wire that needs to be restrung."

"Well," he said, "it's Friday and I go to school at two p.m. today. I could take Tara with me on Saturday morning, around nine a.m., and get to that one pasture we've all been working on. That okay?"

Bobbing her head, Shay said, "That's fine, but I want you to mentor Tara. I'll leave it up to you to find her the right ranch horse. Show her the tack room and all that stuff, and then tell Noah."

Harper quelled his sense of good fortune and kept a serious demeanor. "Of course."

"Great," Shay said with relief. "Listen, I gotta run. Tara? Harper will show you the other bedroom, and I'm sure he'll help you set up your computer with the Wi-Fi we have available here in the house."

"Good," Tara said. "Don't worry about me. I know how to fit in."

Shay got up, giving Tara a grateful look. "If you need anything, drop over to the house or call me. Harper has our landline number."

"I'll try not to make a pest of myself," Tara teased, smiling up at her longtime friend. "Go ahead and leave. I'm sure Harper and I can work things out and get me moved in."

Harper liked that Tara could take care of business on her own. She didn't strike him as a helpless female in the least. And being black ops? Those women were strong and he knew that better than most men. He was positive there would be no bird-with-a-broken-wing routine with Tara.

His ex-wife, Olivia, had been just that: helpless-appearing. With the emphasis on the word *appearing*. But he didn't blame her for their divorce. That was entirely on him. His ex-wife had no patience or the kind of love, he guessed, that could have seen them through that PTSD rough patch of his. It just hadn't worked. They'd married too young, were too immature and not ready for the heavy burden of the PTSD that had split them apart.

He wondered if Tara had PTSD. She seemed awfully calm, wasn't tapping a foot or finger or moving around a lot in her chair, which would be telling of a restless nature. Those were all signs of PTSD among many of his Marine Corps buddies, including himself. He couldn't sit in one place too long. When Tara turned her attention from Shay, after the other woman hurried to the mudroom to don her winter gear, Tara fearlessly held his gaze. It wasn't a con-frontational look, merely a well-what-do-we-do-next kind of expression. Smiling to himself, he finished off his coffee and stood, pushing back his chair.

"What do you have in the way of things to move in, Tara?"

"Not much," she said, rising.

"Let me show you the house and your bedroom. Then we can start getting you situated. I've got chili for dinner tonight. My class at the college gets out at five p.m. and I'd figured on eating at six if that's okay with you?"

"Sounds good. I'm not too bad in the kitchen, Harper. Is there something else you want to go along with the chili?"

"That's good to hear because I'm pretty limited. I was going to mix up some corn bread to go with it tonight."

"Show me where the box is and I'll get it done."

"I like your style. This way," and he turned, sauntering into the kitchen. Might as well start there. He enjoyed her warmth and sincerity. That was unexpected. But nice. Mentally, Harper had two columns in his head: one of good traits and one of not-so-good ones for Tara Dalton. He was sure she had chinks in her armor, too, just like everyone else did. With them being thrown together, living under the same roof, he had to find out her strengths and weaknesses and how they stacked up with his less-than-perfect character.

Tara tried to ignore Harper's eye-candy good looks. The guy had military short, dark brown hair, brows straight across his light gray eyes, and his face was square. He could have been a model instead of a combat corpsman. Until she'd shaken his roughened hand, her heart and body were off-line. The twinkle in his gray eyes told her this guy had a good sense of humor, which was something Tara appreciated in a person. Having taken R & R in France and gone to the Louvre Museum in Paris, she'd walked the marble-tiled halls for hours. She'd always loved the Greek and Roman era and so had chosen those exhibits to look at first. There was one statue of Apollo, white marble, that she'd seen and taken photos of. He had beautifully sculpted lips. And Harper was a twin, in that sense, to the Greek sun god.

He had character in his face, lines at the corners of his eyes and around the corners of his mouth. Tara intuitively sensed he'd seen a lot of combat. Even the corners of her mouth would pull in deeply when they were caught in a firefight with the enemy. And there were certainly some feathery lines at the corners of her eyes, too, because of squinting, even with sunglasses on, in that hot, unforgiving Afghan environment.

As Harper opened and closed different cabinets and drawers, showing her where everything was located, she tried to ignore his quiet, intense maleness. Shay had been right: Harper might appear to be a Type B, but underneath that teasing exterior of his lurked a Type A, no question.

It actually made her feel better. Maybe safer was the word Tara wanted to use as he moved along the cabinets, showing her the contents and explaining where the bowls, pots and pans were stored as well. He was an organized person, but then, he had been in the military, and that was the place where everyone got discipline, organization and the drive to finish what they started.

"This way," he said, gesturing toward the hall where the bedrooms were opposite each other.

Tara followed, enjoying watching Harper walk. He was boneless, and the only way a man made it look that beautiful meant he was in top shape. And whether she wanted to or not, she fantasized about Harper without his clothes, what he would look like. That awakened her lower body big-time.

Unhappy with her response, Tara knew the job was her priority. She hadn't even thought about a relationship, still in free fall from leaving the military and fighting her PTSD anxiety 24-7.

As Harper moved down the hall, she couldn't hear him at all. That told her he was definitely black-ops trained and most likely in a team either with the Marine Recons, the Navy SEALs or Army Delta Force. She knew that, often, the top Navy medics were in demand regardless of branch; 18 Delta medics, trained in the Army Special Forces, took in medics from other services to train them as well. She wondered if he was 18 Delta. Tara would almost bet on it but refrained from asking him that.

"Okay," Harper said, halting and pushing open a door, "this is your bedroom. Actually, it's more like a suite. When Shay and Reese had the blueprints drawn up by Steve Whitcomb, who's an architect, they wanted a large-enough room so you could have a small office, but also your own bathroom as well."

"Oh," Tara said, impressed as she walked in, flipping on the light switch, "that's great." She halted, gazing around. Harper came and stood near her, his hands on his hips as she surveyed the room.

"Shay loves the eighteen-hundreds and antiques, which you probably know if you grew up with her," he said. Gesturing toward a huge oak rolltop desk that had a lamp on top of it, he added, "She chose all the furniture for the homes. I hope you like it," and he looked down into her eyes.

"Love it. Shay and I would root through our only antique store, which was owned by Mrs. Abigail Beazely. She was ancient, but she loved us girls coming in after school let out and allowed us to touch, sit and listen to her about a certain piece's history and provenance."

"Kinda took you for old-fashioned," he said, one corner of his mouth curving upward.

Tara gave a short laugh. "Because I already look like an antique?" she shot back. Instantly, Harper's dark brows flew up and a distraught look came to his gray eyes.

"No," he managed, flustered. "No, not at all."

She gave him a wicked look. "I give as good as I get, Sutton." She saw relief come to his expression, honestly thinking that, at first, she had been insulted.

"Yeah," he said slowly, rubbing his chin, "you do."

"You should be used to it. We're both military."

"Well, yes," he muttered, "but you're new here and I wanted you to feel at ease and welcome. I'd never tell a woman she looked old. That's a death warrant."

Reaching out, she touched his broad shoulder. "Sorry. I guess I've been around SEALs for too long. They play hard and fast and they're merciless about ragging one another." Not wanting to stop touching him, Tara could feel the hard warmth of his flesh beneath the blue-and-white-checked flannel shirt he wore. He had a sheepskin vest over it, and his chest was well sprung. Forcing herself to lift her hand away, she added, "I've been home less than two weeks, so I'm still coming down from being in the teams."

"I forgive you," he said, his eyes twinkling. "You're regaining your footing. Took me a good six-to-nine months after getting out to start behaving more like a civilian than a military type."

"Mmm, I don't want to lose everything about the military," Tara said, walking into the room. "I'll probably always tease the daylights out of you, Harper. But you look like you can take a little baiting. Am I right?" and she smiled into his gray eyes.

Tara noticed when Harper thought he'd called her old-looking, his eyes had gone a darker gray. Now, they were a lighter color. She noticed little things, but that was partly because she was a photographer, and the other part was her training in black ops. If one didn't notice the details, it could get her or her team killed, so they were important to note. His cheeks had gone ruddy, too, when he thought she'd taken his teasing the wrong way. That was endearing because the SEALs she'd worked with never blushed. It told her Harper was a lot more sensitive than the average guy. And he was quick to right a wrong, unafraid to fess up if the occasion called for it. Looking down at his hands, she saw no ring on his finger. Why was she doing that?

"Listen, you check out your room. I need to get going. We'll meet at six p.m. in the kitchen and sit down and have our first supper together," he said.

"Sounds good. Thanks for everything, Harper." She saw him nod, turn and silently leave. The man was an interesting enigma, she thought, surveying her new home. Shay did love antiques, no question. Tara's bed had a brass head- and footboard straight out of the 1850s. There was a bright, colorful quilt on the full-size bed, as well as a hand-braided rug of similar colors, beneath it.

She loved that rolltop desk, walking over to it and sliding her fingers across the sleek, polished surface. The golden wood gleamed with polish and care.

The wallpaper was cream-colored and there was one wall, behind the bed, that had tiny pink rosebuds scattered over it. The other three walls were painted the faint pink color of rosebuds, and Tara liked the feminine appoint-ments. She knew Wyoming winters were long and hard. There were heavy dark-pink-and-white-striped velvet drapes to keep the cold out at night. They were open now, showing a transparent white set of curtains that could be opened, bringing light in from the double windows.

The bathroom had a claw-foot tub, and Tara almost groaned out loud over that discovery. She knew she'd soak in it often, especially after doing a lot of hard, physically demanding work all day long. It would be wonderful to relax in it. There were fuchsia-colored towels on a nearby rack, a hand towel near the pedestal sink and a washcloth. Someone had thoughtfully put out a new bar of soap, also pink, in the dish near the faucet. Picking it up and placing it near her nose, she found it smelled like roses.

Turning, she absorbed the quiet of the place. Outside, she could hear a rooster crowing, but that was about all. The house was well-constructed and there was a nice warmth to the room as she walked through it and then to the rolltop desk. Opening it up, she saw there were electri-cal connections for her computer, printer and scanner. Shay and Reese had thought long and hard about the layout of everything in this room, and Tara appreciated that.

The only shadow in her life now was Cree Elson. Tara wanted to shrug her shoulders, literally, to erase him from her mind. He lurked around the edges of everything she did or thought about. Shay had said he lived in Jackson Hole. Did he ever come home to visit his mother, Roberta? He had always been close to her. She was nutty as a fruit-cake, mentally unstable as far as Tara was concerned. It sickened her to see her manipulate her young son, Cree, making him completely reliant on her, listening to her every word. Shaking internally from past memories, Tara didn't know what to do. She felt fear, threat and unease.

Cree Elson was too close for comfort. Would he begin to haunt her life again? Stalk her as he had before he'd jumped her and kidnapped her?

Wrapping her arms around herself, Tara stood, closing her eyes, trying to beat back the terror that had never really gone away. It had stayed deep within her. Now, it was back. In spades.

Chapter Three

April 3

Harper arrived at his home at six p.m. The April sky was starting to cloud over, but there was a nice pink strip of color to the west that he appreciated.

Stomping off his boots in the mudroom, he tried to tamp down his curiosity about Tara Dalton. He wanted to know a lot more about her for all the wrong reasons. She was trying to get her feet under her after leaving the military. Harper was sure she wasn't interested in developing any type of relationship on top of all of that. Still . . . His heart had other ideas and he grimaced, placing his Stetson on a wooden peg next to his winter coat. He hadn't expected to be drawn to another woman after the debacle of his marriage. And right now? It was the wrong time because he, too, was trying to get back on his feet.

Ears keyed to the nearby kitchen, he could hear Tara puttering around in it. Not wanting to appreciate those sounds as much as he did, and the familiar odor of food cooking, he tried to push it all away. Just having a woman in the house changed the energy, he acknowledged, unbuttoning his long sleeves at each of his wrists, rolling the cuffs to just below his elbows. The place was warm and inviting now. Did Tara have a boyfriend? He wanted to know and tried to ignore the reason why as he stepped into the kitchen.

"Hey," he called, letting Tara know he was present and accounted for, "how are you doing? Need any help?"

She had just taken the corn bread from the oven, placing it on a trivet on the kitchen counter. "Hi. No, all's going okay. But thanks. How's everything out at the barn?"

Ambling over, he gave her enough room but smelled the corn bread that she'd slathered with some butter across its golden top. "Candy and her foal are doing just fine. We're going to have the farrier out tomorrow morning and he's got a lot of horses to trim or shoe. Are you familiar with those kinds of things?" He liked the way Tara's blond hair was pulled into a single braid down between her shoulders.

"Yes." She straightened up and put the butter back into the fridge. "My dad has a five-acre hobby ranch. He bought me my first horse when I was ten years old. Over time, he bought two more, one for him and one for my mom." She wiped her hands down the sides of her jeans. "I don't have total ranch experience, but I'll learn as I go."

He smiled a little and watched her cut the steaming corn bread. "How about repairing barbed wire and replacing fence posts?"

"Done all of that," she assured him, handing him the platter to take to the table. Her fingers briefly touched his. "My dad and I, plus the two wranglers he hired, would go out on weekends with them and do the duty. We all worked at that kind of thing together. I always loved it."

"Not a fun thing to do in my world," Harper said, walking over to the table and putting down the corn bread. Tara had set up the table so one of them would sit at the head, one on the left side. He liked the idea of being close to her. "Fence-post rot is our biggest problem here on the Bar C. Crawford, who ran this ranch before he had a stroke, had let the replacement of fence posts go for seven years in a row. He's an alcoholic and he chased off all his wranglers, so the whole ranch suffered from years of neglect." He walked over to the counter and drew out two bowls for the chili, handing one to her. "As a consequence, we have untold numbers to replace in all the various grass lease pastures. And before we can offer a lease to a rancher to put his cows out to fatten them up during the summer months, those posts have to be strong and solid. No one is going to lease a pasture with bad posts or unrepaired barbed wire. Cows are smart and will test the posts. If they give way, they're very good at pushing them over so they can escape. Same with barbed wire that's sagging or broken from rust and age. I've seen cows get down on their knees and duck under the weak strands and run off, too."

Taking off the lid on the chili, she stirred it with a long wooden spoon, sniffing it appreciatively. "Shay mentioned there was a backlog of work to do but wasn't specific. This smells great."

Harper handed her the ladle. "Ladies first."

Her lips quirked. "Thanks," and she took the ladle from him. She spooned the thick, fragrant chili into her bowl, then said, "Here, give me your bowl. Tell me how much you want."

"Up to the brim," he told her. "Do you want shredded cheese and sour cream on top of your chili?"

"Ohhh, that sounds delicious. Yes, please." She filled his bowl and then replaced the lid on the chili. "My mouth is literally watering."

"Hungry, huh?" he asked, bringing over a pouch of shredded sharp cheddar cheese and handing it to her.

"I think it's because I got a job. I lose my appetite when I'm stressed and things aren't going well for me. When I got home, my mom told me I was way underweight and I needed to regain it," and she pointed to herself with a grimace.

"That's what a mom's supposed to say," he said. "And she's right; you're pretty skinny for your height," he informed her, looking her over. Her clothes were loose-fitting, and that meant weight loss. Some pink came to her cheeks and he realized he had made her blush.

Sprinkling the sharp cheddar cheese across the top of her chili, she said, "I've always been on the lean side."

"Probably the black-ops mission work you did entailed a lot of time pounding the ground for miles." He took the cheese from her, liking that their fingertips met once more. There was turbulence in her willow-green eyes, and he realized he'd triggered a memory, probably from her black ops past.

"Yes," she said, opening the sour cream and rising to retrieve a spoon from the drawer. "As a photographer, I was always jumping in and out of a helo miles from our objective."

Harper gave her a studied look. Her full lips were thinning. "Does talking about that make you uncomfortable, Tara?"

Shrugging, she dropped a dollop of sour cream on her chili. "Yes and no. I'm still more there than here right now, to tell you the truth."

"You've only been home a week. I know when I got home, it took me months to adjust."

"Yeah, it's an adjustment all right," she muttered,

pushing the sour cream in his direction and handing him the spoon. "I hope the walls are thick in this house."

He snorted. "Don't worry. If you wake up screaming or hitting the floor, thinking it's an IED, I'll understand. I do the same thing: flashbacks and nightmares. Usually at least once a week."

She gave him a warm look. "Good, because that's why I wouldn't stay with my parents at their ranch or their home in town. I know I'd scare the hell out of them when I wake up screaming. Or hitting the floor. They've never been in the military and I've tried to explain it to them, but it wasn't going to work."

"I understand," he said, sympathetic. He placed two heaping dollops of sour cream on top of his chili. "I lost my wife because of my PTSD," he admitted, surprised by the words coming out of his mouth. Glancing over at Tara, he saw her worried look relax. Her eyes became filled with sadness as she met and held his gaze.

"I'm so sorry, Harper. That had to be rough on both of you."

"It's in the past," he said, more gruffly than he'd intended. What was the connection swirling between them? Harper felt like he was blathering his most personal information out to Tara. He hadn't intended to do that. The words just popped out of his mouth; he'd been unable to catch them in time. Unhappy, he said, "Let's eat."

Tara sat at his elbow, and Harper was happy to have her near. Those loose blond tendrils around her temples made her look younger than he knew she was. Some of the grind of combat was there, though. The fine, feathery lines at the corners of her eyes were just beginning, but he knew how she'd gotten them. That meant a lot of missions on the ground, out in the hot, bright Afghan summer. It happened whether one wore sunglasses or not. He also saw some white scars on the backs of her hands here and there. Probably gotten during firefights. He decided to probe her past a little more between bites of corn bread and chili.

"As a combat corpsman in Afghanistan," he said, "I was assigned to black ops groups, mostly Navy SEALs but some Delta guys, too. A lot of them worked together on bigger missions. I've met FBI women who were out with the teams from time to time, too. They were along because of their expertise in translation and reading captured documents."

"Yes, there are a lot more women who work in black ops. We had FBI women, some CIA case agents with us, too."

"I never met a combat cameraperson, though. Were you pulled in on certain missions or were you assigned to a team and went out every time?"

Tara buttered a bit of corn bread. "I was assigned to Bagram Army Base. Because there weren't a lot of combat camera people around, I often got shoved into a Night Stalker MH-47 for night missions. Sometimes it was with SEALs, other times Delta Force operators or a Special Forces team."

"So? You were busy all the time?" he guessed, seeing the turbulence, the darkness in her eyes once more. Something was driving him to find out about Tara. He felt how closed up she was, but he knew it came with the territory of black ops work.

"I was never not busy," she said, spooning chili into her mouth.

"Were there other women with you on these missions?"

"Sometimes. There was also a group of combat women who were part of a larger top-secret trial to see how they did under combat conditions."

"Well, that's settled now that the Secretary of Defense

has opened up all careers, including combat, to women, across the board."

"Yes, we were guinea pigs in the trenches, and I guess we proved we had the right stuff," Tara said, wrinkling her nose.

"But you saw the worst of the worst," Harper guessed. "You were the one who had to take video and photos. You were the intel woman out on the front lines."

"Front lines never existed," she snorted, giving him a wry look. "And yes, I saw more than I ever wanted to see, Harper. But as a combat corpsman with black ops groups, you did, too."

"Which is why we both have PTSD," he agreed.

"You've been out how long?"

"A couple of years now."

"Has your PTSD ramped down at all? I'm worried mine is going to stay high like it is now."

Looking around the warm, toasty kitchen, Harper said, "Since coming to work here at the Bar C, being with other vets who have similar issues, I'm sleeping better. I don't get as many nightmares as I did before. We meet every Friday evening over at Reese and Shay's house. A psychologist from Jackson Hole, Dr. Libby Hilbert, comes down and kinda guides us through what the week has been like for each of us."

"Ugh, shrinks."

"Nah. Libby, even though she's a civilian, understands PTSD. She's actually been helpful to all of us over time."

"Yes, but you all know one another. I'm new."

"That will change," he soothed, seeing the concern in her expression. "And you don't have to talk or share if you don't want to. There's no pressure on anyone to speak up. Libby's a very gentle, kind person, and I think the more you see her deal with all of us, you'll come to trust her like we do."

"Well," she grumbled, "maybe it will work in the long run. I just hate baring my soul in front of strangers." She poked and prodded her spoon at the last of her chili.

Chuckling, Harper said, "You're a vet. You're among your own kind, Tara. We aren't strangers to one another because we've shared similar experiences. That bonds us for life. Sit next to me this Friday evening and you won't feel so threatened."

"I've yet to meet Noah, Garret, Reese, Kira, or Dair. I know Shay, which is really a blessing. We were fast friends growing up here in the valley together."

"Yes, and you can count on her. She's solid. I think you'll appreciate the ones you haven't met yet." His tone grew amused. "They don't bite."

Smiling weakly, Tara nodded and set her empty bowl aside, taking one more piece of warm corn bread from the platter. "That's good to know, Sutton."

He grinned. "A day at a time, Tara. You're one of us. And you'll find out these are really good people here at the Bar C. Wait and see."

It was almost nine a.m. The April sunlight was strong through the low-hanging gray clouds. Tara wasn't sure if it was going to snow or not. Probably it would.

She was at the kitchen sink when there was a knock at the back door. Frowning, she dried her hands on a towel and hurried to answer it. Who could it be? Thinking it was Shay or someone else from the Bar C, she was surprised to see a woman wearing a law enforcement uniform standing there. Her heart took off in dread as she opened the door. Sheriff Sarah Carter. Her father, David, had been the sheriff for twenty years in the county before he retired. And Tara remembered Sarah because they went to the same schools here in the valley.

"Sarah, it's so good to see you again. Is something wrong?" She always worried about her father, because some of the men he'd put in prison had sworn revenge once they got out.

The woman sheriff shook her head and smiled a little. "Hi, Tara. Nice to see you. I heard you just got back in town, and I had a talk with your dad two days ago. I'm here on official business. But first, I want to welcome you home."

Tara smiled thinly and gave her old friend a warm hug. Sarah was at least five-foot-eight-inches tall and medium-boned, her ginger-colored hair short, just below her ears. "It's good to see you again. Come in."

"Thanks," and she shrugged out of her heavy brown nylon jacket and hung it on a peg. Taking off her brown baseball cap, which showed an embroidered gold badge on the front of it, reading "Lincoln County Sheriff," she picked up her briefcase. "I need about half an hour of your time. I heard you got a job out here, so congratulations. How about we have coffee, if you have any, in the kitchen? We can talk there."

Stymied by Sarah's unexpected appearance, Tara said, "Sure. I just made a fresh pot." What was this all about? Sarah was very pretty, despite her unadorned khaki, long-sleeved shirt and olive-colored trousers. She wore polished black boots of a combat style, but then, the winters here in Wyoming necessitated heavy footwear.

Sarah took a seat at the table, waiting for her. She drew out some papers from her briefcase and set them next to her hand.

"I know you left here when you were eighteen," Sarah

told Tara as she brought over a tray with the coffee, milk, sugar and cups on it.

"Yes, after being kidnapped by Cree Elson, I had to get away." Sitting down opposite Sarah, she poured coffee into the two mugs. Handing one to Sarah, she said, "I've been meeting a lot of old friends since coming home. I was hoping to run into you sooner or later."

Grinning, Sarah poured cream and sugar into her coffee. "Even though this is official business, I was looking forward to seeing you again. How are you doing?"

"Adjusting to civilian life. It's really tough right now. I know from my mom that you enlisted in the Marine Corps after we graduated, but you went into the law enforcement end of it. I ended up as a combat cameraperson, spending seventy-five percent of my years on deployment to Afghanistan."

"Yes. I came back about a year and a half ago. My father wanted me to run for county sheriff and I wanted away from the combat in Afghanistan. I know you understand."

"Oh, yes, I do. But you look good, Sarah. Life must be agreeing with you."

The woman pulled out a file. "I like what I do and I'm happy. My dad was loved by just about everyone in the county and I want to run it like he did. I don't want people afraid of us. I want them to continue to see us as friends who can help them when they need us."

"So, why are you here? Not that I don't love seeing you." Tara tried to tamp down her fear. Was it Cree Elson? Again? God, she hoped not.

Sarah sipped her coffee, holding Tara's eyes. "I wanted to meet with you personally because I went over my father's notes on your case regarding Cree Elson. I read all the transcripts of the trial and his sentencing."

Wincing, Tara muttered, "Him. I was afraid this was about him. Damn." She saw Sarah's green eyes soften with sympathy.

"I'm sorry," Sarah said. "When I heard from your father, who I'm always running into over at the courthouse, that you were home, he asked me to get involved in your kidnapping case. A snitch who works with Cade, my assistant sheriff, told him Cree was talking about you after he found out you were back. This snitch works for us; used to be a druggie but is clean now. When Cade sat down to interview him about Elson, who works up at a restaurant in Jackson Hole, I got called in on it. The reason I'm here is to ask you to take out a restraining order against him. I wanted to meet with you, find out what you wanted to do about him, if anything. The only thing I can offer you is the restraining order. It will put him on warning not to approach you."

Moving uncomfortably, Tara said, "Do I really need one?"

"I'm trying to assess the situation, figure out if there's still a threat toward you from Elson. My gut is screaming at me to get this restraining order enforced."

"What does your dad think?" she asked. "Because my father admires and respects him. He's worked on many cases involving people here and I'd like to know his thoughts."

"I did discuss it with my dad and he thinks there's good reason to go forward with the restraining order." She pushed the papers toward Tara. "Based on his knowledge and my going over your kidnapping case, I agree with him. Elson works fifty miles north of us, but that doesn't mean he doesn't come to visit his mother or hang around with his three brothers when he's got time on his hands."

Stomach tightening, feeling as if an invisible hand were

gripping it, Tara studied the restraining order form. "My parents haven't spoken to me about this yet. Was my dad in favor of it after finding out the details?"

"I talked to your parents about it last night. Given that your father's a judge in this county and that my office works daily with him, I wanted his advice. We talked about it, and he felt I should be the one to discuss this with you. It's more of a formality, but it's an important one in the chain of events on something like this, should Cree ever try to approach you again. The *i*'s have to be dotted and the *t*'s crossed. I have no problem throwing his ass back into prison because you need to feel safe here, Tara."

"So, my dad thinks a restraining order should be in place?"

Sarah nodded, watching her. "It makes sense under the circumstances. Elson threatened you as he walked out of the courtroom after being convicted and being sent to prison for ten years for your kidnapping. He's been out for a year on parole."

"I haven't really asked my dad about him because, frankly, out of sight, out of mind with that crazy bastard. I guess I didn't want to know. I'm still hiding."

Mouth quirking, Sarah said, "I'm in close contact with Commander Tom Franks of the Teton sheriff's department in Jackson Hole. They know Elson is part of a gang in that area that sells drugs on the side. He's got a part-time job as a dishwasher at the Red Pickup Saloon in town. So far, they haven't been able to find him with drugs or selling them, but we know he's doing it. But he hasn't tested positive for drug use."

"Is he selling drugs somewhere else in Lincoln County, Sarah?"

"We know Hiram, Kaen and Elisha are. But they also

work with a drug lord from Central America, too. Often, they're out of state, and we don't have the manpower Teton County has to follow them around to prove it. This is one of the poorest counties in Wyoming, so my budget can't be stretched as much as I'd like."

"What's your gut say?" she asked, feeling her hands tighten painfully into fists.

"That Cree sells his nickel bags where and whenever he can. We've got a major Guatemala drug cartel in Wyoming that's trying to gain traction locally. We don't know if Elson is part of a bigger drug dealer scene or not. We know his three brothers are involved."

Making a muffled sound, Tara slid her hands around the mug of coffee. She had grown up with Sarah Carter. She was a no-nonsense kind of person but had a kindness to her, too. "His mother, Roberta, is the county gossip. What's she saying?"

Smiling a little, Sarah said, "Not much on that account. On everyone else? Any dirt she can find, she's spewing like the toxic person she is and will tell anyone who stands and listens to her nasty tales."

"Like mother, like sons," Tara muttered. "Nothing's changed since I left at eighteen."

"No, same players, same scumbags, same upstanding citizens. The canvas hasn't really changed much, except that we have a lot of military vets coming home to work in the county."

"That's a good thing," Tara said.

"I think so. I was in the Marine Corps from eighteen until I was twenty-two. After I left, I got a job with the Teton sheriff's department, where I cut my teeth on civilian law and got to know the lay of the land in western Wyoming.

That's why Tom Franks and I are so close. I worked under him."

"And then you ran for sheriff here when your father said he was retiring?"

"Yes."

Looking at the restraining order form, Tara asked, "Do you think by serving Cree with this that he might focus on me even more? If he's focused at all?"

"That's a question I wish I could answer, Tara, but I can't. What I'm trying to do is put legal protection in place for you. I don't want Elson coming into my county causing problems. He's mentally ill, unpredictable, and everyone knows it, but no one can do anything about it. He's not allowed to have a gun. He's been in bar fights in Teton County. I just don't want him bringing it all here. If I can nip it in the bud and give you some protection, I'd like to do it. What do you think?"

Tara nodded, looking at the demands on the restraining order. "We both know it's a worthless piece of paper if Elson doesn't want to obey it."

"I know that. But at least we'll have legal documents on record should he attempt to bother you after I serve it to him. Then? I can arrest him."

Rubbing her face, Tara muttered, "I hate this. I knew coming home would stir up this crap, Sarah."

Sadly, Sarah nodded. "It has to be hard on you. I can't imagine how you feel, your worry that he'll start stalking you again, watching you, as he did when you were sixteen."

Rubbing her arms, Tara said, "Exactly."

"But you're not sixteen. You're twenty-seven now, mature, far more savvy than before. You were in the military, so you know how to defend yourself. Have you gotten a concealed gun license yet?"

"No, I haven't. Shay said all the wranglers on the Bar C have them, and that I should carry, too. I just got here, so I haven't made it a priority yet."

"I think it would be a good idea," Sarah said. "Do you want to sign the order?" and she motioned toward the papers beneath Tara's hands.

"I guess. What are you going to do then?"

Sara finished off her coffee and sat up. "Once I get the Clerk of Courts and everyone who has to sign it taken care of, I'll pay Elson a visit up in Jackson Hole. Tom will work with me on that. They'd like nothing better than to get rid of Elson because they know he's dealing. There's a huge effort to get that Guatemala drug ring out of there, but it's been slow going. The FBI are finally going to send some agents and money our way to try to run the bastard out of our state."

"Not the Wyoming I knew growing up," Tara said, regret in her tone. Sarah had provided a pen along with the order and she picked it up, signing the papers with a trembling hand. "Is there anything I need to do—tell Shay or anyone else here on the ranch?"

"Once I get you a copy of the signed restraining order, I'll inform Shay. I'll ask the Clerk of Courts to send her a copy because you're living on her ranch. I know she holds a Friday-night meeting with Libby Hilbert, which is two days from now. I'll make sure she has a copy of it, as well as you. Let everyone know on Friday. The more eyes we have on you when you go to town or leave the ranch property, the better off you'll be."

Pushing the papers toward Sarah, she muttered, "I feel like I'm in prison. I'm going to have to be watching over my shoulder, remain alert. Like I did when I was rescued from Cree."

Sarah folded the papers and tucked them into her briefcase. "Look at it this way: You were in the military. Your dad told me you were black ops and saw combat. You can use your PTSD to remain alert. That can help you in a perverse way under these circumstances." She pushed the chair back and stood. "If you need help," she pulled a business card from her pocket, handing it to Tara, "call me. I'll have my department up to speed on Elson and this restraining order ready to go by tomorrow morning."

"Do you think he'll try to hurt me?" Her stomach ached with tension and she unconsciously rubbed that area of her body.

"Elson knows the Teton sheriff's department has him under their microscope. If he breaks the law, he's going to spend a long time in a federal prison. I don't think he wants to do anything to jeopardize his freedom."

"I hope you're right," Tara whispered, shaking her head. "He's obsessive, Sarah. Sick and obsessive."

"I know. All we can do is be watchful and alert. I'm hoping Elson will get nailed on drug charges up in Teton County. I don't want him in our backyard. The only time he comes here is to visit his mother."

"How often is that?"

"Maybe once or twice a month. I think he gives her some of his paycheck."

"Okay, good to know. Whether I like it or not, I'm going to have to adjust to my new reality," she offered, standing.

"I'll be in touch with you. In the meantime, welcome home. I know your parents are really happy to have you back." Sarah came over and gave her a quick hug.

If only her PTSD wasn't so bad . . . Looking at Sarah, she suspected she had the same symptoms. She just cloaked them better than Tara. "Thanks for everything you're doing. I really appreciate it."

Sarah placed her hand on her shoulder. "Keep integrating into the Bar C. Let the other vets here help you, Tara. Shay has a tight group of wounded warriors here, and I know they'll be like vigilant guard dogs. They may be able to take away some of your worry and concerns. I'll be in touch."

Chapter Four

Cree Elson felt the rage building in his chest. It always happened when Cory, the manager of the Red Pickup Saloon, yelled at him.

"Get those goddamned dishes washed! My waitresses are out of beer glasses out front! Get on it!"

He worked at the rear of the saloon, enclosed, no windows, hot, humid, and he was sweating like a pig. He hated the manager, who was the son of the owner, Ed Blackwood. He wiped his sweaty brow with the back of his arm, dishes clashing and clanging as he pushed hard to get them all into the huge aluminum dishwasher. Fuck them all! He hated smug Cory, who was all of twenty-two, a snot-nosed brat who called on Dad if things didn't go his way. Cree's red hair clung to his brow as he grabbed a plastic crate that held a lot of dirty beer glasses. They were next into the washer.

He hated this menial work. His mother was always railing against him to quit this crappy job and get something else. But who else would hire an ex-con? Not many, as he'd found out after getting out of prison. From the age of eighteen through twenty-eight, he'd been incarcerated. Another kind of hate, deeper and more malevolent, rose in him. As he slapped the beer glasses into another section of the dishwasher, not caring if he broke them or not, he pictured Tara Dalton's face in his mind. He'd been eighteen when he'd tricked her into coming into a back room of the gym. From there, he'd grabbed her and dragged her outside to his beat-up old Ford pickup. He'd made a clean escape, heading for the Salt River Mountains, where he'd dreamed of building her a cabin and living with her.

Unfortunately, the sheriff had caught up with him within a day of trying to hide in the mountains. Tara was a fighter and wouldn't stop trying to escape, which flustered the hell out of him. Yes, he'd hit her in the face and split her lip. Yes, he'd broken her nose. The sheriff of Lincoln County at that time, David Carter, had tracked them down because there had been a late May snowfall and he'd been easy to find.

When he'd caught up to him, the judge of the county, Tara's father, Scott Dalton, had to recuse himself from the case. Cree had celebrated that, but the other judge, Jeb Parish, a white-haired crotchety old bastard, had handed him a ten-year prison sentence for abducting Tara.

Scowling, he slammed the door on the machine, jabbing a button to get everything washed and cleaned.

"Get out here!" Cory yelled from the open door. "Bus the tables, dammit! You're lazy, Elson. Flat-out lazy! I got customers waiting for clean tables. You're costing me money!"

Cursing beneath his breath, Cree grabbed a huge green plastic tray and marched angrily toward the door, pinning Cory with a look he hoped would kill the little bastard on the spot.

But it didn't.

Breathing hard, Cree knew if he retaliated, he'd get fired. What was worse? Working at a lawful job or selling drugs secretly on the side? It sure as hell netted him a lot more money than being yelled at by this mangy coyote of an asshole kid.

At thirty years old, Cree felt a decade older than his age. Tonight, he'd meet up with some of his customers, pass drugs for money, then go back to the boardinghouse at the end of town. There, he shared the bottom floor with three other men around his age. Two of them were ex-cons, like him. The other, Billy Pike, just hadn't been caught yet breaking the law. Cree could sell enough drugs to pay his rent and have some money left over to give to his mother. The dishwashing job gave him legitimate cover.

He brushed past Cory, storming down the white-tiled hall. Out front there was blaring cowboy music, lots of laughter, hooting and hollering from the tourist patrons who were here to experience the so-called Wild West. The Red Pickup Saloon was known as the place where the action was. Cory paid some actors who pretended to be tourists to start a bar fight at least once a day, usually at happy hour, around four p.m. People would lift their cell phones, videotaping the exciting event. It was entertainment.

What wasn't funny was that the Teton sheriff's department knew what was going on at the saloon and frequently dropped by to keep things quiet.

It was late afternoon when Cree pushed through the swinging, bar-style wooden doors and toward the forty round wooden tables on one side of the saloon. It was filled with patrons. The mahogany, 1920s bar, which was the talk of the town, had leather saddles instead of stools, surrounding its U-shape. That was always a busy area, and one he didn't have to be concerned about. About fifteen tables needed to be cleared, so he got to work.

As he did, his red brows drew down and he glanced out the window of the saloon, and he saw someone he hated: Sheriff Sarah Carter herself, not one of her deputies, dropping in.

What the hell!

She was the sheriff of Lincoln County, not Teton County. He snorted and kept on clearing the table. She was five-foot-nine-inches tall, wearing her khaki uniform, that gun on her right hip. He hated women who were in charge of anything. They were supposed to be subservient to men. His mother had read it out of the Bible, which was his guidepost. Women were to serve men, not the other way around.

Carter entered the saloon and nearly all heads turned her way. She took off her dark brown baseball cap, holding it in her left hand, coolly surveying the patrons. Cree almost snickered when Cory came bursting out of the hall, panic written on his face, afraid law enforcement was going to cause problems and his patrons would leave. He watched out of the corner of his eye, all the while continuing to clear tables. Elated that Cory was sweating as he hurried over to Sheriff Carter, Cree couldn't help but lift his full lips into a wolf grin of delight. Cory was always afraid of a sheriff, whether it was Teton County's or the one next to it, Lincoln, which Sarah Carter ran.

He'd give anything to eavesdrop on their conversation, but the music was too loud to hear anything. Within a minute, the patrons were back to drinking, talking and laughing as the sheriff stood near the entrance, speaking with Cory.

Cree was careful. Because he had a criminal record, he could be searched at any time for drugs and weapons. He wouldn't put it past Sarah Carter to do just that, although she never had before. But sometimes, the Teton's deputies frisked him and gave him a hard time outside his workplace. Oh, they'd like to see him and the others in the boardinghouse out of this town. Cree knew they were considered druggies. Jackson Hole was a glamour spot in Wyoming, a Palm Springs in its own right, with lots of filthy-rich homeowners who looked down their noses at the working class.

So? Why was Carter here? He rarely saw her, especially in another county, so that made him curious about what had brought her here. There was word on the street that there was an undercover FBI agent trying to break into the drug trade in this part of Wyoming. If there was, Cree certainly hadn't run into the bastard. And if he did and found he was a plant? He knew what the Guatemala drug lord, Pablo Gonzalez, would do. That spy would be dead in a heartbeat, his body thrown into the forest, never to be found.

Cree bought his drugs from Gonzalez but refused to be part of the ring. Not stupid, he was aware that the US government had its eye on the drug lord and was just waiting to take him down. No, he didn't need that. He had to stay clean in the eyes of the law or else.

His immediate threat was Sarah Carter, whose spring-colored green eyes narrowed speculatively on him when she lifted her head after talking to Cory. Instantly, Cree's pulse rate shot up and he forced himself to look away, paying attention on cleaning the table in front of him. *Shit!* What did the bitch want with him? Glancing surreptitiously to the right, he saw her leave Cory's side and come toward him. Mouth tightening, he stopped cleaning as she approached, wary about what she wanted. His heart started to beat harder. Carter had no enforcement capability in this county. It wasn't hers to run. God knew, however, she had more than once visited his mother, asking about his alleged drug activity. His mother always rolled over and played the idiot all the townspeople thought she was. It was a ruse, of course, and they often laughed about it afterward.

Straightening to his full six-foot-two-inches, he glared at Carter, who halted about three feet away from him. Most people, when he assumed that stance, automatically backed off. But she didn't. He'd entertained the idea many times in his head kidnapping her and taking her to the cabin he'd built in the Salt River Mountains.

"You want somethin'?" he demanded, a wet cloth in his right hand.

"Yes," she said. "Let's go to the hallway, out of everyone's earshot. You go first and I'll follow you."

He wanted to spit into her calm-looking face. Nothing rattled that bitch. Absolutely nothing. Cree grabbed the plastic tray filled with dirty dishes and glasses, moving around the table and heading toward the swinging doors. Once inside the hall, he went to the kitchen and set the tray aside, waiting for her to appear. She wore a man's clothing, but that didn't hide her femininity in the least, which Cree saw as a weakness. Women weren't better than men. They never had been. His hands tightened at his sides.

Sarah came to a halt just within the opened door to the kitchen, settling the hat on her head, keeping her gaze steady on him.

"Tara Dalton has left the military and is home for good." Her voice lowered. "And you need to know that a restraining order against you was just put into service." She pulled it from the clipboard she carried, handing a copy of it to him. "You can't be within five hundred feet of her at any time. You even so much as look at her? And you're in Lincoln County, my turf? I'll take you down so damned fast it will make your head spin."

He grabbed the piece of folded paper. "I didn't know she was back." That was a lie, but he didn't care.

"My advice, Elson? Stay the hell away from my county. If I find you in it? I'll have a deputy tailing you wherever you go. Got that? You're to leave Tara Dalton *alone*. Don't speak to her. Don't approach her. I'm just waiting to take you in and haul your ass into court again. And this time, there won't be any leniency on breaking your probation. Got it?"

Glaring at her, he stuffed the paper into his back pocket. "Yeah, I got it, Sheriff." He saw her eyes go a darker jade color, her voice low.

"You come into Lincoln County? We have a drug-sniffing dog team now. We know your truck and license number. My deputies have standing orders to pull you over and search you and that truck any time you cross the county line. Got it?"

"Yeah," he snarled, "I got it, Sheriff." He hated her calm expression, hated that game face she always wore. "I have a right to visit my mother!"

"Sure you do. Just expect our drug-sniffing team to be all over you when you do."

Hatred pooled deep within him. Right now, he was torn between who to go after first: Tara Dalton or this bitch of a sheriff. Nothing would give him greater pleasure than to hurt Sarah Carter real bad. "That's harassment," he grunted.

Shrugging, Sarah said, "But it's justified. Let's see, Elson. How many times had you gone to jail for a couple of weeks to a month for selling drugs or having them on your person before kidnapping Tara?" She held up her hand. "Six times in the span of three years you were in juvie. You're not careful. But if I catch you? I'm asking the state attorney general to go after you with everything we can and put your ass in prison for a long, long time."

His upper lip lifted and he barely rasped, "You gotta catch me first."

Tara wished her stomach would relax. Sarah had dropped by in the afternoon with the signed papers. She had taken a copy of them over to Shay, who was in her office at the ranch house. Asking her to stay, they'd walked to the kitchen. Tara could smell a beef stew cooking on the stove. She'd met Reese earlier and he'd gone to town with Noah to get more grain for the horses boarded in the ranch stables.

"How are you doing?" Shay asked, carrying cups of coffee to the kitchen table and sitting down.

Tara sat opposite her. "Not good today. Sarah coming to fill me in on Cree just brought up everything I was trying to ignore."

Shay nodded. "Yes, it's a sticky, awkward situation you came home to. But wipe that worry out of your eyes, okay? Sarah's on top of this. She's working closely with the Teton County sheriff. All you have to do is be alert. Plus, we'll discuss this when Libby drops by for our Friday-night get-together tomorrow night."

"Yes, everyone needs to know what's going on," Tara said glumly. "I just wish things were different. That Cree was out of here. Gone from my life forever."

"I know." Shay sighed and gave her a sympathetic look. "It's sort of like our ongoing legal issues with my father. He lives in Wind River now. We have a restraining order against him; he can't come to Bar C land again, but I hate the possibility of meeting him at the feed store or at Kassie's Café. I'm always nervous about it."

"I forgot about that," Tara admitted. "Even though your father isn't going to kidnap you, that's still a terrible stress for you."

"It sure is. And every day, people in Wind River who see him say he's getting stronger physically. He wants to get rid of his limp and the weakness from that stroke he had and prove to the court that he's fully capable of retaking the Bar C. Reese thinks it will eventually culminate in a jury trial."

"I remember my dad talking about Ray and his father when I was growing up," Tara murmured. "He said Ray was always getting the tar beaten out of him by his old man. And before I went into the military Ray was well on his way to destroying the ranch. It was already beginning to die."

"It was. I got the shock of my life when I came home on a hardship discharge to take over the Bar C because he was in a nursing home, incapable of doing much of anything after that stroke."

Looking around the warm, large kitchen, Tara said, "Well, you've done so much good, bringing the Bar C back to life. You deserve all the credit, Shay; you had a dream, a vision for your home."

"There's days when I feel good about it," Shay admitted. "If not for Reese's love and support, I don't think I could have taken on my father and made a stand against him."

"Reese is a great guy, but then, all the men of the Bar C are."

"Speaking of them, do you think you'll get along with Harper?"

Tara smiled a little, sipping her coffee. "Yes. He's very nice. I don't see any problems arising between us. It's just me getting used to the tempo and pace of the ranch at this point."

"Well, we'll let all the wranglers in on your kidnapping and the fact that Cree Elson's still around; plus, they need to know about the restraining order. Sarah sent me an updated photo of Elson, and I've passed it to everyone's cell phone so they can spot him if they see him around town or anywhere near our ranch." Reaching over, Shay touched Tara's hand. "Don't worry. Everything will settle down and start smoothing out the more you get used to your new, fixed routine known as civilian life."

Giving a weak smile, Tara said, "There's a lot of military here at the Bar C, which makes it a lot easier to make that transition, Shay. And I really do want to contribute."

"You will, in time. I just need you to breathe, take it easy and let Harper guide and integrate you into our ranch rhythm."

"I'll sit down with him tonight and tell him what happened. I don't want to blindside him at the Friday-evening meeting."

"I think that's a good idea," Shay said.

Harper sat in the living room with Tara after dinner. She appeared nervous and tense, as if she had something on her mind.

Sitting at one end of the couch, she poured out the story of her kidnapping by Cree Elson. It took every bit of his control not to reach out and drag her into his arms, to give her a sense of safety. It was painfully obvious that Tara didn't feel safe at all after Sarah Carter's visit and the signing of the restraining order.

Opening her hands, she uttered, "I'm really sorry to drag you into this, Harper. But I felt you needed to know first, not last, what was going on in my life. It wouldn't be fair for you not to be aware I have an enemy out there who could jump me at some point. I don't know what I'd do if you got hurt by Elson. He's crazy and flies into unexpected rages and lashes out." She touched her nose. "When I was with him and tried to escape, he punched me in the face and broke my nose. He told me after I regained consciousness that he didn't know what had happened, that he had no memory of striking me."

Moving slowly, Harper sat up, elbows on his thighs, his hands clasped between them, studying her in the lulling silence. There was such fear in her eyes, and he could feel the tension and anxiety swirling around her. "I think you're pretty brave, coming back here," he said quietly, holding her anguished gaze. "Did you know Elson would be around when you came home?"

Shaking her head, she whispered, "I put him deep down in myself to the point where I buried it all. When I finished my enlistment, my whole life was in tatters. The PTSD was tearing me up and that was my focus. When I got home and my dad told me that Cree was still in the area, that's when it hit me like a sledgehammer. Up until that point, I honestly hadn't thought of him in years."

"Because your focus was on surviving missions and combat," he said, nodding.

"Yes . . ."

"How do your parents feel about this? About Elson being in your backyard?"

"My mom worries he'll do the same thing to me, kidnap me or try to kill me. My dad has full belief that law enforcement will keep me safe."

"The difference between a judge and a mother," Harper said, his mouth pulling inward at the corners for a moment. "What do you want to do, Tara?"

"I wanted to come home, Harper. Have I thought about leaving since I found out about Cree? Yes. But I love this valley. I love all the people I grew up with and I want to be home to try to get well."

"I agree with you. When you come from a happy home, plus a town of people who know and love you, it's good to stay."

"But it's an awful price, Harper. What if Cree attacks me in this house? What if he hurts or kills you? Or Shay, Reese or anyone else who lives on the ranch? I couldn't bear to have that happen. And I know Cree is capable of killing."

"But he hasn't."

"No, not so far, but I saw it in his eyes. He gets angry, snaps and he's a wild man without control." She touched her nose. "I know from experience. I pushed him too far and this is what happened to me. I still feel to this day that he's obsessed with me, and he could kill me if the situation was right."

Seeing the helplessness in her expression, he said, "You have a right to come home. You have a right to be with your family. No one should be able to chase you away."

"That's how I feel, Harper. I'm angry, I'm scared and my imagination is tearing the hell out of me. My PTSD makes it worse because now I'm in a different form of combat, but it's still life and death. I thought by coming home I'd find peace. Healing."

He heard the anguish in her whispered tone, saw the defeat in her eyes. "Look," he said gently, "Rome wasn't built in a day and you coming home after so many years, I'm sure, seems daunting. I believe you couldn't be safer than here on the Bar C. We're all combat-trained vets. Once everyone gets Elson's photo and you share your story on Friday night, you'll have a vanguard of vets surrounding you. We all live with PTSD, which makes us hyperalert." He grinned a little. "And in this case? With Elson potentially skulking around again? Our alertness will keep us more aware than most other people. You'll be safe. And if you have to go into town, one of us can go with you. You don't need to be by yourself, feeling like there's a target on your back. We'll figure something out that works for you. Okay?"

She gave him a grateful look. "Thanks . . . I hadn't thought about our hyperalertness. You're right. I just hate imposing my problem on all of you. And it's not a little one; it's nasty with awful consequences if Cree tries to come after me again."

"Well," he counseled, straightening up, "let's just see what the gang has to say on Friday night. Okay? Because, whether you like it or not, men are very protective of women and children." He held up his hand. "And I know you can take care of yourself, but in this case, the more eyes and ears on the situation can be a huge plus. It will keep everyone safe. If we know who the enemy is, that's ninety percent of the battle."

She looked mollified by his words. Harper wished he could do a helluva lot more for Tara. There was magic between them; he could feel it. He already knew what love was, and his heart was opening for the first time since Olivia had divorced him. He'd never blamed his ex-wife for her actions. At the time he was a certifiable emotional and mental wreck. Now, years later, he'd worked through a lot of his PTSD, he'd matured and life didn't seem quite so threatening to him.

He watched Tara collapse against the sofa, her knees drawn up against her body, her arms around them, afraid. At least she had some hope in her eyes, and if his words, his quiet tenor, could do that to ease her mind, that was good. She was more worried about others being harmed by Elson than herself.

Harper understood that reaction to being part of a team. Serving in the military molded a person to care for their team, squad or platoon equally, usually more than themselves. It was the ability to sacrifice for their comrades that set them apart from people in the civilian world. He knew Tara, without ever thinking, would put her own life in jeopardy to save any one of them from Elson.

His heart opened and the sensations flooded his chest in a way he'd never experienced before. Tara was so damned brave, but she didn't see herself like that. All she saw was that she was a catalyst waiting to get one of them hurt because Elson might stalk or attack her again. Every cell in his body wanted to protect her, shield her from her thoughts and agony and worry. He needed to find a way to focus her attention on something other than the drama of this bastard threatening like a lurking shadow over her life. Harper wanted desperately to hold Tara. She looked so alone, so frightened leaning against the couch. Silently, he promised her that he'd be there for her in whatever capacity she'd accept him into her life.

Understanding he was no pick of the litter because he'd already lost a marriage and a woman he'd loved deeply, Harper held no rosy, idealistic goals for a romantic relationship with Tara. Right now, she needed a steadfast friend who could support her and get her focus off what could hurt her and on to something far more healthy and hopeful. Harper could do that for her. He knew he could.

Chapter Five

Harper made a point of watching the vets as they pulled the chairs, sofa or folding seats into a loose circle for their Friday-night chat at Shay and Reese's ranch home. Libby, her red hair in a topknot, ran the session after dinner. She was in her midforties, and Harper, as all the other vets, entrusted the psychologist with their vulnerable, combat-injured emotional wounds. Maybe it was Libby's pale green eyes, several shades lighter even than Tara's beautiful willow-colored ones, that made her look like a hawk. She was intense and attentive. Libby was a very good listener.

He'd wanted to sit next to Tara but had decided not to do that because he didn't want anyone to know how protective he had become toward her. And he instinctively knew she would pick up on it herself. It was too soon to let her know he was seriously interested in her. Libby would have picked up on that instantly, too. Women had all-terrain radar. Harper wasn't ready to admit to anyone, much less fully to himself, that Tara was opening doors that had slammed shut in his heart. He was still getting used to his heart acting up, and he wasn't sure what to do about it. He'd failed miserably at marriage before and didn't feel he had the necessary skills to be an equal partner in a serious, emotional relationship with another woman. At least not yet. Tara was making him want to engage with her on that level, though. Maybe it was just as simple as that he was lonely and Tara, by accident, was filling that spot in his heart.

Everyone warmed to Tara immediately, especially Kira and Dair. And when Tara finished her explanation of Cree Elson kidnapping her, both women got up and walked across the room to give her hugs of support and sympathy.

He'd wanted to do the same thing but had anchored his butt to the chair instead. At least Kira and Dair could give Tara what she really needed right now: a sense of acceptance and care. He could see the relief in Tara's eyes that she wasn't alone in this ongoing predicament, that she had stalwart friends standing with her. Still, he fought an urge to go over and hold her because he sensed that was exactly what she needed.

Garret Fleming, who was going to marry Kira, gave his fiancée a concerned look when she sat down after hugging Tara. He studied Tara and then said, "There isn't anyone here who won't have your back, Tara. You need to know that."

"Thanks, Garret. My mind knows that, but right now, I'm pretty rocky about the whole issue."

Libby leaned forward, giving Garret and the rest of them a kind smile. "Tara, you've just left the world you've known for many years and stepped back into civilian life. That's enough of an emotional adjustment. But then to find out Cree Elson is still around, and the sheriff insisting on a restraining order to keep you safe; it's enough to make anyone reel. Your reactions are normal. You need to lean on all of us while you make these external and mental adjustments."

"That's right." Noah Mabrey spoke up, giving his fiancée, Dair, a loving look before he held Tara's distraught gaze. "We're all here for you. Anything you need, just ask us."

"Oh," Kira said, her gray eyes stormy with emotion, "you can cry on our shoulders, Tara. Dair and I are great listeners."

"Yes," Dair chimed in, her black hair in braids, "but I think Kira, Shay and I just might drop in unannounced to check up on you every once in a while. You're black ops. You're used to buttoning up and not asking for help from anyone."

Tara gave Dair a roll-eyed look. "Well, you're sure right about that. You work hurt, you don't complain, you stuff your fears and get your job done. Teammates are counting on you to do that. But I don't mind if any of you come up to ask me how I'm doing. I promise I'll spill it all because I'm not black ops anymore."

Garret grinned. "Well, now that you're with us here at the Bar C, I'll just make you a couple of special dinners. You do know we gather every Sunday at Shay and Reese's house at four p.m.?"

"Harper mentioned it to me," Tara said. "I've just been too busy of late to think about it."

"Well, it's Friday," Reese told her, smiling a little, "and we do expect you to show up for Sunday dinner. Okay?"

Harper added, "Tara, Garret is a chef of the first order. Once you taste the food he makes, you'll never miss a dinner here."

Tara gave them all a grateful smile, her hands clasped tightly in her lap. "Thank you—all of you—you have no idea how welcome you make me feel. I promise, despite everything that's going on, I'll carry my fair share of the load here at the ranch."

"Yeah," Noah intoned, giving everyone a silly grin, "we know that one. Work hurt. Don't complain and all that. But here? If you get hurt? You go and see Harper, because he's our combat corpsman on the property. Don't overdo anything right now; I think Libby will agree with me on that."

"Certainly will, Noah," Libby said. "You're still in shock, Tara. Let us surround you. We'll support you. And you're going to have good and bad days. Like the rest of the vets here, you have serious PTSD. And with Cree Elson around, this is triggering your symptoms big-time. I think all the vets will tell you that after about six months here on the Bar C, they felt more at peace, less anxious, and from that point, their PTSD has been gradually diminishing. Am I right?" Libby looked around the circle at each of them.

Harper saw everyone vigorously nod their heads.

"Maybe I'm expecting too much of myself," Tara hoarsely admitted, staring down at her hands.

"Vets are bred to the bone to go the extra mile," Libby said gently. "Just ask for help, Tara. Don't wall us out. You're lucky to be bunking in with Harper because he already has the combat corpsman's healing energy. Utilize him, okay? I'm sure he'll be there when you want him to be."

Giving Harper a kind look, Tara said, "He's already doing that for me, Libby, and I'm so grateful."

"How does he help you?" she asked, tilting her head, holding Tara's gaze.

Pushing some of her blond hair away from her face, Tara admitted in a low voice, "Well, I've never told him this, but when he comes in from the barn and I'm in the house, I can literally feel my anxiety dissolving."

"So, just having him near does that for you?" Libby asked.

"Yes. Or if I'm in the barn helping him with something, the anxiety leaves. I stop thinking about Elson stalking me again."

Libby gave Harper a pleased look. "Nice touch, Sutton."

It was Harper's turn to feel heat stealing into his face. "Well," he stumbled, "I guess it's just because of my corpsman skills."

"Oh," Libby drawled, "I have a feeling it's much more than that, but I'm not going there. Okay?"

Harper realized the very astute Libby saw right through him, and that whatever was going on between him and Tara was much more than just his corpsman skills. Not daring to look at anyone else in the room, he merely nodded. He'd be digging himself in a hole for sure if he responded. Sometimes no explanation was best, and this was one of those times.

When he happened to glance to his left, Garret was grinning like a wolf who'd just nailed his prey. Looking to his right, Noah had a shit-eating grin on his face. *Well, hell!* These guys seemed to sense that his connection to Tara was more than just being a caring medic toward her. Damn. They would razz the hell out of him!

April 25

There were moments when Tara didn't think she'd make it through the day as a wrangler because of her high anxiety levels. She had called Libby Hilbert, who had an office in Jackson Hole, to get some help with it. Libby asked her to make an appointment with a physician's assistant, Taylor Douglas, who lived in Wind River. Seeing her sounded hopeful. She didn't want to be drugged up with antidepressants, though, unable to remain emotionally engaged and enjoy her life.

She had just hung up the phone, getting ready to make lunch, when Harper came into the mudroom, stomping off the slush from another snowstorm that had hit the valley yesterday. He'd spread salt pellets along the wooden sidewalk that lay between the four homes and the arena, as well as to the other barns.

"Lunch is almost ready," Tara called over her shoulder.

"Smells good," Harper said, entering the kitchen after shrugging off his cold-weather gear. He pushed his fingers through his flattened-hat hair. "What did you make for us?"

Tara hungrily absorbed his unexpected closeness as he halted and leaned over her, smelling the soup she was stirring in a large six-quart pot. "It's actually whatever I could find in the fridge," she admitted, enjoying his masculinity, that quiet, intense feeling that automatically surrounded her whenever Harper was near. "I even found a couple of yams, cut them up and threw them in."

"Well," he said, straightening, checking to see if the table was set, "it smells great."

"We had leftover brats and I chopped them up for a protein source." No cowboy was a vegetarian. The work they did required serious protein in their diet.

"You've got corn bread baking, too," he said, pleased as he leaned over, looking into the window of the oven.

"Yep, it didn't take me long to figure out you were a meat, potatoes and bread kinda guy," and she grinned. Tara loved that his gray eyes flared with amusement over her teasing. There were days when Harper didn't shave and she liked the darkness that collected, giving him a very sexy look.

"Guilty as charged," he drawled, rolling up his sleeves. "Anything else you need help with?"

"No. I made us each a salad. You can grab them out of the fridge and put the dressings on the table, too."

"Got it," he said. Harper also pulled out the two types of salad dressing, along with the covered bowls.

"How are Candy and her foal doing? This was the first day you were going to let them loose in the indoor arena."

"Fine," he said, setting the salads on the table. He pulled off the plastic wrap from each one. "Candy was whinnying a lot because her foal thought the arena was a racetrack," and he chuckled. "The little one liked getting out and stretching those long, slender legs of hers."

"I wish I could have seen that." She ladled the soup into two bowls and brought them over to the table. Next came the corn bread, which she cut up and placed on a platter, bringing it over and putting it down at his elbow.

She loved having three meals a day with Harper. It was their time for intimate talk, not ranch business, and she needed that closeness in an emotional sense, more than usual. Tara supposed it was because her anxiety was off the scale. She wasn't sleeping well, getting only two or three hours a night, if that.

"You can see them," Harper said. "Bring your camera with you when you do." He took a sip of the soup and pleasure wreathed his expression. "This is really good," he congratulated her. "That corn bread is delicious."

Tara smiled with pleasure.

"You were on the phone when I came in earlier," Harper continued. "Who was calling?"

"Oh, Libby called me. She gave me the name of a local PA who she said helps PTSD people like us. Taylor has a test she runs, and if my cortisol is out of normal bounds, she can give me something called an adaptogen that supposedly shuts off the cortisol in my bloodstream."

Nodding, Harper cut two large slices of corn bread and placed one of them on a smaller plate next to her bowl. "Yes, Libby's sent all of us to see Taylor."

"Has it worked? I mean, are you still anxious since getting Taylor's medical help?"

Harper shook his head. "No," he said between bites of corn bread, "since taking the adaptogen she gave me, I've been calm. I've never had the anxiety come back. I sleep through the night, I have fewer nightmares and flashbacks. It takes about three days after taking the adaptogen once or twice a day to shut off the cortisol, which keeps pouring into our bloodstream twenty-four hours a day and making us hyperalert."

"Truly?" Tara couldn't keep the amazement out of her voice. She saw his gray eyes turn warm. "We were all on Libby to get you to Taylor sooner, not later, because of this stuff going on with Cree Elson. I'm glad she called you today. Are you going to make an appointment with Taylor? It will be the best thing you've ever done for yourself."

"Sure, with that kind of recommendation," she said. "I'll call her after lunch."

"Good," he said, pleased. "It's been a couple of weeks since you came here. Do you feel like you're settling into some kind of routine?"

She buttered the steaming corn bread. "Yes. I just need to get a decent night's sleep. I lose so much every night. I get up and putter around in the kitchen. I hope I don't wake you up, Harper."

"I was that same way when I first came to the Bar C. Seeing Taylor, getting tested for high cortisol and then taking the adaptogen to turn it off, will give you a new lease on life."

She muttered, "Will it make Cree disappear?"

He chuckled. "No, but I sure wish it could."

"I'd give anything to get rid of this horrible anxiety," she whispered, sipping her soup.

"Taylor will help you on that issue." He reached over, tapping the back of her hand, cupped around the bowl. "After you get done talking with her, bring your camera down and take some photos of Candy and her little one. You need to start snapping some shots again."

"I worry it will interfere in my work around here, Harper."

"Nah, it's not going to bother anyone. That's part of your job, shooting stock photos, It's time you started a file on the Bar C, and who knows? You could sell some of the stock online. That's where you make your money for the ranch."

"It is," she agreed. Looking out the large picture window, she sighed. "And it's so beautiful out. I can hardly wait to see Candy and her foal in the paddock."

"Well, right now with the spring day melting some of the snow and then the temp falling below freezing at night, we have nothing but ice in those paddocks. Come late May, they'll be muddy, but everything will be pretty much melted. Then we can let them outdoors."

Cree sat in his boardinghouse room, ignoring his two friends who helped pay the monthly rent for their Jackson Hole digs. He hated listening to them jabbering with each other when the crazy bastards were high on meth. He had enough constant noise as a dishwasher for the saloon; now he craved quiet. It was cold outside and he didn't want to walk the back streets of the town. Not at this time of night, because there could be ice on the sidewalks. He didn't need to slip and land on his ass.

He studied the restraining order the sheriff had handed him. His mouth flattened. He was already on law enforcement's radar because of his prison record. How stupid had he been? Driven by teenage hormones, blindly in love with Tara, wanting her, wanting a happy life with her, and he'd grabbed her. And got caught. And now? He had nowhere else to go. He didn't dare try to work in Wind River. Everyone knew what he'd done and was angry at him for it, so nobody would hire him. At least in Jackson Hole, fifty miles away, he could get a job. This was a town of the haves and have nots. The rich and famous lived here. Meanwhile, working-class people struggled like hell to hold on by their fingernails, paid next to nothing, and yet they were the worker bees who made the town function.

He wanted to rip up the restraining order, but he didn't. If he came within five hundred feet of Tara Dalton, his ass could be thrown in jail. Or if he went onto Bar C property, where she worked. He wondered where she lived. There was no address other than the Bar C. Did she live there, too? Most wranglers had a bunkhouse or some sort of living arrangement on the ranch they worked for and he guessed she probably did live on the property. Hence, he was not legally allowed on that ranch's property.

His upper lip curled and he felt rage flow through him. It felt like a war within him. On one hand, he wanted to choke Tara and watch her die. On the other, he still obsessed with her. That need for her had never left him. *Never.* His heart pounded briefly to underscore what she meant to him. He was thirty years old and his puppy love for her had begun back in grade school, and it had never diminished. The intensity of his need for her was like an invisible hand pushing him forward, cajoling him to go after her, kidnap her again. Only this time? He'd be a helluva lot smarter about it. This time, he wouldn't get caught and she would finally be his. *Now and forever.*

Folding up the restraining order, he got up and pulled open a drawer on his nearby bed stand and dropped it in. Grabbing a towel, washcloth and soap, he left the large room and headed down the hall to the bathroom on the first floor of the three-story building. His red hair was long and straight and he had it tied back in a ponytail. Once in the bathroom, he stripped naked, removed the rubber band from his dark red hair and climbed into the shower. Scrubbing his hair with shampoo and cleansing himself with the soap, his mind and heart orbited around the need for Tara.

He'd not seen her since she'd left. His mother had called him excitedly, telling him that she'd seen Tara Dalton at the feed store. Cree wasn't sure whether to be happy or sad about it. Scrubbing his hair, lathering the soap into the thick, heavy strands, he closed his eyes, envisioning Tara. How did she look now? Probably more beautiful. More desirable. In every way. His erection sprang to life as he fantasized what he'd do to her after he kidnapped her again.

All his fantasies had kept his obsession to claim her alive and haunting him hourly. The voices that had manifested when he was fifteen whispered to him to make her his own. The voices never stopped, always cajoling, always pushing him to go after what he wanted. Tara was in his blood. In his soul. He needed her like he needed oxygen to breathe.

The asshole shrink he'd seen in prison had squeezed it out of him and he'd talked about his obsession with her. The shrink had tried to make Cree think he saw Tara as an out, his good-luck charm, a lucky rabbit's foot and everything wonderful and happy he yearned to have. Tara represented all that to him and more. It wasn't just about having sex with her, although he knew he'd enjoy that immensely. No, he wanted the nurturing quality that exuded from her. He wanted her to want him. The most powerful emotions arose in him when he visualized her cradling him in her arms, his head pressed to her breasts.

But she never had. Tara had fought like a spitting, angry bobcat when he'd captured her, dragging her off to the Salt River Mountains. She hated him and screamed at him, demanding that she be released. Who the hell did he think he was to grab her and make her his prisoner? Oh, Tara had a mouth on her for sure, and he grinned a little, rinsing his hair beneath the warm water. He tried to patiently explain why he'd done it. That he loved her. That he needed her to live with him. That he needed to be held and rocked by her.

Well, that hadn't gone over well either. He pushed the suds on his face away beneath the water, opening his eyes. Squeezing the extra water out of his hair, which hung halfway down his long, muscular back, he laughed. Tara was fearless. She fought him without ever quitting. She tried to escape, which angered him. Even now, he felt bad about striking her and breaking her nose. He'd felt horrible afterward. That wasn't what he'd wanted to do with her. He'd wanted to love her, hold her and be tender with her. But his anger . . . Well, he'd always raged, had what they termed an uncontrollable temper. The voices would push him into acting and he'd snap and hurt someone. And then he wouldn't remember what he'd done. It was only after he'd come down out of that blinding rage, with Tara sitting there, her hands with ropes around her wrists, tied to the nearby trunk of a spindly pine tree, her nose bleeding, that he'd realized something had happened.

At first, he didn't remember striking her. She had angrily told him, tears running from her eyes, that he'd slammed his fist into her face. How the hell else did he think she'd gotten a broken, bloody nose?

Cree shut off the shower and stepped out, his body glistening with water. Grabbing a towel, he scowled, remembering that stark afternoon in the mountains. He'd struck Tara. The last person in the world he wanted to hurt and he'd done just the opposite because the voices in his head ordered him to punch her to shut her up.

Oh, he'd wanted to hurt plenty of people who made him angry. When Tara'd called him crazy, he'd snapped, he guessed. Well, there was no guesswork about it. There was no one else in the vicinity to break Tara's nose other than him, so even if he didn't remember doing it, the proof was there, staring him in the face. He'd tried to help her, pulling out a small towel from his knapsack, holding it up to her face so she could press her nose against it.

Tara was so angry, she'd lashed out with her tied hands, striking his hand and the towel away. He'd been shocked by her actions. All he'd wanted to do was make up for his hitting her. Mumbling apology after apology didn't soothe her anger and hurt either.

He felt guilty that she wouldn't let him help her afterward. It was then he'd realized he really was the monster his mother and father had always said he was. He'd had these voices screaming inside his head, sudden black rages triggering violence, never remembering them until someone else told him what he'd done. No memory of it. Not ever.

His mother called him an imbecile, an idiot. The shrink in prison had suggested that his old man, his father, Brian, who was an alcoholic, had abused him as a baby and given him a traumatic brain injury. Which was why, the shrink said to him, that the rages short-circuited in the injured frontal lobe of his brain and he would remember nothing, nor did he feel any remorse or guilt while in a fury. He felt dead inside. Always had.

Cree dried himself off, his mind going back to the miserable years he was a prisoner. His mother couldn't afford to drive to Salt Lake City federal prison to see him often. Gas cost money and she had little. He'd hated that time and, finally, he'd served his sentence and was freed.

Disliking that everyone else called him a mental retard, Tara saying he was a crazed monster had lingered hurtfully in his chest. Cree had never forgotten the kidnapping or her despising him for doing it.

He promised to build her a beautiful cabin in the woods, where she'd be happy with him. That's all he wanted. He honestly didn't know what happiness was, but seeing Tara daily in school made his heart feel good. It was the only time he'd ever felt emotions flow through him like sunlight, chasing away the darkness in his soul. Tara made him feel hope for the first and only time in his life. It was her. That wonderful, sunny smile of hers, that husky laugh, that sparkle in her green eyes. All he had to do was picture her in his mind and his whole body vibrated with a wild yearning for her once more. It felt like the world's worst addiction, and he was trapped within it. Besides, the voices told him that Tara wanted him and he should go get her and make her his own, once and for all.

Somehow, he had to rethink his kidnapping her. This time? It had to work. He had to preplan. He had to watch her and get her pattern of daily living so that when he captured her a second time, he'd be successful. And maybe Tara being older, she wouldn't be as wild and angry as she had been at sixteen. But even if she was, Cree believed in his heart that he could tame her with kindness, be good to her, hold her. He was older, too. Patience wasn't his strong suit, but with Tara, he wanted so badly to be just that for her. She might not like being captured and living with him, but eventually, Cree felt, he could wear her down, convince her that he was the only man for her. Yes, that would work. He would be patient with her. No matter if she was angry all over again, calling him names and pleading to be released, he'd stick to his new plan.

Chapter Six

May 1

Ebony raced around the indoor arena, her little broom tail straight up, her spindly legs flying through the sand, her tiny teacup muzzle thrust as far forward as she could stretch it on her short little neck. Tara couldn't stop a chuckle from forming as she watched the two-month-old black filly with the white blaze down her face, scamper around. Like any foal, she kicked, jumped, bucked and slid. Her mother, Candy, stood patiently in the center of the empty arena, watching her baby race around.

Clicking off a series of photos with her Canon 7D camera, Tara felt the thrill of photography envelope her once again. Instead of photographing horrendous photos of torture, death and carnage, she was shooting something hopeful and positive that would make people smile. Harper had coaxed her out the day they'd talked about shooting Ebony in the indoor arena and those photos had been wonderful. She'd already sold a number of them on stock photo websites. They were popular, but then, any baby horse, filly or colt, was cute, in her opinion.

It was midday, the May sunlight spilling brightly into

the arena. She looked up to see Dair and Kira arriving, smiling and raising their hands in greeting. Lifting hers as well, Tara said, "Come and watch Ebony. She's *such* a showboater."

The women's collective laughter echoed through the arena, but it didn't stop show-off Ebony from whirling around on her long, thin legs and running the other way. She made little grunts with her gigantic effort to race at them at the fastest possible speed as Tara continued to photograph her. She saw Dair and Kira come and lean against the pipe-rail fence, hooking a boot over the lowest rung, grinning and watching the foal.

Finally, after sprinting around, Ebony slowed and went back to her mother, thrusting her nose beneath the mare's belly, looking for a quick pickup of milk. She suckled noisily, her tail whipping back and forth like a metronome as she thirstily drank from her patient, nearly half-asleep mother. Tara got all of it on her card.

"Hey," Dair called, "I just saw Harper. He said you'd seen Taylor Douglas about taking that saliva test for high cortisol. How did that go, Tara?"

Tara came over and shut off her Canon, allowing it to hang around her neck. She joined her friends, leaning against one metal post, the rails between them. "Okay, I guess," she told Dair, who was in a light denim jacket, jeans and boots. As always, she had her black hair in braids, her baseball cap pushed up on her head. She was wearing gloves, and Tara knew she was helping Harper clean out the box stalls. It was a daily and necessary duty. "I mailed off the box with my saliva tube in it this morning. Taylor said she'd call me when she got the results, which should be in about five days."

Dair nodded, resting her arms on the rail. "Kira and I

were sent to her by Libby Hilbert about a month after we arrived here at the Bar C," she said. "Best thing Libby has done for us." She shot a look to her left, where Kira stood. She, too, was wearing a lightweight denim jacket, her leather work gloves in one hand. "Wasn't it, Kira?"

"Absolutely," Kira said. "It's the next phase of getting well."

"Maybe not a hundred percent well," Dair told Tara, "but having the anxiety stop has been huge for all of us."

Kira grinned at Tara. "And we're all looking forward to when Taylor prescribes the adaptogen you need to shut off that cortisol once and for all."

"I can hardly wait," Tara agreed, leaning against the post, watching Ebony feed. The little filly was assertive and her mother nearly had her eyes closed, head hanging as Ebony butted repeatedly at her mother's milk bag. Candy had the patience of Job, that was for sure.

"Hey, we're driving up to Jackson Hole this afternoon," Dair said. "Would you like to come along?"

"Why are you going up there?"

Dair gave Kira a warm look. "There's a wedding dress store up there and she's going to find and order her dress. Shay is coming along with us, by the way. We figured we'd use the ranch truck with the extended cab. All four of us will fit into it. Are you interested?"

Tara knew Kira had agreed to marry Garret and that they'd set a date of June 16 to get married here at the ranch. "Sure, I'd love to go along!"

"Maud Whitcomb is going to meet us up there," Dair said. "She's planned a little midafternoon treat at a very upscale restaurant on the main plaza after Kira has chosen the dress and ordered it. Some wine, some munchies. Should be a lot of fun."

Tara nodded. "Sure, let's do it!" She saw no harm in going to Jackson Hole with her friends. It was always in the back of her mind that Cree Elson lived there. So far, though, no one had seen hide nor hair of him in Wind River. And everyone was watching out for him because the locals knew what he'd done to her before.

Little by little, Tara's fear of being kidnapped or harmed by Cree was dissolving. In large part, it was due to Harper's quiet, unobtrusive presence in her life. Tara often wondered what she'd done to deserve a man like him. Every day it was getting tougher to ignore his masculinity, his smile, his teasing and the warmth he always fed her.

Dair pushed away from the rail, looking down at her dusty, dirty jeans. "We're all going to wear nice, clean clothes to go up there," and she brushed off her jeans and grimaced.

Tara asked, "What time? And where do I meet you girls?"

"An hour from now," Kira said. "At Shay and Reese's house."

"I'll be there with bells on. First, I need to tell Harper where I'm going."

"Do it," Dair said, walking with Kira along the concrete sidewalk outside the arena. "We'll see you soon."

"Who's the designated driver?" Tara wanted to know, thinking that drinking wine and eating canapés midday would be fun, but someone had to stay sober.

"That would be Shay," Kira called over her shoulder as they reached the door to the arena. "Her father's an alcoholic and she doesn't touch it. She's going to drive us there and back."

Dair chuckled as she held the door open for Kira. "Yeah, but she'll chow down on the goodies Maud has ordered from this fab restaurant we'll be visiting afterward. It's the Bell Tower. Heard of it, Tara?"

"Oh," Tara said, halting, "that's a five-star restaurant. Wow. Maud is going all out for you, Kira."

"Yes," Kira agreed, smiling. "Maud loves weddings. She's been a huge help to me. I'm not exactly a seamstress and I'm not so much into fashion, but she is."

"It sounds like a lot of fun," Tara agreed. "Okay, I'll see you in an hour!" and she split off from her friends, heading down the path that led back into the boarders' box stalls, where Harper was. She felt her heart lift. This past month, she'd seen the love between Kira and Garret. She was happy for them. If any couple she knew deserved something good to happen to them, it was those two.

The cool breeze flowed past her as she turned down one of the wide concrete aisles. There were fifteen box stalls on each side and, halfway down, she saw Harper cleaning one out, a wheelbarrow nearby and a pitchfork in his hand. Her heart swelled with such happiness as she watched him working. It might be only fifty degrees outside, but the huge sliding doors at the other end were open, giving the horses fresh air and sunshine.

Harper wore a muscle shirt that showed off his powerful upper body and broad shoulders. He wore gloves, and as she walked quietly toward him, Tara liked the way his jeans fit his narrow hips and his long, powerful legs. His hair was always kept short, but she could see the sweat gleaming on his brow as he swung another pitchfork full of cedar shavings and horse poop into the wheelbarrow.

He spotted her, smiled and straightened up.

"Hey," she called, "you're almost done for the day," and she halted near the opened door to the stall. The boarded horse, a black-and-white pinto gelding named Puzzle, poked his head out of the door and nickered to her. Tara went over and patted the ten-year-old horse, who nuzzled her outstretched hand.

"Hey, yourself," Harper said, leaning against the pitchfork. "Did you get enough photos of Ebony in action?" He wiped his brow with the back of his arm.

Tara tried not to be moved by Harper's sexiness. He seemed totally unaware of how beautiful he was. "Oh, she's tearing around as usual. I swear, I think Shay and Reese ought to think of putting her into the quarter horse futurity and racing her. She loves to run."

Chuckling, Harper said, "They *are* thinking about it. Both of her parents have racing blood, so I wouldn't be surprised if they do."

"There's a lot of money in that racing futurity," Tara said. "It could help the ranch."

"Yeah, but that's several years away. Ebony has to grow up, get trained to race and all that, too. I heard from Reese the other day that there's a big quarter horse farm in California looking to purchase Ebony as soon as she's weaned. I don't know what they're going to do."

She moved around the wheelbarrow and Puzzle went back to eating hay out of a net suspended near his opened door. "Me either. I'm going up to Jackson Hole with the girls in about an hour," she said, and shared the reason with Harper. At first, she saw his gray eyes darken with concern. It was never far from her consciousness, Cree Elson being up there. The more she explained it, the less concerned he became.

Pushing several damp strands of hair off his brow after removing his glove, Harper said, "That sounds like a great spring break for you gals. What time will you be back?"

"I don't know. I've never been in a wedding party before."

Smiling, Harper said, "Well, after wine and food

midafternoon, you're probably not going to be too hungry whenever you get home."

"Probably not," and then she added, "I'll bring home a doggie bag with the goodies in it for you. Okay?" Her heart expanded as his smile deepened, but it was the burning look in his gray eyes that set her lower body on fire. Tara had finally decided that what was between them was strong and constant, and now, her hormones were also thrown unexpectedly into the mix. She couldn't resist watching his mouth, constantly wondering what it would be like to kiss Harper. Every night, lying awake, wanting him, wanting more intimacy. Yet, he never made a move to let her know he wanted the same thing from her, although she sensed he did. What was stopping him?

Pulling on his gloves, he said, "Sure, bring those goodies home. We've got some gumbo soup I made earlier this week. We'll have soup and whatever you bring back."

"I'm sure there's going to be dessert, too."

"Even better," Harper said, picking up the pitchfork. "Well, I gotta get Puzzle's stall finished and then we're done for the day."

"Do you want me to go get Candy and Ebony? Bring them back to the broodmare stall?"

"Nah," he said, "let them stay out for a while longer. Good mental health for both of them. Ebony's getting to the age and stage where she needs to be out all the time to become strong."

"No question," Tara agreed. Lifting her hand, she said, "Okay, see you later."

Harper frowned and halted just inside the box stall. "Listen, just be careful up there, okay? I know you're black ops–trained, Tara, but I don't trust Elson."

A chill moved down her spine as she halted. "Yes, I'm jumpy about it, too."

"Well," he drawled, "just stay alert. I don't think Cree will try to bother you if he sees you. And if he does, then you're with a group of women who have seen combat and they'll be there to defend and protect you. But I don't really think it's going to come to that. Just be alert, is all."

Nodding, Tara whispered, "I hate this, Harper."

Giving her a sympathetic look, he said, "I know you do. There's not much anyone can do about it. Elson is allowed to live wherever he wants whether he's a felon or not."

"I know," she grumbled. Lifting her hand, she said, "I'll see you tonight sometime."

"Have fun."

Turning, she moved down the clean, wide aisle and headed for the front door to the arena. Some of her excitement had been dulled by their conversation. Anger burned in her that she had to remain on constant guard. There was nothing fair about being stalked, kidnapped and then having the bastard fifty miles away. Tara longed for the day when she could honestly feel free again at home. She knew her parents worried constantly about Cree. He was a dark shadow that bred terror within her. Even Harper's concerned expression sent fear through her. If she wasn't reading him wrong, it looked like he almost wanted to escort them up there and be a big, bad guard dog for the wedding party. But he said nothing. And she wasn't going to ask him to do it. This was supposed to be a girls' afternoon out. They were going to help Kira find the right wedding dress. She should be happy, looking forward to it.

Instead, as she pushed through the door and then closed it, the sun falling warmly upon her, Tara felt that old sense of dread. It was nothing specific; it was just that old fear creating turmoil in her tightened gut.

She swung off the concrete sidewalk to the wide, wooden path that led up the slightly sloped hill to her home. All four houses sat in a row and the wooden sidewalk had been built earlier for Dair, when she'd been in a wheelchair, recovering from an injury. Everyone on the Bar C had chipped in to build the wooden sidewalk for her and in a day's time and a lot of hard, constant work, they'd done just that. She liked the way her boots echoed on the wood, the sound soothing some of her fear, dissolving it.

Tara knew Maud Whitcomb. Everyone in the valley did. But still, she'd been young when she left and she wondered if Maud remembered her.

Kira, Dair and Shay bubbled over the fifty-five-year-old matriarch of Wind River Valley and her world-famous architect husband, Steve. They owned the largest ranch in the valley; it had come down through Steve's ranching family from 1850 to the present. She was amazed to find out they were millionaires many times over but also very generous with their money. One of the many ideas they were putting into practice was persuading people who drove through the valley to stop here for more than gas. This route led straight to Jackson Hole, which was the gateway to Teton National Park and Yellowstone Park. They were working with businesses and other ranches in the valley to build excitement so travelers would stay one or two days before continuing their drive north.

Tara had been warned that Maud, who was five-foot-seven-inches tall, rarely went anywhere without her red baseball cap on her short black and silver hair. That as she looked around, her light gray eyes were like an eagle's all-seeing gaze. She was wiry and darkly suntanned. Maud was the rancher and ran Wind River Ranch while Steve had global customers for his architecture business. She was a socialite, had good taste and loved get-togethers like this one.

When they pulled into Jilly's Wedding Shop, which was on the main plaza of Jackson Hole, it was one p.m. The cow town, even in early May, was packed with hundreds of tourists walking along the wooden boardwalk that comprised the square. Tara knew she'd have a tough time spotting Cree Elson if he was around.

Across from the small wedding shop and the plaza was the Red Pickup Saloon. Cree worked there. The whole plaza was crammed with parked cars sporting out-of-state license plates, tourists noodling through the businesses that were strung together. It was hectic energy, and as Tara got out, keeping her Canon around her neck because she was the official photographer for today's event, her gaze swung to the Red Pickup Saloon.

It was nothing but hordes of people who had gone there for lunch, people who would stop and peer through the big plate-glass windows, and the wooden saloon doors were flapping back and forth with patrons coming and going. Tara knew Cree worked as a dishwasher, so he wouldn't be out front where she might spot him.

Still, she looked for a long moment before moving into Jilly James's upscale wedding gown store. In the two huge front windows, she saw many different styles of wedding dresses, recognizing the names Vera Wang and Oleg Cassini. Kira didn't have that kind of money for a wedding dress and Tara wondered why Maud Whitcomb insisted upon this shop. The vets were hardworking, but money was scarce and they were all saving, plus giving some back to the Bar C. She was the only one with a reasonably healthy bank account, thanks to her saving most of her pay while she was on combat deployment.

"Maud!" Shay cried as she entered the shop. "Wow, you're all dressed up!"

Tara followed Dair in, shutting the door that had a tinkling bell on the top of it. Dair had lost her lower left leg to an IED, but beneath the dark green pantsuit she wore, no one would suspect she was an amputee. She turned, seeing Maud, who was dressed in a tasteful tangerine linen pantsuit with a white silk tee beneath it. She looked elegant.

"Hey," Dair teased mercilessly, "what happened to your red baseball cap, Maud? I didn't think you went anywhere without that poor, ragged thing."

Maud laughed heartily, coming forward, arms open, embracing Kira, Shay and Dair. "Oh, every once in a while, girls, I do leave that flea-bitten cap at home. Glad to see all of you again!"

Tara stood smiling because the women embraced each other with real warmth. When Maud released them, she moved toward her.

"It's been a long time, Tara, since I saw you last. You were eighteen and getting ready to leave for the military. Welcome to Wyoming once again," and she held out her long, spare hand to her. "We're glad you've come home safe and sound."

Tara shook her hand, feeling the calluses on Maud's palm. She might be the richest rancher in the valley, but it was immediately obvious Maud worked outdoors a lot. "I was ready to leave at that time, as you know. But I'm glad to be home."

Releasing her hand, Maud curved her arm around Tara's shoulders and led her over to the other three women. "We're glad to have you back with us, too. You're one of us now. And I remember you as a little girl, growing up here in the valley. The school plays. You were a sports maniac, good at everything you took on."

Tara knew why so many loved Maud. She was warm, sincere and made everyone feel special and welcome. Maud released her and they all stood in a loose circle. "Oh, those school plays," Tara groaned, watching Maud nod. She knew the Whitcombs had no children, but they had adopted several, and Tara had gone to school with them. The Whitcombs were at every school play, video-taping it like the proud parents they were of their beloved brood.

"Yes, and I remember *Peter Pan*; you got to play him, swinging back and forth on those wires attached to your harness. You were a little thing, then, but so great as Peter!"

Shay nodded. "Yep, Tara was a star, no doubt."

"Wow," Dair murmured, "I'd love to see that video of you, Tara."

Rolling her eyes, Tara muttered, "No . . ."

"I have the video," Maud said proudly, giving Tara a wink. "Maybe we'll plan an all-girls' day at our ranch soon, and I'll share it with you."

Kira gave Tara a wicked grin. "Oh, I'd love that! I'll bet you were a cute little Peter Pan."

"I've never lived it down," Tara lamented, good-natured about the teasing.

"Well, fish to fry for another day," Maud said. "I talked to Jilly beforehand, Kira, and she's got certain gowns for you to try on."

Kira gave Maud a distressed look. "Maud, I can't afford a designer wedding gown. Garret and I just don't have that kind of money."

"Well," Maud drawled, "those of your generation who get married? That's a big deal. And stop worrying about it. Steve and I are going to give you two wedding gifts.

One is that we're paying for whatever wedding gown you desire. The price doesn't matter. Okay?"

Tara heard Kira gasp, her hand flying to her mouth, her eyes huge at Maud's unexpected gift. She had no idea the cost of a wedding gown but was sure it was pricey. And then, Kira burst into tears. They all made reassuring sounds, surrounding Kira, their arms wrapped around one another, comforting her. She saw Maud's light gray eyes tear up. So did hers.

A wedding was a big deal. She knew real love was hard to come by. Her parents had gotten married and then she came along. Her father adored her mother. And he loved her. Tara knew only the good, wonderful side of loving parents.

Jilly came out with her assistant, Mary, who carried a tray of wineglasses filled with champagne. Kira wiped her eyes and hugged the hell out of Maud, who held her tightly for a moment.

Tara liked Jilly James, who was in her late twenties, dressed in pink-linen trousers with a very feminine dark fuchsia long-sleeved blouse, her black hair up in a bun on her head. Her blue eyes were glistening, too. Not a dry eye in the place after Maud's surprise gift to Kira and Garret.

Tara could hardly wait to tell Harper about her girls' afternoon out to find Kira's special wedding dress. She wasn't very frilly or feminine anyway, but she did enjoy girlie things like this. As everyone took their proffered glass of champagne, Jilly made sure Shay received one filled with orange juice, and they all toasted Kira's coming marriage to Garret.

As she sipped the bubbly French champagne, which Maud had purchased for the occasion, Tara stood back, watching how the ranch owner adroitly took Kira over to a rack along the wall, telling her that these were the gowns in Kira's size eight. Tara loved that wedding dresses were in more than just white. She preferred the antique cream-colored ones herself, and she wondered which color Kira would choose.

Dair came over to her. "Nice, huh?"

"Very," Tara murmured. "Wonderful to see Kira so happy."

"Garret's deliriously in love with Kira," Dair said, sipping her champagne. "He adores her."

"That's what real love is about," Tara agreed. "My dad worships my mother to this day. I was lucky; I grew up in a very loving family where my parents really did and do love each other."

Dair met her gaze. "You are very, very lucky. A lot of kids don't grow up in what I'd term a happy home."

"No, most of them are dysfunctional, more or less."

Dair grimaced. "My father used to beat the hell out of me. I hated him."

"I'm sorry, Dair. I didn't know."

Holding up the glass, Dair managed a sour grin. "Must be the champagne loosening my tongue. I'm sure you'll hear me talk about my family in our Friday-night meetings with Lilly Hilbert sooner or later."

Reaching out, Tara murmured, "I'm sure, but still, I'm sorry, Dair. You didn't deserve that. No child does."

"No," Dair sighed, "but it happens way too often. From my experience? About seventy percent of the people who decide to bring children into the world are horrible parents. They don't have a clue what a good parent is and does with their child or children." She grimaced. "Enough of me; this is a happy day and we should be celebrating. Come on, it looks like Kira has found her gown. Let's join them."

Tara felt such sadness for Dair. Not only did she have a

terrible father but she'd lost part of her left leg in combat. Dair was someone she admired and respected because she didn't let a lost partial limb stop her from being a darned good wrangler. And she knew Noah Mabrey had proposed to Dair, and that she'd said she would marry him. She wondered when that might come about as they wandered over to a gown Jilly was holding up for Kira to look at more closely.

"Wow," Tara murmured, "that's beautiful, Kira!"

"Do you like it?" Kira asked her and Dair.

"I like it because it looks like an antique from a bygone era," Dair said, motioning to the cream-colored dress.

"Tara? What do you think?" Kira asked, touching the lace atop the fabric gently, her gaze on the gown.

"I love it because of the top of it and the three-quarter sleeves are pure lace. And the beaded appliqué of leaves over the shoulders really set it off."

"This is a strapless trumpet gown," Jilly told them proudly, gesturing down the front of it. "It's so feminine, with the lacy top and sleeves. The trumpet silhouette flows into an A-line beaded lace skirt. It was designed by Oleg Cassini, and he truly knows how to bring out a woman's beautiful body and make her look elegant."

"Well," Tara said, "I love the lace, the appliqué falling over each shoulder of the top."

Maud came forward, sliding her fingers down the ivory fabric. "Very nice, Kira. What do you think?"

"I think it's lovely. I like the lace that flows over the entire gown, the appliqué of the leaves. I love nature. This is perfect for me, Maud."

"Then," she said with a smile, giving Jilly a nod, "let's get you into it to see how it looks."

Tara sat with Dair and Shay. She had seen Dair going

through some of the gowns in another section, saw her pick up the price tag, frown and then reluctantly release it, moving on. She had moseyed around the elegant shop and seen the price tags, too. Thousands of dollars for each gown. There was just no way any of them could afford such things. Maud was unbelievably generous, and she was glad the ranch owner was springing for Kira's dress. That was such utter kindness and Maud was such a role model. She had millions, but she spread her wealth around to those who would never attain such a lofty economic status or afford such finery.

"This is so wonderful," Shay sighed. "I love days like this."

"Wish we had more of them," Dair agreed.

"I don't know," Tara said, "we're happy at the Bar C. Oh, I know things go wrong all the time, but we get them fixed."

"And you're happy with us?" Shay asked her.

"Completely," Tara said. "My mom and dad are okay with the fact I'm not living with them anymore."

"I know you see them at least once a week," Dair said.

"Yes. I love having lunch with my mom at Kassie's. My dad's schedule doesn't allow him that kind of time off, but I do get to see him when I go over to have dinner with them on Saturdays. It's working out, Shay. Don't be concerned about me. Okay? I know what a worrywart you are," and she gave Shay a gentle smile.

"Okay," Shay said with a laugh, "I'll stop worrying about you."

Sitting back in a satin-covered white chair, Tara sipped the last of her champagne. She was getting a pleasant buzz from it, glad that she only had one glass. Dair had loosened up, too, and that made her smile. She was part Native American through her Comanche mother and was an intense, focused person. Noah, the man who loved her, had gentled some of Dair's rough edges. Just as Harper was helping Tara in his own quiet way.

Leaning back, Tara closed her eyes, picturing Harper in that muscle shirt and jeans. Damn, he looked good! For years, she hadn't thought much about sex. The demands of her military job put that fully aside. But now? Harper was someone she was looking forward to seeing every day. He gave her a sense of peace and contentment. No man had made her feel like making a nest and calling it home, and yet Harper had done just that without saying or doing anything other than being himself. Her heart moved with strong feelings for him. What would it be like to kiss him? To feel his arms come around her? Nightly, she was asking herself those questions again and again.

Where was this going with Harper? Where did she want it to go? What did he think about her? About them? So many questions she longed to know the answers to.

Chapter Seven

May 2

Harper couldn't contain his smile as he ate dinner with Tara after she got back from the Jackson Hole wedding dress party. He knew she'd gone there with trepidation, fearing running into Cree Elson, but it hadn't happened.

Instead, she'd had a wonderful afternoon with all the girls and was slightly tipsy when she returned home because she'd drunk champagne. Kira now had her wedding dress ordered, and Tara had shown him a photo of it on her cell phone. He somberly promised he wouldn't tell Garret what it looked like. After all, the groom wasn't to see his beloved until he stood in front of the altar with the reverend, waiting for Kira to be led down the aisle by her father. Yep, he crossed his heart and hoped to die in front of Tara, he'd keep her secret. She was worried Garret would see or hear about the beautiful dress beforehand. He was, after all, a black ops guy.

"And next week? Dair, Shay and I will be meeting Maud again at Jilly's to choose our bridesmaids' dresses. Kira will be with us and she wants us to be happy with the color and choice." Laughing, Tara said, holding his smile, "Do you know how long it's been since I wore a dress?"

He sipped the gumbo soup he'd heated up earlier. "Seriously?"

"Well, I was in combat all the time. We'd get flown back to Bagram and I'd be exhausted, stumble to my B-hut and crash. There was no place to dress up in a skirt, blouse or anything else."

His smile disappeared as he thought about her explanation. Tara was more excited than he'd ever seen her, cheeks flushed and blue eyes dancing with happiness. "Well, maybe getting out of the military will bring you back to the womanly things you might want to experience once more."

Tara gave him a wicked look but dug into her meal of the spicy-tasting gumbo soup. She loved leftover soup because it was better tasting the day after. "Being a wrangler discourages it, too. I've decided I'm doomed to wear jeans the rest of my life, Harper."

"Nah," he teased. "We could always go to the barn dances held in the valley all year long. They bring in a caller, a fiddler or two, and folks of all ages come to square dance. You probably know all about that because you were born and raised here."

Nodding, she picked up her glass of water, taking a sip. "I love the barn dances! We actually had a circuit around the valley when I was growing up. There are fifteen ranches here in the valley and each one held a dance at some point during the year. Maud and Steve, of course, threw the biggest and best one because they had the money to do it. I know everyone in the valley was touched by their generosity and kindness. And they always held their spring barn dance in March, when we were sick of snow, knowing it was going to last through early June."

"I heard from Garret earlier today that there's a barn dance over at the Red Tail Ranch next Saturday. Would you be interested in going with me?" And he held his breath because Harper would damn near do anything to hold this woman close to him. *Anything . . . just once. . . .* "Come on," he cajoled. "I don't have two left feet, Tara. I promise I won't step on your toes. How about it?"

"Are Dara, Kira and Shay going?"

"I think so. I'm surprised they didn't talk about it with you today."

"Well, we're not exactly a couple, Sutton. Maybe that's why?"

He returned her wry look. "True. But it would get you out of here for a while, you could wear a dress, plus you could see a lot of the people you grew up with at the dance, too. I'm sure they want to welcome you back to the valley."

"I'd love to go with you."

"Great. Now you need a dress, huh?" and he grinned wolfishly, thinking how beautiful she would look in one, his imagination going wild with possibilities. Harper wondered if Tara had decided to go with him because of the idea of meeting some of her old friends and ranch families. Or was it because she wanted to go with *him*? He didn't have the nerve to ask. He couldn't even joke about it because never had he wanted to get to know a woman more than Tara.

Groaning, she said, "Oh, jeez . . . you're right, Harper." She looked up toward the living room. "I don't own a dress. I guess I could go back to my parents' house. They left my old bedroom just the way it used to be. Mom hasn't thrown out any of the clothes I wore in high school."

"Well," he said, "haven't styles changed since then? I mean, I'm sure you'll look great in anything you wear." Harper realized he was sliding into enemy territory. He honestly didn't know that much about women's fashion. All he knew was what he liked. He didn't know one designer from another. He saw Tara wrestling with the idea of going to visit her old high-school closet for something to wear. "Could you ask Jilly when you see her next week? I'll bet she's got lots of nice clothes you could choose from."

"Yeah, but it's the money, Harper. I have a nice nest egg sitting in the bank, but I don't want to spend a lot of money on a new outfit." And then she grimaced. "Sorry, that came out wrong."

He reached out, squeezing her hand. Any excuse would do. "I understand where you're coming from, Tara. You and Shay are about the same height and size. Maybe she's got something you could borrow?" He saw Tara wrinkle her nose. *Oops.* Wrong thing to suggest. Forcing himself to remove his hand, he muttered, "Look, anything you wear will be fine with me. Okay?" He instantly saw the worry leave her eyes.

"I have a nice trouser and blazer set. Do you mind square dancing with me in something that isn't a dress?"

"No, I don't care what you wear." *Or don't wear.* But he clamped his lips shut to stop the rest of his words from escaping. Sometimes his mouth got ahead of his brain. "You'll look beautiful, Tara, no matter what you decide to wear. I'll be proud to escort you." That seemed to mollify her, helped her overcome her anxiety. She was so damned readable. Did everyone else see her that way? Or was Tara only opening up to him? Allowing him that special, intimate privilege of seeing her for who she fully was? That idea warmed his heart. When her golden hair, which was loose, slipped forward over her shoulders, he itched to slide his fingers through those molten strands. More and more, it seemed every day, there was this driving need to get inside Tara's head and heart. Why now? He was so damned poor at relationships and sustaining one. Tara deserved better than that.

May 10

Tara tried to tame her nervousness over going with Harper to the barn dance held at the Dvorak family Red Tail Ranch. The May evening was chilly. It had snowed two days earlier, dumping a new foot of it across the valley. By this time, she was tired of snow, yearning to see green sprouting through the white stuff, heralding their short spring and summer season. Usually, from early June to mid-September, there was lots of sunshine and the valley sprang to rich, green life, which Tara loved.

She tried to tamp down her expectations surrounding Harper. Yet she was eager to be on the dance floor with him. Not all the dances were rousing square dances. There was a slow dance spliced into the evening, too, giving couples a chance for closeness.

The Dvorak barn was huge, a hundred years old, built by the first German family member who had come from that country to set up ranching in Wyoming. Doug Dvorak, this generation's owner, had painted his barn last summer. The bright red sides gleamed in the setting sun. As Harper drove his truck onto the muddy, sloppy ranch road, Tara could see at least thirty trucks, SUVs and other vehicles parked to one side of the barn.

"Wow, looks like the whole valley is here!" she said, excited as she traded a glance with Harper. He was dressed in a pair of black chinos, a neatly pressed white cowboy shirt that was open at his throat, revealing the strong column of his neck. His dark brown hair had recently been washed and was military short.

"I see Maud and Steve's red double-axle pickup truck," he said, making a motion with his hand toward the windshield.

"Those are the same trucks you see at the feed store," Tara said with a grin. "I like that everyone's been able to come. It's a nice time to get to find out how the other ranch families are doing, and hear what's happening in their lives."

Nodding, he parked the truck in the next slot available. Turning off the ignition, he said, "We're here. Excited?"

Laughing, she looked down at her peach-colored linen pantsuit. Tara wore a bright orange silk tee beneath it, her blond hair up on her head held by two bright green plastic combs. "Yes, very."

"You look beautiful," he told her, his voice thickening a bit.

"Thanks," and she nervously smoothed the linen fabric down her thigh. "I refreshed myself on square dancing," she admitted. "It's been a long time since I did any."

Chuckling, Harper climbed out. "Me too."

Tara waited for Harper to come around the truck and open her door. She knew he had courtly manners and enjoyed them. When he held out his hand to her, she took it, feeling the strength and roughness of his fingers closing around hers. She scooted out, absorbing his closeness as she took her white leather purse off the seat. It felt as if he was reluctant to release her hand, but he did. There was a swirl of emotion in his gray eyes she couldn't interpret. But her feelings were certainly clamoring for the possibility of being very close to Harper, touching him and rubbing against him as they were locked in a slow dance with each other. She'd barely slept last night, lost in fevered dreams of possibilities with this quiet, unassuming cowboy.

"Ready?" he asked, locking the truck and cupping her elbow.

"Oh, yes. My mom and dad's car is here, too, I see. They said they'd hold a table for us. We'll sit with them, if that's okay with you?" and she angled her gaze, catching his expression.

"Sure. I've already met them a number of times. Your mom is a wiz at anything mechanical."

Laughing, Tara said, "Yep, Mom is definitely that way. She loves running our hardware store, but I think even more, she truly enjoys teaching others how to fix things and what the right tools and stuff they need to do just that."

Walking at her side along the graveled path leading to the open barn door, Harper said, "Do you think your mechanical ability translated into becoming a photographer? There's a lot of technical expertise needed to work with a camera, much less take a decent photo."

"I had lunch with Mom the other day and she was saying the same thing. I mean, I'm mechanical, but I dearly love getting just the right aperture, the right light, on whatever it is I'm going to photograph."

Harper halted at the door, allowing her to enter first. There was fiddle music, along with accordion music, plus a snare drum, filling the barn. In the background was a caller, and a square dance was in full swing. The music was merry and upbeat. Along the sides of the cavernous barn were tables of varying sizes and shapes. Lights had been strung across the high beams. He kept his hand on

Tara's elbow as she spotted her parents at a small, round table covered with a plastic red-and-white-checked cloth.

Tara went over and hugged her mother, Joanna, who was dressed in a square dance blouse and skirt. She then went and hugged her father, Scott, who was dressed casually in a white western cowboy shirt, jeans and boots. She loved them so much and was glad they'd understood her moving to the Bar C. Turning, she introduced Harper to them, although they had both met him at different times in the past.

"Can I get you something to drink?" Harper asked, pulling out a chair for Tara after shaking her father's hand. Joanna and Scott had drinks already.

Sitting, she said, "Well, you know I don't do well with champagne, so how about some hot chocolate? Jenny Dvorak is well known in the valley for her secret recipe. Everyone loves coming here because her chocolate is so rich and spicy tasting."

Taking off his cowboy hat, Harper set it next to where Tara was sitting. "I didn't know that. Then I'll get two cups." He looked over at Scott and Joanna Dalton, asking if they'd like some, despite their other drinks. Both said no but thanked him.

Tara looked around at the noisy place filled with music and laughter. She sat next to her mother. "Have you danced yet?"

"Oh, yes, we have. Your dad and I are just taking a break."

Tara smiled at her father. She knew it was tough for him to get out much because of his large caseload. "How does it feel to dance a little, Dad?"

Scott Dalton smiled. "Feels good to get my dead butt out of a chair and move around, to tell you the truth."

"It's a good thing we have these fifteen barn dances

every year," Joanna said. "I so look forward to them! Did you know? Jenny made apple tarts! You know how wonderful they are. She makes them with caramel drizzled over them and adds pecans to the apples inside."

"Oh, goody!" Tara said. "Gosh, I've missed the good food everyone makes for these dances."

Scott chuckled. "I'll bet your young man will spot them in a heartbeat and be bringing you back a plate of them."

Twisting in her chair, looking across the busy barn floor, she saw Harper at the food table with a lot of other people. "Yes, he's not one to miss much."

Turning back, she saw how relaxed her father was. Tara knew he carried a lot of responsibility as a judge. He cared deeply for the people of Lincoln County. Often, if a person had a choice of going to jail or getting help, he would talk them into getting the help. A fierce love for her father rose in her, for his understanding, for his empathy. She had the same view of the world: that people were not intrinsically bad or evil. The only time her outlook had failed was with Cree Elson or someone who'd murdered another person. She'd tried to think through the shock of being captured by him, trying to persuade him to let her go, that it wasn't right that he'd kidnapped her and made her a prisoner. But it hadn't worked. Still, Tara knew Cree came from a horribly dysfunctional family situation, and that he'd been regularly abused by his alcoholic father, like all his brothers had been.

"Uh-oh," Joanna said, "look, Tara. Harper has a tray and look what's on it! Two cups of hot chocolate and four of Jenny's world-famous apple tarts!" and she burst into laughter, trading a warm glance with her husband. "What a lovely young man he is, Tara!"

Tara nodded, a lump in her throat, emotions sweeping through her at his thoughtfulness toward her parents. She could see the merriment on Harper's face. He was so darned handsome and her heart thudded to underscore it as he set the tray down in front of her family.

"Everyone, including Doug Dvorak, who was at the food station, told me I'd better steal four of his wife's apple tarts or I'd be sorry because they'd just come out of the oven and wouldn't last long," he said, grinning as he sat down. "I added whipped cream to them, Tara. I know how much you like the stuff." He looked at Joanna and Scott. "I got you two some, just in case," and his smile increased as he handed them each a tart on a paper plate. He then gave Tara a tall mug of hot chocolate and placed his next to the steaming apple tart.

"You're a good man," Scott said, taking the paper plates and passing one to his wife. "Thank you."

"You're welcome, sir."

Scott shook his head. "No, don't sir me, Harper. I was never in the military like you were. Just call me Scott if I'm not sitting on the bench, okay?"

Harper nodded. "Sure will, Scott."

Touched by his unselfishness and ability to think of others, Tara smiled and picked up the other two paper plates from the tray. "You did good, Sutton."

"Harper? We bet you'd return with only two of those tarts," Scott told him.

"I didn't know about them until Doug Dvorak came over and introduced himself to me and Jenny, who had just brought out a sheet of them straight from the oven. He led me down to the dessert section. Said that Jenny's apple tarts are world class and that they'd disappear in another few minutes after word got out that they were available. So, I grabbed enough for all of us."

"Glad you did," Tara congratulated him, cutting into the huge tart with her plastic knife and fork. The warm caramel was thick and had slipped into the tart itself. "Thank you. I'd completely forgotten about Jenny's tarts. I've been gone too long."

"Well, it isn't like you've been home forever," Harper noted, eating his tart, relishing the sweetness and the butterscotch caramel drizzled over it.

Tara saw the Bar C tables about halfway down the south wall of the barn. She spotted Kira, Garret, Shay, Reese, Dair and Noah. Soon enough, they'd go over and say hello. The girls were decked out in square dance outfits and the guys were in jeans, cowboy shirts and boots. She felt a little odd in her pantsuit, then shrugged it off. Harper seemed smitten by how she looked, saying how beautiful the peach color was on her. It made her feel good.

Hating herself for doing it, Tara swept the area, over a hundred or so people within the barn, wondering if Cree was hidden somewhere among them. Her mind said no, that he was very much a loner, never showed up at the barn dances with his parents when she was younger. Could he be skulking outside? Waiting for her? She wished she could just block him out of her mind, but she couldn't.

Harper glanced in her direction and Tara had the distinct feeling he was sensing her worry. The look in his eyes was one of concern, although he said nothing. There was this unvoiced communication between them, and she was grateful for his expression, as if he was silently telling her everything was all right. That she was safe here with him. Harper wiped his mouth with a paper napkin, wadded it up and put it on the empty plate where the tart had been minutes before.

"Want to do this slow dance?" he asked.

Tara had to shake herself. She was so caught up in the snare of her past with Cree that she hadn't realized the fiddlers were now playing a slow dance for the winded square dance crowd. "Sure."

"You two enjoy yourselves," Joanna called. "Your dad and I are older; we're just going to sit this one out and enjoy these delicious tarts."

Harper bit back a groan as Tara came into his arms on the crowded dance floor. There wasn't a whole lot of room and he was glad because he could pull Tara close. Her breasts, hidden beneath the blazer, barely brushed against his chest. That sent keen longing through him as she lifted her chin, looking deeply into his eyes, her hand held gently in his. He liked that her other hand rested on his chest, the skin tightening beneath her palm. The gentle sway of her hips enticed him and he swallowed, trying to stop the burgeoning erection beginning to swell against his zipper.

"This is nice," Tara said. "And you're a good dancer, Harper."

He laughed a little nervously. "What? I'll bet you thought I was a clodhopper with two left feet."

Her lips curved. "No, you've never been clumsy. That's not who you are. And if the truth be known? I love walking behind you."

"Why?" Harper saw merriment in her eyes. He had no idea what she meant by that comment.

"I love the way you walk. You're in such great, athletic condition that you appear boneless when you move. Graceful, in a male kind of way."

"Oh," was all he could manage. Heat flooded his lower body over that huskily whispered compliment. Harper saw something new in her eyes. Something he didn't dare believe could be true. Automatically, his hand tightened a little more around hers. There was such powerful intimacy building between them.

"Men are beautiful, too, you know," Tara teased him.

Heat stung his cheeks. He liked her spunk, her boldness and honesty. He had from the beginning. "Okay," he managed, "I guess I just never thought of men as beautiful, is all."

"Oh, it's a feminine word only?"

Now she was teasing him big-time and his mouth curved faintly. "Fair enough. You're beautiful to me, Tara Dalton. In fact, I can't see one thing wrong with you in any way. I like the way your blond hair is up on your head, like the way the lights above shows how it glistens. And the trousers and blazer you're wearing; the color brings out the beauty of your skin." Fair was fair, and he gloated a little, watching surprise and then pleasure come to her expression. And without a word, she took a half step forward, her body fully pressed lightly against his. He moved his splayed hand against the small of her back, not any lower, however. It was enough to let her know that what she'd done was appreciated and mutual. There was something about a slow dance, the way the partners gravitated like planets orbiting one another that made Harper's heart surge with hope.

He kept telling himself he wasn't good enough for Tara because he'd already blown through a previous marriage. He'd loved Olivia. But he'd lacked the tools, the maturity, to save their marriage, and he blamed it entirely on himself.

Now, because he cared so much for Tara, he was stuck with a dilemma. He wanted her. All of her. Yet Harper knew he'd hurt her because of his lack of relationship skills sooner or later. And the last thing he wanted to do was hurt this woman.

Finally, he leaned down, his lips barely touching the gold strands of her hair. "Tara? I need to tell you something important. And you have a decision to make afterward. Okay?" Harper wasn't going to use her. He was going to tell her the truth and let his past fall where it may. It was Tara's decision to make, not his. He saw her eyes grow darker.

"What? Is something wrong?"

He shrugged, trying to think above the sensations of her body lightly against his own. "Well, I owe you a story from my past because it could change how you see me . . . us. . . ."

Her brows dipped. "Okay," she murmured, "tell me."

Harper didn't waste any words about him falling in love with Olivia and then their marriage falling apart under his watch. He finished the story with, "It was completely my fault, Tara. I take full responsibility for the marriage ending. I just didn't have what it took to keep it together."

Tara looked away for a moment as he slowly turned her on the dance floor. Lifting her chin, she studied him. "I'm sorry you got divorced, Harper. It had to be hard on both of you."

"It was."

"You know, my parents have been married since they were eighteen. They've gone through thick and thin together. I watched them dealing with stuff, with each other, while I was growing up. And every marriage has hard, challenging times, there's no question. And as I grew up, matured, was in the military, I saw a lot of young men and women getting married. I saw a lot of those marriages die on the vine. There's a lot of stress on the veteran, Harper. In this case, it was you. Olivia didn't have a clue what you'd gone through, what you'd survived or what you saw. She couldn't. But you can't off-load what happened to you either. You have to slowly work through it over time."

"Yeah, but my PTSD broke us apart," he said.

"And I'm not making light of the fact that PTSD hasn't broken up a lot of marriages, because it has. I have it myself, and I know on some days, no one, not even Max, Shay and Reese's golden retriever, should be around me."

Harper gave her a slight grin. "Yeah, that about sums it all up for me, too. There were days when Olivia shouldn't have been around me at all."

"But I've also seen some of my friends, who were married, the guy or gal having PTSD and coming home. Those marriages went through a lot of stress, but they hung together."

"Mine didn't."

"No, but it was a casualty of war, Harper. That's the bottom line. I've come to realize where marriages turned toxic because the PTSD monster wanted to tear it apart. Neither party could help what had happened to them. Some marriages hung together. Many didn't." She searched his eyes. "So, why are you telling me this?"

Clearing his throat, he said, "Tara, ever since I met you, my heart started opening up to you. I never expected it. But you mean a lot to me in every way. And I needed to tell you about my failed marriage because I don't want to hurt you." Fear ratcheted through him, and Harper wondered if he'd said too much, judging by her eyes widening briefly over his explanation.

"Oh," she managed, "well . . . I didn't realize . . . I mean . . ." and she stared at him, speechless.

Harper slowed, and they stood between the couples, staring at each other. He wanted to kiss Tara. She looked surprised, and then pleased, and then he saw uncertainty in her eyes. Over what? Him? "Talk to me," he urged. "What are you thinking? Feeling?"

One corner of her mouth quirked upward for a moment. "I guess . . . I guess I thought it was one-sided, Harper."

"What was one-sided?" He saw bright red color flush her cheeks. With her fair skin, she blushed easily.

"Us," Tara choked out, placing both her hands on his chest, their hips against each other. "I've always been drawn to you, Harper, from the day we met. I thought it was just me. You never flirted with me. You never did anything to let me know you were interested. I guess I'm just in shock that you feel the same way I do about you, is all. It's going to take me a moment . . ."

"Take all the time you want. Are you happy about knowing this, Tara?"

She chuckled and nodded. "Yes, I am. I mean, I'm scared for a lot of reasons. Not least is our mutual PTSD. We both have it."

"Yes, but you got that cortisol treatment from Taylor at the clinic and you no longer have the anxiety. I don't have it either, and according to Libby, it was the most pervasive, single symptom that was often the culprit in tearing a couple apart."

He began to move them once again, picking up her right hand and enclosing it in his. "Doesn't the fact I screwed up my marriage scare you, Tara?"

Shrugging, she said, "No. You're very sensitive with me, Harper. You're kind and you're self-aware. I don't meet many guys with that combo, and let me tell you, I love it. I love that you consider me your equal and you ask first, you never assume. Those are all good signals for a healthy relationship."

"Ever since you've come to the Bar C, my life has been

better, Tara." His voice lowered and he held her warm gaze. "I look forward to waking up and finding you out in the kitchen making us coffee, working with you at my side in the arena and then sharing dinner with you at night. I like our talks. You're incredibly intelligent and you've had experiences and insights I haven't. I learn from you every day."

"Funny, I feel the same way about you, Harper. I always find something new about you that surprises me and makes me happy. Maybe it's your medic personality. I don't know. But even the horses—the broodmares especially— love your kindness and gentleness toward them. Why should I feel any different from the way they do about you?"

Harper hadn't realized how much of a load he was carrying on his shoulders until he felt the weight begin to dissolve. The look in Tara's eyes told him the unvarnished truth: she really did like him as much as he liked her. The way her hips swayed against his, the silent promise hanging between them, sent an unparalleled joy through him. "Then we have something to build on, Tara, with each other?"

"Yes," she answered. "I don't know where it's going, Harper."

"I don't either. But I'm willing to give it a try. I just didn't want you walking into this blindsided because of my past. I still feel raw and unsure whether I can grow or do whatever it is I need to do and not hurt you in the process. I don't want to ever do that."

He felt her fingers lace through his as they moved around between two couples.

"Nothing is guaranteed, Harper. You and I as vets know that better than anyone on the face of this earth."

"True."

"I'd like to continue to explore what we have. But we

need to talk about it, too. I had no idea you felt the same as I did until right now. I've seen too many relationships destroyed because the partners didn't talk often enough with each other. I'm not going to let that happen to us. Okay?"

"Okay," he agreed, his throat tight with rising emotion. "I can't believe you're willing to take a chance on me, but right now I'm the happiest wrangler in the valley."

"You don't see yourself as I see you," Tara said. "And I like what I see, Harper. I really do."

Chapter Eight

Tara couldn't contain her euphoria over their quiet talk on the dance floor. Later in the evening, she and Harper visited the Bar C table, danced the slow dances and then came back to her parents' table, which was now filled with ranching friends. How long had it been since she'd been this happy? Harper seemed unsure of just how far to go with her after their honest talk, so Tara solved that problem. She picked up his hand when they walked around the barn floor. And when he tentatively placed his arm around her waist one time, she leaned into him, silently letting him know that she yearned for the intimacy. The look in his eyes registered relief, but also heat. Harper wanted to kiss her.

And she wanted to kiss him so badly she swore she could taste his mouth on hers. This had been weeks in building between them. Tara was tired of waiting, but now she understood the foundation of Harper's hesitancy. He doubted himself because of his failed marriage. It wasn't that he wasn't interested in her. She was relieved by the realization. Just having his large, rough hand around hers made her feel safer than she'd felt since she was sixteen years old. Harper fed her his protectiveness whether he knew it or not. It wasn't that obvious, but she felt it around him as he extended and embraced her with it.

As they started the next slow dance, couples crowded onto the floor, and she liked the closeness of the people. It gave her an excuse to lean into Harper. There was no question he wanted her because she could feel the bulge of his erection against her belly. It did nothing but cause chaos deep within her, hunger combined with impatience and need. She wondered if he felt similarly.

Harper brought her into his arms, his hand enclosing hers. Tara lay her head on his shoulder, content as never before. She wouldn't question where this was going. She wanted their relationship to continue in this direction. And when she got out of here and they were driving back to the Bar C, she would confide that to him. Right now, as her cheek rested on the fabric of his cotton shirt, feeling the heat of his flesh beneath it, the boneless movement of his body, she closed her eyes, sinking blissfully against him, allowing him to hold and guide her.

On a break, later, many of the couples went out to enjoy the coolish spring night. Harper had led her outside after he brought her jacket to her. The graveled driveway kept the mud away as they walked arm in arm with each other. A lot of low voices floated nearby. There were shadows around the massive barn. Above them, the night sky was clear, and Tara could see a growing quarter moon canting slightly in the western part of the sparkling canopy overhead.

"It's so beautiful tonight," she said, resting beneath his arm, her body against his as they ambled down the long slope toward the ranch road below.

"It is. Nights like this make you glad you live in Wyoming," Harper said.

"Tell me about your parents, Harper. Where did you grow up? Where do they live?" and she looked up at his deeply shadowed face. He'd put on his cowboy hat before leaving the barn, although he had no coat on like she did. Just the muscles of his arm around her shoulders tamped down her worry about Cree Elson. In her wild imagination, she thought he might be nearby, hidden in the shadows, watching her, waiting to get her alone so he could kidnap her once again. Being with Harper soothed her fractious mind and she focused on him as a man she truly enjoyed being around.

"Well," he said, slowing as the gravel met the muddy road, not wanting to step into it, "my folks live in Burns, Oregon. My father works for a sawmill, although so many of them are going out of business with the lumber industry slowing down that he worries he might not have a job as a millwright there for long."

"That's not good."

Shaking his head, he said, "No, it isn't. My mother, Irene, is secretarial assistant to the principal at a middle school in Burns."

"Is her job safe?" Tara asked, moving around so that she could lean against the front of him, his hands settling on the small of her back. She saw the consternation in Harper's darkened eyes as he looked out beyond her for a moment.

"Her job is. But my dad's isn't."

"What else could he do if he was laid off?"

"He's part of the generation where things went to high tech and he wasn't trained for the upgrade. He isn't that computer savvy and I worry about that. I've been trying to talk him into going to the vocational school in Burns and getting re-educated into computer sciences. If he could do that, he might be able to get a job where someone needs that skill. Everything is going to computerization."

"All except our jobs," she said wryly.

"Yeah," Harper chuckled, "no computer is ever going to replace a wrangler, that's for sure." He lifted his hand and pushed a few tendrils away from her cheek. "My parents were born in Burns, and so was I. My grandparents on both sides of my family still live there. They're pretty old now, but they still live in their homes and would never think of moving anywhere else. We're a close-knit family that actually gets along with one another," and he grinned.

"They're not going to an assisted living facility?" Tara guessed. Her skin tingled pleasantly as his fingertip grazed her temple. She wanted Harper's touch. Ached for more of it. Her intuition told her that he wasn't a man who moved fast with anything. And maybe his broken marriage was the reason why. Tara knew they had the time to explore and grow whatever it was that had sprung between them.

His mouth curved. "No, my grandparents would never do that. They're pretty set in their ways. My Grandpa Joe says he's dying in his own bed."

Laughing a little, Tara said, "I understand. Maybe because we're so much younger, we don't think about things like that."

"Not yet," he murmured, gazing down at her. "But we all age. We'll all be where our parents and grandparents are someday. I lived with several generations of my family growing up and I saw the process."

"So?" Tara whispered, her hands moving to his shoulders. "What are your dreams, Harper?" She saw his gray eyes alight with amusement.

"Nothing special, Tara. I had always wanted a marriage like my mom and dad have. They love each other to this day. They're the best of friends and they love doing things together. Growing up? I always thought I'd have the same thing. When I met and fell in love with Olivia, I expected it. But things . . . life . . . had other challenges for me."

Hearing the sadness in his soft voice, she said, "But you can try again, Harper. I've always heard my mom say that no one should get married until they're in their late twenties, that we're just too immature and inexperienced to do it any sooner than that." He opened her hand on his shoulder, feeling the warmth of his flesh beneath the fabric. "My parents got married at eighteen and they're still together, but I think they're the exception to the rule."

"I do, too."

"When did your parents get married?"

"Right out of high school. They'd been going together for years. And they had planned on getting married after graduation."

"And here you are, twenty-seven years old and they've been married that long. It speaks to them truly enjoying and liking each other," Tara said.

"And maybe that's the mistake I made with Olivia," Harper admitted. "I've had years to think about my actions, about where my head was at, how I saw her and myself." He grazed her cheek with his thumb. "My mom and dad share a love of hiking. The Cascade Mountains are real close and as kids growing up, their parents were always hiking, having picnics and being in the forest together as a family. I think, looking back on it, I didn't give Olivia and me enough time to get to know each other, to do things together, to find out if we were compatible. My folks love to fish and that's their focus when they go on hikes into the mountains."

"You may be right," Tara agreed, enjoying leaning her hips against his. No question he wanted her; the heat was pulsating throughout her abdomen, telling her he wanted the same thing.

"Do your folks share something in common?"

"Oh, many things. They love card games, bridge especially. They have a circuit here in the valley and a bridge club. I always know where they are on a Saturday evening because that's when the club gets together. My mom is an avid sports fan, loves the Arizona Cardinals football team. My dad loves all the professional football teams. They sit and watch the games together."

"That's good," Harper said. He moved his hands up her back and then slid them to her waist. "What about us, Tara? What do we share in common?"

She laughed. "Cleaning out horse box stalls, riding and repairing fence line."

"You know, since you've come to the Bar C, you haven't done much photography."

"Been a little busy," she said, seeing the warmth come to his eyes. "I'm selling well on the stock photo websites, Harper."

"I've been thinking about that. There's some really nice old, broken-down cabins up in the Salt Mountains. There's a beautiful trail into Prater Canyon. In fact, the end of Maud and Steve's property sits on the edge of the state park. I was thinking that if the weather cooperates, maybe sometime next week we could pack a picnic lunch, throw it into our knapsacks and go to the park. We could take that trail up into the mountains where the old cabins are. I think they would make a good photo. What do you think?"

"Sounds like fun. I'd love that, Harper. But are you big on hiking?"

"Sure am. There are several nice cold creeks up into the Prater wilderness area. I intend to try to catch some trout for us. If I get lucky? I'll catch enough to bring back and fry for dinner that night. What do you think?"

"That sounds fantastic!" Tara said, excitement in her voice. "Before I came into your life, did you fish much?"

"Yes. My dad taught me trout fishing and I love it. I'm not sure which is more important to me—the hike into the area or actually fishing. I like the woods, the quiet; it was very helpful to me after I got PTSD."

"Well, I would love to go with you on a hike and trout fishing," Tara said. "I'm sure there's going to be plenty to shoot because from what Shay has said, the Salt River Mountains are filled with all kinds of wildlife."

Nodding, he said, "They are. We'll carry bear spray on us, for sure. Plenty of grizzly and black bear around."

"Sounds exciting."

He snorted and said, "Oh, you'll feel your adrenaline pouring through you when you meet a big eight-hundred-pound sow grizzly."

"I'm sure I will."

"Then? It's a date?" and he dug into her gaze.

Tara felt his hands tighten just a bit around her waist, and the burning quality in his gaze made her think he was going to kiss her. There were plenty of other couples around, but they were the farthest away from the barn. "That's a date, Harper. Now? Will you kiss me?"

His mouth twitched, deviltry coming to his eyes. "In a heartbeat, Ms. Dalton," and he released her waist, his hands framing her face, gently angling her chin upward to meet his descending mouth.

Tara pushed up on her toes, meeting Harper's mouth. Closing her eyes, her hands resting near the column of his neck, she wanted this more than anything else. The scent of him as a man, the way his mouth brushed hers so lightly, sent a thrill arcing through her. She knew Harper could be strong and powerful with her, but she relished the gentleness he shared with her as he explored her lips. His mouth was cherishing, and she tasted the sweetness of the hot chocolate he'd drunk earlier. A low sound of pleasure vibrated in the back of her throat as his mouth made more contact with hers. Tara could feel him holding back. She wasn't sure why. She was no wilting lily and responded with her fire and need for him, fearless and wanting Harper to know she really could be kissed fully, not as if she were some breakable woman. In the back of her mind, she wondered if Olivia had been, though, and that was why he reined himself in with her. There was so much she didn't know yet or understand about Harper that she wanted to know. Tara wasn't the kind to assume anything. She'd rather ask and drag out the information so she would know where they stood with each other.

She lost herself in the returning pressure of his mouth, taking hers more surely as she had arched into him, her hips tight against his. Oh! There was no question he wanted her, his erection strong against her belly. She wasn't ready to go there yet with Harper. He was still healing from his marriage. Unsure of himself with her, still blaming himself for what had happened between him and Olivia.

As Tara felt his rough hands loosen a little against her cheeks, his finger trailing downward, sending skitters of fire through her, she languished in the heat and need of his mouth taking hers. Now Harper understood she wasn't a fragile thing. She was strong, confident and sure of herself with him, and that seemed to loosen some of the hold he had upon himself. She moved her hands across his chest, glorying in the power of him, his skin growing taut where she caressed him. It was a wonderful exploration and she absorbed the tension in him against her, the need building until she could feel an ache below, telling her just how much she wanted him.

The music of the fiddles and accordion drifted out of the barn. It was a call to everyone that the band was back and dancing was going to take place shortly.

Tara didn't want the kiss to end. There was a subtle tension through Harper as he hungrily took her lips, kissing her deeply, unleashing his desire as he cupped the back of her head, ravishing her lips. She drowned in the emotion he shared with her, his need, his adoring her as he gentled his kiss toward the end, kissing each corner of her mouth, brushing her wet lips one more time before he reluctantly eased away.

Lifting her lashes, she drowned again in the raw need burning in his eyes. There was no mistaking that look: This was a man who worshipped his woman, wanted to please her even more than he had already. It was a wonderful discovery, and Tara cried inwardly as he released her head, helping her to stand on her own two feet. She felt heady, euphoric and dazed all at the same time. Never had she been kissed like this. There was so much more to Harper. Vaguely, she realized in her erupting lower body and thudding heart, that he was a man of few words; he let his actions speak for him.

All Tara could think was: Wow. *Just . . . wow . . .*

Harper could barely think straight as he placed his arm around Tara and led her back to the barn and the music. He longed for some quiet, uninterrupted time with her, not at all interested in the dance or socializing anymore. That kiss had changed everything for him. Everything. As he walked to the Dalton table and sat down to chat with Tara's mother and father, he tried to focus on them, not his overjoyed heart.

"Harper, Tara tells us that you're working toward a degree to become a paramedic."

Harper held the judge's gaze. "Yes, sir, I am. I've already got the approval from the fire chief of Wind River FD to apply for a job opening they have waiting for me once I graduate."

"Isn't that dangerous work?" Joanna Dalton asked.

"Not compared to what I was doing in the military," he said, trying not to smile. Harper understood that civilians didn't understand the rigor and stress on those in combat. But maybe, in this case? They knew Tara was under a lot of pressure and wanted to know more about him. He wondered if they'd already picked up the fact that he and Tara liked each other. Were they doing some questioning of him to find out who he really was? Seeing if he measured up to Tara or not? Harper thought so but didn't become defensive about it. He saw Joanna's expression turn thoughtful at his answer.

"Can you tell us more about yourself?" Scott Dalton urged.

Okay, Harper got it. Clearly, Tara's parents saw them as more than just employees working at the Bar C. He wondered if Joanna's radar—that woman's intuition—had tipped her off and she'd mentioned to her husband. More than likely.

He gave them the short version of his family history. They were working middle class, nothing fancy, and he wondered if that disappointed them. Was this going to turn into something of a comparison between the two families? Would they see his family as less than their own? Think he wasn't good enough for Tara? All those fears moved through his mind at lightning speed. Harper didn't want her parents set against him. Glancing to his right where Tara sat, she appeared at ease. Maybe he was gun-shy because he remembered meeting Olivia's parents, who were very rich and didn't think anything of him at all.

"I know they need a full-time paramedic over at the fire department," Scott said. "How much longer before you graduate?"

"One more year," Harper said. "I'm carrying an A in all my classes."

"I would imagine," Scott added, "that because you were a combat corpsman, you find the paramedic route a little boring?"

Grinning, Harper said, "In some ways, but saving lives is my focus. The teachers have already asked me to do a PowerPoint presentation on combat medicine and the golden hour. I can share some of my experiences from over in Afghanistan with the students because combat medicine is different in some respects from the paramedic/EMT medicine practiced here in the USA." He saw Scott give him a pleased look.

"That speaks well of your teachers, to recognize that your skills are superior in areas they probably have never been taught about."

Harper liked Scott Dalton's understanding, and it surprised him. The man hadn't been in the military, but maybe because Tara had been, he'd done his homework. "Yes, it does. I'm enjoying the classes at the college and they're teaching me the way it's done now, here, in this country."

"Well," Joanna piped up, "you're such an asset to the valley, Harper. We're all glad you're here. There's a real need for a full-time paramedic with our fire department.

As it is now? We have to rely on helicopters to come from Jackson Hole to pick up a sick or injured person."

"Yes," Tara said, "and people can die en route on a fifty-mile helo ride. With Harper getting his degree, he's going to be able to stabilize the patient so we can hopefully prevent tragedies from occurring." She gave him a warm look filled with pride.

Harper realized all his fears about not being good enough for Tara were caused by his own anxiety. Scott and Joanna Dalton were looking at him with respect. It was such a huge difference between the way Olivia's parents had treated him.

When Tara reached out, covering his hand on the table with her own, squeezing it, he wondered if she was reading his mind. But then, they did have this magical, invisible tie to each other. And she had to be picking up on his concerns and anxieties. Just the warmth of her hand for that brief moment quelled all his fears, saw they were turning out to be baseless.

"Well," Scott said, "we'd like to have you and Tara over for dinner on Saturday. Are you available?"

Harper glanced over at Tara. "I am. How about you?"

She grinned. "I love having dinner with my mom and dad." She turned to her parents. "We'd love to come over. What time?"

"Make it four p.m.?" Joanna said. "That way we can sit and chat for a bit beforehand."

And ask me more questions, Harper thought. But now he wasn't as wary because he felt Tara's parents genuinely accepted him. Whether he wanted to admit it or not, that was important to him. He knew that, in part, Olivia's parents had derided her, while he was deployed in Afghanistan, for marrying someone "out of her class." He often wondered how much of her parents' cajoling her had played a part in the final demise of their relationship. Harper realized he'd never know for sure. But at least now? Tara and her parents accepted him, admired and respected him. Another huge, invisible load slid off Harper's shoulders that he hadn't realized, until that moment, had been there all this time.

Chapter Nine

Tara was barely able to contain her excitement as she followed Harper up the Prater Canyon trail. The late-morning temperature was in the fifties, but the sky was blue, the sun warming her as they hiked the evergreen-clothed canyon. Up ahead, she could see snow-clad Prater Mountain, one of the taller ones in the Salt River chain. She wore her heavy denim coat, a bright blue knapsack on her back, plus gloves to keep her fingers warm. Right now, she appreciated the warmth of a knit cap over her head and ears. She had a hiking stick in her hand.

Harper, walking at her side, seemed impervious to the chill and was wearing a dark blue baseball cap that had US Navy embroidered on the front of it. He, too, carried a knapsack on his shoulders, as well as a hiking stick. The ground was thawing and so their heavy, thick-treaded boots were picking up the mud. This was a well-used, popular trail, one she'd hiked many times as a child and teenager. He carried a .30-06 rifle on his left shoulder because grizzlies were everywhere, and no one wanted to suddenly confront one and then get killed by it. The rifle was there as a precaution; Tara knew Harper didn't want to kill a bear either. But at this time of year grizzlies were hungry after coming out of hibernation.

The day was incredible, the air fresh and cool, a blue jay in the distance squawking its warning that people were coming down the trail and into the deep canyon. She had her Canon camera around her neck, a 200mm lens on it. She hoped to see elk or deer, but it was pretty late in the morning for that. These animals were nocturnal and, by dawn, were usually bedded down to sleep during the day. Still, Tara held out hope of spotting one or two. Maybe even a fawn because this was the time of year when they were born.

The area was alive with life, birds flitting around them, nest-building materials in their bills, swooping up into the tall pine trees near the edge of the flat, open canyon floor.

Drawing in a deep breath, Tara had never been happier. It had been nearly two weeks since she'd kissed Harper. And he'd been so busy between taking classes at the college and getting his wrangler duties done around the Bar C that they'd had little time to sit down and talk at length. Today, he told her, they were going to get that time together or else. Tara had laughed, but she'd agreed. Her life was ratcheting up, too.

Last week, she'd loved going back to Jilly's Wedding Shop in Jackson Hole to have Kira help them choose the bridesmaids' gowns they'd wear for the wedding on June 16. Maud Whitcomb was there and insisted on paying for them. It was a wonderful gift, and they'd hugged the hell out of her for her continuing generosity.

Kira loved lavender and, fortunately, so did she, Dair and Shay. She was pleased that the dress design chosen was something she could wear after the wedding. The knee-length dress would be available should she want to wear it after that. Harper had seen a photo of it from her cell phone, but the dresses wouldn't be ready until the end of May. The material was real silk, and Tara had marveled at the velvety quality of it. It felt good against her fingertips. Maud lauded the praises of silk to all of them, saying it was wonderful to wear. Tara wouldn't know. About all she'd ever worn was cotton or polyester fabrics. Silk cost too much and her mother was practical. Silk wasn't something she could ride in, or do barn work or anything else.

The look in Harper's eyes when he'd studied the cellphone photo of the dress had made her smile. He liked it for a lot of other reasons, she suspected. Was sex on her mind? Oh, yes. She'd enjoyed the stolen moments when they kissed. It wasn't often enough, but Tara understood. They were too busy, there were too many demands from their jobs and his intensive college program. She was so glad when Harper had suggested this morning that they take off and go for a hike, have lunch at the old cabin above Prater Canyon and talk at length with each other.

Tara was so focused on her thoughts that she nearly ran into Harper. He'd stopped and was pointing to the right. There, along a group of pines, were three elk mothers with their babies.

She grinned a thanks to him, quickly lifting her Canon and took some shots. And then she took some more because the mothers and their babies didn't duck back into the dark, shadowy pines to hide.

Keeping her voice low, she asked, "Why do you think they're out at this time of day?"

"Grizzly," he murmured, eyes squinted, looking down the canyon where the elk had come from. "They've just come out of hibernation. They're hungry and they know there are fawns around to be eaten."

Grimacing, Tara said, "These babies are so cute. I hate the idea some of them might be killed by a bear."

"Yeah, I know, but it's survival of the fittest and you know that better than most. You grew up in this valley."

"I try to avoid thinking of those things," she murmured, kneeling in the wet grass, focusing on a tiny baby trailing her mama.

Lifting the cap from his head, Harper said, "I know. You're a big softy, Ms. Dalton."

Her lips lifted as she kept the camera focused. "I just don't like killing."

"And you were in combat. Does that figure?"

His teasing made her pull the camera away from her eye. Looking up, she felt the warmth of his look cascading around her. "No, it doesn't. I'm glad to be back home, Harper. I never liked killing and I never will. I didn't join the military to kill. Defend our country? Absolutely. But not to kill if I could avoid it."

He leaned over, caressing her shoulder. "Anyone in their right mind doesn't want to kill another human being, so you have lots of company on that one."

Her gaze fastened on his mouth and her entire lower body went hot with need. Did Harper realize just how sexy he was? Tara didn't think so. He wasn't a braggart, arrogant or pushy like so many men. "I haven't met a vet yet who doesn't agree that peace is the answer. Anyone who's gone into combat sees what war does. There are better answers than killing one another."

"Hey," he said, lifting his gloved finger, "take a look down there, about a tenth of a mile behind those elk."

Swinging her head, she stood, frowning. There was a cinnamon-colored grizzly sniffing and following the small group. "Damn," she muttered. "I was hoping to avoid this."

Harper came to stand next to her, pulling the rifle off his shoulder, locking and loading it. "Me too, but it's spring. They're starving and they need to eat, so they're going to smell out where the elk are laying down for the day and try to kill one of their fawns."

Tara was no stranger to grizzlies, and Harper seemed to understand a lot about bear activity. "You've seen one this close before?"

"Yes, on horseback. I was riding fence line last spring and fixing a downed section when a huge male, about eight hundred pounds, popped out of the woods. Scared the living hell out of me," and he hefted the rifle into position so it was ready to use in case the grizzly charged them.

"What did you do?"

"I carried a pistol on me. Bears have lousy eyesight. I wasn't sure he saw me as much as he saw my horse, probably thinking it was his meal. I fired off three shots and the sound scared him and he hightailed it back into the woods."

"Might have to do it with this one," Tara said, taking photos of the approaching bear.

"That bear will eat four-legged before he'll think about a two-legged meal," Harper said. "Come on; time to move to the other side of the canyon. I don't want to spook the grizzly, but I also don't want to be standing where we are now. That's way too close."

Tara agreed, quickly moving with him. Harper put her in front of him, bringing up the rear, his gaze always on the approaching grizzly. She saw the bear was trailing the scent of the elk mother and didn't seem to be looking around, his focus on getting food for his shrunken belly. She saw the elk begin to trot up the canyon, the fawns running to keep up. Above all, she didn't want to see that grizzly kill one of the babies. She couldn't stand to see it. Hurrying, she lengthened her stride. Harper kept up with her easily, staying at her left shoulder, the rifle ready in case they needed it.

Remaining silent, Tara tossed a quick glance over her shoulder; the grizzly was probably about three hundred yards from them. That was only six hundred feet. A bear could run at twenty-five miles an hour and cover that distance in a heartbeat. She heard Harper place a round in the chamber of the rifle, flicking off the safety. He, too, knew that the bear, should it decide they were his meal, would be on top of them in a blink of a human's eye. Quite literally. They were that fast, that nimble and quick.

"Keep moving," Harper said in a low tone. "The bear's still on the elk's scent. In a moment he's going to smell *our* scent. I don't know what he'll do . . ."

"We have bear spray, Harper."

"I know, but I'm not willing to risk our lives on spray if that bear charges us."

She heard the grim determination in his voice. "We should stop if he decides to come toward us."

"Yes. You stay behind me. I'll shoot."

Tara knew that if a grizzly charged, the first one was usually a feint. The second charge was for real. And there was no way to read the animal's mind to know if he would feint on the first charge or not. She risked a glance over her shoulder again, seeing the tension and focus in Harper's face as his gaze tracked the bear's trek. He was coming up on where they had been standing near the path the elk had taken.

The grizzly halted, woofing and turning around in a larger circle.

"He's picked up our scent," Harper warned in a low tone.

Tara heard the disappointment in his voice. "Should we stop?"

"Not yet; he's still sniffing. He's not sure what he's picking up."

"He can still see the elk ahead of him."

"Yeah. As bad as his eyesight is, I'm hoping he'll leave our scent alone and go after something he knows for sure. He's acting as if he doesn't know the scent of us."

"Good."

"Let's stop."

Her heart started a slow bang in her chest. She stood near Harper's left side because if he had to shoot, he'd be using his right arm. There was no way she wanted to impede him getting a bead on the grizzly because he'd only have a few seconds to lift that rifle and sight the bruin. The bear moved in a circle once more. Then he lifted his nose, whuffing and sniffing loudly into the cold air.

"The wind is in our favor," Tara said quietly to Harper. "It's blowing toward us. We're upwind of him. He won't catch our scent." She saw Harper barely nod his head, his gaze riveted on the animal less than a thousand feet from where they stood. It was way too close, and Tara swallowed against a tightening throat.

Suddenly, the bear rose up on its hind legs, ten feet tall, looking directly at them.

"Oh, God," Tara choked.

"Don't move . . ."

She remained frozen. It was well known that if a person tried to walk or run away from a grizzly, it would charge. The only thing they could do was remain like statues, unmoving. If they tried to turn to run, the bear would think them quarry and swiftly catch up to them, killing them. It brought back all the terror and anxiety that combat had caused her.

Tara didn't move, wondering if she was going to die. That thought alone made her want to cry out because she'd just met Harper a short time ago. They had something good going between them. She wanted the time to get to know him, herself and deepen their relationship.

The bear lifted his nose, snorting and then inhaling.

Tara could feel a breeze against her face. "The bear might not be able to see us," she squeaked, her voice off.

". . . Maybe . . ."

The grizzly stood up so he could see more of the area where they were. Tara knew he was looking for movement. They remained statue still. Her heart was banging away in her throat. The sound was so loud, she couldn't hear anything else, adrenaline pouring into her bloodstream.

Without warning, the grizzly suddenly dropped to all fours, and charged toward them.

Tara didn't even have time to shout a warning.

Harper jammed the rifle into his shoulder.

The huge, booming sound made Tara's ears ache. She winced, stepping backward, her gaze on the charging bear. It happened so fast!

The grizzly dropped, it's front feet collapsing, his wide, wedge-shaped head plowing into the thick, green grass. His huge body was still moving forward. The animal flipped, went into a slow-motion roll and then flopped out on its belly. All four of his legs splayed outward.

Tara made another squeaking sound of disbelief as the bear collapsed fifty feet in front of them. The animal had been so fast, she didn't think she'd been able to blink twice.

Harper kept the rifle up, finger on the trigger, tensely watching the bear. There were several jerking movements, but he didn't get up again. His gaze snapped to the bear's flanks, watching for his breathing. Because if he was still breathing, that meant the bear could rise and come at them again. He kept a bead on the head of the bruin, where he'd buried the first bullet.

Tara gulped. "Is he dead?" She anxiously watched the bear.

"Give it another half minute," Harper replied in a rough voice, his rifle sighted.

"I wish he hadn't charged," Tara whispered, tears burning her eyes. "I hate killing anything."

"So do I, Tara. This couldn't be helped. I'm sorry . . ."

She reached out, barely touching his shoulder, not wanting to destroy his line of sight on the bear. "I know how much you love wildlife. You're not a hunter. You're a fisherman."

"Yeah," he said, slowly lowering the rifle, still watching the unmoving bear. "I don't like killing anything . . ."

He was a medic. Harper saved lives, he didn't take them. Although she knew combat medics did carry weapons and would kill if attacked or their team was under fire. It was in his DNA to save lives, though, and as she slowly walked around his left side, she saw the suffering in his eyes. He'd hated killing the grizzly, too.

"We need to call the Forest Service up in Jackson Hole," she said, pulling out her cell phone. "This has to be reported."

Nodding, Harper said, "Just wait a moment. I need to go check to make sure he's dead. He wasn't wearing a tracking collar either."

Most of the grizzlies in the Teton National Park and at Yellowstone had been tranquilized and had a radio collar fitted around their necks so the rangers could keep tabs on their whereabouts. "No, this bear isn't wearing one." She reached out, gripping his upper left arm. "Be careful, Harper. Grizzlies have been known, even after being shot, to bite or take a swipe at hunters."

"Shay warned me about that first thing when I came to the Bar C a year ago," he said. "I'll be careful. You stay where you're at."

"I won't move. I promise." Some of the adrenaline was leaving her and she was beginning to feel the crash that always came afterward. "I'll wait to call the rangers."

"Yes, let me check the bear out . . ."

"Be careful, Harper . . . please?"

"Promise . . ."

Approaching such a huge animal, knowing how dangerous it was, Tara didn't want Harper to go near the bear. She knew he had to. The whole day they'd planned had gone south. They would have to report this to the Forest Service and then wait here until a ranger came to take their statement, take photos and then get the grizzly removed. Harper wouldn't be charged with killing a bear. This had been about protecting their lives and the rangers would understand that.

Harper approached from the rear of the bear, watching carefully for any sign of breathing. Tara understood his being cautious in approaching the bruin. She could see blood leaking out of a hole in the animal's head, still feeling badly that they'd had to take its life. But if they hadn't, one or both of them would have been mauled, bitten or possibly killed. Grizzlies were well known to go after hikers if they ran.

Leaning down, Harper remained at one end of the bear. He slung the rifle across his shoulder, placing his large hand on the bear's foot, pulling at it a little to see if it moved.

It didn't. Moving to the center of the bear, he placed his hand on its thick fur, feeling for breathing.

Tara watched the hardness in Harper's face. Was this what he looked like in combat? There was no sign of weakness in his expression, his gray eyes so pale they reminded her of an eagle tracking its quarry. There was tension in him, but he moved soundlessly, working his way forward toward the bear's massive hump and shoulders. He'd stop, place his hand on top of the fur, press down, still trying to feel for any breath sounds. There was such a thing as a limbic action of the bear's brain that could still react, even if it was dead, for minutes afterward. Tara knew Harper was very aware of that possibility, which was why he'd started at the rear of the bruin and was quietly and slowly working his way forward toward the head.

By the time he leaned forward from the bear's neck, placing his hand on his head, the animal's eyes were glazed and unblinking, Tara knew the grizzly was dead. Harper made a point of not getting within range of the bear's massive front paws and those five-inch curved claws it had. He straightened and moved back a good six feet from the bear before looking over at her.

"Go ahead and call the Forest Service."

She nodded and made the call. Harper came around the bear and talked with the supervisor from the Teton National Park, telling him what had just transpired. Then the bear would be taken away, checked by the Forest Service and a thorough forensics study performed on it.

Clicking off the phone, she said, "How are you doing?" His eyes were still nearly clear and Tara realized that when he felt in danger, the color changed. She knew that when he looked at her, desiring her, his eyes became a darker, smoky gray color.

"Feeling bad I had to kill the bear," he muttered, giving the animal a look of regret. "I was hoping he wouldn't get riled up over our scent, but he did."

"I thought for sure he'd follow the elk and try to kill one of the babies."

He slid his left arm around her waist, easing her around and away from the bear. "I had a bad feeling about it."

"That gut intuition?" she asked, leaning into him, wrapping her arm around his waist, wanting his closeness, his protectiveness.

"Yes. Having PTSD comes in handy sometimes, doesn't it?" he joked, cocking his head in her direction, holding her gaze.

"Yes, but most people aren't going to run into a hungry grizzly," she murmured. Squeezing him, she said, "I'm feeling so sad for the bear. I know you had to take him out, but I wish he'd made a different choice."

Shaking his head, Harper led her to the other side of the canyon. "We all make choices all the time, Tara. The bear was no different. It just wasn't the right one for him today."

Hearing the heaviness, the thick emotions barely concealed in his tone, Tara pressed her brow against his shoulder, wanting to comfort him. "You're a good shot."

"I'd better be. We had one bullet standing between him and us."

The derision in his tone was partly black humor, and Tara realized it was his way of starting to let down from the incident. She slowed as he eased the strap of the rifle off his shoulder and placed it against a nearby pine tree. Shrugging out of her pack, she leaned it against the trunk. Harper did the same. He lifted his cap, rubbed his hair and then grimaced, looking back at the bear.

"Hey," Tara called softly, coming around, facing him, sliding her arms around his shoulders, "come here." She hugged him, burying her face in the column of his neck, tightening her arms around him. The tension in Harper was palpable as she aligned herself against him. For a split second, he froze. And then she heard him groan her name, sweeping his arms around her so tightly the air whooshed out of her lungs. He pressed his face into her hair, clinging to her.

Sensitized to him, Tara felt a deep quiver within him, felt as if he wanted to cry, scream or shout out his regret over having to take the life of such a beautiful wild animal. Harper wasn't a killer and never had been. Her closed eyes filled with tears as he kissed her hair, holding her so tightly, as if to breathe her into himself, to hold her forever.

Her heart opened wide and she relaxed, allowing herself to melt into him, to let him hold her as tightly as he needed. For an instant, Tara almost felt as if she were like a life preserver to him and if he released her, he would be lost forever. It was such a deep, eviscerating realization that it shocked her. Harper had never been needy. Even now, she wouldn't say that he was. But emotionally? Yes, he needed her, needed some comfort, needed that moment where life was stronger than death. Tara understood that more than most because she'd been in combat. She'd seen people killed and injured. She understood that perhaps Harper was in the middle of a flashback to a time when such a thing had happened to his team. Never had a man held her as tightly as he did right now.

Even through her sadness, she thought she understood what was going on within him, and joy rose in her heart, warmth spreading through her chest. She tightened her arms around him, silently letting him know she was there for him. That he could lean on her when he needed to. And that was the exact sense Tara was feeling from Harper. She wished they were alone. She would kiss him, hold him, make him feel better, not worse. New tendrils slowly opened within her heart. She recognized those fragile new feelings. She was falling in love with Harper.

Chapter Ten

Harper tried to hold on to his explosive flashback as he stood in Tara's arms in that canyon. He'd broken out in a sweat, his heart thundering in his chest, feeling quivery inside, fear eating him up as he struggled to control it. He had no idea how she knew he needed her to throw her arms around his shoulders and pull him against her, but it saved him in ways he could never give words to. Just being able to bury his face in her loose blond hair captured by the knit cap she wore, steadied him. The spiral into that horrifying flashback made him grip her so hard he heard the air rush out from between her lips.

Eyes tightly shut, he clung to her, trying to wrest himself from the roar of gunfire, the screams, the blood and carnage around him on that cold Afghan dawn when they were attacked by the Taliban just outside a village. It was barely light when the attack occurred. Even now, as he sucked in a huge draught of air, he needed to smell something of life, that special honeysuckle shampoo Tara used on her hair and not the stench of metallic blood filling his nostrils instead.

As the grizzly charged them unexpectedly, the flashback simultaneously slammed into Harper. He didn't know how he'd been able to shoot the charging bear in the head, stopping him. Even with his eyes open, he saw the flashback instead of the bear. It was a miracle he'd hit the animal at all.

With his eyes shut, his five senses ballooned, overwhelming him. He tried to stop all the sensations, to avoid the blips, like grainy, visceral photographs, but a flashback always captured him and he would relieve everything. Every last damned thing. Every death. Every scream. Every smell cloying into his nostrils, making him gag. He felt so damned helpless that cold March morning. Lives were lost. He couldn't save everyone and guilt tore through him.

Only Tara's warm, supple body pinned against him, his arms tight bands around her as he held her, kept his sanity, kept him stable. He needed to smell life, not death. He needed her warmth and softness, not the hard, brutal reality he saw playing out against his tightly shut eyes and across his brow like a horror movie. His mind tumbled, his emotions raw, eviscerating and in control of him. All he could do was hold her even tighter.

The blood on the bear's head had thrown him into a deeper spiral as he'd opened his eyes, walked toward it to make sure it was really dead. He was torn between the past and the present, on a sanity-insanity tightrope.

After making sure the bear was dead, he wanted to protect Tara. He grabbed her by the waist, hauling her away from the carcass, wanting to place distance between them. Harper kept seeing the past overlaying the present. He had to get Tara across the floor of the canyon. He wanted that distance between them and that bear. He knew it was dead, but his other emotions, other needs to protect those in his team, made him more frantic inwardly, and it all focused on taking care of Tara.

His mind was like a bowling ball in a marble room where it rolled around, making him feel as if his control were going to slip away from his grasp. The past overlaid the present. Sometimes he'd see the green grass they walked through toward the pine tree grove on the other side of the canyon and then a splice of the firefight would slam in front of his eyes instead. He felt like he was living in two different realities at once, struggling to stay in the one with Tara. Just having his arm around her waist gave him purchase, gave him the driving need to stay in the present. Now. Not the bloody past.

By the time he'd leaned his rifle against the pine tree trunk, the flashback was beginning to overwhelm him. And to his surprise, Tara came to him, as if sensing his need for her. Amazed by her incredible intuition, Harper had never been more grateful than right at that moment, with her. He shook in her arms and he felt less of a man, worried that she wouldn't understand what was really controlling him. When her gloved hand moved soothingly across his hunched, tense shoulders, something old and hard broke within him. Somewhere deep within him, untouched by the flashback, Harper knew Tara understood exactly what he was in the throes of, and she pressed herself even more surely against him, to steady him, nurture him, in her own special way.

And then he felt her lips brush his temple, her words low and broken.

"It's all right, Harper, it's all right. You're here with me, not back there. . . . Just hold on to me; it will pass . . . hold on to me . . . I won't let you go. . . ."

The words rushed through him, filling his heart, sending a calming sensation over the raging waters of his whipsawing emotions. He held her, fought to focus on her small, healing kisses along his temple, his hair and neck.

God, he needed this! He needed her! Hot tears burned behind his lids. They leaked out of his eyes even though he wanted to stop them, worried that Tara would see him as weak if she knew he was crying. Olivia had accused him of being less than a man because he'd shake, cry and wouldn't be able to control his emotions when flashbacks struck him. He'd be on the floor, in a corner, trying to hide; they were that overwhelming and powerful. She had been disgusted by his behavior, saying a man never cried.

Tara's low voice continued to overlay his flashback. Words he couldn't make out, but he could hear the tone of care and comfort in her voice. He was too torn apart to think coherently. Only the strength of her arms surrounding him, cradling his body against hers, small kisses meant to heal, her hand moving slowly up and down his back, was what he concentrated on. Little by little, the flashback began to lose its grip on him. It was because of Tara, who was strong when he was presently weak, that had helped chase it back into that demon hole where it burned angrily in his soul.

Harper had no idea how much time had passed. The quivering in his stomach, the gripping tightness around it, began to ebb away beneath Tara's guiding him through the process. As his mind canted more and more to the present, leaving that horrific flashback to sink to the bottom of his psyche once more, Harper knew she realized what had just happened. Her touches were meant to calm and heal. Her kisses were soft and soothing. This wasn't about sex. It was about one human being caring for another when they were hurting so deeply. The doors to his heart flung wipe open and he'd never felt the depth of feelings he now felt for Tara. She was unselfish, giving back to him, doing her best to help him get through it.

Lifting his hand, he released her, and she stepped away

from him. He self-consciously wiped his eyes, avoiding her gaze, too raw to deal with her reaction to his tears. He wouldn't apologize for them because he'd cried in the medevac as two of his teammates died en route to Bagram. He couldn't stop crying at that time either.

"It's all right," Tara said quietly, lifting her hand, settling it on his shoulder. "Flashback? Killing the bear brought it on?"

His voice was rough. "Yeah . . ."

"It always helped if I did some slow, deep breaths when I was coming out of one."

Barely glancing at her, he saw her expression was one of understanding, not condemnation or judgment, as Olivia's had been. He made one more swipe at his cheeks, drying them. "I'll be okay." He saw her lips twitch, her blue eyes shadowed with knowing. "Maybe in a little while," he added thickly. Her hand moved slowly up and down his shoulder, still soothing him. It actually helped him orient back to right now. The past was fading quickly, far more so than before, and he realized it was Tara and her unflappable, calm way. "How did you know?"

"I saw it in your eyes when you looked up at me when you were checking to see if the bear was dead or alive."

"My eyes?" He wiped his hands down the sides of his jeans, straightening, lifting his chin, holding her upturned gaze. There was such tenderness in her gaze that it made a lot of his self-consciousness dissolve. There was no censure in Tara's expression . . . just sympathy and understanding.

"I once looked in a mirror when I was starting into a flashback," she told him with a slight shrug, her hand slipping from his shoulder. "I hated what I saw. I looked like a crazed, insane animal. It scared me so much."

"So you knew."

Nodding, she said, "I could feel you starting to fly apart, Harper. I could feel you struggling to contain that monster. All I could think to do, all that I'd always wanted when a flashback hit me, was to be held tightly. Held and protected." She managed a sad quirk of one corner of her mouth as she studied him. "That's when I came to you once you put that rifle down against the tree trunk. I wasn't sure what you would do. I know some guys strike out, fight back. I wasn't sure . . ."

He stared at her intently, watching the breeze lift a blond curl against her pale cheek. She was rattled. It had been hard on Tara, too, Harper was sure. "I wouldn't ever hit you."

"In my heart of hearts? I knew you wouldn't hurt me, Harper. It's not in your DNA to strike out at others. You're a combat corpsman. You're there to calm and care for the injured, not lash out at them."

"Logic is faultless," he murmured, giving her a small smile of thanks. He felt more stable emotionally now and added, "It hit me out of nowhere. When the grizzly charged us, it triggered it." He saw Tara's expression sag in shock. "Yeah," he grumbled, "that veil of the flashback dropped over my eyes. I couldn't even see the bear anymore, Tara. I shot anyway. I was trying to push the flashback away, but it was too strong. It overpowered my sight."

"My God," she whispered, her hand moving to her lips as she stared up at him.

"I got lucky," he groused, shoving his hands into the pockets of his jeans.

"Oh," Tara murmured, reaching out, grazing his jaw, "it was much more than luck. You're a combat corpsman. You'd shoot straight even if hell was charging you."

He managed a snort, avoiding the pride and respect in her gaze and voice. How unlike Olivia was Tara. It was so black and white that Harper could hardly believe it. In the military, it was wrong to cry at any time. But that dawn firefight and subsequent flight to Bagram in the medevac had torn Harper in two. The men who died on the deck of that helo he'd been with on three earlier deployments. They were brothers to him, not just comrades in arms. His throat tightened, but he forced out the words, "I couldn't let you be injured or hurt, Tara. It was the last thing I'd ever let happen. What was left of my mind at that point was that the grizzly was going to have to go through me first to get to you. I shot because I had nothing to lose at that point."

Tara stared, her lips parting. "Oh, Harper . . ."

Making himself look at Tara, he saw tears of gratitude in her eyes. Not censure. Not anger. Just . . . humanity. One human reaching out to touch another. His heart thudded, but this time, it was all those wonderful, wildly escaping feelings of goodness spreading throughout his chest as she whispered his name and came forward, opening her arms to him.

Tara came and leaned against him, her arms around his waist, her head on his shoulder, her brow resting against his jaw. Harper wrapped his arms around her, this time gently, not squeezing her as he had before. Kissing her knit cap over her hair, he rasped, "You're the most important person to ever walk into my life, Tara. You have to know that . . . believe it . . ." He nudged her cheek, asking her to lift her chin, and she did. Never had her lips tasted as sweet, as wonderful as right now, sliding against his. A groan came from deep within him as he felt her push her belly against him, letting him know just how much she needed this connection, too. Somewhere in his shorting-out mind, the wash of the flashback emotions meeting and surging with newer, more heated ones, told him how important Tara was to him.

He heard her make a happy sound in the back of her throat, her arms tightening around his waist, her breasts solidly against his jacket. If only they were back at the ranch, back in their home, he'd have instantly picked her up into his arms and carried her to his bed and loved her until she fainted from pleasure. The scent of her velvety skin against his, their breathing growing ragged and harsh, the urgency to absorb her into every cell he owned, became primary. Tara was life. She instilled hope within him once more. She was his. And never had Harper known it more than just now. He understood as few others did that a near-death experience made a person want to prove they were alive, that they had survived. Her mouth opened and he took her with new fierceness, glorying in her wetness, her eagerness and hunger that matched his own.

It was only after he reluctantly eased from her glistening lips, eyes barely open, staring into hers, that Harper realized there were no remnants from his flashback. That amazed him because it usually took hours, sometimes half a day, before he was fully back in the present, back into his body, in the here and now.

Stunned by the realization, he framed Tara's face, drowning in her lustrous blue eyes that were barely opened. He could feel how dazed she'd become as their mouths had clashed urgently with each other. She was no less affected by the danger they'd suddenly found themselves in. Luckily, she'd escaped being triggered into a flashback.

With his gloved thumb, he smoothed it across her cheek. "What we have," he began in a growl, "is something I've never had before, Tara. When I look at you? You're like a lake, smooth as glass, beautiful, but you have such depth. I want the right to explore you, hear what you have to say, what you think . . ." He saw her lashes sweep downward.

". . . Yes," she whispered, "I want the same from you, Harper. Nothing less . . ."

Tara waited patiently beneath the boughs of the pine tree where the rifle sat. Within an hour, a vehicle bearing a wildlife biologist and two rangers arrived. Tara had never seen a grizzly killed while living in Wind River Valley, so she didn't know the protocol or how the rangers were going to react to the event.

Because they'd had an hour alone, Harper had been able to climb out of the depths of his flashback. By the time the Forest Service people arrived, he was his normal, unflappable self. The woman ranger, Wendy Jenkins, had taken Tara's statement on what had happened. The male ranger, Thomas Bosveld, had taken Harper's statement. They had separated them, and Tara could guess why. They wanted to compare each of their stories. If they matched, all was well. In the meantime, a gray-haired biologist carrying two big suitcases of equipment checked out the dead grizzly. No one seemed upset about the event.

Later, after the statements were taken and compared, Harper was allowed to come to sit near her. The rangers went to help the wildlife biologist. Tara frowned. "Are we in trouble?"

"No," Harper said. "Bosveld said this happens. While there's no hunting of grizzly, these kinds of unfortunate meetings do occur, especially in the spring."

"I would think they would be happy we weren't mauled to death."

Grinning a little, Harper said, "You're getting testy. Are

you hungry?" He reached for their packs, bringing them forward. "It's noon."

Her stomach grumbled.

Harper laughed a little, opening his knapsack. "I made peanut butter sandwiches. Would you like one?"

"Yes, I guess I'm coming down from the shock of the bear charging us. I'm hungry now," and she reached for the neatly wrapped sandwich, thanking Harper. Sitting there and munching on it, she said, "What will they do now?"

"The biologist has to take all kinds of tests, blood and otherwise, lots of camera shots and measurements. Each bear is tracked, and if they're killed or die, that data is added to their main headquarters database in the Tetons."

"How do you know so much about this?" she asked, canting a glance in his direction.

"Garret had to kill a grizzly last year. He was out in the Tetons, on a heavy-equipment job, when a male attacked him in the yard where he was digging a trench line."

"Oh, no," Tara said, worried. "What happened?"

"Garret carries a Glock 19 on him. He has a legal license for open carry. He put two slugs in the bear's head and killed him instantly. He got swiped by him, though. The bear had charged and his claws ripped up his jeans on his lower left leg. He had to be taken to the local hospital for about thirty stitches from those claws."

Tara stared at the bear in the meadow. "We were lucky."

"Very," Harper said, munching on his sandwich. "I'm afraid we're not going to make it to that cabin today, Tara. We'd have another five miles to hike up the canyon before we reached it."

"This was enough excitement for one day," she agreed.

"Bosveld said this bear isn't from around here. He has a tablet with the bear database for this area. He thinks it was a five-year-old looking for new territory he could hunt in. Normally," and Harper made a general gesture to the north of where they sat, "the rangers have tracking collars on the grizzlies that live within the park boundaries. They know their habits, their trails, and they can get people out of those areas, protecting them in the spring and rutting season in September."

"But out here," Tara said, waving her finger up and down the canyon floor, "we didn't know the bear was in the area."

"Well," Harper admitted, "there's a website the rangers share with the ranchers, and I went onto it this morning before we left. This area was said to be free and clear of bears. But this one is a wanderer, so there was no way anyone could have known he'd be in our vicinity."

"It was a shock," and she gave him a concerned look. "How are you feeling now with the flashback receding?"

"It's pretty much history." He finished the sandwich, wiping his hands in the surrounding dried pine needles. "Thanks to you."

"What do you mean?"

He glanced over at the cluster of rangers around the bear and then devoted his attention to Tara. "Just between you and me? When I would get a flashback, it was usually a sound or something that spiked my adrenaline, and then that firefight at dawn would download. It would take me a minimum of a day to dig myself out of it."

"You don't look burdened by it right now, Harper. Or am I wrong?"

"No, you're not wrong." He reached over, smoothing his hand across her jacketed shoulder. "It was what you did that helped it dissolve. I've never had it leave so quickly, Tara." He dug into her widening eyes. "It was you, what you did, holding me, talking me back to now, helping me to pry away from the past with your voice." Giving her a shy look, he added in a lowered tone, "I wish I could give it the words it deserves, but I can't put them together. You have magic."

Heat stung her cheeks and she looked away for a moment, trying to tame her explosion of feelings. "I knew the bear must have triggered your flashback," she said, turning her gaze to him once again. "I have them myself. I recognized the signs, Harper, that's all."

"And I got that you did. I was trying to control it, control myself."

"But it doesn't work that way."

Shaking his head, he muttered, "No. I wish to God I could control it. That whole dawn firefight passes over me like a steamroller. I can't stop it. I couldn't stop it when the bear suddenly charged us either."

"I'm glad I could help you. I felt pretty helpless really. You were shaking and I wanted so badly just to hold you, to make you feel safe when I knew that was the last thing you were feeling at the time."

He watched her brush a strand of hair away from her cheek after taking off the knit cap and laying it nearby. "You have no idea how much it meant to me. Being held? That was an incredible gift you gave me, Tara. And your hand just smoothing across my shoulders and back stabilized me so fast it stunned me. Your voice? Well, your voice called me home, to you."

Swallowing hard, Tara stared down at her hands around her drawn-up knees. "I . . . didn't know . . . thanks for telling me. That sounds pretty miraculous in itself."

"No disagreement," Harper said thickly. "But we've probably never been in a situation where the person or people around us knew what was happening and figured out what we needed. This was a first for me."

"I know," Tara murmured in a low voice, picking up a dry pine needle and breaking it between her fingers, "when I got home, I warned my parents about my flashbacks. But they weren't ready for my screams, my wildness, my craziness once I was caught up in it. I can't blame them. They didn't know what to do to help me. And I was so worn out and emotionally exhausted afterward, I just didn't want to talk. I try not to think about it, Harper. Just thinking about it makes it come back sometimes, and it scares me. That's why I moved out of my parents' home. No one was getting much sleep."

"I know that one," he admitted, frowning. "Only mine was with Olivia. She was a civilian. She didn't know military. I was over in Afghanistan for deployment after deployment. She was safe and sound stateside. I'd come home and not want to sleep in the same room with her because I was afraid I'd hurt her in one of my flashbacks. I couldn't control when they might happen and I never wanted to hurt her during one."

"Oh, that . . . yeah . . . My dad tried to pick me up off the floor one time and I swung on him." She grimaced, her voice filled with regret. "I gave him a black eye. It was awful. They'd never laid a hand on me growing up, Harper, and here I swing on my dad. I didn't see him, I didn't know it was him . . . I was so caught up in that firefight."

"It's rough on everyone. Olivia didn't understand. There were times I'd scream so loudly that it would wake her up in the bedroom across the hall where she was sleeping. She'd come in and I'd be caught in the flashback and it scared the hell out of her. I don't blame her. I was out of control. I was back there, in Afghanistan." His mouth curved inward at the corners. "My PTSD broke our marriage wide open. I never blamed her for wanting a divorce.

I couldn't talk about it. I clammed up. I was at fault in that more than she ever was."

"But you didn't strike out at me, Harper."

"Well, you know from seeing Taylor and getting that adaptogen? How it calmed my anxiety?"

"Yes."

"At the time I was married, the only thing the military doc had was antidepressants and sleeping tablets. I refused either one. But since taking that adaptogen last year, I don't have the anxiety any longer. Anxiety is gasoline being poured on the fire of a flashback."

"I don't have it anymore either. I think it's incredible and I'm so grateful that Libby Hilbert urged me to make an appointment to see Taylor about getting my cortisol level checked. It's wonderful not to have that constant hyperalertness and anxiety always eating at me."

"Yeah," Harper said, giving her a sour grin, "you've definitely ramped down since the medicine shut down the cortisol in your bloodstream. You're not so nervous and restless. You sleep through the night. You're getting a good eight hours, and that helps so much."

"It does," Tara agreed. "So? You think the difference between then and now is the anxiety being gone? That when I went to hold you, you wouldn't lash out at me?"

"Yes, I do. It took away my sense of dread that someone was lurking around to kill me. All those emotions make you ready to fight back. Today I had the flashback, but I didn't have the anxiety. That made a huge difference in how I reacted."

"A good one. Too bad that adaptogen can't stop our flashbacks."

He laughed a little. "Yeah, I told Taylor that and she agreed. But just getting rid of the anxiety? I feel damn near human again. Except," and he waved his hand toward the bear, "when I get charged by an animal with five-inch fangs and claws coming at me at the speed of a freight train."

Laughing with him, Tara said, "Well, anyone would have had an adrenaline reaction to that."

"Yeah, but in my case, it triggered the flashback."

"How long has it been since you had one?"

"Six months. This one took me completely by surprise."

"Getting charged by a mature grizzly is enough to jolt anyone, Harper."

He said nothing for a moment, moving several dried pine needles between his fingers, frowning and staring down at them for a moment. He looked over at her. "Whatever we have between us, Tara? It's good. It's decent and it's two-way. What you did for me today? I feel nearly normal now, and I shouldn't. This stuff hangs around me like a bad cold for days afterward. But it's gone." Mouth lifting a little, he said, "I'm not glad about the bear triggering this, or that I had to kill it. The good thing that has come out of this day is the affect you have on me."

Chapter Eleven

May 16

Cree's mouth turned into a slow smile as he read the *Tetons Gazette*, the county newspaper. There, splashed on the front page, was a dead grizzly that had been shot by Harper Sutton. Even better? Tara Dalton's name was mentioned. He was on break from his dishwashing job at the saloon and had grabbed the paper. Always looking for a better-paying job, he'd wanted to look at the sparse want ads for Jackson Hole. Instead, the big photo on the front page had snagged his attention.

So? Tara was hiking in the Salt River Mountains. It irked the hell out of him, made him angry that she had a boyfriend. He wanted to kill the bastard. Tara was his. And this time? He wasn't going to screw up with kidnapping her and make good on keeping her.

Still, his mind turned over the possibilities. He had grown up in Wind River Valley and he knew the Salt Mountains area. Prater Canyon was a big tourist attraction, a very popular hiking spot. There were several miners' cabins up farther above the canyon itself, well beyond where most tourist hikers would venture. He'd made the mistake of going to the first broken-down cabin in a meadow to keep Tara there. Scratching his unshaven jaw, Cree folded up the paper after reading the brief article. He knew of a mine ten miles beyond that area where the bear had been killed. And it wasn't a cabin either.

He'd been looking for a place to take Tara, one that would help him make sure she didn't escape this time. On his day off, he would hike that area and check out that mine. Very, very few people even knew it existed. He doubted it was on any maps, but he worried about topographical maps that did have things like mines on them. That could prove an issue. He wasn't going to worry about it just yet. First, he'd buy the topo map for that area to see if the mine was indicated on it or not. If it wasn't? Well, that made his hideout even better because he was sure a group of men would be looking for him and to rescue Tara.

Not this time. No, this time she was going to pay for fighting him and trying to escape. He wouldn't make that mistake twice. And Cree was clear that with this second attempt, if he did get caught kidnapping Tara, they'd put his ass in prison and throw away the key forever. Her father would see to that, being an influential county judge.

Mouth flexing, he quickly perused the want ads, seeing nothing. He was stuck at the saloon. Well, that was all right. Everyone who owned a restaurant needed a dishwasher, and this job served him well. At least for now.

May 24

Just the rhythmic movement of a horse between her legs lulled Tara into a dreamy state. Ahead of her was Harper on Ghost, a gray quarter horse gelding with a black mane and tail. They were repairing fence posts this afternoon under a clearing sky, the wind coolish, the sun warming her head and shoulders.

Socks, an eleven-year-old chestnut gelding with four white socks, was an old pro at this fence-fixing routine. Tara allowed the quarter horse to grab mouthfuls of the rich green grass that was growing swiftly now that most of the snow had melted. There were still stubborn white patches here and there along the pasture fence line where they rode. Harper wore his cowboy hat, had long, leather chaps that were splotched with the wet grass when he knelt onto the ground to dig around a rotted post. Her chaps were spotted with wet grass, too. She had on a gray down vest over her long-sleeved red-and-black-flannel shirt to drive off the cold air sweeping the valley after a chilly front had just passed on through.

When the grizzly had been killed, it upended their quiet lives on the Bar C. Neither had expected it. Both had turned down interviews locally, regionally and even from major news organizations out of the East.

She watched the way Harper rode Ghost, with that boneless ease. He was so damned sexy, and her dreams had escalated with each kiss they shared. They both had so much baggage to work through that she wanted the time to get to really know him, to show him their continuing compatibility in so many areas with each other.

Harper had some ongoing nightmares, too. The bear had been killed on the 15th, and since then, he'd been wrestling with his PTSD, which had spiked. Tara wouldn't admit that his screams on some nights didn't bolt her out of bed, her heart pounding, adrenaline coursing through her, trying to tamp down her own reaction. She'd heard screams like that before: her own. And it brought back memories of terrible firefights she'd been caught in, too. Neither of them were getting much sleep.

That's why she looked forward to a whole afternoon out on the land. Nature always settled them, she'd come to find out. This was the first time they'd been assigned fence-mending duty together and she'd silently cheered over it. She knew how tough it was for Harper to speak about his emotions and what was bothering him. Tara hadn't let him know he'd kept her up nearly every night, too. He didn't need that burden right now. He was dealing with enough because he'd been forced to shoot that grizzly.

Since the bear killing, he'd retreated in some ways from her, and Tara had felt the loss of the warmth and intimacy Harper had given her. Inwardly, she had cried over it, but she understood why. Her parents, after being awakened by her screams during a nightmare, had wanted to help her, too. And now, Tara didn't want to crowd him to tell her what the nightmare was about; that was something Tara wouldn't do. She never wanted to tell her parents; to give voice or words to what she'd seen or what she'd survived. To give it words meant her parents would forever remember it, too, and she didn't want to go there. *Not ever.*

Heaving a soft sigh, Tara leaned down, rubbing Socks' thick, winter-coated neck. The horse's ears flipped back and forth, acknowledging her touch. Smiling a little, Tara watched Harper ride with that cowboy slouch of his. He'd been born to a saddle because his parents had given him his first horse at age seven. He'd ridden with his father and mother, practically born to horses. His mother, in particular, loved horses, and they always had some on their small family ranch of twenty acres. It was a hobby and pastime, but Tara could see Harper truly was completely in sync with Ghost. It made her feelings for him bloom once more in her chest.

Tara had to laugh at herself. Since the bear charging them, she'd barely thought about Cree, that he was in the vicinity. With PTSD, her hardwired mind went to the latest threat, not an old one from years past. And for that, Tara was grateful. On Wednesday, tomorrow, she was going to Jackson Hole with Shay, Kira and Dair to pick up their bridesmaids' dresses. They were ready to be tried on. Kira was so excited. The wedding would be on in a few weeks, and everyone in the valley was more than ready to celebrate. She was glad there was still quiet time, though, because of the reoccurrence of Harper's PTSD. Just as he'd laid open his heart to her out there in Prater Canyon, she knew he could open up that vat of horror he'd survived to her in the future. But it would take time. Patience. And trust.

Trust was strong between them and growing every day. Harper had saved her life out there in Prater Canyon. Although caught in the terror and the grip of the flashback, he'd managed to kill the bear. Tara found that amazing. There was never any doubt within her that Harper wasn't a trustworthy man. And how she ached to give him a reprieve from these recurring nightmares. She hurt for him, feeling helpless, unable to support him when he really needed it.

Later, as they were working on a particularly snarly barbed wire issue between two posts, Harper had connected the loose strands. He was down on one knee and Tara was on the other side of him, holding the ends taut between her elkskin leather gloves.

"Phew," he muttered, "this one is a rat's nest." He

quickly wrapped the broken wire around newly strung wire. "You doing okay?"

Tara was a foot away from him, the barbed wire between them. "Yeah."

"Arms getting tired?" and he glanced over at her.

"Just a little."

"Wouldn't fib, would you, Ms. Dalton?"

Grinning, Tara said, "Not to you, Mr. Sutton."

"I wonder how many women would be out here doing this?"

She chuckled. "Not many."

"Builds character *and* muscle," he said. "You can let go now. Let's see how the wire sits."

Releasing it, Tara sat back on her heels, her hands resting on her wet, splotched chaps. At least her jeans were dry, the leather keeping them that way.

Harper tested the tautness with his glove. "Feels about right." He looked over at her. "Nice job. Thanks for your help on this one."

Tara saw the pride in his eyes for her part in the process. "It's easy when working with you." She saw his expression relax and he, too, sat back on the heels of his boots.

Harper took off his gloves, holding her gaze. "Our quiet, private lives have been pretty upended since I killed that bear."

Groaning, Tara muttered, "It's the media, Harper. If they'd just leave us alone. I'm not glorifying the killing of such a beautiful wild animal and I know you don't want to either."

"Well," he said, wrapping the gloves in his left hand and resting it against his chaps, "I guess I was kinda talking about something more personal. About us."

She gave him a blank look. "Oh . . ." Tara saw the

tenderness in his gray eyes as he silently regarded her. "I don't understand."

"You and me." Harper quirked his lips. "Since killing that bear, I've had nightmares nearly every night. I wake myself up screaming. I know I wake you up too, Tara, even though you haven't said a word about it."

"Why should I?" She shrugged. "It happens to people like us, Harper."

"Yeah, I guess so," he muttered, frowning. "You should have told me I was waking you up in the middle of every night."

She compressed her lips. "You didn't ask."

He gave her a dark look and considered her answer. "You've got shadows under your eyes," and he gestured toward her face. "I keep trying to figure out what to do."

"What do you mean?"

"I'm going through a cycle of nightmares. It will probably last another two or three weeks, Tara. I don't want to keep waking you up like that."

"I'll handle it," she said. "It would be different if I didn't know why you were having them, Harper." She saw his scowl deepen, worry in his eyes. "Really. I can," and she held up her hands. "This will pass."

"It's not what you signed up for," he said heavily. "I was worried about this from the time you were assigned to the house."

"I have nightmares, too, Harper. Don't I wake you up some nights?"

"Sometimes . . . not often. . . ."

She gave him a frustrated look. "The biggest thing that bothers me about you and your nightmares? It's waking up, sitting there, wanting to go to you and not doing it." She saw surprise in his face, his mouth moving as if to stop a backlog of emotions from being unleashed within him.

"Why would you want to come to my room after I woke you up like that, Tara?"

"To hold you." She stared across the barbed wire, her voice choked with feelings. "I don't know, Harper. I don't know what to do or how to help you. I feel so damned helpless. I hate that I'm too much of a coward to get up, walk out of the room and knock on your bedroom door. That's what I *really* want to do. But I don't."

He swallowed hard, looking down at the green grass. Finally, he lifted his head. "That's funny . . . I mean, it's not but . . . When you arrived? I'd hear you screaming and I knew what was going on. The first time it happened? I leaped out of bed and was halfway down the hall, getting ready to open your bedroom door before I stopped myself."

"Really?" and she gawked at him.

"Yeah. I was torn out of sleep, wasn't thinking and my brain finally got engaged before I ripped that door off its hinges to reach you."

She saw the tenderness in his eyes, felt teary and pushed it all away. Now wasn't the time to cry. "I know the first two weeks I was having a lot of waking up at night . . . I'm sorry, Harper."

"Why apologize? We do it to each other. You can't help it any more than I can, Tara. Do I feel bad when I wake up screaming? Knowing I've probably jerked you out of desperately needed sleep? Yeah . . . well, we're two of the same kind."

Nodding, she reached down, moving a thick blade of damp grass between her thumb and index finger. "Can we handle this any better with each other than we did with our civilian counterparts?" she wondered.

He lifted the hat off his head and pushed his fingers through his hair. Settling the Stetson back on his hair, his voice wry, he said, "We need to try. At least, that's how I feel, Tara. How about you? What are your thoughts on our situation?"

"My reaction the first time you screamed, Harper, and it woke me up was to run to you and just hold you."

They sat there staring at each other for a full minute. Tara absorbed the sun's warmth, the breeze lifting some strands of her hair caught up in a ponytail. She took off her baseball cap, studying it. "Sometimes," she managed in a soft, torn voice, "it's so hard to talk about how I feel. I know much of it has to do with my military training, with my deployments."

"Same here," he admitted, pulling the gloves back on. "I know men don't show many feelings, and yes, the military definitely brings that point home. But you know what, Tara? When you held me, sensing my flashback in that canyon? That was the best thing that's happened to me in a long, long time. You holding me short-circuited a lot of it. Usually, I'd go days afterward, dazed and not really connected back to life the way I wanted to be. But your holding me helped so damned much that I'm still in awe of it all. Aren't you?"

"I've always believed in holding. It makes us feel safe, Harper. Don't you think?"

"I've been going over that ever since it happened, Tara. I keep wondering when I get hauled out of a deep sleep, screaming, if you holding me would help." He shook his head, frustration lacing his tone. "I haven't brought it up to you because I was afraid you'd take it the wrong way. That you'd think I was asking for other reasons."

"I was thinking the same thing, Harper. I was looking

at myself. I was afraid you would think I was coming on to you. I guess I was afraid my actions would be misunderstood."

"I hear you," he said, watching her sad look. "But I didn't take it the wrong way in Prater Canyon when you turned and threw your arms around me."

"No, you're right. You didn't. I guess," and she opened her hands, "I was afraid. I'm still working through so much, Harper. I'm still decompressing from my life in black-ops combat. I can't always trust myself in this civilian world yet. I feel pressure to keep up my end of the bargain with Shay and Reese and their ranch. I need to sell a lot of stock photos to make money there, too."

"And then we have each other," he said wryly, giving her a kind look. "We're exhausted by dinnertime, we need long, hard sleep so badly and yet, when we go to bed, it's broken up by nightmares and screams."

"We're a pair, aren't we?"

"Yeah, but I wouldn't trade you as my roommate for anything."

"These PTSD nightmares ebb and flow. I know that from my own experience, Harper. You didn't have one last night and we both got a decent night's sleep."

"True. It's almost who's going to outlast who. Will our collective sleep loss total us? Or will we be able to gut through it and get in a quiet spot with each other again."

"Before something else ramps it up in us again," she grumped.

"It's tiring."

"I've never been able to talk to my folks or my friends about this," she admitted, giving him a look of thanks. "It actually feels good to talk about it, get that weight off my shoulders. How about you?"

"Yeah, I was thinking the same thing. Friday nights when Libby visits, it's helpful."

"But this is different."

"I know." He studied her. "I don't know what that means."

"Neither do I." She slid him a glance. "But I'm willing to find out if you are." She saw merriment come to his eyes.

"Always the risk taker, aren't you, Ms. Dalton?"

"Kept me from getting killed too many times to count, Mr. Sutton."

"Amen. Me too."

Tara luxuriated in the pride, desire and respect she saw in his expression as he held her gaze. It was as if Harper had somehow magically enclosed her in his arms once more, just as he had out at the canyon. It was the nicest feeling in the world, and one Tara hungrily absorbed. She wondered if he knew how it affected her. She'd longed for a moment just like this and felt fear coupled with anxiety, but she had to speak up.

"We're drawn to each other," she said, seeing his eyes darken a little. "I mean, it's mutual." She opened her hands. "I've never been in a situation like this. And I'm so torn. One part of me, the healthy part that didn't get slammed with PTSD, wants some kind of deepening relationship with you. My other side, the dominant one with PTSD, makes me feel unsure, unprepared, not knowing what the hell my emotions are doing to me at any given hour of the day or night."

"Olivia used to call me an emotional yo-yo," he said. "I was all over the place. When things would get bad, I'd clam up and storm out of the house or go for a drive because if I didn't, I felt like I was going to let my anger and irritation out on her. And I didn't want to do it. But my decision to protect her from myself ended up driving her away from me, too."

"There's just no middle road with PTSD," Tara said, her voice scratchy with frustration. "And that's what I'm afraid of, Harper. I'm not afraid of you. I'm afraid of me," and she put her thumb against her vest. "I'll admit that since the adaptogen stopped the anxiety, I'm not so easily angered or irritated. I finally feel safe enough to let down for the first time since I was in the military. That," she said, holding his gaze, "is in part thanks to you. Being around you always makes me feel safe."

"You do the same for me, Tara. And I've got the same anger and irritation as you do. I try not to take it out on others, which is why the type of work I do now is great. I'm alone, horses don't trigger it, and it's actually helped calm me down. But when you came to live with me? Just your presence did something incredible for me."

Tilting her head, Tara asked, "What?" Because she had no idea she had such influence over Harper.

"You calmed me down. I can't explain it, but that's what happens when I'm around you."

"That's nice to know." She drew in a ragged breath and whispered, "When you're around me? In the house or nearby? I feel safe. Really safe. I stopped feeling safe when Cree kidnapped me. It's horrible being a captive, feeling that you've been abandoned by everyone." She managed a small smile. "You make me feel normal, Harper. And that hasn't happened to me since I was sixteen."

Harper frowned and moved, slowly getting to his feet, brushing some of the mud and grass off his chaps. "That makes me feel good. I'm glad I'm a good influence on you."

Oh, it was more than that. They hadn't kissed since that day in the canyon. The event had sheered through their fragile new life as civilians, ripping away the veneer and putting both of them back into combat and nightmares. She slowly got to her feet, pulling on her gloves. She leaned over, wiping off the mud on her lower chaps. Straightening, she felt Harper's gaze on her, warming her, holding her invisibly in his embrace once more. "I'm just scared and unsure, Harper."

"Me too."

"We're so wounded," she muttered, walking around the fence, opening the gate and then shutting it.

Harper picked up the reins on Socks, who was trained to ground tie, and handed them to her. She took them and he kept his hand around hers. "Even the most wounded vet has a heart, Tara, that feels emotion. It doesn't mean he or she doesn't dream of a more hopeful life, despite the wounds we carry."

Lifting her other hand, she rested it on his upper arm, holding his gaze. "You have more hope than I do, Harper."

"You just got out," he told her gruffly. "In time? The hope grows, so let it. I know we have down days, but we have up ones, too, so let's just celebrate those lighter moments, huh?"

She slid her hand gently up to his shoulder, giving it a squeeze. "Anyone ever tell you, Sutton, that you're a great cheerleader, too?"

"Oh," he said, releasing her hand, "on some days. Let's celebrate if one of us is down. Because it means the other one is up and can help us out of that black vat we find ourselves in."

Chapter Twelve

"So, Tara?" Shay said, drawing her aside in Jilly's bridal shop after they'd finished trying on their bridesmaids' gowns, "you're quiet. What's going on? Are you having flashbacks because of that bear run-in?"

Tara sat down in the white satin chair near the wall with Shay. Kira was fussing over Dair's gown. Dair was self-conscious over her amputated lower leg, that the outline showed when she moved in the dress. "Since Harper had to kill that grizzly, he's been waking up every night from a nightmare."

"I'm not surprised," Shay said, nodding. "That had to scare the hell out of both of you, a bear suddenly charging you like that."

Snorting softly, Tara smoothed the dark blue wool fabric across her thigh. "Yes, it did."

"Are you both having PTSD reactions to it?"

"Yes." Giving her a sorrowful look, she said, "You know how it is. A sight, a sound, a smell, a crisis or superstress will trigger us in a heartbeat. And then we shake for days, even weeks afterward."

Reaching out, Shay placed her hand on Tara's white, long-sleeved silk blouse. "I know."

"Do you and Reese have that happen, too?"

Shay rolled her eyes. "Oh, yes. For Reese, it's the smell of gasoline. He was a company commander in Afghanistan, had a hundred and twenty Marines under his command. They had an IED lob over the fort wall and hit the fuel facility. Gasoline exploded everywhere. A number of his Marines died or were badly burned and he never forgave himself. So, when he smells gasoline, that day, those casualties and his burned Marines, slam back into him."

"Like it does all of us." She studied Shay, who was dressed in bright orange slacks, wearing a pale peach tee beneath it. "What happens, then?"

"Oh, Reese dives into the flashback. If I'm around when it happens, I sit with him, hold him. That really helps him to come back to the present, not be dragged and trapped in the past."

"That's nice," Tara murmured. "Does it interrupt his sleep, too?"

Smiling softly, Shay said, "Before we got together, he'd wake up screaming. Scared me awake in my bedroom across the hall from his."

"That's what's happening to us right now," Tara admitted, frowning.

"You have shadows under your eyes and Harper looks exhausted. Garret came over a few days ago, alerting us to your situation. He's worried for you, too. He knows what it's like."

"I hate it. I hate that it tears us apart, Shay. It seems never-ending."

"But it does improve over time." She slid her arm around Tara and gave her a quick squeeze and released her. "Just keep your faith. It does get better."

"That's what Harper keeps telling me," she grumped.

"There are days I believe him, and then there are days when I lose all hope."

"That's because you're sleep-deprived. You know how your emotions get their knickers in a twist when you've lost night after night of sleep. I went through a couple of years of that before it started ramping down. Getting that adaptogen from Taylor really was the first window of hope to open for me. I hated being anxious and feeling threatened twenty-four hours a day. And you've just gotten your prescription within the last month or so. It takes time."

Grimacing, Tara muttered, "I'm impatient. I've always been that way, Shay."

Laughing, she patted Tara's arm in a motherly fashion. "We're all Type A's; there's no getting around that one."

Tara felt better. "I'm glad I'm talking to you about this."

"There's always a pot of coffee on over at our house, so come over any time you want, Tara. You can't get through this alone. We're all here to help one another. Each of us needs support every now and then." Her eyes sparkled. "Let's talk about happier things. Is there something sweet going on between you and Harper?"

"Yes and no," Tara said. "Yes, we have a connection. But it's stalled because we're in this cycle of PTSD and we're no good to ourselves or to each other. It's just getting through and surviving every day. You know how that is?"

"I do," Shay said gently, giving her a sad look. "The bear incident triggered both of you big-time, as it would anyone. When something like that happens and you're a vet who has PTSD, it's a hundred times worse on us mentally and emotionally. Are you two managing or are you at each other's throats?"

Tara heard the amusement in Shay's voice, but she knew the woman wasn't teasing her. It wasn't a funny situation. "We avoid that at all costs, Shay. If Harper is having a bad evening, he'll go down to the tack room in the arena and repair leather until he can work through what he's dealing with. Or I'll go into my bedroom, shut the door and work on my stock photo website. We know when we're getting edgy and just seem to naturally want to protect each other from the worst side of ourselves."

"That's as good as it gets. When Reese first came to the Bar C and stayed in our house because we didn't have wrangler homes built yet, I was really fearful about it. I had my ups and downs, too. But we talked, and that was the single most important decision we made between each other. Talking helped us understand each other's predicament."

"Was that after you fell in love with each other?"

Shaking her head, Shay said, "Oh, no. It was like we had this mental telepathy from the moment we met. Our emotions were so raw and on the surface anyway that we picked up on the slightest emotional or mental change in each other. We started doing it right after he took that room in our home."

"Harper and I seem to have that connection, too," she said, wonder in her voice.

Lips lifting, Shay said, "Well, I'm not surprised. We saw the way Harper looked at you during the barn dance at Red Tail Ranch."

"What do you mean?"

"I told Reese the other day that I thought Harper was falling in love with you, Tara."

Staring at Shay, she gulped.

"Don't you see it?" and Shay tilted her head, smiling.

"No," Tara said abruptly. "I mean, I've kissed him. I've enjoyed it. But I'm scared, Shay. And I told him that."

"Scared of what?"

"That I'm very unsure of two PTSD vets sharing anything but hell on earth, violent ups and downs of emotion, sleepless nights, flashbacks . . . it's a never-ending cycle," and her voice dropped off into an aching whisper. "There's no such thing as normal anymore, not for either of us."

"Listen," Shay said, becoming more reassuring, "love transcends even PTSD, Tara. At least if you both have the same symptoms, you know what to do to avoid hurting the other person. Or if they're having a bad day, you know how to support them and understand what's really going on inside them to a degree. Those aren't minuses in my book, those are plusses."

"You know Harper lost Olivia, his wife, to his PTSD?"

"Oh," Shay growled, "that bitch."

Brows raising, Tara sat up and stared at Shay. She wasn't one to use curse words at all, so it startled Tara. "Shay, that's not like you. I've never heard you call another woman that."

She saw anger coming to Shay's blue eyes. Her small hands fisted in her lap.

"And I'll just bet Harper has told you his failed marriage was all his fault, because of his PTSD? That Olivia was an angel?"

"Well . . . something like that. You're really upset. Why?"

"Harper is the kind of guy who, if he can't say something good about someone, he won't say anything at all. He glosses over others' eccentricities and mistakes and takes on the burden himself."

"Well," Tara said, "he was a combat medic. He's got that kind of nature: gentle and caring. I think I've heard two curse words out of him in the months I've been living with him."

Pushing her fingers through her short hair, Shay muttered, "All of that's true and I know Harper is going to make a wonderful paramedic after he graduates next year. We're going to be very lucky to have someone like him here in the valley. But Olivia?" She blew air between her lips, her brows dipping. "She was a spoiled little rich girl, Tara. She fell in love with Harper when he was on leave between deployments. Her parents said he was beneath her socially and economically, that he was only a sailor. But she married him anyway, I think, for spite against her parents trying to control her because she had just turned eighteen. She never really loved Harper. He was a victim of her manipulations in her war with her parents."

Tara's throat tightened and she whispered, "Tell me. It's important, Shay. Please? He paints a picture of her as being the one who was hurt in that marriage because of his PTSD."

"You need to talk about this with Harper. I'm not going to tell what I know. This has to be between you and him. If he cares for you as much as I think he does, he's going to tell you the truth. All of the truth. He tends to shoulder the blame, even if it's not his to take on. That's all I'll say. Olivia wounded him severely. He was already wounded by so many deployments. But she cut out his heart."

Pain drifted through her chest. The trembling in Shay's voice told her the rage the other woman held against Harper's ex-wife was genuine. "Okay . . . I'll do that. When there's a time that's good for both of us."

Shay gave her a wry look. "Timing is everything. You and Harper have gone through a lot together in an intense, short amount of time. Catch him on an up day, Tara. And you be up, too. Okay?"

Nodding, Tara reached out, squeezing Shay's hand. "Yes . . . I will. He's important to me. Every day, I discover something new about him that I like."

"You're falling in love with him whether you want to admit it or not," Shay said in a low tone, gripping her hand, holding her gaze. "I know you're not ready to go there yet, Tara. But you two are good for each other. And I understand the hurdles between you. Reese and I had them, too. And as a matter of fact, Garret and Kira had their hurdles to scale before they could reach out and love each other. So have Noah and Dair. It's going to take time. Just be patient with yourself and with Harper."

May 31

"I love the idea of a picnic lunch out in this pasture," Tara told Harper.

It was Memorial Day, and that was a special day for all of them at the Bar C. They had attended services as a group at the local church that morning and said prayers for the military fallen and their families. They had then gone to the local cemetery, which had a section for veterans. They laid flowers on the graves and said a prayer for all those who had been laid to rest. All of them had been in combat, so they understood how precious life was and how quickly it could be taken away.

The temperature was in the midseventies, a rarity, with the sun shining brightly, a few puffy white clouds drifting across the valley from west to east. Tara saw Harper's eyes grow warm as he brought over the leather saddlebags carrying their lunch. He knelt in front of her, opening them up next to the small green-and-blue-plaid wool blanket Tara had laid out.

The horses had their bridles removed, the halters on with lead ropes wrapped around the saddle horns, so they were able to eat their fill after Harper had placed hobbles around their front pasterns. Both animals would willingly graze the thick, rich green grass along the slope beneath the grove of pines.

"Our first picnic of the year," Harper agreed, handing her the plastic boxes containing the food. He set the thermos of coffee down near his knee. "We were trying to picnic during that Prater Canyon hike, but that didn't work out so well," and he smiled a little.

"Have you been looking around for grizzlies?" she asked, amusement in her tone as she opened two of the plastic boxes, each containing a turkey and cheddar cheese sandwich. She poured hot coffee into two plastic cups, setting them nearby. Harper stood and removed his chaps, hanging them over Ghost's saddle. They'd been repairing fence posts after returning to the ranch. It had been his idea to spend an hour together at the pine grove in one of the largest lease pastures.

Harper removed his Stetson, set it on the corner of the wool blanket, and then sat down, crossing his legs, facing her. "I have been watching for bear," he admitted ruefully. "The horses aren't spooked or wary. They're our initial warning." He gestured to the slope. "And we'd see one coming a mile away. The horses would hear him first, though."

Glancing over at Socks and Ghost, Tara smiled as she handed him his sandwich. "Right now, our horse friends are oblivious to their surroundings. They've gone to horsey heaven in this nearly knee-high green grass. I've always marveled at how thick and lush our valley grass was in the spring and summer. It's amazing. It grows so fast."

Harper munched contentedly on his sandwich, his elbows resting on his knees. "That's why grass leases are something Shay and Reese want to be able to give out to cattlemen. This grass is rich with all kinds of nutrients. Cattle fatten up fast on it."

"Shay told me at one time, before her alcoholic father let the Bar C fall into this state, he was one of the richest ranchers, with the exception of Maud and Steve Whitcomb, here in the valley. Grass leases are a huge moneymaker for any rancher if they've got the acreage."

"There's a lot of land with this ranch," Harper agreed, giving the surrounding area an appreciative look. "I know Reese is looking to get all the lease pastures back up and operational by next year. This year, it's strictly fence-mending time. Shay's father let this place fall into shambles. It's a shame really."

"Alcoholism not only destroys the person who drinks, it also destroys his or her job and the family as well."

"Yeah," he sighed, biting into his sandwich. "Shay and Reese have had a really tough time bringing the Bar C back. Have you heard anything else from your dad about Crawford suing the ranch?"

"Not yet. But it's coming. Shay said something about it the other day. Ray is putting in papers with the Clerk of Courts pretty soon, I guess."

"They don't need this. The old man, if he gets this ranch returned to him for legal reasons, will end up destroying it completely. Garret was telling me that Crawford ran off all his wranglers and his foreman, he was such a mean son of a bitch to them when he was drunk."

She munched on her sandwich, seeing how relaxed Harper was. This was a perfect day. "And he'll do it again if he manages to take this to court and in front of a jury.

I'm just hoping that when that day comes, he'll be his old, nasty self."

"Yeah," Harper said, grimacing, "him showing up drunk at court. That would do it."

"He's crafty, from what Noah told me when we talked about Ray one time. He's sneaky, manipulative and abusive. After he told me what kind of man he was, I felt so sorry for Shay. I never realized until that time what she'd gone through growing up with him. I can't even imagine it. I count myself lucky to have two great parents who loved me and didn't abuse me like Shay was abused."

"Me too," Harper said. "We're the lucky ones."

"Did you ever have a dream of what your marriage partner would be like once you met her?" Tara asked him. "I mean," and she laughed a little, wondering if this was the right tact to take with Harper about Olivia, "I always dreamed of finding a man like my father. Did you dream of a wife something like your mom?"

Shrugging, Harper finished off the sandwich and picked up his plastic mug of steaming hot coffee. "I guess I never really thought about my life that way. I was more focused on what I wanted to be, that I wanted to go into the military and serve." He gave her a wry look. "Marriage wasn't on my radar, but it happened."

"You never dreamed of the kind of woman you wanted to marry?" She found that hard to believe, knowing she sure had dreams of the man she'd like to marry someday, if the right one came along.

"Don't you think it's more a woman thing?" he teased, the corners of his eyes wrinkling.

"Probably," Tara groused, an unwilling grin pulling at her lips. "But did Olivia fulfill your idea of a wife?" She knew she was on thin ice with Harper, but he was in a good space today and so was she. He gave her an amiable look.

"She was eighteen, a wild child, rebellious, and I was twenty-one when I met her by accident in San Diego. I was between deployments, on my thirty days of leave, soaking up the Southern California sun and being a beach bum. She looked damned good to me in that little black bikini she wore when a bunch of us played volleyball on the beach."

"Tell me more," Tara urged, realizing Harper had reached a point with her of deeper trust. That alone made her heart yearn even more for this kind of personal, intimate exchange.

"Not much to tell. She had one hell of a body, was beautiful, willful; what guy could resist her?"

"Did she come on to you or did you chase her?"

"She chased me, but I let her catch me."

She saw some sadness in his thoughtful-looking gray eyes as he continued to sip the coffee. "You said she was a wild child. What did that mean?"

"Her parents were very, very rich. Owned a palatial estate in La Jolla. Father was a movie producer, big name, and he had a lot of power. Her mother had been a Hollywood actress until he married her. Olivia was the result." He straightened and pulled over the thermos, pouring himself more coffee and filling her mug up to the brim while he was at it. "Olivia was wild to get out from beneath her parents' control would probably be the best way to put it. She had just turned eighteen and was now an adult. Her big gripe was that they could no longer tell her what to do. She had a really nice apartment facing the beach on the main street and invited me over for a party she was having that evening."

"That was probably quite a party," Tara said.

"Well, it was interesting," Harper said. "Most of her friends were other Hollywood teens like her. They were wild and rowdy. I felt like the old man in that group."

"Drugs?"

He grimaced. "Didn't see any, but they all acted like they were on something. That comes from being a combat medic and recognizing it in some of the guys I had to treat from time to time."

"Was Olivia a drug addict?"

He squirmed. "She didn't behave like one," he muttered. "But later? Yeah, she liked cocaine. I didn't realize it until after we were married about three months. She was enamored with military guys. And I fell for her because I was nose-diving into PTSD, even though I didn't realize it at the time. I wanted something fresh, clean, upbeat and positive. Olivia was all those things to me. Looking back on it? I shouldn't have married her. She was too young and immature and I was a grown-up who had seen too much. We did share a love of the beach, surfboarding and the water."

"It must have been quite a change for you." She could see the regret in his eyes, although he said nothing for a moment, staring out across the green pasture, deep in thought. Tara swore she could feel Harper wrestling with a lot of sudden emotions.

"I'm afraid Olivia wasn't prepared for how I'd come home after nine months of combat. It was hard on her."

"And hard on you, too?"

"Yes, I suppose so. I was afraid to sleep in the same bed with her when I came home. She took it the wrong way, really hurt her feelings and trust in me."

"You must have had a pretty bad deployment. A lot of combat?"

"Yeah, you could say that. I was waking up fighting,

striking out. I was afraid if she slept with me, I'd hit and hurt her by accident. I tried to explain it to her."

"But she didn't have the maturity to understand?"

"She tried," he said quietly. "But yes, age does make a difference, especially in something like a marriage."

"Did she have a temper?"

"Yes. And mine was hair-trigger, too, because of my PTSD. We both lost our tempers and I would yell at her. And she'd yell back. I wasn't exactly mature about it either."

"At least you had a reason," Tara muttered. "I see you on some days, Harper, when you're feeling edgy because of the PTSD, get out of our house and go to the barn to work."

"I learned through my marriage with Olivia not to stay to try to sort it out when I'm feeling like that, Tara." He gave her a concerned look. "I'd never want to hurt you when I'm in that space. Olivia was my whipping post and I didn't have the brains to figure it out until it was too late."

"But she never figured it out either? Was she as defensive as angry when you were? Did she verbally attack you?" Tara knew Olivia was a spoiled, willful child, not a woman who had maturity. She was pretty sure Olivia got her way with her temper tantrums with her parents and, later, she was playing it out on Harper. Tara couldn't imagine the stress on him if Olivia didn't grow up and lose her narcissism and selfishness.

"No, she was pretty self-centered. But what teen isn't? I know I was. I'm sure you could look back and see it in yourself."

"I don't know," she answered, "because my parents taught me early on to care for others. I'll bet your parents were like that with you, too. They didn't let you fall into that me, me, me syndrome that a lot of kids do."

"Yeah," he said wryly, "my parents were an awful lot like yours: responsibility, duty to others and respect for all regardless."

"How did her parents respond to you?"

"Not well." He sighed. "But at the time, I didn't care. All I knew was that when I was with Olivia, I felt alive. I felt . . . well . . . normal. I could hide in her effervescence. She was in love with life and she infused me with it, too, and that was exactly what I needed. I'd seen too much killing and suffering. She was like life, the life I wanted." Finishing off his coffee, he added, "But it was the wrong reason to marry her. I was running away from everything. Libby Hilbert has helped all of us who are here to see how we try to escape the horrors we've seen and survived. I was using Olivia to escape. And now, I realize what I did. It wasn't fair to either of us really."

"You didn't know. But I understand about the hiding. I never used drugs or alcohol to escape, but I loved getting paperbacks from charities like Operation Gratitude and buried myself in novels."

"Far healthier than what I did," Harper said, giving her a look of pride.

Tara was finding Harper always looked at the positive side of life, not wanting to say too much about the negative or dark things that haunted him. She understood it was his combat corpsman disposition, and that it came naturally to him. She saw a tiredness in his eyes, realizing that talking about his failed marriage was like an anchor pulling him into deep water again. "Did you and Olivia just sort of drift apart? You were gone most of the time. I'm sure she had her Hollywood friends to keep her entertained."

"Yes, it sort of disintegrated over time. I wouldn't sleep with her when I returned from deployment, and that made her furious with me. She just couldn't or didn't want to understand that I was in a continual war zone."

"Most civilians can't begin to put themselves into what we've seen or survived," Tara said sympathetically.

"For Olivia, I was an old man who was no fun anymore. She wanted to go to parties and I didn't. I couldn't handle the loud music. She wanted to go out all the time to five-star restaurants, and we didn't have the money. In the end," he said, "she asked for a divorce and I gave it to her."

"She doesn't strike me as someone who was very kind."

"No, that wasn't a part of her," he agreed. "Looking back on it, we were like oil and water and never mixed. She was enamored with the concept that the only real man for her had to be from the military. I'm afraid I disappointed her badly on that score. I was no hero."

"But by the same token," Tara pointed out, "she idealized you and you would never be able to live up to it."

"Correct," he muttered, reaching inside the second saddlebag and pulling out their dessert. Shay had made everyone peanut butter cookies yesterday and brought some over to them. "But I was running and hiding, too. I used her as much as she used me."

"She probably wounded you with words."

He gave a one-shouldered shrug, handing her three cookies. "She's a highly intelligent person and, yes, she had a mouth on her. She's got a bear-trap mind and thinks faster than most people, including me."

"So," Tara murmured, biting into a cookie, "you got the receiving end of a lot of verbal abuse?"

"Any time Olivia was angry, I was blamed for it some way. It was never her fault, and she never took responsibility for her part in our dance with each other. Lack of maturity," he said, munching his cookie, a look of satisfaction coming to his expression.

Nodding, Tara said, "I avoided getting married. I knew that deployments were changing me, that something inside me was happening and I was different from before. And because I was unsure, scared of it, not getting a full picture of what was going on within me, I didn't want to get into a relationship. I knew I could hurt someone with my out-of-control temper and the irritation that hit me sometimes."

"Well," he said, raising a brow, "you at least had the self-awareness, as Libby calls it, to realize that you were wounded and that you could turn around and wound someone else with your words and actions. Olivia never gave that two seconds of thought before she'd lash out at me."

"Probably hard to take?"

"In the end, it was really tough. She said some pretty bad things about me, and at the time, it scored my heart and soul. I was raw emotionally anyway from the PTSD. But coming home to her was like getting another dose of combat, just a different kind, was all."

Aching for him, Tara could only give him an understanding look. Now, Shay's comments made more sense to her. And it helped her understand Harper in a new way. "And that's why you're so tentative about us, what we might have?"

He gave her a sad look. "Yes, it is."

"I'm nothing like Olivia."

"No, you're not. But I still worry about my PTSD. I handle it, I control it, but there's days or nights when I don't do very well with it. I don't ever want to hurt you when I'm in that space."

"I see you take evasive action every time you're caught up in it," she noted gently. "But I'm in the same boat with you, Harper. My PTSD has its ups and downs, too."

"Yes, and I see you go hide away in your room and shut the door. That's when I know you're feeling edgy."

"At least we don't take a pound of flesh out of each other. That's a huge step forward for both of us."

"We're self-aware now. We can feel the PTSD starting to stalk us and we know what to do to protect our partner or the people around us. That's positive and it's a healthy step forward, as Libby has often told the group."

"I really like you a lot, but I'm afraid . . ."

"I know you are," he said gently, reaching out, squeezing her hand resting on her knee. "And it's okay. I understand. I'm no prize myself."

She gave him a round-eyed look, disbelief in her tone. "Oh, yes, you are!"

Chapter Thirteen

Tara had surprised herself with her unexpected outburst as they ate their lunch. Harper sat back, both brows moving upward.

"Well," she sputtered, "you *are* a prize! You're loved by many people, Harper. Don't you take them into account, also? Why do you listen to one person's viewpoint on you, take it to heart and not listen to the many, many others who know you to be a good man?" Her voice was quavering with emotion, but she didn't care. Leaning forward, Tara poked him in the vest he wore. "I don't *ever* want to hear you say that about yourself again. Okay? Because it's not true! You were a good person before you met Olivia and it sure as hell hasn't changed after you divorced her. One person's opinion of you shouldn't count for more than another person's. You have so many other people who truly like and love you, Harper. You do so much for everyone else. That's rare nowadays because many people have become self-centered and selfish, but you aren't and you never have been." She sat back, breathing raggedly, staring hard at him, just daring him to refute anything she'd just said. Her hands curved into fists on her knees for a moment and then she forced herself to relax.

Harper studied her beneath his short, spiky lashes. His mouth drew into a wry half smile. "Remind me to hire you next time I need a more balanced view of the world," he teased.

"I meant every word I said, Sutton, so don't think this is funny, because it isn't. You're hitting a nerve in me. I truly dislike anyone who would put someone else down. I've stuck up for myself, and I've stuck up for others, all my life. You're important to so many people. You need to be reminded of that. Olivia's snarky, self-serving comments that tore you up don't account for anything. She used you as her whipping post, not the other way around." She saw his eyes widen slightly, giving her a shrewd look.

"Were you born this way, Tara?"

Scowling, she snapped, "What way?"

"Defender of the poor, the lonely and the helpless?"

She realized he was gently mocking her, but not in an unkind fashion. There was a burning look in his darkening gray eyes that made her yearn for him in every possible way. He was close to her physically, as well as emotionally, in that charged moment. Tara wanted to feel his mouth against hers once more. Since the bear incident, they hadn't kissed at all. It was as if the PTSD had thrown both into opposite corners and had stunted the intimacy that had sprung up between them.

"Yes," she said, all the petulance leaking out of her voice, "I do stick up for those people who need support. We all need help at times, Harper. My mom and dad are that way, too. I saw them help many people while I was growing up. I saw their kindness and I wanted to be just like them."

"Don't ever lose that quality," he said gruffly, getting to his feet. "That's one of many things I like about you, Tara."

Their time was up. The hour had sped by much too fast,

to her chagrin. It felt as if they'd just sat down ten minutes ago. She hungered for deeper, searching talks just like this one with Harper. He was a damned onion, so many layers to him. Peeling one back, she learned something new about him every time. But he wasn't giving up his layers to her easily, and now she had an idea why. Shay had been right to make her ask Harper about Olivia. No wonder she had called her a bitch. Olivia was a child in a woman's body, never having to take responsibility for her actions or words.

Harper held out his hand. Tara took it, relishing the warmth and strength of his fingers around hers as he eased her to her feet. He released her hand, but his gaze never left hers. She stood less than two feet away from him. There was turbulence in Harper's gray eyes, stormy-looking, burning with something, a need she couldn't translate. But it drew her powerfully toward him and she swayed a little. If only she could get that wall out from between them!

Harper wrapped his fingers around her upper arm. "We need to do more of this type of talking, Tara. Just you and me."

His gritty, low voice, the intensity in his sharpened gaze dug straight to her heart and then flared throughout her. She swore she could feel him fighting his desire for her just as she was for him.

"But we have a brick wall between us, Harper," she said, her voice strained.

"Okay, so we're infected with PTSD." His mouth flexed and he kept his hand around her arm. "Today? Maybe we took a brick or two off that wall." His voice lowered and he pulled her to a stop and nudged a few tendrils of hair from her cheek, tucking them behind her ear. "I'm in for the long haul with you, Tara. If this is what it takes, I'm fine with it. How about you?"

Every time she experienced Harper's raw, honest courage, she wanted to weep over his suffering. Tears she fought, wanting to hide them from him. "I think you know I'm in this for the long haul, too. I'm just scared. And so are you."

"We are." He eased the pressure of his fingers around her arm, caressing her shoulder. "We'll just live with the fear like we did in our deployments, that's all. It never stopped us from doing our job over there. We kept moving ahead, Tara. You know how to do that. Only this time? It's personal and it's between you and me. We aren't in Afghanistan anymore. The war is over there for us. We're home now, and we're safe, even if we rarely feel that way."

Giving him a steady look, she whispered, "Don't ever kid yourself, Harper, the Afghan war lives within us to this day, this hour and this minute. The PTSD we got there is the baggage we carry all the time."

He smiled tentatively and released her shoulder, "I want my life back just like you do. I'm starting to climb out from beneath my divorce from Olivia, and I want to live again. I know the PTSD steals from us, but it hasn't taken over within us, and it never will. We're strong survivors, sweetheart. And that accounts for my hope for both of us to keep taking down that wall that stands between us, a brick at a time."

Sweetheart. The word had been spoken so quietly, but with such emotion, that Tara stood, absorbing it because she needed that sign from Harper, despite their messy lives and wounded emotions. She wanted to cry and looked down at the blanket, bending over and picking up the emptied saddlebags. "Shay said something to me the other day," she confided, handing them to Harper.

"What was that?"

"Reese and she have the same issues we struggle with daily. She said that the most important thing was that they talked on a personal, honest level with each other all the time. Every day. And secondly," her voice became hoarse, "she said that when you love a person, that love transcends the PTSD. It doesn't cure it, but it has helped them live their lives in such a way that it's good for both of them. Instead of tearing each other up, they know when to walk away and not hurt the other. To me? That's as good as it can get under the circumstances."

Nodding, Harper didn't move. "That's good advice she shared with you. Garret and Kira, Noah and Dair are going through the same things we are. It's not easy. It's the hardest thing in the world from where I stand."

"But it's worth it, Harper."

He dragged in a deep breath, looked toward the hobbled horses eagerly eating grass. Lifting his head, he met and held her gaze. "That only works if both people want the same thing and have the same objective."

Her throat hurt with unshed tears as she stood and watched him turn and walk toward the two horses. Did she have the courage to continue to deepen her relationship with Harper? Her heart clamored loudly that she did. But her PTSD-soaked brain was pessimistic, answering the question negatively. Gathering up the blanket, she shook it out, then folded it neatly, carrying it over to where he was putting the bridles on their horses.

In her eyes and heart, Harper looked so strong and steady. He was a cowboy. He was a military vet. He'd saved untold lives in combat, and Tara was sure he'd risked his own life many times in order to save one of his comrades. Silently, she promised him that she did want to try to figure out the morass that stood between them.

Having PTSD changed everything and demanded that both people involved find new ways to protect their partner from themselves. It was a terrible risk, but it had to be taken.

Tara didn't know if she had what it took, but she liked Harper so much that she didn't see it as a choice she had to make. It was the path she wanted to walk with him. After he bridled the horses, he took the blanket, rolling it up and tying it behind the cantle of his saddle.

A blue jay swept over them, calling raucously as it did so. Jays were good sky guard dogs in Tara's opinion, and she looked to Harper, who was studying the darkness within the nearby thick grove of pine.

"You think there's a bear snuffling around in there?" she asked.

"Maybe." He looked at Ghost, whose ears were also pricked up from the direction the jay had flown and called out a warning. "Let's mount up and ride up that slope to the fence line. We'll continue our mending, but we'll watch our horses for any other signs a bear might be active and in our vicinity."

Nodding, Tara took the reins, pulling them over Socks' head. He, too, was fully focused on the interior of the pine grove. "Is there a collared grizzly the Forest Service knows is in this area, Harper?"

He held the reins while she mounted Socks. "Yes. We have a sow and her three-year-old cubs that live in this area. We've not seen them on Bar C property, but Shay said she'd seen them in one of the lease pastures after she'd just had the cubs. The Forest Service came in, tracked her and tranquilized her, putting the collar on her."

Taking the reins, Tara said, "Okay. Well, maybe she's back on Bar C property."

Harper mounted. "We'll keep an eye out. If we do see

her, we'll try to get a cell-phone photo of her for the Forest Service. If she's the one that's collared, she's probably the local bear and she's in her territory hunting." He motioned to Tara to move ahead of him and start up the slight incline.

"They travel about twenty miles a day in search of food," Tara said over her shoulder, nudging Socks forward with her heels.

"Yes, but if that's the local sow, how did she get onto Bar C property? Probably through some broken-down area of our fence line we haven't spotted yet," Harper said, unhappy.

Grimacing, Tara nodded. "We'll stay alert." She hated the idea of a grizzly in the immediate area. Both of them carried .30-06 rifles in leather sheaths behind their saddle fenders. And both knew how to use them if they had to defend themselves against such a bear. What was worse? The sow had cubs and she would be superprotective and more willing to charge anyone she thought was an enemy to her babies. One thing Tara knew for sure: one never got between the mother and the cubs. That was a sure death warrant for the stupid person who did it. A sow would charge anyone who cut her off from protecting her babies. Leaning forward in the saddle, she urged Socks into a slow trot up the grassy knoll.

June 16

Tara loved her pale apricot bridesmaid's dress. It was knee length, with a heart-shaped bodice and lace around her shoulders and down her arms. She felt feminine and beautiful.

She stood with Shay and Dair as Kira walked down the aisle in her antique cream-colored wedding dress, her father, Les, looking proud of his beautiful daughter as he slowly escorted her to the man she was going to marry. He was teary-eyed, self-consciously wiping his eyes every now and again. On the other side of the Unity minister, Monica Doharty, stood tall and handsome Garret Fleming. Beside him was his best man, Reese. Noah and Harper flanked him as proud-looking groomsmen. They were all wearing tan cowboy business suits, black ribbon ties at their throats, their best set of cowboy boots cleaned and polished, their black Stetsons in place, standing with their inherited military posture with shoulders thrown back. Her heart swelled with the organ music, and she gripped the small bouquet of red, orange and white roses in her hand. There were two-foot-long ribbons beneath it, the same color as the flowers. The church was packed with everyone in the valley, coming to celebrate Kira and Garret's wedding. The temperature of the June afternoon was in the seventies, sunny and perfect as far as Tara was concerned.

Tara remembered going to this church since she was a child. Monica, the minister, was forty-five years old and the mother of three grown children. She had taken over the position as minister from Myron Campbell, who'd retired four years earlier. Tara had grown up with Reverend Campbell on the pulpit. She liked the warmth of Monica, her alto voice, her obvious maternal care for her flock. She loved coming to Sunday church services, finding strength in Monica's sermons from the Bible, as did so many others in the valley.

On the groom's side of the aisle were her mother and father in the second row. Tara loved her parents so much. They were trying their best to embrace and understand the toxic PTSD symptoms she'd gotten. She'd had many long, deep talks with them about them the past few months.

They'd only grown closer, more supportive of her, knowing what to recognize in her when she was having a bad day. She loved them for trying to understand the hellish storm that lived within her.

Gaze drifting across the assemblage, she saw Kira was radiant in her shoulder-length lace veil. Looking toward Garret, she saw tears in his eyes; he was struggling to battle them back. Her own throat tightened. And to get a small piece of happiness like this? Tara was overwhelmed with sudden emotion, Kira's face blurring for a moment as she sniffed and tried not to cry herself.

There were very few dry eyes in the church as Monica later pronounced Kira and Garret man and wife. The reception was going to be held in the huge church hall, an annex to the main red-brick building. It could handle up to five hundred people. After Garret proudly walked his wife down the aisle and they left to walk over to the annex, everyone genially followed.

It was nice to fall into line after the new couple with Harper at her side. He gave her a wink and a tender smile, and she felt warmth cascade through her. If only she could read what was in his eyes! Was he thinking that someday they might fall in love so deeply that they couldn't imagine life without each other? Knowing that her dreamy, idealistic side was taking hold of her, Tara shared a tremulous smile in return, moved by the wedding. She made no apology for the tears streaming down her cheeks, not caring if it mussed the little bit of makeup she'd put on with Shay's help. There was lots to do to help Kira and Garret open all the wedding gifts that were stacked on many tables and helping with the catered food that had been provided by Kassie from the restaurant, as well as the western band that was setting up right now in the annex.

Once they got to the roomy building, Tara loved how it

was decorated, gold and white ribbons emanating from a central chandelier that sparkled brightly with crystals. Everything was perfect. Shay, Dair and Tara had worked long into the night, making sure it looked like a beautiful fairyland for Kira and Garret.

There was nothing greater than working with other vets because they knew how to come together as a flawless team to make the 450 people who were to attend the reception feel at ease and welcomed. Kira was teary and Garret held and kissed her several times. It made Tara's heart melt. The fierceness that these male vets had for their women impressed her so much. They were a special group of men who adored their women. More than once, Tara would look up and see Harper across the room, pulling out chairs for the visitors, and glance in her direction. The warmth that had begun in the church only tripled because the look he gave her was more than just lust. There was something new in his expression, a thoughtfulness, a realization of some deeper connection with her, was what she could sense in the moment.

How badly she wanted to be with Harper right now, but there was simply too much for her to do along with Dair and Shay, to keep things on track and moving forward. Maybe tonight, after Kira and Garret left for the Jackson Hole Airport to take their Hawaiian honeymoon, she could once more be with him.

"How are you doing, Tara?"

Harper walked at her side, his arm around her waist, the night sky twinkling with stars thrown across the black vault of the heavens. It was chilly and he had taken off his coat and placed it around her shoulders once they had stepped outside the annex. It was almost ten p.m. and the valley folks were making the most of the western band inside, dancing until ten thirty p.m., when they would call it a night.

"Better now," she murmured, looking up into his shadowed features. They walked slowly through the crowded church parking lot.

"Good. I think we pulled off a good reception for Garret and Kira, don't you?"

Nodding, she rested her head against his shoulder. "Absolutely. It went off perfectly. Vets work so well together. There wasn't a hitch in it. Kira and Garret got to relax and just enjoy this special time with each other, which is what we all wanted."

"And even though the bride was beautiful," he said, kissing her brow, "you were, too. First time I've seen you in a dress, Tara, and I gotta tell you, you look incredible."

She laughed softly as he stopped and unlocked the door to his pickup. "Thanks. I'm glad Kira let us wear low, comfortable sandals. I never wear those foot-damaging torture devices called heels. All they do is ruin a woman's foot and cause horrible bunions."

He smiled as he opened the passenger door for her. He inhaled the honeysuckle scent of her shampoo. For the wedding, Tara had left her hair down, the blond strands gleaming, emphasizing the beauty of her wide blue eyes that he wanted to drown himself within. The rustle of the sleek fabric, her graceful movements, all conspired to make him ache for her. Did he want her? Yes. But he wasn't the type of man to chase women for sex. There had to be something more, much more, than just lust involved. It had to be meaningful. And judging by the yearning looks she'd traded with him off and on throughout the reception, they were on the same level of understanding. Where would tonight lead them?

Chapter Fourteen

Harper was driven to kiss Tara as they entered their home. He'd seen it in her eyes throughout the evening. They were too busy making sure everything went smoothly for Kira and Garret to do anything about it. Now? They were alone. And he was desperate for some intimate, quiet time with her.

"Hey," he said, touching her elbow as they entered the kitchen, "would you like to have a glass of wine or something with me in the living room? We barely got to say five words to each other tonight."

"Yes . . . I'd like that . . ." She stepped away from his hand on her elbow and picked up the sides of her dress. "I feel like a princess, but right now, I'm more like Cinderella and it's approaching midnight."

He stepped back, his gaze moving from her shoes up to her head. "You're not going to turn into anything else but who you are." His voice lowered as he saw a flush spread across her face. Harper reached out, barely grazing that warm, smooth cheek of hers, watching her eyes go soft with longing—for him. He could feel it. Wanting to taste her lips on his once more. "Are you going to change first?"

She made a muffled sound and dropped the fabric,

giving him a grin. "Well, I'm waffling because I hate wearing bras and I want to get out of this one."

His brows rose. "Really?" The color of her cheeks deepened. Her shyness was endearing to him. "I hadn't noticed."

"Oh, sure, Harper. Your whole life is about seeing details. I'm sure you knew I don't wear a bra when I work around here. I only wear one if I go horseback riding or something special, like tonight."

It was his turn to feel heat crawling into his face as he held her teasing look. She looked so beautiful to him, her gold hair slightly mussed, framing her features. Beneath the lamplight above them, he could see caramel and sunshine colors intermixed. He wanted to slide his fingers through those silky strands. "Mmm," he said. "How about I get you some wine? I'm pretty tanked up and topped off with that punch from the party," and he touched his belly area.

"Okay," she said, a little breathless. "I'm going to change and I'll meet you on the couch."

Harper wanted nothing more. "I'll climb into some familiar clothes, too," and he grinned. Watching her pirouette around, the fabric shimmering against her lithe body, the lace across her shoulders and enclosing her arms, Harper enjoyed the photo of Tara that he took with his heart. Turning, he followed her, and they each went to their own bedroom.

No one was more surprised than he was later when he sat in the corner of the couch, having gotten Tara her glass of white wine and setting it on the coffee table in front of him. He'd opted for a red T-shirt, jeans and sock feet. She reappeared in her soft gray gym pants and a loose-fitting, sleeveless pink tank top. Her hair was brushed, a gleaming cape around her shoulders. Best of all, she was barefoot.

Smiling, Harper was going to stand up as she drew near, but she waved him to sit back down.

"This looks good," she said, giving him a grateful look, reaching for the wineglass.

"You weren't hitting the punch bowl like I was," he offered, smiling as she settled down next to him, nestling her hip and then her long torso against his left side. Harper was surprised by her move. Since the bear incident, their familiarity had dissolved, much to his frustration. Lifting his left arm, she leaned into him after curling her legs beneath her. He liked her snuggling up.

"I wasn't anywhere near the punch bowl. Me and the girls were at the gifts table, opening them up so Kira and Garret didn't have to spend time doing it themselves."

"I should have thought about that," Harper said, frowning. They were across the way at the food tables, helping Kassie and her staff keep the appetizers coming out warm. It had been a hungry crowd. And the food had been delicious.

Sipping the wine, she licked her lower lip and relaxed completely against him. "You guys were just as busy as we were. Don't feel bad about it."

Moving his fingers lightly up and down her upper arm, he said, "You're worth remembering, Tara."

"Well," she said lightly, "it appears Noah and Dair are thinking about getting married, too. They haven't set a date, but we'll be old hands at this the next time around," and she smiled.

Her lips were sculpted, without any lipstick on them, and it took everything Harper had to remain relaxed even though his body was burning up with need for Tara. She was happy, and it was the first time since the bear incident he'd seen her buoyant. "Those two are definitely in love, no question."

"Dair is hesitant, but I understand why." She slanted a look up at him. "Her PTSD stuff."

"But she's got to see that Reese and Shay have worked it out. And so have Kira and Garret."

"I know, but she's an amputee, Harper. It's tough to have the lower half of one of your legs missing. She makes it hardly noticeable, and I admire her so much for her grit and wanting to fit in."

"If anyone can convince her, it will be Noah. He's good with horses and women," and he grinned a little, watching her lips lift.

"You're right. Noah has a special touch, but with Dair, he's exactly what she needs."

"I've watched Dair since she got here and she's made huge, positive strides," Harper said. "I think it's the environment at the ranch, the fact we're all PTSD vets. She arrived pretty tense and defensive, but over time, she shed all of that and relaxed. She's a lot happier than when she first came. But then again? We were all where Dair was when we took a job here at the Bar C. And it's taken us time to relax, too."

She sighed and nodded, sipping the wine. "I don't know about you, Harper, but for the last few days I've ramped down off that PTSD cliff." She gave him a warm look. "Have you?"

"Yes," he admitted, his hand stilling on her shoulder. "Maybe we were looking forward to something happy. Seeing Kira and Garret so damned high on each other? The wedding? What do you think?"

"I think you're right. It's so nice to be part of something that's good and positive. It's great to focus on a happy event." She leaned forward, placing her wineglass on the coffee table. Returning to his embrace, relaxing against him, she placed her hand over his heart. Lashes lifting, she whispered, "I so want us to get back to where we were before the bear intruded. Do you?" and her voice dropped into an aching whisper, her fingers pressing more firmly across the soft fabric.

For half a heartbeat, Harper was stunned by Tara's trembling admission. Automatically, he eased his hand through her silky hair, holding her gaze. "I want you in whatever way you want to share yourself with me." He hesitated, his voice dropping. "I know you have issues, but I think they're surmountable. And yes, the bear charge tore both of us loose from our fragile moorings. And I want to kiss you . . ."

She lifted her chin. "Kiss me, then."

His whole world anchored and Harper unconsciously held his breath for a moment as he tipped his head forward to meet her parting lips. His mind canted, he lost the ability to think, only drown in the cushiony softness of her lips meeting his, firm, eager and filled with promise. His heart exploded with a fierce joy as Tara leaned into him, her breasts pressed against his chest, her hand sliding warmly up to his neck, pulling him closer, tighter to him. There was nothing in his life he wanted more than just this with her.

Harper wasn't going to lie anymore to himself. He was falling in love with this woman who struggled daily to maintain some kind of normalcy in her ripped-apart life. She was so strong, and he felt that strength as her lips glided wetly against his, taking and giving, her breath ragged. He slid his fingers into her thick hair, relishing the feel of the strands, his nostrils flaring as he inhaled a scent that was purely her. A soft moan rose in her throat and he hungrily absorbed it into himself, his entire body erupting in fire and need for her alone. She was so fearless and vulnerable with him.

In his tumbling thoughts, washed ashore with glowing emotions of joy, he realized Tara trusted him. Harper kept his hands where they were. He wanted to caress her shoulders and back, but he didn't feel her giving him permission to move or do anything else other than enjoy this life-changing kiss with him. It was enough, and a thread of sweetness flowed through him as he lifted his mouth from hers, kissing each corner and then pressing a soft kiss to each of her closed eyelids.

Tara sank her head against his upper chest, her arm sliding around his torso, holding him. Harper knew it was love, whether the word was ever verbalized between them or not. The way Tara looked at him, the way she touched him, told him that. There was lust in her grazing touch, and so much more. The awe in her expression, the respect and pride she had for him, was present. It made him feel like the man she had searched for but never found until now. And he wasn't disappointing her, which was a huge relief.

Slipping his arm around her back, his other hand cupping her cheek as she lay her head against him, he closed his eyes, savoring the intimacy with her. This was what he needed, had always wanted but thought it impossible to ever have. Olivia had never been cuddly or maternal or wanted this kind of wonderful closeness. Right now, lust took a backseat to greater, more important emotions that clamored brightly within his heart, bringing light to his darkened soul. Tara filled him with hope that despite how broken he was by PTSD, her love, her intimacy with him, filled those cracks and crevices within him and were healing him.

Never had he felt the welling up of love that he felt for Tara right now. Her honesty gut-punched him and made him realize that his first marriage had been a total sham because both of them had been so immature. Tara brought truth and honor to them as a couple. She played no games. She wasn't manipulative and she was mature far beyond her years. How brave she was. And she deserved no less from him. Harper kissed her hair, smoothing some strands back against her temple with his fingers.

"I cherish every moment with you, Tara. I have from the day I met you." Swallowing, his throat tight with nearly overwhelming feelings, he rasped, "You need to know that you're a bright and shining light in my life. I never thought I would ever experience what I do in your arms, with your kisses. You make me feel hope, make me feel alive, and I dream . . . I dream of something so much better for both of us if we can just keep talking and showing how much we mean to each other." He pressed another kiss against her hair, the honeysuckle scent rising into his nostrils.

"I feel the same, Harper," she whispered against his T-shirt, nuzzling into his chest with her cheek. "I feel so wonderful when we're like this. You make me feel safe."

"I always want to be there for you, sweetheart. And I will be if you'll let me. We're going to have ups and downs, but it's moments like these that bind my wounds and I know what we have can help heal us together, Tara."

Nodding, eyes closed, Tara tightened her arm around his middle, content to rest against him, wanting nothing else. "I don't want this moment to end. . . ."

"Me neither . . ."

Tara tried to steady her voice, her heart pounding so hard that she hesitated for a moment before speaking.

"Do you really think we can do this, Harper?" She saw him give her a lazy, boyish smile that melted all her building fear.

"I've been waiting for you from the day I met you, Tara. I know I'm a bad risk, having been married and divorced, but I'm older now. I know what caused it to fall apart." He smoothed his thumb across her cheek. "I think our feelings for each other are strong enough, still growing toward each other, to take this shot at happiness. You make me happy, Tara. I always feel so damned good when you're around me. You have no idea how much I look forward to having breakfast, lunch and dinner with you. I want to know what you're thinking because you're smart, sensitive, funny and sympathetic. I like to see the world through your eyes, your thoughts and ideas."

His earnest, gruffly spoken words feathered through Tara and she felt her heart expand until she thought it might burst open with such profound joy that she might die of euphoria. "I—I guess I never knew you felt like that about me."

Grimacing, Harper slipped his hand to her shoulder, gently smoothing out the material across it. "I haven't exactly been the most demonstrative person with you. That's my fault. But we've been through some pretty hectic ups and downs since meeting, too. It seemed we went from one crisis right into another one. There was no quiet time, no backwater where we could relax and honestly open up to each other. First, it was Cree Elson. Then, the bear incident."

"God, this stuff happens in threes," she muttered, shaking her head, enjoying his hand gently moving along her shoulder. "I hope I'm wrong about that . . ."

"Maybe we'll get lucky this once," he said. "Two's enough in my book. We deserve some down time."

Snorting softly, Tara said, "I've never had luck, Harper. It doesn't figure in my world, believe me. I have to earn everything I get."

"Well," he rasped, leaning over, kissing her wrinkling brow, "that's going to start changing right now."

His lips brushed her flesh, sending wonderful sensations of pleasure through her. She felt her breasts tightening, her whole body catching fire, simmering, wanting Harper. As he drew away, his hand coming to rest over hers, calmness in his gray eyes, she felt the bubbly joy moving through her. "I hope you're right."

"Tell me what you want right now, Tara. Talk to me."

Her voice was soft and filled with emotion. "I want more than your kisses, Harper. I want you. All of you. The wounded part of me is unsure. The healthy part of me is positive I want to get past all these hurdles and be with you."

"We've been through so much, Tara. I think if you look back at your life in the military, you'll see you were always a risk-taker. I was one in my military job, too. We both need to use that risk-taking side of ourselves and use it now. We did it and survived combat. You and I aren't in combat with each other. We're trying to find a way, a passage, toward the other. If you look at all you've survived in the military, you'll know in your heart that we're a risk worth taking. You and me," and he held her gaze, waiting for her answer.

Harper was right. She tucked her lower lip between her teeth for a moment, glancing away, hearing the deep emotion, the yearning, the need for her, in his strained voice. "I remember my mom telling me that life wasn't for the weak. Living was always going to be challenging. It takes courage and bravery to live. She warned me that there would be times when I'd be so scared that it would paralyze me. And she was right on all counts." Melting beneath his tender gaze, she managed, "It's time I risk my heart. I can't keep listening to the negativity in my head. I need you, Harper. All of you. I'm willing to try . . ." and she choked, tears burning in her eyes over her decision.

He grazed her temple, looked beyond her for a moment, then settled his warm gaze on her.

"We'll take this a step at a time, Tara. There isn't going to be a rush or an urgency, and even though I feel like it inside, it's not the right track to take with you, with myself, right now. Do you agree?"

Giving a jerky nod, she whispered, "Yes, no hurry, no expectations, Harper, because I'm so damned scared I feel like crying and running away sometimes."

He sighed and gathered her up against him, his chin resting against her head. "Then we'll be afraid together, okay? We'll run toward each other, not away from each other when that happens. Fair enough?"

Closing her eyes, pushing back the tears, Tara managed, "Y-yes . . ."

"Look," he said patiently, "the worst scenario is that we discover through a process of trial and error that we aren't meant for each other. It's all right, because at least we tried. We found out, Tara. And that's better than living the rest of our lives wondering if we'd had the guts to walk toward each other, instead of running away from possible happiness. We just won't know until we give ourselves permission to try. Do you agree?"

She managed a croak of a half laugh. "You're always so logical and calm. Yes, I agree."

He smiled and pressed a kiss to her temple. "The worst

is out of the way, sweetheart. And you're the one who has to set the ground rules for us. Tell me what you want and I'll try to give it to you. Just because we're trying to explore what we have doesn't mean this fragile relationship of ours is a done deal one way or another."

"I need to hear that, Harper, I really do."

"We respect each other, Tara. We care about each other. And we're sensitive to each other's moods and ups and downs. We're doing the best we can even though we're pretty well fractured by PTSD."

"Are you scared?" and she lifted her head from his chest, searching for and finding his warm gaze. His mouth, such a beautiful part of him, twisted a little.

"Scared just like you. But everything we've ever dreamed about having is always a challenge," and he caressed her cheek. "We'll do this even though we're scared out of our minds, we'll inch forward at your pace. You'll talk with me, Tara, you'll tell me what you want so I know where my boundaries are with you. I'm no mind reader. This is going to be tough going because neither of us is used to working on a relationship like ours. I tried and it ended in divorce."

"Yes," she sighed, "and I've been avoiding it like the plague, knowing I was broken in so many places."

"Yet you're a good human being, sweetheart. You're kind and caring and you aren't selfish. Despite your wounds, you're whole in ways so many others aren't. Don't you see that?"

"I guess," she muttered, shaking her head. "My parents raised me to be a responsible person to others; the world didn't revolve around me. I've always been that way."

"And you have no idea how much that appeals to me, Tara. I like you just the way you are."

"Thanks," she whispered, touching his roughened jaw.

"Where do you want to start? What's comfortable for you? And we'll take it from there."

"You have a say in this, too, Harper."

"Of course I do, but I'm on a learning curve right along with you. I learned by clamming up with Olivia that I lost the marriage. I'm going to force myself to talk with you, to let you know where I'm at emotionally. Otherwise? It's not going to work. I'll be making a lot of mistakes, Tara, and I hope you realize I'm far from perfect."

"My mom always told me there was a man out there for me, the perfect puzzle piece, like a jigsaw puzzle, who would fit me perfectly."

"I like how your mom sees the world," he said, touched.

"Mom is a jigsaw puzzle addict. She loves putting puzzles together." Tara laughed. "I don't like puzzles, but she loves them. She's always got two or three sitting around on her desk, or at one end of the counter at the hardware store, or wherever she can start a new one."

He chuckled. "Well, I kinda like the idea of fitting another person. That's a nice way to see us."

Her smile softened and she leaned up, her lips against his. "I want to sleep with you tonight. I want to love you and I want you to love me. I know it won't be perfect, but it doesn't have to be. Are you game? Is this what you want, too?" and she allowed her lips to barely brush his, feeling his immediate reaction, his arm tightening around her.

"We want the same thing," he managed, his voice low and thick with so many emotions.

Chapter Fifteen

The anxiety of being imperfect, the scars on her body received from years of deployments in combat, whether Harper would think her desirable or not, raged through Tara as she stood naked in front of him. His bedroom was cool with the mid-June night air slipping in beneath a partly opened window at one end of the quiet room. Her heart was beating rapidly, as much from fear of being rejected by him as from wanting him.

The moonlight was silvery as it slipped around the edges of the drapes across the only window, lending a muted radiance that silently surrounded them. Harper had undressed along with her, their clothes in piles here and there on the cedar floor. Tara was old enough to know that no one was perfect body-wise, but she still cared deeply what Harper thought of her. She managed a nervous half smile and whispered, "I'm feeling so unsure of myself with you." Instantly, she saw Harper's gaze sharpen and hone in on her upturned face.

"Hey," he growled, settling his hands on her shoulders, "don't go there. I'm beat up, too, inside and out, Tara."

"Yeah," she choked, absorbing the callused warmth of his hands smoothing along her shoulders, as if she were a fractious, scared horse that needed to be calmed. Well, she was nervous. "I see the scars on your body, Harper, and it really brings home to me how hard deployments were on you, too."

Mouth flexing, Harper slid his hand down to her flared hips, halting at a long two-inch scar. "You have your fair share of them, too."

"Oh, I got plenty of nicks and dibits," she joked as he lightly stroked the scar with his fingers, his brows moving downward, concern in his eyes as he studied it.

"And like me," he said, holding her anxious stare, "I'll bet just by looking at a scar or touching it, the whole episode comes back to you?"

Making a sound of frustration in her throat, she began to feel her worry dissipate as Harper continued to graze her waist and hip lightly, stroking her, as if to erase her anxiety. "Yes. Worse? The emotions come roaring back with it, which makes it even more difficult sometimes." She made a helpless gesture toward her right hip. "I try not to look at myself when I'm naked. I avoid it. I don't want to remember."

"I do the same thing," and he grinned a little, his hands following the curve of her hips, holding her, but not so close as to make her uncomfortable. "I tend to pay attention to shaving this face of mine but wash the rest of my body by Braille."

"Does it bother you that I have so many scars?" She was afraid of the answer. There were swellings on her legs and hips particularly that would never disappear. Discoloration came along with each one of them as well.

Looking deeply into her eyes, Harper rasped thickly, "No, Tara. I like you just the way you are. You're beautiful in my eyes . . . my heart," and he slid his hand behind her nape, asking her to come forward, and she did.

The look in his slate-colored eyes, burning with a fire that made her heart triple in beat for a moment, told her so much. So much. Taking that halting step forward, trying to push all her reservations aside, her worries and fears away, she lifted her hands, placing them lightly against his darkly haired chest. His flesh was warm, firm, and she felt the muscles leap beneath her fingertips.

His mouth gently claimed hers and she became lost in the heat, his strength and the tenderness he imparted to her, his hands outlining her shoulders, drawing her even closer to him. Lost in the building haze of his desire, his mouth telling her of his need, she felt all her fears being burned up in the heat that flamed between them. The moment Tara leaned languidly against him fully, his erection pressing into her belly, all her coherent thoughts turned to ashes. Feeling him control the amount of strength he exerted against her mouth, his hands cupping her shoulders, worshipping her, making her feel sacred and as necessary as breathing, a soft sound of pleasure vibrated in her throat.

Just feeling so cherished beneath Harper's mouth giving and taking with hers, convinced her that she had nothing to worry about and everything to celebrate with him instead. She'd had lovers before, but never this sensitive, never monitoring her as he did right now. It spoke to Tara about the depth of his commitment to her, his wanting her as an equal partner, wanting to learn what pleased her and what didn't. What a far cry from the other men earlier in her life. That was the last conscious thought Tara had because in one fluid movement, Harper lifted her up into his arms, her body pressed sweetly against his as he carried her over to the bed. Depositing her on top of the quilt, she slid toward the center, giving him room to stretch out beside her.

The luminescence of the moonlight did nothing but accentuate the planes of his face, showing the hunter-like intensity in his shadowed eyes, his highly developed muscles moving, contracting, relaxing as she welcomed his advances. There was great satisfaction in moving her gaze across Harper's silhouetted body. His powerful masculinity reminded her of a cougar who was all lithe beauty coupled with an underlying danger that vibrated close to the surface.

She wasn't ever a passive lover. As Tara slid her hand across his broad shoulder, she once more was reminded of his strength as a man, pulling him down upon her, lips parting, wanting to taste Harper once again. This time, she shared her hunger with him, her lips firm, gliding, letting him know that her desire for him was equal to him wanting her. She felt him shift as he hungrily took her lips beneath his, his other hand sliding across her hip and cheek, bringing her belly flush against his warm, thick hardness. Fire leaped to life within her. As she moved sinuously against Harper, her hardened nipples entangled in the silken hair dusting his chest. A gnawing ache throbbed deep within her.

Harper knew from talking with her that the best way for her to get an orgasm was for her to be on top of him, and he was fine with her choice of position. Slipping his hands around her waist, he ended their kiss and then lifted her up and over the top of him, her long thighs bracketing his hips. There was an unspoken concert between them, and Tara closed her eyes, sitting atop his warm, hard erection, the slickness of her own juices making her moan with pleasure. The moment he cupped her breasts, his thumbs brushing the tips, she gave a small cry, but it was a sound filled with utter gratification, not pain. Just the way he stroked her, teased her, lifting his hips, meeting her swollen gate, sent sheets of burning heat upward into her. She trusted him fully with herself. She knew he was focused on her pleasure right now, not his own, although she could hear his growl of satisfaction as she slid atop him, yet to have him enter her.

Her whole world came apart as she eased down upon him, her body opening to him, widening, accommodating, the silky juices allowing him to slide deep within her. A low cry of raw fulfillment tore from between them as he teased each of her nipples with his lips, suckling her, making her lose her mind, shifting to that animal part of herself that enjoyed the act of lust with someone whose heart was a part of this heated dance between them. She felt Harper's large, roughened hands curve around her hips, holding her, thrusting slowly into her, little cries of delight vibrating in her throat. The rocking motion he established dismantled her in the best of ways. In moments, her body convulsed inwardly, the explosiveness of the powerful orgasm making her cry out in surprise and pleasure.

Tara floated, her palms against his powerful chest, fingers digging into his flesh as he brought her to a second orgasm within minutes of the first. Never had she come so quickly or so strongly, understanding that it had to be her heart engaging wholly with Harper that had allowed these amazing moments. Never had she felt so close to a man, wanting to be a part of him, feeling him melt into her until she felt as one with him. And when he released within her, he groaned out her name, his fingers tight against her waist, freezing in his own rapture of release. It triggered a third orgasm within her and she nearly fainted from the sizzling ringlets of throbbing, widening fire consuming all of her.

Tara felt herself falling forward, her arms weakened, collapsing fully against Harper. He guided her so she lay like a warm, soft blanket across the length of his upper body, her head coming to rest upon his left shoulder, her damp brow pressed against his sandpapery jaw. They were breathing like two winded animals, clinging to each other, appreciating each other as never before. Harper moved his hands across her shoulders and slowly down her spine, cupping her cheeks, moving just enough to tease her wildly throbbing body once again. Tara uttered a groan, embracing him, arms sliding around his neck. He gave a low uttering of her name, and she felt him absorbing her as he gently rocked her against him, continuing to initiate ringlets of fire that still arced teasingly between where they were melted into each other.

Harper couldn't stop reveling in the silky tightness of Tara surrounding him. She felt so damn good. It had been so long since he'd had sex. Olivia had crippled him, always pointing out his scars, the swellings that would never go away or his bruised flesh that would never lose those colors. She didn't understand that each injury, each scar was a story, usually devastating to him personally, and saying his body looked ugly to her had affected his manhood and his heart. Because of that experience, he understood Tara's earlier nervousness about all her injuries and how they might appear to him. More than anything, Harper had wanted to put her at ease, and he had.

As Tara moved off him, kneeled next to his right arm and leaned over, she softly kissed a three-inch scar that had curved around his right shoulder. Her fingertips were warm as she lifted her lips from the wound that he'd gotten during his first deployment.

He lay there, watching her through half-closed eyes, absorbing the thoughtfulness in her expression, the sympathetic look in her blue eyes, watching the grace of her hand as she leaned over once more. The strands of her golden hair tickled his sensitized flesh as she placed a warm kiss over another scar near the left side of his waist. There was no censure in her expression, no disgust in her eyes over his wounds; she understood what it was like to be wounded in combat.

Grazing his left hip, her fingers whispered across an oval, swollen area. His flesh tingled at her healer's touch. Her long, thick hair loose and mussed, strands cool and teasing against his skin once more as she kissed the spot. Straightening, Tara moved down below his hips, sliding her fingers across his thick, curved right thigh. He had a lot of healed cuts on it, as most soldiers did. He was forever skidding to his knees, hitting rocks or pieces of broken tree limbs during firefights. His lower body had taken a pounding.

Closing his eyes, his hands behind his head, Harper surrendered to her tender touch, each kiss opening his heart more and more. It was as if she were mentally memorizing him, mapping him in her heart because her touch was butterfly light, filled with care for him alone. Tara worked her way around to the other side of his body, missing none of his injuries.

When she knelt near his head, she leaned down, kissing him on the mouth, and for a long, long time. As her lips lifted away from his, she whispered, "Turn onto your stomach now."

Without a word, Harper nodded and did as she asked, tucking a pillow beneath his chest, his cheek resting against his folded hands on the mattress. Closing his eyes, he felt Tara's lingering touch across his short, dampened hair, and her lips brushed against a scar on his left shoulder blade. It was as if his soul was relaxing, fractured as it was, for the first time since all the injuries occurred. The caress of her lips against his flesh, the brush of her finger-tips afterward, as if sweeping away all the sordid memories associated with each scar, was nothing short of magical. No woman had ever done this for him. It was, for Harper, an act of selfless love he'd never experience from another person. The tenderness Tara shared with him as she worked from his shoulders down to his feet staggered him emotionally.

By the time she had completed her journey with him, giving unselfishly back to him, tears stung against his tightly shut eyes, wanting to be released, too. It felt as if a fist were pressing upward into his chest, squeezing his heart, which still recalled so much agony inflicted by each wound. Yet Tara's soothing kisses and touches took the raw, visceral emotions away, dissolving them, leaving him in awe of her.

Tara lay down beside him, her brow against his hair, her arm spanning his broad back, and Harper felt her nurture him in another way. They lay quietly against each other, and he could feel the soft beat of her heart against his upper arm, where her breasts pressed against him, felt the moisture of her shallow breath flowing across his nape and shoulder. The relaxation thrumming through him, the sexual release that had drained him, overwhelmed him, and he drifted off to sleep, never having experienced such an incredible level of human care as he just had from Tara.

Much later, it was the night's coolness in the room that slowly woke Harper. Groggy, he felt Tara's warm, curved body following the line of his from his head to his feet.

Her arm lay across his waist, her cheek resting against his neck and shoulder. Her moist, slow breath feathered across him and slowly brought him awake enough to realize where he was and what had happened.

At first, it felt like the most delicious dream he'd ever had, and he didn't want it to ever end. This woman, who was so damned hot, yet so kind and thoughtful, was holding him with her woman's strength. He luxuriated in the silence, the soft whisper of wind through nearby pine trees, their scent lingering lightly in the room. The coolness of the night sighed against his skin.

Tara was wrapped around him, almost in a protective measure, in his wandering, sleep-filled mind. He'd never felt that from any woman before. But then, Tara wasn't most women. She had been a combatant. She knew life and death, and Harper was sure she had felt the same within him, wanting to guard him as he slept with her at his side.

It brought a new awareness to him about his relationship with his ex-wife and the present one with Tara. They were a universe apart in every possible way. His appreciation of her maturity, her ability to open herself up to him, totaled him emotionally. She was honest, innocent in some ways, trusting and, most of all, vulnerable with him. Harper wanted to shake his head over the unexpected luck of her walking into his life. From the first, it had felt like a magnet had awakened in his chest, his heart yearning wildly and constantly for her. And yet? They'd had so much to overcome within themselves, much less with each other. How brave was his woman.

There was no longer moonlight. It was dark now as he barely opened his eyes. In the distance, Harper listened to the crickets singing outside the window, a natural symphony of different insects, which added to the mellow sounds of the night surrounding them. Tara was here. Naked. Beautiful. *His*. Never had he felt such an overwhelming sense of protection as he did toward her. Oh, he knew Tara had survived a lot, had shown she could defend and protect herself without him being around. She could have died the many times she'd deployed with black-ops groups. Yet the curved lushness of her long body aligned with his made his heart fly open with fierce love for her. Harper had thought he knew what love was when he'd fallen helplessly for Olivia. But he hadn't known. *This* was love. *Real love . . .*

Closing his eyes, he savored that realization, feeling the unparalleled euphoria enclose his heart, making him feel hope, now able to dream of a happy future he'd thought he'd never experience.

The room was chilly and they were laying naked on top of the bed. Harper hated to move. It was the last thing he wanted to do. This felt like the most beautiful dream he'd ever had and he was loath to end it. But Tara was real. And so was he. And they'd made love to each other hours earlier, falling exhausted into each other's arms afterward, utterly and completely fulfilled. Dazed by the beauty of her love for him—and he did know without a doubt that Tara loved him as he loved her—he wanted this to be the foundation for their new, burgeoning relationship. Their lovemaking was too special, too beautiful, profoundly touching his heart and soul, to not experience it again and again. This was the woman he wanted in his bed, sleeping beside him until he drew his last breath on this earth.

He slowly eased out from beneath Tara's arm and leg. She mumbled something unintelligible, frowned and then snuggled down on her belly, into the folds of the rumpled quilt, her cheek resting on the fabric, still fast asleep. Getting up, he padded silently to the bathroom and then to the linen closet. His eyes had adjusted to the gloom, and as he brought a huge white cotton down-filled comforter to the bed, Harper could see her scars. She had as many, maybe more, than he did. And he wanted to kiss each of them just as she'd done for him.

His heart was wide open to Tara and he came to her side of the bed, gently spreading the warm comforter over her. She stirred but didn't awaken, and he was glad. Just the thought of getting to slide back into bed, gather her into his arms, their bodies melting against each other again, tunneled through Harper. The gold of her mussed strands glinted dully as he eased into the bed and slid over to Tara, easing her back into his arms and against his body.

". . . Harper?"

He smiled to himself, hearing Tara's drowsy voice as she partially awoke as he embraced her. "It's all right," he rasped, kissing her hair. "Go back to sleep, sweetheart. You're safe. . . ." And he always wanted Tara to feel as safe as she did right now, burrowing into his arms, against his body, her arm slipping across his waist, drawing him as close as she could get to him. Cherishing the moment, Harper relaxed, allowing Tara to get comfy against him, hearing her breathing slowing into sleep once more. He had slid his arm beneath her neck, encircling her shoulders, drawing her close, and the last sound he heard was a little vibration in her throat, telling him she was happy. That was all that mattered.

Closing his eyes, he tried to settle down his awakening lower body. He had no doubt they would make love again when they woke closer to dawn. Unable to believe how buoyant and joyous his heart felt, he savored the feeling as never before. Harper knew from too many other times in his life how the bad mixed with the good. Only good happened a lot less frequently than bad for him. *Until now. Until Tara.*

They were meant for each other. His mind canted to his parents, who were deeply in love with each other and expressed it daily in many small but important ways. Sometimes, in his late teen years, he'd see his dad drop a kiss on his mother's cheek. Or they'd touch each other's hand or arm. Sometimes, it was the special meals his dad liked and she never forgot to make for him. And his dad knew his mother loved Shasta daisies, so one time he'd brought home a pack of seeds for her. And the very next evening, before dinner, he'd begun to dig along their fence to prepare a place where she could plant them. Harper had grown up, luckily, with parents who knew how to say *I love you* in hundreds of different ways.

His arm tightened a little around Tara's shoulders as he thought of so many little ways he wanted to let her know he loved her, too. She needed a new printer, the old one nearing the end of its life. The idea of taking her on a surprise picnic in the Salt Mountain Range, to another beautiful spot where she could photograph wild animals and blooming flowers, appealed strongly to him. She loved having dinner with her parents at their home. Often, she would reneg, though, and now Harper silently promised her that they'd see her parents on a weekly basis. He knew it was healing for Tara and he'd make it happen.

As sleep claimed him once more, the last thought Harper had was to take Tara to lunch at Kassie's, her favorite place to eat out. They both deserved time away from the ranch, to focus more on each other. And although the café could be noisy, he would time it so that they were both in a reasonably stable state where noise wouldn't grate harshly on their tender, exposed nervous systems. Liking his potential plan, Harper promised to put more nice surprises in Tara's life. She deserved them. And so did he.

Chapter Sixteen

June 18

Tara didn't try to ignore or minimize her love for Harper as she drove toward Wind River. Even now, her lower body glowed in memory of waking up yesterday morning with his arms around her, his body cossetting hers. Never had she felt so safe. So . . . loved . . .

It was early morning, near seven a.m., and she needed to drive in to pick up a special order of feed for the broodmares that had arrived at Charlie Becker's store yesterday. Needing to be back at nine a.m. to work with Harper out in the arena with Candy and her foal, Ebony, she was glad there wasn't much traffic on the two-lane highway. The sky was a light blue, the sun's rays streaking across the oval valley, highlighting the Wilson Range on her left and the Salt Mountains on her right. She loved that this valley was bracketed like bookends, by two different ranges. To her, it had always felt like a pair of Mother Earth's arms around this special place she loved so much.

Harper. . . . She sighed and tried to keep her focus on driving. The highway was empty, so it wasn't that stressful to divide her attention. Her heart was full of so much happiness she didn't know what to do with herself. It was as if she was finally opening up, trusting a man and, in doing so, had opened the floodgates of her heart to a whole new world. One that she hadn't anticipated. She felt as if she were in some kind of luscious, ongoing dream that she was afraid would suddenly disappear. Knowing it was the PTSD, the sense that something bad was about to happen to her, as it had in the past, and would happen again in the future, was like an old tape.

Libby Hilbert had taught her how her mind would replay bad tapes and that she had to ignore them, not invest in them. To connect with the memory emotionally kept it alive. When the memory popped up, Libby said to consciously force herself to think of something good that had happened in her life. Replace a negative tape with a positive one. And it was working. The past didn't have the same claw-like hold on her as before. Meeting Harper, having a job with sister and brother vets at the ranch, were healing her. As it was healing them all.

Harper was offering her an incredibly happy world in the present and future. Tara didn't fool herself that there wouldn't be issues, but his patience and understanding allowed her hope to fully blossom. He hadn't said he loved her and she hadn't said the words to him either. She suspected they were both gun-shy of such a powerful word, that so much bad had happened to them in the past, they were going to be circumspect about admitting love now. Oh, how she wanted to, though! They were both coming out from a long, long journey with their military service, their brutal experiences and learning to live with PTSD. Tara didn't fault herself or Harper for not saying what they felt in their hearts for each other. Bad always seemed to follow them and they were always looking over their shoulders. Maybe in time, Tara thought, they would see that something good was happening for them, something hopeful and beautiful. Then? They could tell each other that they were in love.

Suddenly, a rusty-looking red-and-white pickup loomed in her rearview mirror. Tara froze for a split second, the vehicle roaring up on her, the grille taking up her entire rearview mirror. She was driving a half-ton truck. The one bearing down on her was a three-quarter ton, much heavier and larger. Instantly, she gripped the wheel a little harder. Before she could step on the accelerator and avoid being hit by it, the vehicle smashed into her right rear fender.

There was a shattering, crunching, metal sound ripping through her cab. Her ears hurt from the screeching as they collided. Tara didn't have time to scream. Her truck suddenly swerved sideways, turning around and around, out of her control. In seconds, the truck was airborne, and everything slowed down to painful single frames for her, as if she were in some kind of movie. As the truck flipped through the air, the seat-belt strap yanked hard on her shoulder. She screamed.

The truck slammed into her berm, the sound of buckling metal roaring all around her.

The airbags had already deployed, blinding her.

Tara was jerked and yanked one way and then the other, pain shooting through her neck, shoulders and chest. Her hands were torn off the wheel as it plunged down the steep berm. More metal shrieked as it was torn away by the rocky slope. Another cry came out of her as she was blinded by the airbags, unable to see or do anything except take the brutal physical punishment. Her mind blanked for a second as the truck slid to a halt on its side. She was hanging in the seat belt, trying to push the airbags away. She smelled smoke, and panic seized her. Breathing hard, she struggled, slapping at the now-deflating airbags. She had to get out!

Escape! She had to escape! Frantic, she twisted in the seat, her shaking fingers trying to locate the seat-belt release. The airbag was in the way, stopping her from reaching it. Cursing in frustration, all her combat training took over, and Tara jerked her hand downward toward the leather belt where her Buck knife was located.

The door above her was savagely jerked open.

Tara looked up.

Cree Elson stood on top of the truck, holding the door open, grinning down at her.

No!

Her mind blanked as she stared up into his slitted green eyes. His red hair was long, in a ponytail across the shoulder of his camo-colored T-shirt. His thick lips twisted into a triumphant smile.

"You're mine, Tara."

The words caromed through her skull and she whimpered, still trying to get to her knife. She had to fight him! She had to escape! But as she moved and jerked at the imprisoning seat belt, dizziness swept over her. For a moment, she lost her bearings. Feeling warm blood trickling down the left side of her temple, she realized she'd slammed into the door frame at some point. Escape! She had to get away from Cree! The look in his eyes was one of rage, triumph and desire.

"Sit still!" he shouted, getting down on his knees, hauling out a five-inch hunting blade from a leather sheath. "Stay still and let me cut you out of there!"

Breathing raggedly, Tara froze. She saw fire suddenly appear beneath the bent hood of the truck. Black smoke started to roil upward. Cree leaned over and she smelled whiskey on his breath as he grabbed her shoulder strap, swiftly cutting through it. Instantly, Tara fell toward the passenger seat, hanging against the deflated airbags.

Cree cut the other strap.

She fell hard into the side of the truck that lay against the ground.

Before she could twist and get to her knife to defend herself, Cree leaned in, his large hand grabbing the left shoulder of her jacket, hauling her up and out of the cab as if she weighed nothing.

Grunting, Tara flailed her arms, trying to strike out at Cree as he jerked her out of the truck. In seconds, she was flying through the air, away from the burning truck.

Landing hard, Tara rolled a few feet across the rocks before stopping near the rear of the truck. She saw Cree scowl and come after her, the knife in his right hand, anger leaping to his tense face. Trying to scramble to her feet, she made it, but dizziness felled her. With a cry, she pitched to the right, throwing her hands out, trying to escape Cree.

Too late!

"Damn you!" he breathed, grabbing her shoulder, yanking her around.

Tara stumbled in the rocks, falling against Cree's hard body. She grunted, struggling. "Let me go!" she screamed. Lifting her knee, she jammed it up into his crotch.

Cree howled, releasing her.

Run!

Gasping, Tara clawed herself upright, weaving, stumbling, trying to get off the slope and onto the smoother, dirt berm. Frantic, she looked for any traffic either way. There was none!

God! No! No! Not again!

Dizziness assailed her as she stumbled. She heard Cree grunting and cursing behind her. She'd seen him fall to his knees, his hands grabbing at his crotch, bent over. She'd meant to mangle the son of a bitch. And she hoped she had. It would be the only way to stop him from capturing her.

Making it to the berm, she dug the toes of her cowboy boots into the soft, gravely dirt, straining, pushing herself, wobbling unsteadily. She fought the dizziness. Jerking a look over her shoulder, adrenaline spurted into her bloodstream. Cree was getting up, his face dark with rage, his eyes on her, lurching to his feet, his lips drawing back from his teeth.

No! No! Faster! Run faster!

Tara's mind wheeled. She ran hard, running away from Cree, following the empty highway. If only a vehicle would come by! If only! But the road was utterly deserted. The look in Cree's eyes told her he was going to kill her. He'd taken up his knife again, holding it in his fist, launching himself in her direction.

Breath tearing out of her, she had to think. As she ran, she jerked the snap off her leather sheath, pulling the Buck knife out. Her fingers were so trembly, she had a hard time pulling out the one-and-a-half-inch blade. It was her only defense. Her cell phone was still in the truck.

She heard the heavy footfalls of Elson coming upon her. Tara knew she couldn't outrun him.

It took everything she had to stop, suddenly turn around and face him.

Cree was running hard, hatred in his expression. He hadn't been prepared for her to suddenly stop and face him.

Tara gripped the knife, closing the gap as he suddenly stumbled and tried to halt his hurtling toward her, surprise in his eyes. She knew from combat that surprise could make the difference between living and dying. And she knew she was going to die if she didn't face her attacker. Never again would she be his prisoner! *Never!*

She'd had good training from the black-ops groups she'd worked with. Tara knew you never extended your knife hand toward the enemy. Instead, you closed the gap with their body, holding the knife at your side, ready to strike when close enough. That way, the enemy couldn't knock the knife out of your hand. She saw Elson's face twist, hatred combined with shock as she launched herself at him. Tara knew she had nothing to lose. A momentary thought of some driver finding her lifeless body lying beside the highway gave her the superhuman strength she needed. There was no way she was going down without a fight. Teeth clenched, her lips lifting away from them, she used her left shoulder, slamming heavily into Elson.

He woofed out a loud sound, his arms flailing outward like a windmill as she knocked him off his feet.

Her hand came forward and she jabbed.

Elson twisted.

Her knife slashed into his left upper arm, ripping through the T-shirt, blood flying as the point sank deep into his upper biceps.

Cursing, he landed on his ass, sprawling, yelling curses.

Tara turned, spun around and continued to run. She hadn't hurt him enough! A short blade like hers could never kill someone unless she got to his heart, and that had been impossible under the circumstances. She knew a blade could be turned aside when it met bone. Had she wounded him enough to stop him from chasing her?

Barely turning her head, she saw him sitting on the berm, utter shock in his face as he tried to stop the bleeding from his upper arm. His knife was sitting beside him on the highway.

Let a car come by! Winded, Tara pushed herself, the

dizziness making her weave unsteadily. Her vision blurred. And then it sharpened. Dammit! Her heart felt like it was going to leap out of her chest. The cool air tore by her as she continued to run as fast as she could. There was nowhere to hide. It was the flat of the valley floor. She could see half a mile ahead of her and there were no vehicles coming toward her. It was so early in the morning. No one was up and about yet.

Her breath was tearing out of her burning lungs. Her legs felt wobbly. She turned, looking back.

Elson was on his feet, picking up his knife. He was coming after her. This time, she saw murder in his face. If he caught her, he was going to kill her. There would be no mercy.

Helplessness, terror and knowing she was going to die roared through her as she heard his heavy footsteps approaching. For a split second, Tara thought of Harper, thought of his tenderness toward her. She'd never see him again. Never be able to tell him she loved him.

A blow came, striking her in the neck, hard.

Tara grunted. She was flung forward, flying off her feet, releasing the knife. Cree had struck her as hard as he could with his fist right between her shoulders, deliberately stunning her. Tara heard herself scream as the ground came roaring up at her.

And then . . . darkness . . .

"Charlie, is Tara at your store?" Harper's hand tightened around his cell phone. He stood in the broodmare barn. It was eight a.m. Something felt wrong to him and he couldn't explain the dread surrounding him. He'd decided to call Charlie because Tara wasn't answering her cell phone. That didn't make sense either; she always answered when he called her.

"No, she's not here, Harper. Why? Was she comin' to pick up that horse feed for the Bar C?"

"Yes, she was. She left at seven a.m. this morning. She should be there by now."

"Maybe she got a flat tire on the way here?" Charlie asked.

Grimly, Harper said, "She has her cell phone with her. She'd have called me." His mind spun. What the hell had happened to Tara? He tried to tamp down his wild emotional response, the fear starting to nip at him.

"Oh," Charlie said. "Gosh, Harper, I don't know. Can you get in your truck and come this way? Maybe she broke down on the side of the road? Maybe her cell phone isn't working?"

"I'll go find out, Charlie. Thanks for your help." Harper had no sooner clicked off on that call when another came in. It was Sheriff Sarah Carter calling. It felt like his stomach fell out of his body.

"Harper here," he answered, holding his breath.

"Harper, we just had a motorist along Highway 89 call in to say there was a truck accident and fire. We asked her for the license number and she gave it to us. It's your truck. Are you all right?"

Terror screamed through Harper. "Sarah, Tara was driving that truck to Charlie's to pick up some feed at seven this morning."

"The motorist called the fire department. I have a deputy on the way out there as well."

"I'm leaving now," he said. "Did the motorist see Tara?"

"No . . . the truck is fully engulfed in flames."

Harper violently slammed the door shut on his emotions. "Is the motorist there now?"

"Yes. She pulled up at a safe distance. But as she drove up, she saw a man dragging a woman with him into another truck. A rusted, red-and-white Ford, and he took off at high speed. He raced past her, heading north on 89."

Harper stood paralyzed for a second. "That's Cree Elson, Sarah. He's kidnapped Tara." The words came out low and tortured. His eyes blurred momentarily and he fought back the reaction. He was gripping his cell so hard he thought he was going to snap it in half.

Sarah's voice changed. "There's no positive ID yet, Harper. Why don't you drive to the scene? I'll meet you there. We have to figure this out."

"I'll tell Shay and Reese before I leave," he growled.

Harper didn't know what to do with his emotions. It was a quick fifteen-minute drive to where he saw the black, thick clouds of smoke rising from his overturned truck. The vehicle lay on its side far below the rocky slope. The fire department was there, quickly putting out the fire. He saw the motorist standing beside her car, spotted Sarah and the other deputy talking with the eye-witness. Pulling up behind a Toyota Camry, he quickly got out.

Sarah greeted him as he came up. "Good news. Tara is *not* in that truck of yours. Fire department just put out the fire and there's no body in the cab."

Nodding, Harper's gaze moved to the young woman.

"This is Cindy Long," Sarah said, "a tourist driving through. Let me tell you what she saw," and she launched into the details of the woman's report. Harper stood there, knowing full well it was Cree Elson who had rammed his truck to get to Tara. When Sarah mentioned a pool of blood on the berm that had soaked into the soil, it got Harper's attention.

"Blood?" he said, numbed by the thought it was from

Tara. Harper knew she wouldn't go down willingly to be kidnapped again by Elson.

"Yes," and Sarah pointed in the direction of where the blood was located. "My forensics team is on their way out here. They'll get samples. I found out from Taylor that Tara's blood is at her clinic, so we can quickly see if there's a match or not."

Mouth tight, Harper peered at the smoking remains of his truck. "Can you positively identify it was Elson?"

Sarah said, "I showed Cindy a photo of Elson and she said the man looked like him. She was about a quarter of a mile away when she saw what happened."

Harper looked at Cindy, who was short and slender, her face white, her eyes dark with worry. "Did you see the woman he had?"

"Y-yes . . . she was pretty tall and she was unconscious. He was dragging her along by her jacket. I couldn't believe it. I didn't know what to do," and she gave him a look of apology.

"You called us," Sarah told her gently. "You did the right thing, Cindy."

"Did you get a good look at the woman?" Harper asked again, trying to get more details. He wanted to scream but knew he couldn't.

"N-no, not really. I just saw her blond hair over the denim jacket she was wearing. I—I'm sorry, I wish I could tell you more, I really do."

Harper realized he was scaring the hell out of her. Reaching out, he briefly touched her tense shoulder. "No, you did fine, Cindy. We really appreciate your help."

"The woman? Tara? Is she your wife or something?" she asked Harper.

"Not my wife . . . but someone I love very much," he admitted, his voice rough with emotions.

"Well," Sarah told him, "I'm assuming it was Tara. I put out an Amber Alert already, Harper, along with her photo and Elson's photo. If he's on any major highway, someone will call us. It's not hard to identify a rusted red-and-white Ford pickup."

"Yeah," Harper rasped, taking the hat off his head, pushing his fingers through his dark hair, "but what if he takes a back road? There are so many of them in this valley."

Sarah nodded. She thanked Cindy and had her deputy finish up with the questions.

Taking Harper by the arm, she led him toward her cruiser, near the fire truck. "Listen," she told him, "we're moving ahead with this. As far as I'm concerned, unless proven otherwise, Elson rear-ended Tara's truck, throwing it off the road. There was a scuffle, because you can see deep toe prints dug into the berm. There are places along the berm for a quarter of a mile where there was a struggle. I'm hoping the blood belongs to Elson, but we can't be sure yet. I'm sorry."

Settling the cowboy hat on his head, he rasped, "What do you think Elson will do to her?"

"I don't know, Harper. I honestly don't. The fact there's blood on the berm," and she gestured toward the blackened truck down below them, "and he rammed her to stop and kidnap her? He's violent this time. The last kidnapping, he didn't hurt her until he had her in the cabin up in the mountains and she tried to escape. Then he struck her in the face, breaking her nose."

Swallowing hard several times, Harper wiped his thinned mouth. "What do we do now?"

"Pray that a motorist sees that pickup and calls our office. I have three other deputies on Highway 89 from Jackson Hole southward. If he's on that stretch, one of my deputies will see him and call it in."

Helplessly, Harper studied the serious-looking woman sheriff. She was competent and on top of things. For that, he was grateful. "What can I do, Sarah?"

She reached out, her hand on his slumped shoulder. "Go back to the Bar C. Wait to hear from me. Until we can locate Elson, we have no idea where she's at. I've alerted the Highway Patrol in Idaho, as well as Utah. All the information, the photos, are out to them. Everyone is on a manhunt for him and Tara. We just have to wait for a break, and that's the hardest damn thing in the world to do."

Chapter Seventeen

Harper sat with everyone from the Bar C around the wooden trestle table in Reese and Shay's kitchen. Everyone was grim. He saw the worry in their eyes. They sat with coffee in hand, the tension thick.

"We've decided not to tell Garret and Kira about this," Shay told them quietly. "They just started on their honeymoon. We want them to enjoy their time together."

"Yeah," Noah said, "because Garret would be back here in a flash if he knew what had happened."

"Kira wouldn't be far behind him," Dair muttered, frowning.

"For now," Reese said, "let them enjoy their happiness. I know they love Tara like a sister and they would be back here in a heartbeat."

"We still have no proof it was Tara who was taken," Noah said.

Harper knew his friend wanted to give everyone hope, so he didn't argue with him, but he knew without a doubt Tara had been kidnapped.

He moved the thick white ceramic mug slowly around between his hands, sitting opposite Dair and Noah. It had been an hour since Harper had returned to the Bar C, called a meeting and told them what had happened. They huddled together, as if feeling there was strength in the team being one at times like this, and Harper appreciated that. He knew there was so much daily work that needed to be done, but everyone was sitting with him until Sarah called with news. He could barely sit still. He wanted to do something—anything—to end this waiting. Tara was out there with Elson, who would hurt her, might kill her. The sour taste in his mouth turned bitter as he shut his mind off from going down the dark, haunted path of her being raped and murdered.

Shay sat nearest him and placed her hand on his forearm, "This is so hard on you, Harper."

Shrugging, he said, "We all knew Cree Elson was in the background, like a coyote circling his prey. We were aware that he might try to kidnap Tara again. At least she and I thought it was a possibility." He felt her fingers grow firmer around his arm, and he saw tears in Shay's blue eyes. He wanted to cry himself but didn't dare because if he started, he wouldn't stop.

Glumly, Shay whispered, "I know. . . . Reese and I talked about it, too. Elson is unstable. He's proven that over and over again."

"Probably all of us willed that thought away," Dair said. "None of us wanted to believe Elson would come after her again."

"We didn't want to think of it," Reese agreed. "Part of it is that the Bar C is a place of safety. We can let down here. Heal."

Harper swallowed hard and took a sip of his coffee, burning his tongue. There was no question his friends were just as deeply upset as he was.

The phone rang.

Harper jerked, snapping his head up, his gaze whipping

to the wall phone. Everyone at the table jumped, the tension tightening in the kitchen.

"You take it," Reese told him, gesturing toward the phone.

Quickly rising, Harper answered it.

"Sarah here. We've gotten a piece of luck. Cree Elson's truck was spotted going into Prater Canyon in the Salt Mountain Range. On a hunch, I called the Forest Service right after you left the scene, Harper. I asked one of the civilian employees who has an RV and parks out in the parking lot of different Forest Service camping sites to drive over to Prater Canyon. The reason I asked him to do that is because the first time Elson kidnapped Tara, he took her to a cabin up above Prater Canyon. I asked him to keep an eye out for Elson. I gave him a description of the truck and told him to keep his cell phone available in case he drove into that lot."

"And?" Harper growled.

"Elson came into the parking lot and he has Tara with him. My office assistant is sending photos to all your cell phones right now. The good news is that Tara's alive, but she's injured. One photo shows a lot of blood down her left temple and the side of her neck. Elson is wounded, too. He's got a bandanna wrapped around his upper left arm and there's blood down his left arm. Was Tara carrying a Buck knife on her? Most wranglers do."

"Yes," he breathed, "she was."

"That explains Elson's wound, then."

"What about her head wound? Was she walking okay?" Being a medic, Harper had to know.

"We think she got the injury when the truck flipped. Our contact, who's in his sixties, said she was walking but appeared dazed. Check your phones for those photos now."

Harper turned, his heart beating hard in his chest,

telling everyone to pull out their cell phones to look for the pictures. He went to the table and retrieved his and brought it back to the wall phone, picking the receiver back up. "I got the photos," and he zeroed in on them. Cree had tied Tara's wrists with rope in front of her. He was gripping her by her right arm, practically dragging her along. The man was wearing a dark green knapsack that probably weighed close to fifty pounds on his broad back. Harper felt his gut turn icy as he studied the photos. "He's got a pretty big knapsack."

"Yes, we think he's going to take her up into the canyon again, like he did before. There are several broken-down old log cabins up at seven and eight thousand feet. We believe he may choose one of them to hole up in with her."

"Which is why you set a lookout at the entrance to that canyon," Harper congratulated.

"Yes," Sarah said. "Cree isn't right in the head. He has brain damage. And my gut told me because of the circumstances, he was going to repeat the same pattern. And he has so far."

"What now? What do we do?"

"I'm getting a posse together, along with a SWAT team from the Teton County sheriff's department. Commander Tom Franks is helping us. They're a much bigger organization than we are. The Forest Service is bringing in horses by trailer. They'll arrive at the canyon in another hour. There's an ex-military drone pilot who works with us coming into the office, and he'll be traveling with us to the site. We'll all be there shortly. He's going to fly the drone into the areas where I think Cree is taking Tara. If we can locate him with a drone, that will save a lot of man-hours of trying to find him by horseback and on foot patrol."

"Yes," Harper rasped, "that will be a great help. What can we do?"

"Nothing. Just stay where you are, Harper. I know you want to come, but you can't. You're not trained."

He snorted. "It's fine that everyone at the Bar C stays here, but I'm sure as hell *not* going to wait with them. I'm coming to meet you at the canyon whether you like it or not. I was in combat, Sarah. I've had years of black ops in Afghanistan. You *want* me there. I can be of help with strategy and tactics. I'll bring my paramedic bag with me, too. Someone could get hurt."

"I knew you wouldn't sit this out."

"Hell no. I'll meet you there."

"Don't do anything, Harper, once you arrive. Wait for us, okay?"

"I'll wait," he promised roughly.

Tara struggled to keep up. Cree had bound her wrists with a cotton rope and he had strung about eight feet between them, the other end attached to his belt as she walked behind him. He'd taken her watch off her, searched her for a cell phone and found none. She'd barely stood his hands frisking her, lingering at her breasts, her butt and then her thighs. It had sent a shiver of dread so deep within her that she wanted to scream. But he was wounded, losing blood, and he was in a foul mood. His eyes looked half-crazed, just as they'd been the last time he'd kidnapped her. That look scared her more than anything else. It made Cree unpredictable. Explosive. One minute he could be nice, but the wrong tone of voice, the wrong expression on her face, would send him into an uncontrolled rage. That was how her nose had gotten broken that first time. She'd asked for some water because she'd been dying of thirst.

She struggled on the steep mountain that was taking them to near the eight-thousand-foot level. They were above the canyon now and on the slope. Unused to such hard, constant hiking, she was breathing heavily. So was Cree. Blood was still leaking from where she'd sunk the blade up to its hilt into his upper biceps. He'd forced her to tie a dark green neckerchief above the wound to create something like a tourniquet. It didn't stop all the bleeding; fresh red blood was constantly dripping down to his elbow and then dropping off into the pine needles beneath their feet.

The calves of her legs were starting to cramp; she wanted to ask him to stop so she could rest, but she knew him well enough to be sure he had a destination in mind. Cree was big, strong and in good shape, so he doggedly kept going up the deeply forested area. Her mind turned to wondering if anyone had seen them after the crash. She recalled a gray Toyota driving up to the scene as Cree dragged her, semiconscious, toward his truck. She couldn't call for help because she was barely aware, except to register a silver-looking car had stopped. Had the person seen them? Had they called 911? What if they hadn't? How would Harper or Sarah at the sheriff's department know their whereabouts? It all seemed so hopeless to Tara.

"Hurry up!" Cree snapped, barely turning his head, glaring at her, giving the rope a jerk.

"I need to rest, please!" Tara knew she didn't dare get too bossy with him or he'd hit her. She'd been young, angry, scared and foolish the first time he'd kidnapped her. Now, she was older and more mature. Cree was emotionally imbalanced and she felt if she looked at him the wrong way, he'd unexpectedly attack her. She worried about him raping her. Tara knew he'd try to sooner or later. An icy sliver of terror coursed through her. He was limping and she guessed it was because she'd kicked him squarely in the balls. It gave her a tiny bit of satisfaction.

Cree suddenly halted.

Tara nearly crashed into him, stumbling, dizzy and collapsed onto the pine-needle floor, landing on her hands and knees.

He removed the rope from his belt and tied it around a branch just above Tara's head. "You need to drink water," he muttered. Looking warily around, he shrugged out of the heavy pack and set it at his booted feet. Grabbing a quart of water, he thrust it toward her. "Drink your fill. I want you alive."

Looking up at him, seeing the hatred mixed with so many other emotions she couldn't even begin to interpret, Tara gratefully took the water bottle. When their fingers touched, she jerked her hand back. His glare intensified.

"Can't stand me touching you?" he jeered, pushing the plastic bottle into her hand. Straightening, he added, "Get over it."

Drinking deeply, Tara knew she had to remain hydrated. Even though she was still terribly dizzy and her head wound ached, screaming at her like an unrelenting banshee, she continued to look for ways to escape. She saw no pistol and no rifle on the outside of Cree's massive pack. That didn't mean he didn't have one inside it, however. Water dribbled down her chin as she continued to gulp it down.

She winced when he grabbed the bottle out of her hands.

"That's enough. Don't be a selfish bitch. I need some, too."

He pressed the bottle to his lips, tipping his head back, drinking the last half of the contents. Wiping his mouth afterward, he stashed the empty bottle in the knapsack, drawing out another full one and placing it in a side net pocket.

Tara sat there, leaning back on her boot heels, grateful for the rest. She glanced around. Up above them was a rocky slope where the pine trees were thinning out because of the high altitude. Above that area it was nothing but bare rock and a lot of snow that had yet to melt. She figured they must be somewhere around eight thousand feet and that they were on the tallest mountain in the valley. They'd already passed up the old, broken cabin where Cree had taken her captive and kept her before. She wondered where he was taking her this time.

The pine needles were dry, and that meant they'd be slippery, tough to run across and hard to keep her balance on—at least what little she had left. Did anyone know where she was? Assuming they didn't, Tara realized she had to get out of this on her own. There was no way to rely on help, even though she secretly longed to know that Harper and those who loved her were out searching for her right now. Would Sarah realize Cree was repeating his actions? If she did, she'd have someone in place to search Prater Canyon.

Tara had glimpsed an RV sitting off in one corner of the parking lot, which had made her hope whoever was in it had seen them. The fact that Cree had tied her hands in front of her before they left the cab of his truck should tell anyone in the RV that something was wrong. Had anyone seen them, though? If they had, had they called 911? Tara tried not to let her spirits rise because the person in that vehicle could have been asleep and not seen them at all. Her hope deflated.

"Let's get going," he snarled at her, hauling the knapsack onto his shoulders, settling it against his back.

Judging by the sun, it had to be around ten a.m. Tara

sorely missed her watch. Taking her time, her muscles protesting, she placed her hands against the trunk of the tree to steady herself as she stood on weak knees.

Cree approached her and she tensed, watching him without any trust. His red hair was badly mussed, some of it escaping from the ponytail. His beard was at least three days old, emphasizing his narrow, gaunt features. He didn't seem as out of sorts as before, more focused and, therefore, steadier emotionally, she hoped.

Untying the rope, he looped it around the left side of his belt and retied it.

"Cree, you don't have to do this," she said, keeping her voice calm, watching him glance in her direction. "You could let me go. I wouldn't press charges. Just let me go."

He snorted and stood there, hands on his hips, studying her. "You don't get it, do you?"

"I guess I don't."

"You're *mine*. You've always been mine. This time, I'm not letting you go." He wagged his finger in her face. "You try to escape this time and I'll do more than bust your nose. Understand?"

He was insane. Obsessed and insane. "I'll never be yours, Cree. Not *ever*," she hissed, tensing, waiting for him to strike her.

A twisted smile came to his lips. "We'll see. Over time, you'll come to appreciate me. I'll be good to you, Tara. You'll see. Now, come on. We gotta make that old salt mine before noon. They're gonna start hunting parties soon enough, lookin' for us."

Blinking, Tara's mind spun with that information. The Salt Mountains got their name precisely because the Native Americans had found salt in certain places within the mountain range. As she slipped on the pine needles, she caught herself, straightened and moved up the slope, knees protesting. Tara dug into her memory. At one time, there had been a couple of mines built by prospectors in the range. Salt was expensive and always in demand. Even though it didn't command gold prices, it was called white gold by the prospectors-turned-businessmen in the area. The salt that came out of these mines had made them rich. Until the vein ran out. Tara was aware there was an old salt mine near nine thousand feet above Prater Canyon, but she'd never been to it, only heard about it from her father.

Maybe Cree had learned his lesson in keeping her in a run-down old log cabin. It had been an obvious place that law enforcement who had hunted for her had first checked out. Now, Cree had upped the ante. Would anyone think about that old salt mine? Tara doubted it. She'd lived here the first eighteen years of her life and never visited the historic mine, which was now shut down. It had run out of salt in 1900 and quickly fallen into disrepair, essentially forgotten by people of the twenty-first century. She wondered if it was even on the Forest Service maps. Certainly, a regional topography map would have it.

Maybe . . .

Was that his objective? His new hideout? Tara hadn't been in any mines, so she had no awareness of what it was like to be there. Moving her eyes first one way and then the other, she tried not to let Cree know she was looking for an escape route. Every once in a while, he'd turn his head, catch sight of her and then turn away, focused on the ever-steepening slope in front of them. Wanting to search the sky, Tara didn't dare as the woods began to thin out more and more. They would be easy to spot from the air now, a lot of ground between each tree. Keying her hearing, she found no noise except for the call of birds every now and then.

She tried to keep her imagination leashed. She had to

focus, instead, on escape. Already she'd spotted several good-size downed limbs. Could she scoop one up without Cree seeing her do it and hit him over the head, knocking him unconscious? Tara shivered at the thought of him catching her in the act. She was sure he'd come unhinged and kill her with the knife he carried in a sheath.

Her mind turned at a thousand miles an hour, looking at every possible escape route. She'd gone through two weeks of evasion training because she'd been a combat photographer. There had been many times when she'd been out with black-ops groups that she'd learned stealth at a much higher level. How to hide in plain sight. How to evade. To be patient. Take her time and survey every possible weapon that might be of use to her survival. And right now? Those pine limbs all over the floor of the forest were her primary weapon.

For an instant, Tara felt fear of dying. She'd come so close so many times before and cheated death. But would she this time? She didn't know. On the heels of that fear serrating her came an overwhelming love that she'd quietly developed for Harper. She loved him. Miserably, as she scrambled up and over some rocks, cutting her fingers, she couldn't stop the grief over the loss of him. Would she ever see Harper again? Or would he find her beaten and dead? Her heart tore and a soft sob broke from her lips. She bowed her head, tears stinging her eyes. Above all, she couldn't let Cree see her this way! She just couldn't. Battling back all those grief-stricken emotions, needing Harper so badly right now, needing his arms around her to make her feel safe once more, came like an avalanche over Tara.

Staggering, she dragged in a deep breath, shoving everything down, down, down within her. She'd had to do this in combat, too. It was no easier now than it was then.

In some villages, children had been kidnapped out of homes, the mothers screaming and crying, begging her team to find the kidnappers. Bring their children home. It was a refrain she'd heard too often, and the one that gutted her as nothing else ever would. Taliban were stealing the children to sell to sex traffickers waiting near the Afghan-Pakistani border. Those children would be taken across to Pakistan, never to be seen again. The money would be spent on weapons to rearm the Taliban.

Tara had identified with them too easily because Cree had stolen her from her home, too. And he'd tried to have sex with her, but she'd fought him off and wouldn't let him touch her. Those children weren't in that position. They were too small, too weak to defend themselves against such sexual monsters. Shivering inwardly, Tara tried to push away all the ugly memories she'd had to deal with in Afghanistan too many times. Now, it was here again.

Again.

Once more, she was pursued. Hatred rose up in her as she watched Cree balance the heavy backpack against the challenges of the slope ahead of them. He could easily outmuscle her, no question. And he would. Sooner or later, he would. Her mind turned into a chain saw, tearing into her fear, releasing it. The way he looked at her made her stomach turn with nausea. Like those poor Afghan children, she, too, was going to be turned into nothing more than a sex slave, owned by a brutal male. In the end, Tara knew it was about power over a woman or child fueling the sick male.

She'd never forgotten Cree's mother, Roberta. She'd grown up with her father discussing some of the permissible information about the cases that passed through his court. At least once a year, for as long as she could remember, Roberta would press charges against her husband, Brian, who was a drunkard and a drug addict. When he wasn't high on drugs, he was a brutal animal, beating up on her and her four sons. Brian Elson was well known for being an ugly drunk. Everyone in Wind River Valley steered clear of him when he drank at the local bar. She tried to feel sorry for Cree but couldn't. Had his father sexually traumatized him? It was entirely possible. Tara remembered her mother saying sadly, one night at the dinner table, that Cree was "little more than Brian's punching bag."

Chapter Eighteen

Harper waited impatiently for Sarah to gather everyone so they could plan a strategy to find Elson and Tara. It was nearly noon, the overhead sun bright, the temperature in the seventies and climbing in Prater Canyon. There were ten USFS horse trailers, two animals in each, saddled, with rangers standing nearby, ready to hunt down Elson.

The most crucial part in this whole plan was Terry Larson, who was the drone driver. He was with one of Sarah's volunteer deputies. Terry's son, Josh, sixteen, was assigned to watching on a Mac laptop for anything the high-flying drone could see far above Prater Canyon. Harper had hesitantly left the milling group and went to look over Josh's left shoulder, peering intently into the picture being sent back by the drone.

He wanted things to move a lot faster. Noah and Reese joined him, intently watching the screen of the laptop with him. They had loaded up their own ranch horses, were already saddled, waiting in their four-horse trailer off to the south side of the parking lot. They had deliberately parked far from the law enforcement effort and trailers, wanting to stay out of the way. Harper knew the rangers wouldn't share any of their horses with them. That was fine with him. Nearby, he could see the glacier-fed river, that milky, opaque green color that started up high, around thirteen thousand feet in the Salt Range, where it wound down one side of Prater Canyon.

Eventually, the deep-flowing water would empty out into the Snake River, which ran about half a mile farther down from the canyon opening. He glanced over to see Noah and Reese intently studying what the drone camera was videotaping. The drone was at ten thousand feet and Terry, who was in his forties, promised everyone Cree wouldn't hear it if he was in the vicinity. Besides, at that altitude, it gave the drone a much wider range of visibility to spot Cree.

How badly Harper wanted confirmation that Cree had Tara captive and was somewhere far above them. The back of his neck prickled, a warning that his intuition was right. The drone had already checked the two broken-down cabins at seven and eight thousand feet, with no sign of life around either of them. Sarah looked disappointed about that intel. Larson told her there was an old, abandoned salt mine at nine thousand feet. As a kid, he'd played up near that mine and said that often, during his high school days, boys would hike up there to drink beer. But that was a long time ago. He was sending his drone to check it out.

Sarah had asked the head ranger to bring over the topographical map of the area, and they spread it open on the asphalt parking lot, all of them kneeling around it, looking closely at all the lines drawn, trying to locate the ancient salt mine.

Larson couldn't help because he was flying the drone. The river that flowed up in the Salt Range paralleled the route to the salt mine, so he used it as a natural guide as he stood near his son, dividing his attention between flying the drone and looking at the camera footage on the laptop. Father and son were a good team, and Harper was grateful they'd volunteered to help find Tara.

Sarah had the captain of the SWAT team, the head of the regional USFS, her six deputies convene. She worked with them to lay out a plan of action once they got confirmation from the drone whether Cree had been spotted. There was no sense sending anyone on horseback up above the canyon unless they could verify Tara and Elson were there.

Harper tried to hold on to his shredding patience.

"We found them!" Larson called out excitedly to the assembled group huddled around the topo map.

Josh straightened, his grin wide as he pointed triumphantly to the laptop. He gave his dad a thumb's-up.

Instantly, Harper was bent over the laptop, squeezing in between Reese and Noah. Shading his eyes, he could see two stick-like figures moving between the trees. "Where are they?" he demanded of Larson.

"At about eighty-five hundred feet and right in line to get to the salt mine," Larson said, a congratulatory grin across his mouth.

"Can Elson hear your drone?" Harper demanded. More people crowded around them, everyone wanting to catch a look at the computer screen.

"No. I have a very quiet drone because I do a lot of close-up commercial footage of wild animals. Elson will never hear it until it gets within five hundred feet of where he's standing."

Anxiously, Harper got down on one knee, his hand on the back of Josh's metal chair in front of the table where the laptop sat. His heart amped up and he felt shaky inside as he saw Larson begin to orient the camera toward them for a much closer look. In moments, the zoom lens showed

Cree. Fear and joy swept through Harper as he saw Tara looking well enough. She was on an eight-foot leash, the white cotton rope strung between her tied wrists in front of her and the loop of the rope at the rear of Cree's belt as he struggled with the rockier, steep slope ahead of them.

"What's she doing?" Josh asked, turning toward Harper.

Scowling, Harper moved closer. He saw Tara lifting her bonds, chewing on them with her teeth as she made sure she walked directly behind Cree, the huge pack hiding his ability to see what she was doing. "She's trying to untie the knot with her teeth," Harper guessed.

"But why?" Josh wondered. "If Elson finds out . . ."

Harper didn't need him to finish his thought. Scanning the video, he saw the river no more than fifteen feet away from where they were climbing. The river was damned icy cold, glacier-fed, deep, fast and at least a hundred feet wide. A little farther down from where they were located was a thirty-foot waterfall. Terror started leaking through him. Before he could speak, Reese leaned over.

"I think she's trying to get free and then she'll run to the river and jump in to try to escape him, Harper."

Dread filled him. "Jesus," he whispered, "she's willing to go over the falls? The water's so damned cold that hypothermia will set in within five minutes. She could drown even if she survives the thirty-foot fall." Worse, she could strike a rock on the way down, or break her leg in the pool below. So many bad things could happen to Tara, it knotted his stomach.

Reese studied the situation. "That's my hunch," he said, giving Harper a worried look. "Where else can she go? She can't outrun Elson. She has no other way to protect herself."

Pointing at the screen, Harper said, "No, those branches on the ground are baseball bat in size and length. She could grab one of them. Maybe that's her plan. Get her hands freed, grab one of those and coldcock Elson, knock him unconscious. Then run, following the river down to Prater Canyon."

Nodding, Reese said, "That's another possible plan." He rubbed his jaw, worry in his tone. "Either way, it's risky as hell."

"Tara would try to escape," Harper said grimly. "She's been trained in escape and evasion tactics in the military. She's not going to meekly go to slaughter. That's not in her DNA." He buttonholed Reese. "I'm taking my horse and heading up in that direction. I'm not waiting for law enforcement to get saddled up."

Reese looked at Noah. "We've got two-way radios on all of us. Harper and I are going to take off to try to get up and reach her." Grimly, he looked at the gathered group around the sheriff. "Let's just quietly leave on horseback and move toward the river."

Harper nodded. "Good idea. There's a lot of brush and trees at the far end of this canyon that hides the trail climbing up and out of it. They'll never know we left."

Noah said, "Get going. I'll stay here and work with Josh and Terry to keep you two apprised of any changes."

Now, all of Harper's anxiety melted as he and Reese casually walked back to their horse trailer, which was parked farthest away from the assembled group. It would be easy to mount up and ride at a walk toward the river, half a mile away. Even better? The land sloped downward near the end of the parking lot so that if any of the law enforcement types saw them leave, they'd see them heading south, not up into the canyon. It was a sleight-of-hand tactic, and he saw Reese grinning like a wolf as they walked to the trailer.

As they disappeared around the four-horse trailer,

Reese opened the front of the trailer, pulling out two rifles and handing one to Harper. "Put this in Socks' sheath."

"Got it," Harper agreed, taking the .30-06. He placed a cartridge into the breech, then put the rifle on safety. If they needed firepower, they wouldn't have time to load a bullet into the chamber.

"Black-ops time," Reese said, setting his rifle aside. He reached into a box and handed Harper a black nylon holster with a Glock 18 in it. "One for you and one for me. Here's a Kevlar vest. It's holding two more magazines."

Satisfied, Harper quickly pulled on the heavy, camo-colored vest. In front were two magazines for the Glock, plus pouches for the bullets for the .30-06. They weren't going after Cree Elson without adequate firepower. "We'll use the slope to cover our progress to the other end of the canyon, then slip into the woods where the trail leading up and out of it is located."

Reese nodded, hauling on the vest. "Roger that."

"Damn good thing we've all been in black ops. Makes this mission easier to pull off."

"Yeah," Reese said. "Let's get Socks and Ghost unloaded and then leave quietly like the shadows we are. Once we get below that slope, we're trotting all the way to that canyon trail. It's a hard climb for the horses and I don't want to wear them out too soon."

"Copy that," Harper agreed, going to the tailgate and flipping open the handles so the ramp came down. The horses were already saddled and ready to go. Their bridles were hanging on the saddle horn, and as soon as the horses backed out, Harper and Reese would slip the bridles on over their halters, mount and take off.

Harper tried to keep his worry under control. Tara was trying to escape the only way she knew how. And this law enforcement group was moving too slowly to help her if she succeeded.

Mounting Socks, Harper watched Reese easily slip into the saddle of Ghost, his usual wrangling mount at the ranch. Nodding to his boss, they clucked to their mounts, keeping the huge, long trailer as a wall between them and the group on the other side of the parking lot. They would use it to hide their escape. No one would see them leave and that was a good thing. Harper's heart wouldn't settle down. He loved Tara. And he hadn't told her. His leather-gloved hand tightened around the reins for a moment. If only he'd told Tara. If only . . .

Tara gnawed on the cotton rope with her teeth, her gaze always on Cree's back. If he turned around to check on her, she couldn't be caught doing this. She had to escape! Without her wrists free, she was helpless. Her heart was pounding heavily in her chest. She divided her attention between the rocks, the slippery dry pine needles on the ground beneath her feet and trying to ease the knot open. Breathing hard, she saw the forest was thinning out more and more as they continued to climb to nearly nine thousand feet.

Cree was breathing rapidly as well, his hiking pace slowing. They had been pushing hard and fast. Even he was tiring. Up ahead, Tara peered at a huge black butte where there was a lot of dirt on the surrounding slope consisting of disturbed rock and soil.

Her mind clicked off variables. The river was as close as it ever had been because he'd angled toward it, the ground a little smoother, a little less rocky. Far above them, she could hear the roar of another waterfall, but she couldn't see it yet. They had just passed a lower falls area minutes earlier. Tara knew the heavy snowpack above them, as it melted, flowed down this water course every year and into the Snake River, far below. The water was always a milky, light green color, indicating it was glacier melt runoff.

She kept searching on the ground for a pine limb that would be the right size for her purposes. The closer she could get to one, the better. Should she be able to slip free of her bonds, she had to make a split-second decision. Either a limb was nearby or it wasn't. If it was? She was going to grab it, hit Cree over the head and knock him out. There was danger to the plan because if he saw her move suddenly to sweep up a nearby limb, he could turn on her, and then her surprise advantage was gone. Tara knew he could easily overpower her strength-wise. And he'd draw his knife. Or, worse, he might throw the knife at her and injure or kill her if he was any good. She just didn't know.

The choices weren't good ones. But she had to try to escape. Her saliva soaked into the ropes as she hurriedly gnawed and tugged at the knot. It was loosening! Heart amping up, feeling like it would rip out of her chest or that Cree would hear it, Tara kept her gaze fixed on him. Anxiety washed through her. The other choice on her plate made her gut clench. Once she was free, she would run for the river, jump in and swim as hard as she could to the other side, hoping Cree wouldn't follow her. She had no idea how good a swimmer he was. Did he have a pistol hidden in his pack? If he did, he'd have to run after her, get the pack off his back, then find the weapon before he could start shooting at her. How good a shot was he anyway? Again, Tara had no clue.

Because of her military evasion and escape training, she knew the glacier-fed water would sap her internal body heat within five minutes of entering it. And then she'd start floundering, carried downstream by the swift, hidden current toward that lower waterfall. And if she couldn't get to the other bank within that critical five minutes, she could die either from hypothermia or being swept over the rocky waterfall. It was a thirty-foot drop. High enough to kill a person. Tara swallowed against her tightened throat, gnawing more quickly at the rope, feeling the knot loosening with every tug of her teeth.

She swiftly gazed around her, not finding a big enough limb close enough for her to grab. That meant she had to run for the river. Oh, God, what if she drowned? What if Cree caught up to her before she could jump into the river? Tara knew she would die. He wouldn't tolerate her leaving him again. He'd kill her for sure.

For that next minute, Tara tried to focus, tried not to allow her frantic emotions and fear of dying to blot out her thinking. The one thing she regretted the most in her life was that she'd never confided in Harper that she'd fallen in love with him. Her heart cringed with anguish and she made a soft, grunting sound, feeling the bonds loosening rapidly around her wrists. Circulating blood poured into the whitened flesh around her wrists, causing her excruciating pain for a moment. It kept her focused and she wriggled her fingers, willing feeling and life back into them.

Her only escape was the river because there were no limbs nearby.

Tara wanted so badly to live, to see Harper again. To see her parents. To live her life.

Why had it come down to this terrible moment?

She watched Cree's head movement, praying he wouldn't turn at this moment. She rapidly got rid of the bonds, falling to the ground, dragging behind him. Without a sound, Tara turned, digging the toes of her boots into the hard, rocky soil. Everything slowed down for her. She wanted to run directly toward the river, keeping Cree's back in alignment with her escape route. When he turned around, he'd see she was gone. He normally didn't look for ten or so minutes at a time. The wind tore past her as she sprinted, leaping over downed branches, not wanting to make noise to get his attention.

Let me live, let me live. . . . It was a litany in her head, pounding into her temples. She tried to run smart. Tried not to step on anything that would make a sound.

The river was less than a hundred feet away.

"*You bitch!*"

Elson's scream pummeled Tara's ears. She automatically ducked her head and cringed, her speed increasing.

Run! Run!

She had to make it to the water!

Tara tripped over an unseen limb hidden by pine needles. She went flying.

Hitting the bank of the river with an *oomph*, Tara was dazed for a second. Adrenaline shot through her.

Scrambling to her hands and knees, which were bruised and bleeding because of the jagged, hidden rocks around her, she jerked a look toward her pursuer.

Cree Elson was racing toward her. His face was black with fury, his knife drawn in his fist.

He was going to kill her.

And then Elson's charge toward her suddenly stopped.

Tara sat up, scrambling to her feet as she watched the rope dragging from the back of his pack and get tangled around a small pine tree. He was yanked backward off his feet. The knife flew out of his hand.

Run!

Leaping in midair and turning, Tara headed for the

milky-green waters of the wide river. This was her only chance to escape!

Elson was cursing, turning, yanking on the rope to try to free himself from around the pine tree.

Without hesitation, her boots on, she leaped feetfirst into the water, clearing the bank by five feet.

The cold water shocked her. Tara was instantly dragged below the surface.

She felt the powerful pull of the current like invisible hands grasping at her. She twisted, kicking out. She only had five minutes before the hypothermia began to slow her muscles and she could drown.

Head popping up to the surface, she yanked a look back. Her intake of breath was noisy and raspy. Elson was shedding the pack, cursing loudly, and she saw him draw out a pistol. He was going to shoot her. Tara felt a spur of dread, turning, striking out strongly toward the opposite shore. The water splashed and she felt her heart sinking as the downward pull of the water continued. Her boots filled with water, and the added weight made it three times harder to remain on the surface. The bank was fifty feet away.

She was being carried swiftly downstream.

Now, her whole focus was the waterfall coming up. Terror shot through her. A little sound of panic escaped her contorted lips as she struggled to aim for the other bank.

She'd misjudged the current.

Oh, God!

Frantic, Tara saw the rocks jutting up where the waterfall began.

No! Oh, no! I can't go over it!

Her hands were numb. She couldn't feel anything, the icy coldness of the water seeping quickly into her vulnerable body. Her legs felt like concrete dragging her down, and she heard Cree screaming at her, but his voice was drowned out by the roar of the approaching falls.

Tara lunged forward, kicking with all her might. The boots were so heavy! Water washed over her, blinding her momentarily. The current seemed to increase in speed the closer she got to being pulled over.

No! No!

She had no training for being swept over a cataract. She had no idea how to survive it. Or if she could.

The rocky bank loomed before her, filled with wet, glistening rocks as the current eddied and swirled madly just above the falls.

Help me! Help me!

Tara felt her entire body going numb because of the coldness of the water. Hypothermia was setting in. Stretching, her fingers gleaming with water as she sluggishly thrust it above the surface, she clawed frantically at a passing rock sticking out of the side of the bank.

The waterfall was only thirty feet away.

Her speed toward it was increasing.

It felt as if invisible, powerful currents were tugging at her weary legs and boots, pulling her out toward the center of the river once more.

Tara cried out, making another lunging attempt. If she didn't make it this time, she was going to be swept over the falls.

Everything slowed down to a painful crawl for Tara. Her widened gaze was riveted on a rock ten feet away from her. She was only twenty feet away from the falls. It was a long, wet, black rock. It almost looked like a hand being offered to her. But her fingers had already slipped off the other rock because there was no purchase. Everything was slippery.

Kicking with the last of her strength, grunting with effort, the roar of the waterfall surrounded her. The white-water curled, bubbled and eddied at the top.

She cried out, giving one last try to grab that rock on the bank.

Her fingers clawed and grasped at its sharp, roughened surface. Desperate, Tara felt her strength ebbing, felt her legs not working right. She was hypothermic. Her mind was beginning to wander.

Harper! I love you! I love—

The current ripped her fumbling hand off the rock.

She was going over.

Screaming, she twisted, feeling as if she were swimming in peanut butter. At the last second, she oriented herself feetfirst toward the falls.

It was almost instinctive to cross her arms against her chest, her boots facing the roiling, swirling falls, and she was carried with unbelievable speed toward the center of the river. The powerful current pushed Tara between two huge rocks and then she shot outward.

One second and she was in the water.

The next second she was sailing through the air, her arms and legs flailing.

The cry she heard was her own.

Everything was in excruciatingly slow motion. Tara felt like she was heading toward that round, circular pool below. Her mind blanked out as she was whipped by spray, her gaze momentarily blinded. Her whole focus, her whole life, riveted on that beautiful, blue-green pool below, racing up toward her. It looked so calm beyond, where the water fell at one end of it. She was flying. The wind slapped against her face. The spray felt like stinging ice crystals against her face. Her boots were below her and she was dropping fast. What seemed like a long, torturous minute took only seconds.

Tara hit the water hard. Her body plunged deep, deep down into the pool, her feet and lower legs taking the brunt of the contact. She felt pain in the soles of her feet, her ankles and then her knees, the water closing in over the top of her head, burying her beneath the surface, and yet she still continued downward. Opening her eyes, all she saw was cloudy green, milky-looking water surrounding her.

Lungs feeling as if they would burst, she felt herself slowing her downward plunge. Lifting her arms weakly above her head, she twisted onto her stomach, heading for the sunlit surface above her. It was barely a glow, not light, because of the cloudiness of the water.

The surface seemed so far away. She needed to take a breath of air.

No! She couldn't! She'd drown!

Her chest ached. Her lungs felt as if they were on fire as she kicked erratically, trying to propel herself to the surface. Would she make it in time? Or not?

Tara didn't know. Closing her eyes, she began to release the air in her aching lungs, the bubbles racing toward the surface as she floundered and weakly fought to rise. The need to draw in a breath was nearly overwhelming. If she did, she'd fill her lungs with water and die.

The last thought she had was that Harper would never know she'd fallen in love with him.

Chapter Nineteen

Harper pushed his quarter horse up a steep dirt-and-rock path. They'd just reached the top of the canyon. Socks was breathing hard, his fur wet, his mane, short, sticking to his neck as he powered his way upward, his hindquarters pumping hard like pistons. Right behind him was Reese on Ghost. They were both listening to the almost constant soft voice of Josh as he watched the video of his father bringing the drone within two thousand feet of where Tara and Elson were hiking.

Taking off his gloves, Harper jammed them down in his back pocket as Reese came alongside him on the top. Somewhere, two thousand feet above them, was the woman he loved. Would he get to her in time? His throat ached with so much tension it felt like a hard lump was stuck in it.

Reese also shed his gloves. He leaned down as the horses snorted and took off at a fast walk. "We're about half a mile from them."

"Yeah," Harper managed, his voice ragged with worry.

Reese pulled out the .30-06 from the leather sheath, placed a round in the chamber, the safety off. "Let me go ahead. Elson is armed with a pistol and a rifle. And he's carrying a knife. If something happens, I want you to focus on getting to Tara. I'll take care of Elson."

Grimly, Harper nodded. Reese had been a company commander. He'd led 120 Marines in Afghanistan on three yearlong deployments, often working with black-ops groups of SEALs and Delta Force as well as recon Marines. "You got it." He automatically touched the Glock resting in a nylon holster on his thigh. Only a safety strap kept it in the holster, and it was locked and loaded, the safety off. "Good plan," he said, urging Socks into a ground-eating trot.

"If we can intercept them," Reese said, "we could save Tara from having to try to escape."

"Sounds good." Never had Harper wanted anything more than that. He loved Tara. God, how he wanted the chance to tell her that to her face. If only . . . if only he could—

"Tara escaped!" Josh shouted into their earpieces. "She's dropped her ropes, turned and is heading directly for the river!"

Instantly, both cowboys laid their heels into their sweaty, hard-breathing mounts. Harper took the lead, Socks' nose stretched out, nostrils flaring, ears back as he pushed the quarter horse to its limit. There was a long slope, peppered with pine trees, and Harper gripped his galloping horse with his legs, pushing him in that direction at top speed. They wove in and around pine trees, and as they thinned, Harper got his first sight of Cree Elson. He had tripped and fallen, the rope that had captured Tara earlier twisted around a small pine tree.

Jerking his head to the right, he spotted Tara, but it was too late. She'd jumped into the frigid waters of the river, disappearing. He hauled Socks to a halt, the horse nearly sitting down on his hindquarters, sliding to an abrupt stop.

His gaze never left Tara as he watched her struggle against an unseen current.

"I'll get Elson," Reese yelled, galloping past him.

"I'm going down to the pool below," Harper called, whipping Socks around. The horse spun easily, lifting his front legs and pivoting.

"She's going to go over the falls!!" Josh cried.

Harper choked as he headed down the slope, Socks flying at top speed.

Above him, he heard Cree yelling Tara's name. And then, he heard gunfire.

Torn for a split second, Harper had to let Reese handle the situation, no matter what happened. His gaze clung to the top of the falls. Three quarters of the way down the slope, heading Socks toward the pool below, he saw Tara being spit out by the river, shot out like a cannon at the top of the massive, roaring falls.

Her scream made him want to sob out her name. The wind whipped by him, the horse thundering in and around the pines, the air burning his eyes, making them water. He saw her pitched outward by the swift current, arms and legs flailing. To his relief, he saw her miss a jutting rock sticking out just below the falls by inches.

His whole life, his heart, his soul, focused on her righting herself, positioning her entry feetfirst into the pool below. Harper didn't know how Tara did it, but she did. He pulled his horse to a halt, Socks skidding in the dried pine needles and grass near the bank of the pool. Leaping off, Harper watched as Tara plunged downward. The terror on her face tore at him.

Throwing off his hat, yanking off his boots and tearing the heavy vest off his upper body, as well as ridding himself of the holster, he dove into the quiet, lapping pool.

Tara hit the water just as he dove in, the water feeling like a punch to his jaw, shockingly cold.

Tara disappeared instantly beneath the surface. Stroking out toward her, each length made by his long, corded arms, took him closer and closer to where she'd been. Harper kept up the hard, cutting splashes through the water. Where was she? Where? His heart shattered as he thought of her losing consciousness as she hit the water. If she had? She'd breathe in water and die.

No! No! I love her. God, let me get to her in time. Let me—

Tara suddenly bobbed to the surface five feet away from him.

She was unconscious.

With a supreme effort, Harper lunged, grabbing her, sliding one arm beneath her left armpit and across her chest. He brought her against his shoulder, her head lolling to one side, her arms floating listlessly.

"Tara!" he gasped, turning on his back, kicking like hell, trying to get back to the shallower water. "Tara! Wake up! Wake up!" His voice was hoarse, terror-filled. He divided his attention between stroking outward with his right arm and how close he was coming to the shore. Looking up, he didn't see Reese. He didn't know what was going on up above the falls.

It was impossible to think. All he could do was feel. Tara was like sawdust, unresponsive, her face the color of white marble. He saw blood on her left temple, realizing that was the wound she'd sustained before going over the falls.

Suddenly, Tara jerked and began to cough violently. Her arms flew upward and she began to fight him.

"Tara, you're okay," he rasped, tightening his grip around her chest. "Stay still. I'll get you to land in a second. . . ."

Harper heard her gagging. She vomited water, trying to listen to his orders but dazed, barely conscious.

His feet hit the sandy bottom. Instantly, Harper stood and then hauled Tara backward, wanting to get her out of the freezing water as swiftly as possible. By the time he'd dragged her out, getting her to lay on her side and stretch out, he saw her eyes were cloudy. She was stunned, in shock.

"Stay here," he ordered her as he laid her out on the grassy bank, "I'm getting a blanket for you," and he rose, quickly trotting to where Socks was ground tied. Untying the blanket roll behind his saddle with trembling, numb fingers, he yanked it off, racing back to Tara. She was sitting up, looking around, looking at him, confused.

"H-how?" she croaked as he knelt in front of her. Harper quickly got her out of her heavy, wet clothing, bringing the thick, wool blanket around her shoulders.

"Long story," he rasped. "Are you all right, Tara? Look in my eyes," and he peered intently into them. Her flesh was porcelain in color, eyes shocky-looking, and she was trembling badly, pulling the blanket around herself.

"I—I didn't think I'd live," she sobbed, giving him a terrified look.

"You did." He pushed wet strands away from her face, cupping her jaw as he knelt there. "I love you, Tara. I love you . . ."

Huge tears welled up in her eyes as she stared up at him. "Oh," she whimpered, "I never thought I'd get a chance to tell you the same thing. Oh, God . . ." and she broke down, weeping deeply, her knees drawn up against herself, burying her face against them, her sobs loud and hard.

Harper wanted so badly to hold her, care for her, but he worried about what was going on up above him. Had

Reese captured Elson? Or had Cree shot his friend? He didn't know and hadn't heard anything over his earpiece from Reese. "Listen to me, Tara," he whispered urgently, moving his hand against her tangled, wet hair, "I have to ride up above the falls. Reese is with me. He went after Elson while I came down here to rescue you. I don't know what's happened. You need to stay here." He had shed the holster and dragged it over, laying it near her. "The Glock is locked and loaded. I've got to ride up above to find out what's happened to Reese and whether he captured Elson. If you see Elson is loose, shoot to kill."

Jerkily, she nodded, reaching for the holster and weapon. "O-okay . . . be careful, Harper. Please, be careful," and she tried to stop her tears.

Harper smiled and kissed her cold lips swiftly. "I'll be back. Don't worry . . ."

Getting up, he hurriedly hauled on his cowboy boots over his wet socks. They didn't want to go on, but brute force got them back on his feet. He made a leap into the saddle, grabbing Socks' reins, whirling the horse around, sinking his heels into his flanks. As he rode, he pulled the .30-06 out of the sheath beneath the fender of the saddle beneath his leg. The quarter horse wove in and around the pines, climbing rapidly, sweat gleaming against his hide, foam on his neck from the brutal exertion being asked of him. A horse couldn't run forever. They, too, needed a rest and recoup period. Harper knew he was asking everything of Socks. The valiant animal surged up the hill, his mane flying, his short tail raised up like a flag, flying.

As Harper crested the hill, he saw Reese down on the ground, leaning over Elson, who wasn't moving. Nearby, Ghost was ground tied, his flanks heaving in and out. Pulling Socks to a stop, Harper did a flying dismount, running toward Reese, who had a grim look on his face. He kept the rifle ready, never trusting Cree.

"He's dead," Reese told him, looking up as he approached.

Relief wove through Harper as he halted a few feet from where Reese knelt next to the kidnapper. "What happened?"

"He pulled out a pistol and was shooting at Tara as she was being swept toward the falls. When he saw me, he turned and started firing at me." Satisfaction wreathed his soft voice. "One shot. One kill."

Harper knew they had snipers in Reese's Marine company; that was a sniper term. And although he was sure Reese wasn't one, his aim had been true. Elson lay on his back, his red hair around his face, hiding it. The blood on his chest told Harper everything. Reese had fired one round and it had hit the man in the heart.

Kneeling opposite Reese, he said, "Tara is going to be all right. She made it over the falls. She's shaken, but she's down by the pool. I put the bedroll blanket around her. She's going to be okay." He saw instant relief come to Reese's face.

"Best news yet." Reese slowly rose, the .30-06 rifle cradled in his left arm. "I'm going to call Sarah on the radio to let her know what's happened."

"I'm sure Josh is telling them, too; they must have caught all this on the drone's camera," Harper said, standing.

"Most likely. Still, they don't need to bring anyone up here. We'll put him over my saddle and I'll ride behind him. You and Tara can ride down together on Socks."

Tears suddenly stung Harper's eyes and he blinked a couple of times. Tara was alive. She loved him. He loved her. His voice became gruff. "Yeah, sounds like a plan. Let me help you get Elson over the saddle. We'll tie him on so he doesn't slip off."

Tara couldn't get warm. Her cold, wet T-shirt and jeans stuck to her body. She anxiously watched the hill, not knowing who might show up on it sooner or later. Had they captured Cree? Was Reese okay?

She sat on the bank and couldn't believe she was alive. She'd managed, somehow, to not break bones or kill herself when she went over the falls. Gripping the wiry wool blanket around her, she could feel the raw cuts, the smarting sensation slowly coming back to her icy, deeply bruised flesh.

The day was warm, the sky cloudless, the sun shining. Everything looked so peaceful, and yet she'd nearly died. Closing her eyes, Tara rested her head against her drawn-up knees, feeling grateful to be alive and yet so torn up over being kidnapped once again. Something had broken inside her when Cree had dragged her out of that wrecked car. The insane look in his eyes, the glee over capturing her once more. Her stomach revolted and she thought she was going to vomit.

Tara rolled to the right, vomiting up more water she'd swallowed earlier. She got to her hands and knees, the blanket warming her now. She wiped her mouth with a shaky hand, straightening, resting her butt against the soggy heels of her boots. Looking toward the hill once more, her heart thudded hard.

Harper!

Her gaze blurred for a moment as she watched him trotting a very wet, very weary Socks down that slope once again. Never had he looked so good to her, his back straight, riding bonelessly in the saddle, a part of the animal. He was so strong, so confident, and an incredible frisson of love blossomed powerfully through her as he turned Socks down into the pool area. His eyes never left hers. She saw he looked peaceful, tension no longer in his face or in his body. Dismounting, he walked to her and knelt down opposite her.

"Elson is dead," he told her.

Blinking once, she stared at Harper. "What?" Had she heard right?

He reached out, grazing her jaw, now dry and feeling warmer. "Did you realize Cree found his pistol in his pack, got it out and was firing at you as you dived into the water?"

Shaking her head, she caught his hand, feeling his fingers gently wrap around hers. "N-no . . . I didn't hear anything except the noise of the waterfall. I just ran."

"I would have done the same thing." He released her hand. Kneeling behind her, he eased Tara into his arms and she flowed against him. "Let me hold you for just a little while," he murmured against her damp, tousled hair. She settled against him and he heard a sigh, ragged and long, expel from between her lips. Nestling her brow against his jaw, her hand against his chest, he enclosed her. Rocking her slightly, he rasped against her hair. "When Elson saw Reese gallop up and over the top of that slope, he turned and started firing at him. Reese had a .30-06 and he stood up in the stirrups and fired at Elson. Dropped him with one shot. Through the heart."

Turning her face into his chest, she gave a little cry of relief. He held her tighter, keeping the blanket around her. "It's going to be all right, Tara. It's over. Really over."

The words careened around in her head as she pressed

her cheek against the rough, damp chambray of his shirt. Just hearing Harper's heartbeat soothed some of the hysteria rising within her. She needed his strong, caring arms around her as never before. First, the tears came, hot, burning, salty and streaming down her cheeks, wetting the material beneath her cheek. And then, the sobs started, slow at first, feeling like battering rams being thrust up through the center of her body. Then they came tearing out of her mouth. Her whole body shook.

Harper held her tightly. He kept whispering soothing words to comfort her, even though she couldn't make out anything he was saying over her sobbing. It didn't matter because with his other hand, he grazed her hair, smoothed his palm across her tightened shoulders gently up and down the length of her back. It felt as if she was crying from the time she was sixteen years old, when Cree had first captured her. She'd been so young then, naïve, unworldly, immature. And then, not wanting to come home after she left at eighteen, afraid he'd come after her a second time. And he had. With a vengeance. And then the mortification of being caught and kidnapped again. It was just too much for Tara to process. All she could do was cry, sounding like an animal who'd gotten its paw caught in a trap, filled with pain, remorse and guilt, wanting to run away from all of it.

Finally, she ran out of tears. Hiccupping several times, trying to breathe evenly, she felt Harper loosen his embrace around her. His thighs were on either side of her hips, cocooning her, making her feel safe for the first time since this kidnapping had started. With trembling fingers, she tried to push the last of the tears off her damp cheeks.

"H-how did you find us? I gave up hope, Harper. I didn't think anyone would ever find us."

He continued to move his hand from her neck to her waist, the motion calming her. "We got lucky," and he gave her the short version of Terry Larson and his son Josh, who had a drone-operating system and a high-powered lens on the camera that had found them.

Tara lay very still in his arms and absorbed him holding her, still not quite believing she was really safe. Harper and Reese had rescued her. They'd saved her life. Weakness stole through her limbs and she whispered, "I feel like a paper doll, ready to collapse."

He kissed her temple. "You've been through hell, Tara. It's enough to make anyone feel like that." He eased some loose, damp strands of hair away from her wan cheek. "In a few minutes, Reese will be coming down with Elson's body over the saddle of his horse. He was going to call Sarah, who was coordinating the search for you, to let her know what's happened. You and I are going to ride Socks. I'll help you get up and mount on him."

"Poor horses," she murmured, lifting her chin, looking at Socks, who was hanging his head from all the brutal physical demands. "He's just as tired as we are."

"He'll get us down to the parking lot," Harper promised. He was sure there was going to be hell to pay with Sarah. It was small penance for being able to get up here in time to save Tara's life. Reese would make all the apologies she wanted, but in the end, he'd do it again the same way, no questions asked.

"God, I feel so sorry for Roberta, Cree's mother."

"I'm sure Sarah will send a deputy out to tell her in person. She can't not expect it. The sheriff had gone to her house and asked if he was there and that's when she found out he'd kidnapped you again."

"It's a sick family. He paid a horrible price."

"Hey, don't go feeling sorry for him. He tried to kill you, Tara. Forgive him if you want, but that bastard deserves no sympathy in my book."

She nodded, feeling exhaustion stealing through her. "You're right," she mumbled, nuzzling into him.

"It's over, Tara. It's really over. Cree won't be hanging around, following you and waiting to grab you a third time."

Sighing, she muttered, "I know. . . . I just can't believe it's finally over. Really . . ."

He squeezed her and saw Reese slowly coming down the slope on Ghost. He had one hand on Elson's back to keep him in the saddle and the reins in the other hand. Harper wouldn't admit how wiped out he suddenly felt, knowing it was the adrenaline crash after the threat that had stalked them.

"Listen, when we get down to the parking lot? I'll have Reese run interference for us about what we did. I want to check you over thoroughly, Tara. There's an ambulance and two paramedics waiting down there if they're needed."

Making an unhappy sound, she said, "I'm fine, Harper. I don't want to go to a hospital." She held up one hand. "I'm scratched and bruised, that's all. No broken bones. Okay?"

Harper chuckled. "Okay. I think you'd rather let me give you an examination than one of them?"

"Better believe it."

Chuckling, he said, "I thought so."

Reese pulled up. "How are you feeling, Tara?"

She roused herself and slowly sat up, repositioning herself so she could look at Reese. Just seeing Cree hanging dead over the saddle made her stomach roll with nausea. "I'm going to be okay, Reese. Thanks so much for coming to help me. I wouldn't be alive if you two hadn't shown up." The thought was stunning to her, going so deep within her that she wanted to cry again.

"Well, you're here with us in no small part due to your own efforts, Tara. We watched you on drone video getting your ropes unknotted so you could make a run for the river. You're a gutsy warrior. You saved yourself."

Weariness washed over her in waves. Tara managed a small, appreciative smile at Reese. "Like all military vets, we work as a team. The team saved me."

Harper's mouth curved. "Okay, I can settle for that, sweetheart. Feel like getting up and walking over to Socks? Or do you want me to carry you over and toss you into the saddle?" he teased.

"No . . . I can manage."

Harper nodded, stood, then helped her up to her feet. He kept his hand on her elbow and made sure the blanket remained across her shoulders. To her chagrin, her knees were so wobbly, she found she couldn't even slide her boot into the stirrup to mount.

"Let me help you," Harper urged.

Before she could protest, he'd lifted her easily into the saddle, as if she weighed nothing. He wasn't a bulked-up, muscled man, rather lean and wiry, but he was strong. It felt good to curve her legs around Socks. Even little things like that were important. She'd get to ride again. She'd get to photograph things she loved to shoot. Most of all, Harper would be with her. *Always*.

Chapter Twenty

"How's Tara doing?" Shay asked Harper as they sat down at the kitchen table over late-evening coffee.

"She's sleeping like there's no tomorrow," he said, weariness in his voice.

Shay rubbed her face. "Reese is asleep right now, too. He's exhausted."

"I'm not surprised. It was a helluva day for everyone, Shay." Harper appraised her with a concerned look. "How are you holding up? I imagine Reese is going through all kinds of hell over shooting a man at close range, and the fallout is on you. I had to kill an enemy combatant during a firefight and it's with me to this day. I still see the guy's face."

Grimacing, Shay sipped the coffee and said softly, "Reese is pretty much totaled emotionally. I mean, he was a company commander of Marines in Afghanistan. He was in combat a lot. But none of us joined the military with the idea that we'd have to kill the enemy. We would if we had to, but pulling the trigger is a very different thing."

Harper made a sympathetic sound of agreement, drinking his coffee.

Shay raised a brow and then muttered, "I had to kill a

combatant over in Afghanistan. I didn't want to, but I had to. I've never forgotten that day for a moment, Harper. I know it's going to be with me until I die." She gave an abrupt but quiet laugh filled with derision. "Maybe it will haunt me in the afterlife, as well."

"You have a lot of company, Shay," and he reached out, sliding his hand across hers, wanting to somehow comfort her. "Reese is going to have to go through his own kind of hell just like Tara will. Shock does funny things to a human being, but I think you know that pretty well by now."

Shay nodded. "It's true, he's going to go through hell. I don't know of anyone who was in combat who doesn't afterward."

"Being vets, we all have things we had to do that we didn't want to do. We saw things we want to forget but never will."

"Yeah," she whispered wearily. "I just wish Cree Elson and his insanity hadn't happened. With my father filing that lawsuit against us and the ranch, we have enough to contend with. Tara getting kidnapped just pushed me way over my personal edge. I feel numbed out by everything hanging over our heads here at the ranch right now. We just don't catch a break."

"I know, Shay. But Reese is on top of that lawsuit. You've hired a good lawyer. You have to get some distance on it if you can."

"When your own father sues you, it's hard to take."

"No disagreement."

"A day at a time."

"Right now, yes."

"How do you think Tara is going to do? I just can't wrap my head around her being kidnapped twice by the same crazy person. I can't."

"I don't think she can either," Harper admitted quietly. "Did she eat any supper?"

Harper shook his head. "I got some soup down her. After we brought her back to the Prater Canyon parking lot, she collapsed. The paramedics gave her an IV of fluids, which helped. And they let me examine her for injuries."

"Reese said she has a lot of bruises and her hands are pretty well cut up."

"Yes, that's all, though. It could have been worse when she went over the falls."

"Tara had a guardian angel watching out for her on that one," Shay said fervently.

"I saw her go over," Harper said, his emotions still twinging over it. "I thought I'd lost her," and he looked down at his cup, scowling. He felt Shay's hand touch his momentarily.

"Reese thought you two had fallen in love with each other. Is that true?"

Nodding, he glanced at her. "I didn't think I'd ever get to tell Tara that I loved her."

"She didn't know before this happened?"

"No . . . I didn't want to push her, Shay. She was dealing with enough."

"You poor thing," she murmured sympathetically, giving him a caring glance. "Does she know now?"

One corner of his mouth lifted a little. "For sure she does now. I didn't know she loved me either. We both were holding back for different reasons."

"Jeez," she said, shaking her head.

"Maybe now," Harper said, lifting his head, "things will quiet down around here and we can get on with dealing with life without this other stuff cropping up out of the blue."

"There's enough to juggle on our plates daily," Shay agreed. "Thanks for the coffee, Harper. I'd better get back home. I left Reese a note in case he woke up, but I don't want to be gone too long. He might need me."

"Yeah, he probably will," Harper said, rising, walking Shay to the back door. "I'm feeling the same way about Tara. I don't want her out of my sight. Don't worry, though; I'll start doing my regular routine tomorrow morning. I'll just be coming back to check on her more often until I'm sure she's out of the woods." Harper knew they were stretched thin at the ranch. They actually needed more wranglers, and he'd heard Shay talk about it at their last Friday meeting with Libby. Two more would be a huge help.

"Great . . . thanks. Listen, if you need anything, either one of you? Just call over and ask us. Okay?"

Shay was a petite thing, but Harper had learned a long time ago that despite her size, she had the heart of a lion and the bravery to go with it. He opened the door, pushing the screen aside for her. "Thanks for bringing over two pieces of your world-famous coconut cream pie for us. Tara loves it, and I know she'll be grateful you thought about her right now. But if you or Reese need anything, Shay, we're here for you, too. Don't forget that."

Shay walked down the concrete steps, her hand on the pipe railing. Harper had turned on the porch light so she could see easily. Dusk was deep, a red ribbon outlining the peaks of the Wilson Range to the west of them. Turning, she gazed up at Harper's deeply shadowed face. "Thanks, I will."

Harper snorted. "Sure. You never ask for help, Shay." He wagged his finger at her. "Remember."

Giving him a gentle smile, she lifted her hand at the bottom of the stairs. "I'll drop over sometime tomorrow afternoon to see how Tara's doing. Good night, Harper . . ."

He moved quietly back into their home. He was stiff

and sore from the earlier activity, having pulled a muscle in his back from rescuing Tara from the pool after she'd tumbled over the falls. A hot shower would work wonders on it.

The house was quiet. Too quiet. He yearned for Tara's laughter, to listen to her talk about seeing something on the Internet or showing him one of the photos she'd recently shot. He stood in the living room, wanting to go to her. And he would. Looking around, he began to realize just how close they'd come to never seeing each other again. His heart felt crushed as the shock began to wear off and harsh, unblinking reality settled in.

His emotions were like an out-of-control train if he didn't keep busy and distracted. Losing Tara would be losing everything.

Rubbing his face, he walked down the hall. Quietly opening her door, he saw she was sleeping deeply. He'd helped her get out of her dirty clothes, taken them out of the bathroom and then returned. The hot tub of water was what she'd wanted and he'd washed her hair later after she got out and dried off. He'd helped her put on a knee-length white cotton gown. By then, Tara had been almost asleep, the day just too much for her to handle emotionally. Sleep was the antidote for shock.

She had pulled up the sheet and a blanket to her waist and buried her face in the goose-down pillow.

How badly he wanted to join her. But she hadn't asked him to. He'd helped her into her bed, covered her and she'd promptly fallen asleep. Closing the door without a sound, Harper walked to his bedroom. Weariness was bludgeoning him. He hadn't changed his clothes and he smelled of river water. The corners of his mouth tugged upward. He was just as much of an emotional mess as Reese and Tara were. But at least when he woke up tomorrow morning,

Tara would be here. Alive. And his. How much he loved her; he felt the fierceness of his love rising in his chest.

After a hot shower, his back felt almost normal. Wearing a pair of gray gym pants, a towel across his neck, he opened the bathroom door, steam escaping into the hall. He'd spent nearly an hour cleaning up, wanting to get the smell of the glacier water out of his hair as well. He'd shaved, brushed his teeth and done the things he normally did in the morning. He didn't want any reminders. He knew he'd sleep poorly tonight and wasn't looking forward to tossing and turning, with images of today's events slamming nonstop through his brain.

Barefoot, he traipsed into the kitchen, shutting all the lights off except for one. Getting a glass of water, he drank deeply.

A door opened down the hallway.

Turning, glass in hand, he saw Tara come out of her room. She looked wan, her hair mussed, the cotton gown wrinkled, hanging around her badly bruised knees.

"Hey," he called softly, setting the glass on the counter. "Do you need something, Tara?" and he walked toward her, seeing her lift her head, puzzlement in her murky gaze. She was barely awake, from what he could tell. As he drew near, he saw huge tears forming in her eyes, her lower lip quivering as she stood there, looking helpless and fragile.

Reaching out, Harper gently folded her into his arms. She came willingly, wrapping her arms around his waist, resting her cheek against his naked chest.

"Ohhh," she whispered, "this is what I need: you." She nuzzled against him, eyes closed, leaning against his body.

Harper knew this wasn't sexual. It was one human needing another. He ran his hand from her hair down her back. "You're okay, Tara. You're safe," he rasped against her hair, placing a kiss on the strands. Instantly, she sagged fully against him, a little sigh escaping her lips. It was exactly what she needed to hear. Protectiveness swam through him and he simply held her, feeling the warmth and softness of her body contoured to his harder one.

"How can I help you?" he asked against her hair, smoothing his hand slowly up and down her spine.

"I want you to sleep with me," she uttered. "I just want to feel safe. . . ."

"You got it," he promised thickly, squeezing her. "Are you thirsty? Want some water?"

Shaking her head, she tightened her arms around his waist. "Just you, Harper . . . that's all I'll ever need. . . ."

Those were the sweetest words he'd ever heard. In his past marriage, comments like that never had been shared between him and Olivia. It wasn't a very close marriage, not like the relationship he was presently sharing with Tara. She invited his intimacy, remained vulnerable with him even now, in her fragile state. She trusted him, while Olivia had never given him her trust. It made his heart burst open with such keen feelings for Tara that all he could do was be rocked by them. "Ready to go to bed, then?"

Another nod. But Tara didn't move.

Harper smiled tenderly and gently eased her arms from around him. "How are your knees feeling?" Because they had been badly bruised, the skin scraped open on both. Luckily, there were no torn ligaments.

"They hurt like hell," she muttered, slowly lifting her chin, staring up into his eyes.

"You up for me carrying you off to my bed?" he teased, grazing her cheek, putting a few of those errant strands against her temple. For the first time, he saw a small smile come to her lips.

"I'm not a little girl, Harper."

Chuckling, he slipped his arms around her back and beneath her knees, easily lifting her up against him. "You're a featherweight," he teased, smiling down into her drowsy, half-closed eyes. Tara was totaled emotionally. Her gaze was murky and dazed-looking. Harper knew she was still slogging through the shock of it all.

Nestling her brow against his jaw, her arms around his neck, Tara said, "You feel so good to lean against."

"I'll always be here anytime you want to lean," he told her, crossing the living room. He saw all the stress dissolve from her expression. She relaxed fully, eyes closing, a new contentment on her face. Harper knew it was because she truly did feel safe with him. It made him feel strong and good.

He deposited Tara in his bed, then closed the door. There was a very small night-light near it, just enough to help him see where he was going and not stub his toes on the heavy wooden leg of the massive king-size bed. Tara had already moved to the center and he joined her there, pulling up the covers. Sliding his arm beneath her neck, he lay parallel to her and brought her up against him. She groaned, but it wasn't from pain; it sounded more like she'd just entered heaven. Smiling to himself in the near darkness, he waited while she got comfortable against him. Her one leg moved across his. Now, he wished he wasn't wearing a pair of gym pants, wanting that direct contact with her warm flesh.

"This feels wonderful," she whispered, "so right. . . ."

Harper placed his arm around her hip, bringing her flush against him. "Sleep, sweetheart. I'll be here if you need anything." He felt her nuzzle her lips against his neck, kissing him softly. And then, she melted bonelessly against him, sleep swiftly claiming her. Shock was responsible for such tiredness.

Laying on his side, Tara against him, her one arm draped across his waist, a joy he'd never experienced before began to build within him. He couldn't help but compare sleeping with Olivia with sleeping with Tara. All the aches and pains from the day's challenges disappeared as he focused on her warm, sweet body against his. He knew he shouldn't feel sexual, but he did. Part of love was loving the other. The scent of her hair, the strands tickling his jaw, made him smile with a newfound contentment.

Harper knew tough weeks lay ahead of them. What he didn't want to happen was to have Elson's death derail the love they had for each other. Tara was going to need special attention and care. And no one wanted to take care of her more than he did. It would be a balancing act because they were shorthanded at the Bar C. He wasn't sure Tara would be able to carry out her duties for at least a week or two. Her knees were a mess and she needed time for them to fully heal before doing any kind of wrangling work.

Knowing Reese and Shay would give Tara the time she needed, he was concerned for them, too. Worse, Garret and Kira were in Hawaii and hadn't a clue what had happened to Tara. Harper knew there would be hell to pay from the newlyweds when they returned to the Bar C to continue their lives together. Garret, especially, would be incensed that he hadn't been asked to join them in the hunt to find Tara. He'd get over it once he understood how fast things had moved after she'd been kidnapped. Garret couldn't have gotten home in time to help him and Reese find her.

Still, Harper knew it was pressure and stress on Reese and Shay. He was sure Reese would be going through a rugged time because he'd killed Elson. Harper knew from what Shay had said that Reese had to go back to the sheriff's office tomorrow morning to give another statement to the county attorney about it. Apparently, Elson's mother was raising holy hell, saying her son had been murdered. She was threatening to have her sons shoot Reese. That was crazy shit, Harper decided, but Sarah, the sheriff, had to take such threats seriously. Reese had blown it off, angered by the threat, nothing more.

Nowadays, threats could turn out to be real. More and more people were resorting to shooting others who angered them or who they felt had crossed them. Harper worried about that. The Elson clan, as the residents of the valley commonly referred to them, had the them-against-us mind-set. They were outcasts, drug dealers, constantly battling the law in the county. Roberta was the queen of the clan and Cree's three older brothers, all of whom had been in prison at one time or another, were to be wary of. They were a dysfunctional family, and Harper doubted they shared one full brain among them.

What Reese and Shay didn't need was for the Elsons to try to kill him to avenge Cree's death. Harper wanted to talk to Reese about this, and bring Noah in on it, too. When Garret returned from his honeymoon, he was going to get an earful about the events that had come down after they'd left. Harper knew he wouldn't be happy to hear the Elson clan was all wound up over Cree's death. Already, from what Reese had told him earlier in the day, Sarah had called him to warn him about the three brothers screaming for revenge.

Snorting softly, he buried his face in Tara's silky hair. All he wanted to do was forget about life outside the entrance to the Bar C and concentrate on Tara.

She was going to need his help and he intended to be there for her. Nothing else mattered. He loved her.

Chapter Twenty-One

June 23

"Will this ever end?" Tara asked Harper as they left the sheriff's office in Wind River.

He slipped her hand into his as they ambled down the wooden sidewalk to the asphalt parking lot behind the three-story red-brick building. "In time," he murmured, giving her a concerned look.

"It's horrible that Roberta is stirring up her other sons to go after Reese."

"Reese has already been warned by Sarah," he soothed.

"In some ways, I wish I didn't know." But she'd had to go in for another interview regarding her kidnapping with the prosecuting attorney for the county. Sarah had met them in the hall afterward, inviting them into her office, where she'd filled them in on Cree's three brothers.

"Better to know and be on the lookout," Harper said. He squeezed her hand gently.

Shrugging, she looked around at the sunny late morning and the clouds coming over the Wilson Range. There was a call for thunder showers in the area this afternoon.

"I'm surprised they're not coming after me, too. To hear Roberta talk, it was my fault Cree came after me a second time. What a sick, dysfunctional family, Harper."

"Bad blood. Some families never get a break. Brian, Cree's father, was abusive to all his sons. Roberta, from what Sarah told us, was badly abused as well. The brain changes when you live under those kinds of life-and-death threats for years. Cree changed. I found it sad that the medical examiner's autopsy found blood in his brain. He was really damaged mentally."

"I know," she said softly, waiting for him to unlock the truck so she could climb into the passenger seat. "In part, it explains his obsession with me, I think."

Harper opened the door for Tara. "I agree. Although I'm not a doctor or a shrink, Cree was mentally unstable."

Tara wished this whole episode would go away. But it wasn't about to. Roberta had already filed a lawsuit against Reese for killing her son. Now, the county prosecutor and Sarah's office were in defense mode. She knew that eventually Reese would be cleared of the charges. Terry Larson's camera-toting drone had shown very clearly that Cree had fired three shots at Reese before he shot back and killed him. It was self-defense. Sarah didn't seem that concerned in that regard. What she was worried about were the three sons being stirred up by the mother to go after Reese and then go on a shooting spree, killing the vets who lived on the Bar C as well.

Harper climbed in. "What do you say we get an early lunch at Kassie's Café? I'll buy."

She wasn't hungry for food, but she was hungry to be with Harper. "Sure, I'd like that."

"Gonna eat?" he goaded, driving the truck out of the parking lot.

She managed a weak smile. "I'll do my best." Since

being rescued, Tara had little appetite, still cycling up and down from the shock and nearly dying. Every night, she had nightmares about Cree or about being dragged over the waterfall. And every night, Harper awoke, bringing her into his arms, holding her, making her feel safe.

They sat in one of the black leather booths, the popular café quiet just before the lunch crowd wandered in. It was a small place with large windows, sunshine pouring in, the chatting quiet between customers and plenty of smiles and laughter from the ranchers who greeted them when they entered. Tara knew most of them, recognizing a number of the older men in cowboy garb, sitting and having coffee together.

Harper slid in on the opposite side, hanging his Stetson on a nearby hook. He pushed his fingers through his dark hair, giving her a measured look.

"I'm okay," she said. "Really." She saw Harper's face lose some of that tension.

The waitress came over to take their order, then left to get them coffee.

"It'll be good to see Garret and Kira again," she said, wanting to get off the darkness of the Elson clan that had forever changed their lives.

Harper brightened. "Yeah. Noah and Dair are going to pick them up at the Jackson Hole Airport tonight."

Grimacing, she said, "Poor Noah. He's going to get his ears chewed off by Garret when he learns what happened to me."

"Nah, Noah will take care of himself. I'm sure Garret will be upset, but when he hears you're safe, he'll put it all in perspective. Black-ops types don't blow things out of proportion."

"That's good," she said, thanking the waitress who brought over their coffee.

Harper rested his elbows on the table, hands around his coffee mug. "I want to talk about us, Tara."

She heard emotion in his voice and saw a tenderness come to his eyes. Her heart melted beneath that look that said so much. "What about us?"

"I know it's too soon and you're still unraveling from Cree kidnapping you, but I'm the kind of guy who plans far into the future." He gave her a shy grin.

In that moment, Harper was boyish, and her heart yearned to be with him at home, in their bed, loving him once again. Even now, her lower body grew warm with memories from two nights before. "I know you do. That's not a black-ops thing to do," and she laughed a little, caught up in his infectious smile, the light gleaming in his gray eyes as he held her gaze.

"When I married Olivia, I thought about getting out of the service and settling down. That didn't happen, but it didn't stop me from wanting a relationship where love came first."

"What was your dream?" she asked him softly, sipping her coffee, drowning in the love he was showering on her.

"I've always dreamed of having what my parents have, Tara. I was an only child, but I was brought up with a whole lot of love. I've always dreamed of having a family. Not a big one, but maybe one or two children my wife and I could love, nurture and watch grow up before our eyes."

Her heart blossomed. "You know I'm an only child, too. And my parents are still, to this day, deeply in love. We're both so lucky to come from similar homes."

"I know," he rasped. "Do you know where we might go with each other?"

She leaned back in the booth, hearing his thickened words, seeing anxiety in his gaze for a moment. Knowing how much family meant to them, she said, "When I had my therapy session with Libby the other day in Jackson Hole?"

"Yes?"

"I told her I'd never been happier than with you. And it wasn't because you rescued me either. I feel we have something so rich to share with each other, Harper. I know you have to get through your paramedic courses and get your certification so you can take that job at the fire department. Me? I have to get through this emotional gauntlet of coming to terms with being kidnapped again and then Cree's death." She opened her hands, stumbling. "I told Libby there were hurdles in front of both of us, but that I dreamed of a time in the future when we could be together permanently. She asked me if I had any desire to have a child and I told her yes. I want two or three. I love kids, Harper. I always have."

Giving her a studied look, he said, "I love you, Tara. I'm not falling out of love with you. That's not how I feel in my heart and soul. You're the woman I've always dreamed of meeting and marrying." He held up his hand. "I know a lot of our generation doesn't marry. They just live together." He swallowed hard and then said, "Whatever you want is fine with me. I want to wake up with you in the morning and I want to go to sleep at night with you in my arms. Everything else? It's whatever you need, Tara. I need you. I figure if we continue to live together, we'll know some point in the future when things look serious enough that we consider having a child."

Her heart widened with a river of love so profound that it chased away all her worries and dread. "I want the same thing, Harper. I don't care where we live. I'm happy living my life with you."

Tara saw his expression turn soft and his eyes darkened, but it was something she'd come to discover meant he was happy. "Does that help?"

He nodded, swallowing several times. "Yes. It takes a big load of worry off my shoulders to tell you the truth."

"Don't ever stop talking with me, Harper. I want to know how you're feeling, what you're thinking."

"You always will," he promiscd her. He hitched a thumb toward the door of the café. "I thought—well . . . I was in Bell's Jewelry Store a few days ago."

She saw redness tingeing his cheeks, realizing he was blushing. Now, Harper was more like a nervous little boy, and that endeared him to her. "What were you doing over there?"

"I went in to ask Bell if there was such a thing as a pre-engagement ring. You know? Something semi-official a woman might wear as a symbol of her love."

"Oh," she whispered, feeling a glow in her heart, "sort of like what my mom would call a friendship ring?"

"Yes, something like that." He gave her a hopeful look. "I wanted to do something for you that would lift your spirits, Tara. At least, that's what I hoped. Would it bother you to wear a friendship ring that symbolizes us?"

"I wish this table wasn't between us."

His grin broadened. "Really?"

"Yes. Really."

"Then you want to amble over to Bell's after lunch? Pick out something you like?"

Touched, she felt tears sting the backs of her eyes and pushed them away. Tara felt like she'd cried ten years' worth of tears since being rescued by Harper and Reese. Libby comforted her by saying that the deluge would slowly turn off, but that it was important to get her tears out, too. She agreed. "Yes," she said, her voice cracking, "I would love to do that with you."

Bell Kennedy was a slight woman of forty-five, a brunette with large blue eyes. Tara remembered her husband, Billy, who had died of prostate cancer just before she left for the military. The small but pretty jewelry store was neat, clean and had lots of light pouring through the windows. Bell was dressed in a summer yellow-and-orange sundress, her long hair artfully arranged on her head. Tara liked that Bell always dressed so beautifully, a true fashion plate. She didn't wear a lot of jewelry, but it was obviously a real gold collar around her throat and ten or so slender bangles around her left wrist. The gold earrings were tasteful, set with white pearls.

"Tara, good to see you," Bell hailed from behind her glass counter. "Been a long time since I last saw you," and she came around the end of it, opened her arms and gave Tara a big hug of hello. While squeezing her, Bell lifted her head and smiled over at Harper, who touched the brim of his Stetson to her.

"It's been too long," Tara said. She eased out of the hug. "Mom and Dad said they were having a barbeque in two weeks and they were inviting you. Did you get their invite?"

"Sure did," Bell said. "I imagine you and Harper are attending?" and her eyes sparkled with amusement.

"We will," he said. "It should be a good time."

Bell curved her arm around Tara's left arm and led her to a center octagonal glass display. "Now, I'm not a mind reader, dearie, but your young man was in here a couple of days ago asking about a friendship ring. Is that why you're here today?"

"Sure are," Tara said. Bell moved away after showing her to the front of the display and got the key, opening it up. Harper came to her side and she smiled at him. The look in his eyes made her want to kiss him silly.

Bell opened the top of the case. "A lot of couples love a bracelet," and she motioned to at least a dozen of them on display to the left of Tara. "But others like a ring because it's easier to wear. Not every woman likes to wear a bracelet." She held up her own. "I'm a bracelet nut," and she jangled the silver, gold and copper bangles.

"Well, wrangling would probably tear a bracelet right off me," Tara murmured. "Either that or rip my hand off my wrist if I got it caught in the wrong place."

"No, no, we wouldn't want that," Bell agreed briskly, bringing out a tray of friendship rings. She set them in front of Tara. "Look them over. I can get them in any size you need. There are twenty different designs here. If you don't like any of them, I have the catalog, and I can send it home with you to look at."

"Thanks, Bell," she said as the woman turned to leave them alone. Bell had always trusted people, and Tara was grateful for the privacy with Harper.

"See any that call to you?" he asked, giving her a warm look.

"I like this one . . ." and she picked up a sterling silver ring that had three small hearts across it.

"Bell said friendship rings go on the right hand," he suggested.

"Umm, leaving the ring finger empty?" Tara asked as she slipped it on that hand and finger. She saw Harper's brows raise marginally over her choice of hands. Holding it up, she looked at it. The ring was a quarter of an inch wide, the three hearts shining against the light from the windows.

"Well," Harper said, resting his hands on his hips as he

watched her move the ring in the light, "it's your ring. You wear it wherever it feels right."

"This lays flat," she said, brushing her index finger across the hearts. "It won't catch when I'm pulling on my work gloves and I can't possibly snag it on anything."

He picked up her hand, taking it gently into his, studying the ring. "Looks like it was made for you."

She absorbed his callused, rough fingers around her own, drowning in his dark gray gaze. "Ask me why I chose three hearts instead of the other rings that had one or two of them." She saw him smile a little.

"Tell me?"

"It symbolizes you, me," and her voice lowered with emotion, "and the third one is what I hope will be our family someday, Harper."

He groaned, released her hand and wrapped his arms around her shoulders, bringing her tightly against him, holding her for a long time, their heads resting against each other.

Tara closed her eyes, feeling the joy radiating from around Harper. He hadn't said anything, but he didn't have to. She knew how much family meant to him. It meant the same to her. They just had to get into a quieter backwater with one another, leave the drama of the kidnapping behind and get her PTSD to ramp down. Then, Tara thought, suggesting to Harper they get married and she get pregnant soon after might be the right time for that family they both wanted.

Pulling away just enough, she brushed her lips against his. "I love you, Harper Sutton. And I never want to leave your side again."

He kissed her gently, moving his hand across the crown of her hair. Lifting his mouth from her lips, he smiled into her eyes. "We were meant for each other, sweetheart. I'll always be here for you."

Please turn the page for an exciting sneak peek at

WIND RIVER LAWMAN

by Lindsay McKenna.

Coming to your favorite bookstores and e-tailers
in September 2018!

June 1

Sheriff Sarah Carter didn't know what the hell to do. She stared down at the ad she was going to place in the Jackson Hole, Wyoming, newspaper. Her finger hovered over the Send button. Had she gotten this right? Had she shaded or shaved off the truth of the person she was looking to hire? Conflicted, feeling as if the devil on her right shoulder was shouting at her to cut out some of the work qualifications she'd put in and the angel on her left saying it was fine as is, she sat back, frustrated.

Lifting her chin, she stared unseeingly at her staff. Her office was glass-enclosed on three sides, with a red-brick wall behind her squeaky desk chair. Outside, the deputies for Lincoln County were getting ready for a shift change at four p.m.

It was Saturday, and that was always a brutal day for drunks on the roadways. Every Saturday she had assigned a small task force during the summer months to pull over suspected drinkers and give them Breathalyzer tests. The Wind River Valley stretched a hundred miles long, hugging the western border of the state with Idaho and Utah.

It was a fifty-mile-wide valley, bracketed by the Wilson Range on the west and the Salt River Mountains on the eastern border.

What to do? What to do? Her red eyebrows bunched as she studied the computer screen. *WANTED: Wrangler with skill-set in wrangling and with a medical background. Duties include assisting an older woman with age-related tasks. Send résumé.*

Was that enough of a description? Wrangler and caregiver? Actually, she had little hope that any man who applied for the position would have both criteria. Sarah desperately needed a male wrangler to fill in and help her spry seventy-five-year-old grandmother, Gertie Carter. She was her father, David's, mother. And the word *spry* was actually less than what she would use: *rocket* was more like it. Type A, unbound. A go-getter. Or, as Gertie would say, no moss *ever* grew under her feet. No siree bob!

Her lips twitched. She dearly loved both her grandmothers, Gertie and Nell. Both were intelligent, accomplished businesswomen but in completely different realms. Nell sold grass leases to cattlemen from other western states every spring and summer, so they could fatten their cattle on some of the greenest, richest grass in the US. Gertie Carson's husband, Isaac, had died a year ago. They'd been married at eighteen, started the Loosey Goosey Ranch and the rest was history. Together, they'd built an organic egg empire with free-range chickens. Today, they were the largest company in the country, providing organic eggs and fryers to all the major grocery chains. Gertie's egg empire was $300 million.

Now, Gertie needed some male help. Isaac had always taken care of the chicken and egg business while she tended the finances, the contacts with the grocery stores, orders and such. Without Isaac, and having arthritis in both her wrists, Gertie couldn't possibly fill Isaac's missing shoes. No, she needed a wrangler. But she also needed a man who had a medical background because Gertie would get sudden, unexpected dizzy spells and lose her balance. She'd fallen many times. And each time, she called Sarah on the cell phone, asking for help instead of dialing 911.

The problem was, Sarah was often involved in law enforcement situations as the sheriff of the county, and she couldn't just pack up and drive back to the ranch to help out her grandmother. Gertie needed help. Desperately. Right now, her father was filling in, but he couldn't do it forever. No, they had to hire someone much younger.

But who? Who would want to be known as the chicken wrangler of Wind River Valley? Maybe she should tell the prospective applicant he'd be an egg wrangler. Clearly, there was no pride in telling folks he was a chicken wrangler. With a sigh, Sarah put down her private phone number, hit the Send key and prayed for the best, not really expecting anyone to answer the help-wanted ad.

Dawson Callaway was sitting at a café in Jackson Hole, having just driven to the cow town an hour earlier. He'd come from his parents' Amarillo, Texas, ranch. They'd tried to dissuade him, but he'd always wanted to find out what it would be like to live in Wyoming. No, it didn't have the Alamo. No, it didn't have the history of being the largest state in the Union. All those reasons from his father, Henry, fell on his deaf ears.

He'd managed to survive as a Navy combat corpsman assigned to a U.S. Marine Corps company, from age eighteen through twenty-nine. When his enlistment was up? He went home to Texas, back to being a wrangler on his father's small ranch, where they raised cattle. But it didn't fulfill him.

He was restless and wanted to strike out on his own. How many times had he dreamed of coming to Wyoming? Too many. Well, this was his chance. And as he read the help-wanted ads, one caught his eye: for a wrangler with a medical background. That was him. And because his Grandma Lorena had helped raise him while both his parents worked, Dawson had a soft spot for older men and women, seeing his own grams in all of them. Okay, he'd answer the ad as soon as he got a big breakfast at this café. He'd find a local motel, use their business computer, fill out his résumé and see if he could get hired.

June 2

Sarah's eyes widened. There on her personal computer the next morning was a résumé for the ad she'd placed! She quickly scanned the email.

My name is Dawson Callaway. Enclosed is my résumé for the position you advertised.

She sat at her office chair in her own small home, a block from the courthouse building where the sheriff's department was located. It was seven a.m. and she was due to go to work at eight a.m. The only thing good about being the sheriff was that she wasn't on a shift schedule, which she hated but had done for too many years earlier. Trying to quell her excitement, she opened the file that was labeled "Résumé."

Leaning down, looking at her Apple Macintosh laptop screen, she watched the file open. As she rapidly scanned the résumé, her heart beat a little harder in her chest. This man was a Texas-born ranch wrangler, thirty years old, single and had been in the US Navy as a combat corpsman for over ten years before his enlistment was up.

What were the chances? Sarah let a soft sigh escape from between her lips, staring at the résumé, reading it again to make sure she hadn't missed anything. This sounded too good to be true. Was it?

In her business as sheriff, she saw the dregs and the worst of society, not the best. Without thinking, she touched the screen with her fingertips. Dawson Callaway sounded perfect for the job, but she cautioned herself. First, when she got to work she'd run a thorough search on him via law enforcement channels. There was no way she wanted a felon or someone with a bad teen background working with her beloved grandmother. No way. That was first. Next, after ruthlessly researching his background for criminal issues, Sarah would contact a friend she had at the Pentagon. He would get her the man's DD Form 214, and that would fill in another huge blank about his entire military service, what kind of discharge he got and if he had any problems within that time frame. People lied all the time. Or they told half-truths or half lies, thinking it was all right. And it wasn't. She wanted to know everything about this Texan—if indeed he had been born in Amarillo, Texas—before setting up a meeting with him to pursue the possibility of being hired as Gertie's assistant.

She wished she had a photo of him. So, she ran a Google search on him and came up with nothing. That was strange. Most people nowadays had social media accounts, and he had no Facebook page, no Twitter account . . . no . . . nothing.

That raised a red flag up to a point. He was a US Navy medic, a combat-trained one, assigned to a Marine Corps company. She was intimately familiar with the Corps because she'd joined at age eighteen and left at age twenty-two, but not before serving over in Afghanistan in Helmand Province, one of the most dangerous areas to have a deployment. Yes, every squad in a company had a Navy combat corpsman assigned to them. So that part fit and was likely accurate.

Sitting back, she wiped her face with her hands, feeling the weight and stress on her shoulders. Funny how she could let the stress in her sheriff's role slide off and was much less troublesome than family stress. Family was as personal as it got, and Sarah understood why it was taking a toll on her. She dearly loved Gertie. And she wanted to protect her and find someone to help her who was damn near an angel in quality and mentality and very compassionate. And she knew just how long the odds were of finding a man like that.

Her mind canted to the past, to the Navy corpsman in their squad. He was kind, quiet and listened a lot but didn't say much. Most of the ones she'd met in those years in the Corps were like that. They were someone you'd want at your side if you were bleeding out, knowing you were going to die. There was a streak of compassion in them, a humanity that Sarah rarely found in anyone but the medical first-responder world, whether an EMT, paramedic or combat corpsman. There was no question that those in the medical-service field were a certain personality type. She hoped with all her heart that Callaway possessed that same kind of demeanor, but she'd only find out if he passed the first series of rigorous searches. What did he look like? She was dying to find out because she had a knack for reading faces.

June 3

Dawson looked at his cell phone that morning when he got up at six a.m. The motel where he was staying was the cheapest he could find, on the outskirts of the wealthy corporate community. Jackson Hole, he'd found out real quick, wasn't for the poor, the disenfranchised or even the struggling middle class. When he looked at house sales, he realized very quickly that Palm Springs, a very rich community, had been transplanted to Jackson Hole. No one without a lot of money could afford to live in this western town. Him included.

Rising to his six-foot, two-inch frame, feet bare on the oak floor, he stretched fitfully. The bed was lumpy and not supportive, leaving him with a backache that would probably sort itself out by noon. He ambled over to the desk, where there was a coffeemaker, and made a cup. Turning, he walked to the window, seeing the sky was a pale blue, the sun tipping the horizon, the town just beginning to wake up like him. He'd left the phone number of his hotel when he'd sent the résumé. Wanting to hear, he opened his cell-phone email. The note was cryptic:

I've received your résumé, Mr. Callaway. I will contact you in two days. Thank you. SC.

Well, he wasn't black ops for nothing. He'd been ordered to Recon Marines, their stealthy branch, and served in that capacity for ten years. More than likely, this SC, whoever that was, was checking and vetting him about now.

He grinned a little and sipped his coffee, heading to the bathroom to take a hot shower. It didn't bother him that SC was giving him a thorough background check because he had a grandmother, too, and he'd want to protect her from any man who wasn't on the up-and-up. Nowadays, people lied too easily. And fake news was believed, unfortunately. In the world he came from, you didn't lie at all.

Or if you did, you were tossed out with a bad reputation and no one wanted you around them, a pariah.

His curiosity rose as he wondered if SC was the individual who'd placed the ad. Man or woman? He didn't know. Finishing off his coffee, he pulled open the plastic shower-stall door.

June 5

Deciding to take in the scope of Wind River Valley this morning, Dawson had spent the last couple of days nosing around about potential work in the Jackson Hole area. Now, it was time to explore this valley south of the big town.

The small burg of Wind River had 965 inhabitants, or so the sign said. It was built up on both sides of Route 89 and looked more turn-of-the-century—the twentieth one—to Dawson. He'd gone to the Tucson wild west show and the OK Corral staging of that historical shoot-out. This town's footprint building-wise reminded him of that time. The only impressive place in town was a three-story red-brick building midway down on the right, the courthouse. He saw a number of deputy cruisers on the left side of the large, 1910-style building. The jail was also part of the sprawling complex. It had Victorian touches, with white wooden decorations, black, freshly painted wrought-iron fencing around the entire area, plus lots of nicely trimmed bushes and colorful foliage, with a rich green lawn in front of it.

It was clear to Dawson that this was a ranching town. Coming into the city limits, he'd seen at least four different three-quarter-ton pickup trucks, with four different ranch names painted on their side doors. There was Charlie

Becker's Hay and Feed store, and he swung in and parked because the lot was full and busy with ranchers. He saw a number of men who seemed to be employed either by the ranchers or by the store hefting hundred-pound sacks of grain or using hay hooks to place alfalfa or timothy hay into the backs of the waiting trucks in line at the two busy docks. This would be a good place to find out if there were any jobs for wranglers in this lush, verdant valley. Climbing out, he saw a sheriff's black Tahoe parked with the other trucks, with gold on the sides: Lincoln County Sheriff.

Dressed in a pair of clean Levi's, a plaid gold, orange and white shirt, the sleeves rolled up, he wore his comfortable, beat-up cowboy boots and settled the tan Stetson on his head as he mounted the long, wide wooden steps up to the double doors. Men and women were coming and going. They all looked like outdoor types, the men darkly tanned thanks to the coming summer, the women looking fit, firm and confident. Most of them wore their hair in pigtails or a ponytail, all sporting either a straw hat or a Stetson. Working ranch women, just like his mother was, along with her many other duties.

As he entered, he saw a gent in his sixties behind the counter, silver hair, a pair of bifocals perched on his nose and a canvas apron over his white cotton cowboy shirt and dungarees. He was sitting on a four-legged stool and punching an old-time calculator. But what got his attention was the tall, statuesque woman standing nearby in a sheriff's uniform. Her ginger-colored hair was caught up in a ponytail and she wore a black baseball cap on her head. He liked the strength of her body purely from a combat standpoint: medium boned, about five-foot-eight or nine inches tall, shoulders thrown back. An easy confidence radiated from her. Dawson swore she'd been in the military. He could only see her profile, but he would bet anything she had a heart-shaped face. From a male point of view, she was the whole package. Long, long legs encased in those tan trousers that were pressed to perfection. The huge black leather belt around her waist sported a pistol, and several other leather pockets, plus a flashlight, and other things such as pepper spray and a pair of handcuffs, on it as well. It blocked his view of her waist and hips. The long-sleeved tan blouse she wore couldn't stop anyone from realizing she was a woman, however.

"Ha ha!" a woman called as she came in the rear door of the large store. "Here they are, Charlie! Brownies with walnuts! Come and get 'em!" and she took a huge cookie pan covered with foil and placed it on the coffee table in the rear.

Charlie grinned and looked up at the sheriff. "There you go, Sarah. I think Pixie made enough for your shift-change people. Grab a box below the table where they're sitting and put one in for each deputy coming on duty, eh?"

Sarah grinned. "You know that's why I dropped by, Charlie," and she laughed huskily, lifted her hand in thanks and swung around the end of the long L-shaped counter, heading for where Pixie was.

Craning his neck, Dawson saw the huge amount of brownies being uncovered by Pixie. His gaze drifted back to the gentle sway of Sarah's hips. He liked her more than he should have. Walking up to the empty counter, Dawson said, "Brownies?"

Charlie grinned. "Hello, stranger. Saw you come in the door. I'm Charlie Becker. Who might you be?" and he thrust his hand across the counter toward him.

"Dawson Callaway, sir. Nice to meet you."

"What can we do for you, son? Or did you hear that my wife always brings baked goods here around this time every day and you'd like to eat some of them?" He grinned and waggled his silver eyebrows.

Releasing the man's paper-thin hand, Dawson said, "No, sir. I'm checking out if there are any wrangling jobs in the valley. I figured a feed store would know about such things." And then he added with a sliver of a grin, "But those brownies do smell good."

Nodding, Charlie finished adding all the items on his calculator, then ran the tape. Looking up, he said, "Well, Sarah Carter, our sheriff, is lookin' for someone who has a wrangler and medical background. That's the only job I know about right now." He waved his hand toward the rear, where Sarah and Pixie were filling a large cardboard container with enough brownies for the oncoming shift at the sheriff's department. "Might go over and introduce yourself, son. Sarah doesn't bite," he added, his smile increasing. "And grab one of Pixie's brownies before the horde comes through the door after seeing my wife slip in the back door bringing all those goodies."

Lips twitching, Dawson said, "I'll do that. Thanks."

So, Sarah Carter was the one who'd put the ad in the paper. The *SC* he'd seen signed on the email clicked. His mind worked at the speed of light—back into combat mode, he supposed—as he slowly approached the two women who were gabbing and laughing with each other. Because of his combat duties, Dawson rarely missed anything. He liked the slender length of Sarah's hand as she daintily chose brownies from the cookie sheet to place in the cardboard box she held in her other hand. Pixie, who was very short and in her sixties, was giggling about something the sheriff had whispered to her, helping her pile the gooey, frosted brownies into the container.

It was impossible, even in so-called male clothing and wearing a baseball cap, that he'd call Sarah mannish. That just wasn't gonna happen. Sarah wore loose clothing, but not too loose. Nothing was tight or body-fitting. But she sure filled out those pants and shirt nicely. Tucking away his purely sexual reaction to the woman, he saw her briefly glance in his direction, as if sensing him approaching her from the rear.

"Coming back for some brownies?" she asked him, amusement dancing in her green eyes.

Dawson halted and met her teasing grin with one of his own. "Yes, ma'am."

Sarah stepped aside, placing the lid on the box and setting it on the table. "Help yourself. And drop the ma'am, okay?"

He liked her style and her low, husky voice. Turning to Pixie, he said, "Ma'am? May I take one?"

"Of course you can!" she said, pointing a finger at them. "Are you new? I don't recognize you. I'm Pixie, Charlie's wife," and she grabbed his hand, shaking it warmly.

Pixie's friendliness was engaging, and he gently held her small hand in his. "Nice to meet you, ma'am. I'm Dawson Callaway."

"Oh," Pixie muttered, shaking her head, "I'm just like Sarah: don't ma'am me."

Hearing Sarah make an inarticulate sound in the rear of her throat, he turned back to her. He extended his hand toward her. "I'm Dawson Callaway."

He saw the shock in her eyes, recognizing his name. And just as quickly, she recovered and extended her hand to him.

"Sarah Carter."

He enjoyed the firm strength of her fingers wrapping around his. Not bone crushing, but a woman who was fully in charge of herself and her life. "I know. I think you're the SC I sent my résumé to a few days ago?"

She released his hand. "Yes, I am."

Pixie tilted her head. "Oh, I saw that ad, Sarah." She gave Dawson a thorough up-and-down look. "And you're applying for that job, Mr. Callaway? To be Gertie's assistant?"

"Yes, ma'—I mean, yes, I am."

Sarah gave Pixie an amused look. "I've had his résumé and," she turned, looking up at him, "I was going to contact you via email after the shift change. You beat me to it."

He noticed a faint pink blush come across her wide cheekbones. And sure enough, she did have a heart-shaped face. Tendrils of ginger hair had escaped her ponytail, collecting at each of her temples, emphasizing the light sprinkling of freckles across her nose and cheeks. "I didn't mean to," Dawson said, reaching for a brownie and the paper napkin Pixie gave him. "I've spent the last few days nosing around for any wrangler work up in the Jackson Hole area and decided to drive down here today to scope out the valley."

Sarah nodded. "Kind of serendipitous that we met here."

The brownie was mouthwateringly sweet as he chewed on it. Pixie was looking up at him expectantly, hands on her hips.

"Well? How's it taste, Mr. Callaway?" she demanded pertly.

With a chuckle, he said, "Best brownie I've ever eaten, Pixie. Thank you for making them for all of us. Do I owe you or the store some money for taking one of them?"

"Oh, heavens, no!" Pixie muttered, giving him a dark look. "Anyone who ambles into Charlie's store is welcome to them. There's no charge. I like makin' people happy."

"Thanks," he said between bites. "It's really good." And

it was. He could feel Sarah's gaze on him and felt his skin contracting in response. Maybe because of his black-ops background, he could always feel the enemy's eyes on him, his skin crawling in warning. But this wasn't about a threat. He inhaled her feminine scent, light and citrusy combined with her own unique fragrance. Sarah didn't wear any perfume, that was for sure, but his nose and ears were supersensitive; honed by years of knowing if he wasn't hyperalert, he could get killed.

Pleased, Pixie patted his arm. "Well, I'll leave you two alone. I'm gonna go up and give Charlie two of these brownies or they'll be gone before he can walk back here to grab some for himself," she tittered.

Dawson watched the small woman bustle off with two brownies in hand. He could feel Sarah's intense inspection. She stood about six feet away from him. Turning, he connected with her assessing dark green gaze, and said, "I didn't mean to put you on the spot."

Shrugging, Sarah said, "I don't feel like I'm in a spot, Mr. Callaway, so relax."

"Not much gets your dander up," he drawled. "Does it?" Again, he saw those full, well-shaped lips of hers, without lipstick on them, curve faintly upward at the corners.

"Not in my line of work. Doesn't pay to let one's emotions run roughshod on someone else. Never ends up well, and I don't like to see a confrontation escalate."

She chose her words carefully. He wiped the last of the chocolate frosting off the tips of his fingers. "I don't care for them myself."

"No, I can see you don't." She lowered her voice. "I was going to email you later to ask you to meet me at Kassie's Café, across the street, to talk further with you about the job possibility."

He stood there listening to the tone of her low voice, understanding this was personal business, not law enforcement because she was the sheriff. "Sure, that's doable." The corners of his eyes crinkled and he added, "I'm assuming I passed your deep, broad background check on me? Pentagon? Law enforcement?" The corners of her mouth deepened and he could feel or maybe sense her humor about his knowledgeable comment.

"Yes," she answered coolly, "you did."

"Check out my DD Form 214, did you?" Dawson wanted her to know he realized, as a law enforcement officer, she would do such an investigation about anyone applying for a job, especially with an elderly person, who was probably her grandmother. She needed to know that he expected such research on her part. The humor transferred to her eyes.

"You were in black ops, Mr. Dawson. I figure you knew I'd be doing something to dig up the dirt on you when you were in the Navy."

A rumble came through his chest. "Indeed I did, Sheriff."

"Call me Sarah when we're alone," she said.

"Call me Dawson any time you want."

"I like your style, Dawson."

"And I like yours."

He saw pinkness once more stain her cheeks, realizing she was blushing. She might be all business, cool, calm and collected, but there was a mighty nice personal side to her, too. "We have a good place to start, then." He felt her hesitancy. Worry, maybe? He sensed it, but she had her game face in place. Was she ex-military? He was itching to know. Because she sure as hell fit the bill to a tee.

Sarah had opened her mouth to speak when the radio on her left shoulder squawked to life. She held up her finger to him and then devoted her attention to the incoming call from Dispatch.

Dawson listened intently to the short conversation. There was a rollover accident on Route 89, ten miles south from where they were. The only ambulance owned by the Wind River Fire Department, which had paramedics, was twenty miles north at another accident scene, tending victims. He saw the darkness come to Sarah's eyes. Then, she glanced over at him.

"Hold," she told the dispatcher, lifting her hand off the radio key. "Mr. Callaway? On your résumé you said you were a licensed paramedic. I checked it out and it verified you're up to date and can practice. I need someone like you to come with me right now. Our other two paramedics are north of here and can't make it to the scene."

"I'll come with you." He made a gesture with his chin toward the door. "I always travel with my paramedic bag. It's in the truck."

"Good. Come with me. We'll grab it and go." Sarah was on the radio once again, giving the intel to the dispatcher, and then signed off. "We're between shifts right now. All my men and women are coming into the courthouse as we speak," she said, hurrying toward the door, box of brownies in hand.

Dawson easily swung past her to open the door for her. She looked shocked by his action, but then shook it off, diving out the door and rapidly taking the steps to the gravel parking lot. "Yes, and not all your people coming in are there yet, right?"

"Right. Get your bag and meet me at my Tahoe cruiser?"

"On it."

Dawson split from her at the bottom of the stairs. It felt good to be needed. He'd always liked being a combat corpsman and he'd saved many lives with his knowledge. And he liked Sarah.

Pushing her out of his mind, he opened the door to the cab, reached in and grabbed the hefty red canvas bag by the wide, thick nylon straps. In moments, he had locked up his truck and was trotting in the direction of the Tahoe, which was now in motion, heading in his direction, lights flashing on the bar on top of the black roof.

Without preamble, he pulled open the backseat door, throwing in his paramedic bag. Shutting it, he opened the passenger door, quickly climbing in. She put the pedal to the metal and the Tahoe growled deeply, moving swiftly out onto Route 89. He didn't need to be told to buckle up. All her focus was on driving; they must have hit seventy miles per hour after getting outside the city limits. They were heading down a long, flat expanse now, with few cars on the highway.

"I'm officially deputizing you, Mr. Callaway. I can't have a civilian without any medical license in the state of Wyoming being a medic to potential injury victims in that rollover. Lawsuit time if I don't."

"Fine by me. I accept being deputized."

Her lips twisted. "I like your no-nonsense approach."

"Comes with the territory."

"You're okay with this?"

"Absolutely. I feel like I'm back in Afghanistan on a black-ops mission," and he tossed her a grin.

She gave a snort. "Good to know."

"Call me Dawson. Okay? I don't stand on much cere-mony."

"Okay, Dawson." And then she cast him a warm look. "Thanks for picking up the slack on this. You didn't have to and I know it."

"Glad to help." And he was. There was a nice balance

of business and vulnerability within her. That drew Dawson strongly. He didn't see a wedding ring on her left hand, but in her business, just as in the military, she probably didn't wear it for many good reasons. Did she have children? She was in her late twenties, he would guess, and his logic told him that she was either engaged or married. Sarah Carter was way too good-looking not to be in a relationship. That saddened him, but he let it go. Since his marriage to Lucia Steward, and subsequent divorce three years later, he hadn't been interested in another relationship.

Until now. What a helluva twist!

Connect with Us

Visit us online at
KensingtonBooks.com
to read more from your favorite authors, see books
by series, view reading group guides, and more.

for sneak peeks, chances to win books and prize packs,
and to share your thoughts with other readers.

**facebook.com/kensingtonpublishing
twitter.com/kensingtonbooks**

Tell us what you think!

To share your thoughts, submit a review,
or sign up for our eNewsletters, please visit:
KensingtonBooks.com/TellUs.